THE UNDYING THING AND OTHERS

Barry Pain c. 1891

THE UNDYING
THING
AND OTHERS

Barry Pain

Edited, with an Introduction, by S. T. Joshi

Hippocampus Press

New York

Published by Hippocampus Press
P.O. Box 641, New York, NY 10156.
http://www.hippocampuspress.com

Cover illustration by Allen Koszowski.
Cover design and Lovecraft's Library series logo by Barbara Briggs Silbert.
Hippocampus Press logo designed by Anastasia Damianakos.

First Edition
1 3 5 7 9 8 6 4 2

ISBN 0-9748789-0-1

Contents

Introduction

The weird fiction of Barry Pain (1864–1928) constitutes a distinctive element in the work of a writer whose focus was largely elsewhere. Pain early gained a reputation as a comic writer: from as early as 1890 he contributed to some of the leading middlebrow publications of the day—*Punch*, *To-day*, *Black and White*, the *Idler*, the *Sketch*, and numerous others. He, W. W. Jacobs, and Jerome K. Jerome were quickly branded the New Humourists—a term initially coined in derision because it was believed by highbrow critics that these writers (all of whom, curiously, wrote the occasional weird tale) were deliberately seeking to satisfy the lowbrow tastes of the rapidly increasing British middle class. His first book, *In a Canadian Canoe* (1891), chiefly contained humorous tales, but does include one grim tale of psychological terror, "'Bill,'" in which a lower-class boy struggles to deal with the death of his infant sister. It is a searing portrayal of the wretched fate to which British society condemned its working classes at that juncture in history. The volume was the first of nearly sixty books that Pain published in a career that spanned nearly four decades; his uncollected tales and sketches (the great majority of them humorous, but with apparently a few weird items buried among them) number in the hundreds.

Stories and Interludes (1892) contains two weird tales that contain more promise than fulfilment—"The Glass of Supreme Moments" and "Exchange"—and, sadly, much the same can be said for *Stories in the Dark* (1901), a choice item for the weird collector but one that doesn't quite deliver on the potential of some of its premises. This slim collection—it is well under 30,000 words—features a number of tales with powerful ideas that are not executed quite as effectively as one would wish. "The Diary of a God" could have been a powerful tale of psychological horror in its depiction of a man who becomes increasingly isolated from humanity and develops a fierce misanthropy, but its development is crude. "This Is All" is a somewhat more effective sketch of the universal fear of death, and "The Magnet" is another non-supernatural tale that underscores a scarcely less universal fascination with tragedy and catastrophe. But even the volume's lengthiest and most impressive story, "The Undying Thing," leaves us vaguely unsatisfied. It powerfully etches a generational curse in its ac-

count of an anomalous creature, born of one of the ancestors of the own-
ers of a venerable English castle, that dwells in the woods near the estate;
but Pain's refusal to specify the nature of this entity seems less an instance
of artistic restraint than a failure of imagination.

Nevertheless, one can see why H. P. Lovecraft found the tale powerful,
even though he did not read it until 1934. At that time August Derleth had
given Lovecraft a copy of *Stories in the Dark,* and Lovecraft waxed enthusiastic about the story: "Ugh! I really half-believe I ought to mention this in my
article."[1] He is referring to his history of weird fiction, "Supernatural Horror
in Literature" (1927), a revised version of which was then running in the
Fantasy Fan (1933–35); but although he noted the story in a list of "Books to
mention in new edition of weird article," he had apparently already prepared
a revised version of his essay and sent it to Charles D. Hornig, editor of the
Fantasy Fan, and so there was no opportunity for him to cite "The Undying
Thing." As it happened, the *Fantasy Fan* folded before it could run the chapter of "Supernatural Horror in Literature" (chapter 9, "The Weird Tradition
in the British Isles") in which the story would presumably have been mentioned, and Lovecraft had no other occasion to submit a newly revised version of his essay for magazine or book publication.

The final story in *Stories in the Dark,* "The Gray Cat," is a powerful tale of
metempsychosis—a theme that Pain had already treated in a different way
in "Exchange"—and perhaps set the stage for his novel-length working out
of the idea, *An Exchange of Souls,* already reprinted by Hippocampus Press.
That novel is clearly the pinnacle of Pain's weird work, but later specimens
among his short stories are worth more than fleeting discussion.

"The Unfinished Game," in the collection *Here and Hereafter* (1911), is a
routine ghost story about billiards, while "The Unseen Power" is a scarcely
less conventional tale of a haunted house. *Stories in Grey* (1912) contains
two powerful specimens. "Smeath," the longest of Pain's weird short stories, is a richly complex tale about hypnotism and clairvoyance, with a
grisly ending that even today's splatterpunk devotees can relish. "Linda" is
a powerful and moving tale of love and terror that again broaches the metempsychosis theme.

Pain wrote hundreds of short stories, and many of them are uncol-

---

1. HPL to August Derleth, 8 September 1934; in *Essential Solitude: The Letters of H. P.
Lovecraft and August Derleth,* ed. David E. Schultz and S. T. Joshi (New York: Hippocampus Press, 2008), 2.660.

lected; the great mass of them are humorous tales, but a few weird specimens can be found among them. One of these is "Celia and the Ghost" (*Strand*, December 1916), which—if one discounts a very curious story in *Stories in the Dark*, "The Bottom of the Gulf," about a Roman encountering a strange entity under the earth—is a unique instance of Pain's attempt to mingle humour and horror. The result is perhaps not entirely satisfactory, but the story—which also features a sentimental romance element that Pain also employed in much of his work—is of interest from the weird perspective in its depiction of a ghost from the future.

The untitled volume of short stories published in the series "Short Stories of Today and Yesterday" (1928) contains some of Pain's most assured work; it is regrettable that it appeared in the year of Pain's death, for it augured an impressive seriousness of conception and ability to handle complex interplays of emotion that Pain might have used in later weird work. "The Tree of Death" is perhaps the most curious item in Pain's weird repertoire, a kind of Eastern fantasy in the manner of the *Arabian Nights*, told in a stately and archaic diction that is highly evocative and convincing. "Not on the Passenger-List" is a powerful tale of supernatural revenge that brings the earlier tale "The Widower" to mind. "The Reaction" vaguely echoes Arthur Machen's "Novel of the White Powder" in its account of a strange drug that has unexpected effects, while "The Missing Years" is a strange and apparently non-supernatural narrative about amnesia.

The Shadow of the Unseen, a novel that Pain published in 1907 in collaboration with James Blyth, is worth some attention. Little is known about Blyth (1864–1933), a British novelist who also wrote about agriculture, and there is no way to tell the exact degree of each collaborator's contribution to the novel. It is an interesting experiment in hybridisation—an attempt to mingle the society novel, the romance novel, even the comic novel, with the tale of the supernatural. As such, it has a different texture than almost any other supernatural novel ever written—a point that, in addition to its extreme rarity, may suffice to justify its reprinting. In spite of its generally light and bantering tone, *The Shadow of the Unseen* develops a cumulative power in its indirect and insidious suggestion of witchcraft, as embodied in the figure of Judith Jennis, a descendant of a purported witch of the same name, who now seeks to avenge what she believes to be the unjust death of her ancestor. Whether Judith has any actual supernatural powers is never clarified; the one genuinely weird episode—Judith's apparent ability to depict the future by means of a mysterious substance poured into a silver cup—passes relatively quickly. Nevertheless, there is a pervasive atmosphere of weirdness in the work, even if the most powerful scene in it is a purely physical scene of a man in a death-struggle with Judith's huge black goat.

The many years that Pain devoted, however sporadically, to producing novels and tales of natural and supernatural horror bespeaks a fascination with the genre that belies his dominant interest in comic writing. That writing has all but passed from view, but his weird work remains as a suggestive instance of what even writers of very different leanings can do when they find themselves compelled by some inner necessity to portray terror and weirdness in works long and short.

—S. T. Joshi

A Note on This Edition

The stories in this volume are derived, with one exception, from Pain's published short story collections.

"'Bill'" is taken from *In a Canadian Canoe, the Nine Muses Minus One, and Other Stories* (London: Henry & Co., 1891).

"The Glass of Supreme Moments" and "Exchange" are taken from *Stories and Interludes* (London: Henry & Co., 1892).

"The Diary of a God," "This Is All," "The Moon-Slave," "The Green Light," "The Magnet," The Case of Vincent Pyrwhit," "The Bottom of the Gulf," "The End of a Show," "The Undying Thing," and "The Gray Cat" are taken from *Stories in the Dark* (London: Grant Richards, 1901).

"The Four-Fingered Hand," "The Tower," "The Unfinished Game," "The Unseen Power," and "The Widower" are taken from *Here and Hereafter* (London: Methuen, 1911).

"Smeath" and "Linda" are taken from *Stories in Grey* (London: T. Werner Laurie, 1912).

"The Tree of Death," "Not on the Passenger-List," "The Reaction," and "The Missing Years" are taken from the untitled volume of Pain's stories in the series "Short Stories of To-day and Yesterday" (London: George G. Harrap, 1928).

"Celia and the Ghost" is an uncollected story that appeared in the *Strand* (December 1916).

This volume also includes *The Shadow of the Unseen* (London: Chapman & Hall, 1907).

—S. T. J.

The Undying Thing and Others

"Bill"

THE STORY OF A BOY WHOM THE GODS LOVED

Bill came slowly up the steps from a basement flat in Pond Buildings, crossed the pavement, and sat down on the kerbstone in the sunshine, with his feet in a delightful puddle. He was reflecting.

"All that fuss about a dead byeby!" he said to himself.

He was quite a little boy, with a dirty face, gipsy eyes, and a love for animals. He had slept the deep sleep of childhood the night before, and had heard nothing of what was happening. In the early morning, however, he had been enlightened by his father—a weak man, with a shuffling gait, who tried to do right and generally failed.

"Bill, cummere. Last night there was a byeby come to be your sister if she'd grow'd. But she didn't live more'n hour. An' that's why your aunt's 'ere, an' mind yer do whort she tells yer, an' don't go into the other room, an' don't do nothin' 'cep whort yer told, or I'll break yer 'ead for yer, sure's death, I will!"

Then Bill's father had gone away to his work, being unable to afford the loss of a day; and Bill's vehement, red-haired aunt had come into the kitchen, and shaken him, and abused him, and given him some breakfast. Bill's aunt was one of those unfortunate people who cannot love one person without hating three others to make up for it. Just at present she was loving Bill's mother, her sister, very much, and retained her self-respect by being very strict with Bill's father, with Bill himself, and with the doctor. She instructed Bill that he was not to go to school that morning. He was to remain absolutely quiet in the kitchen, because he might be wanted to run errands and do odd jobs. For some time Bill had obeyed her, and then monotony tempted him to include the little yard at the back in his definition of the kitchen. All the basement flats in Pond Buildings have little yards at the back. Most of the inhabitants use them as drying-grounds. In some of them there is a dead shrub or the remains of a sanguine geranium that faded; in all of them there are cinders and very old meat-tins. Now, when Bill went out into the yard, he found the black cat, which he called Simon Peter, asleep in the sun on the wall. Simon Peter did not belong to anyone; she roamed about at the back of Pond Buildings, dodged anything that was thrown at her, and ate unspeakable things. She had formed a melancholy and unremunerative attachment to Bill; her name had been suggested to him by stray visits to a Sunday School, forced on him during a short season when his father, to use his own phrase, had got religion.

"Siming Peter," said Bill, as he scratched her gently under the ear, "Siming Peter, my cat, come in 'ere along o' me, and 'ave some milk."

It is not at all probable that Simon Peter was deceived by this. She must have known that, with the best intentions in the world, Bill could not do so much as this for her. Yet she blinked at him with her lazy green eyes, and followed him from the yard into the kitchen. Bill filled a saucer with water, and put it down on the ground before her. "There yer are, Siming Peter," he said; "and that's better for yer than any milk." Simon Peter put up her back slowly, mewed contemptuously, and trotted out into the yard again. Bill, dashing after her, trod on the saucer and broke it, and overturned a chair. In another moment he was in the clutches of his fierce aunt.

"Do you want to kill your blessed mother, you devil? Didn't I tell yer to sit quoite? An' a good saucer broke, with the poor dead corpse of your byeby sister lyin' in the next room. Go hout! You're more nuisance nor you're worth. See 'ere. Don't you show your ugly 'ead 'ere agin afore night. An' when yer comes back I'll tell yer father of yer, an' 'e'll skin yer alive. Dinner? Not for such as you. Hout yer git!"

So Bill had been turned out, and now sat with his feet in a delightful puddle, reflecting for a minute or two on dead babies, injustice, puddles, and other things. It was a larger puddle, as far as Bill could see, than any other in the street, and it was this which made it so charming. But a puddle is of no use to anyone who has not got something to float on it. If you have something to float on it you can imagine boats, and races, and storms, and it becomes a magnificent playground for the imagination; otherwise the biggest puddle is simply a puddle, and it is nothing more. So Bill started down the street to look for something which would float—a scrap of paper or a straw. He was stopped by a lanky, unkempt girl with yellow hair, who was leaning on a broom that was almost bald, outside an open door. She was four or five years older than Bill, and she was very fond of him. The girls of the wretched neighbourhood for the most part petted Bill; they did so, without knowing their reason, because he was quaint, and pretty, and idle. He was rather dirty, it was true, but then so were they; and for the most part they were not so pretty.

"Bill," said the yellow-haired girl, "why awn't yer at school? You'll ketch it, Bill."

"No, I 'ont. They kep' me, 'cos we've got a byeby, an' the byeby's dead. Then they turned me out for breakin' a saucer when I was goin' after Siming Peter what I were feedin'; an' I ain't to 'ave no dinner, an' I ain't to come back afore night, and when I do come back I'm goin' to be walloped. I wish I was dead!"

"Oh, Bill, you *are* a bad boy; what are yer goin' to do?"

"Play ships at that puddle. I was lookin' for sutthin' what 'ud do for ships, an' can't find nothin'."

"An' what'll yer do about dinner?"

"I ain't goin' to 'ave no dinner," said Bill solemnly. "I'm goin' to starve. They don't keer. Dead byebies is what *they* like."

The lanky girl leaned her broom against the wall, sat down on the doorstep, and commenced the research of a pocket; the pocket yielded her one penny.

"Look 'ere, Bill," she said, "you take this and git yourself sutthin' to eat."

Bill shook his head, and pressed his lips together. He was much moved.

"I 'ad it give me a week ago, and I sived it 'cos there warn't nothin' that I wanted. So you take it. I don't want it. If yer like, yer can give me a kiss for it." She pressed it into his hand. "There ain't no other little boy I know what I'd give it to," she added rather inconsistently.

Bill nodded his head, and the lips grew a little tremulous. He had been treated cruelly all the morning, and this sudden change to sympathy and generosity was almost too much for him. He kissed the yellow-haired girl—once timidly, and then suddenly with great affection.

"Why, Bill," she said, "I ain't done nothin' to 'urt yer, yer look ommust as if yer was goin' to cry."

"No, I ain't," replied Bill, finding words with difficulty—"but—but I 'ate ev'rybody in the world 'cep' you."

Then he walked away with great dignity, and every nerve in his excitable little body quivering. He felt on the whole rather more wretched than before. The contrast made him feel both sides of it more deeply. He had forgotten now about the beautiful puddle and his intention to play at ships. He wandered down the main street, and then down a side street which led behind a grim, frowning church. And here he found something which attracted his attention. It was a dirty little shop which a small tobacconist, and an almost microscopical grocer had used successively as a last step before bankruptcy. It had then remained for some time unoccupied. But now the whole of the window was occupied with one great bright picture, before which a small crowd had gathered. It represented a beautiful mermaid swimming in a beautiful sea accompanied by a small octopus and some boiled shrimps. Her hair was very golden and very long; her eyes were very blue; she was very pink and very fat. Underneath was the announcement—

THE MERMAID OF THE WESTERN PACIFIC!
POSITIVELY TO BE SEEN WITHIN!!
FOR A FEW DAYS ONLY.
ADMISSION ONE PENNY.

An old man was standing in the doorway, with a tattered red curtain behind him, supplying further details of the history and personal appearance of the mermaid. He looked slightly military, distinctly intemperate, and very unfortunate; yet he was energetic.

"What it comes to is this—for a few days only I am offering two 'igh-class entertainments at the price of one. The performance commences with an exhibition by that most marvellous Spanish conjurer, Madumarsall Rimbini, and concludes with that unparalleled wonder of the world, the Mermaid of the Western Pasuffolk. I have been asked frequent if it pays me to do this. No, it does *not* pay me. I am doing it entirely as an advertisement. Kindly take notice that this mermaid is not a shadder, faked up with lookin' glasses. She is real, solid, genuine, discovered by an English officer while cruisin' in the Western Pasuffolk, and purchased direct from him by myself. The performance will commence in one minute. If any gentleman is not able to stay now, I may remark that the performances will be repeated agin this evenin' from seven to ten. What it comes to is this—for a few days only, etc."

Of course, Bill had seen shows of a kind before. He had seen a 'bus horse stumble, and almost pick itself up, and stumble again, and finally go down half on the kerbstone. That had been attractive, but there had been nothing to pay for it. Again, in his Sunday School days, he had been present at an entertainment where the exhilaration of solid buns and dissolving views had been gently tempered by a short address. That, too, was attractive, but it had been free. And now it would not be possible to see this beautiful buoyant creature in clear shrimp-haunted waters unless he paid a penny for it—the only penny that he possessed. Never before had he paid anything to go anywhere. The temptation was masterful. It gripped him, and drew him towards the tattered red curtain that hung over the entrance. In another minute he had paid his penny, and stood within.

At the end of the shop a low stage had been erected. On the stage was something which looked like a large packing-case with a piece of red baize thrown over it. There was a small table, on which were two packs of play-ing-cards, and a brightly-coloured pill-box, and a tired, fat woman in a low dress of peculiar frowsiness. As the audience entered she put a smile on her face, where it remained fixed as if it had been pinned. The perform-ance commenced with three clumsy card-tricks. Then she requested some-one in the audience to put a halfpenny in the painted pill-box, and see it changed into a shilling. The audience felt that they had been weak in pay-ing a penny to see the show, and on this last point they were adamant. They would put no halfpennies in no pill-boxes. They were now firm. So also was the Spanish conjurer, and this trick was omitted. She intimated that she would now proceed to the second part of the entertainment—the exhibition of the Mermaid of the Western Pacific, She removed, dramati-cally, the red-baize cover, disclosing a glass-case. The audience pressed forward to examine its contents. The case was filled for the most part with those romantic rocks and grasses which conventionality has appointed to be a suitable setting for stuffed canaries, or stuffed dogs, or anything that is stuffed. There was a background of painted sky and sea; and in the front there was a small, most horrible figure, looking straight at Bill out of hide-ous, green, glassy eyes. It was not the lovely creature depicted in the win-dow outside. It was a monstrous thing, a contemptible fraud to the practised intelligence, but to Bill's childish, excitable mind a thing of un-speakable horror and fascination. The lower half was a wilted, withered fish; then came a girdle of seaweed, and then something which was near to being human, yellow, and waxy, with a ghastly face, a bald head, and those eyes that would keep looking at Bill. He shut his own eyes for a second; when he opened them again the monstrous thing was still looking at him.

There were two men standing near to Bill. One of them was a very young and very satirical carpenter, with a foot-rule sticking out of his coat-pocket. "So that's a mermaid?" he remarked. "Yer call that a mermaid? oh, indeed, a mermaid—oh, yes!"

"Seems to me," said the other man, middle-aged, cadaverous, and dressed in rusty black, "that it's a sight like a dead byeby."

"Well, you *ought* to know," replied the satirical carpenter, grinning.

Bill heard this. So in that basement flat in Pond Buildings, Bill's home, there was something lying quite still, and waiting for him, to frighten him! He had never thought what a dead baby would be like. His mind began to work in flashes. The first flash reminded him of some horrible stories which his red-haired, vehement aunt had told him, to terrify him into being good. He had objected at the close of one story that dead people could not walk about.

"You don't know," his aunt had replied, "nobody knows, what dead people can do." In the second flash he imagined that he had gone home, had been lectured by his aunt, and beaten by his father, and had cried himself to sleep. He would wake up at night, when all was quiet—he felt sure of it—and the room would not be quite dark. He would see by the white moonlight a horrible yellow waxy thing crawling across the floor. It would be his dead baby sister, and it would have a face like the face of the mermaid, and it would stare at him. He would be unable to call out. It would come nearer and nearer, and at last it would touch him. Then he would die of fright.

No, he would not go home, not until the dead baby had been taken away.

As the audience crowded out through the narrow doorway, Bill touched the man in shabby black—

"Please Sir, 'ow long is it afore they bury dead babies?"

The man stared at him searchingly. "What do yer want to know that for? Depends on the weather partly, and on the inclinations of the bereaved party. 'Soon as possible' 's allus my advice, but they let it go for days frequent."

Bill thanked him, and walked aimlessly away. He could not get the terror out of his mind. He walked through street after street, so absorbed in horrible thoughts that he hardly noticed what direction he was taking, and only just escaped being run over. He had been wandering for over an hour when he came across two boys, whom he knew, playing marbles. This was companionship and diversion for his thoughts. For some time he watched the game with interest, and then one of the players pulled from his pocket two large marbles of greenish glass, and set them rolling. Bill turned away at once, for he had been reminded of those green eyes. He imagined that they were still looking at him; but, in his imagination, they belonged, not to the mermaid, but to the dead baby. He wished again and again that he had never been to that show. He was growing almost desperate with terror. Of course his state of mind was to some extent due to the fact that he had eaten nothing for eight hours. But then, Bill did not know this. Suddenly he gave a great start, and a gasp for breath, for he had been touched on the shoulder. He looked up and saw his father. Now Bill's father had drunk two glasses of bad beer during his dinner-hour, and, in consequence, he was feeling somewhat angry and somewhat self-righteous, for his head was exceedingly weak and poor. He addressed Bill very solemnly.

"Loit'rin' in the streets! Loit'rin' and playin' in the streets! What's the good o' my bringing of yer up in the fear of Gawd?"

Bill had no answer to make; so his father aimed a blow at him, which Bill dodged.

"All right," his father continued, "I'm sent out on a jorb, and I ain't got the time to wallup yer now. But you mark my words—this very night, as sure as my name's what it is, I'll knock yer blasted 'ead off!"

At any other time this would have frightened Bill, but now it came as a positive relief. There is no fear so painful, so maddening, as the fear of the supernatural. The promise that he should have his head knocked off had in itself but little charm or attraction. But in that case he knew what to fear and from whence to fear it. It took his thoughts away for a few minutes from the horror of that dead baby, whose ghastly face he pictured to himself so clearly. But it was only for a few minutes; the face came back again to his mind and haunted him. He could not escape from it. He was more than ever determined that he would not go home; he dared not spend a night in the next room to it. Already the afternoon was closing in, and Bill had no notion where he was to go for the night. For the present he decided to make his way to the green; he would probably meet other boys there that he knew.

The green to which he went is much frequented by the poor of the south-west. The railway skirts one side of it, and gives it an additional attraction to children. Bill was tired out with walking. He flung himself down on the grass to rest. His exhaustion at last overcame his fears, and he fell asleep. He slept for a long time, and in his sleep he had a dream.

It was, so it seemed to him in his dream, late in the evening, and he was standing outside the door of the basement flat. He had knocked, and was waiting to be admitted. Suddenly he noticed that the door was just ajar. He pushed it open and entered. He called, but there was no answer. All was dark. The outer door swung to with a bang behind him. He thought that he would wait in the kitchen by the light of the fire until someone came. He felt his way to the kitchen and sat down in front of the fire.

It had burnt very low, and the furniture was only just distinguishable by the light of it. As he was waiting he heard very faintly the sound of breathing. It did not frighten him, but he could not understand it, because, as far as he could see, there was no living thing in the room except himself. He thought that he would strike a light and discover what it was. The matches were all in a cupboard on the right-hand side of the fireplace. He could only just reach the fastening, and it took him some little time to undo it. The moment the fastening was undone the door flew open, and something yellowish-white fell or rather leapt out upon him, fixing little quickly-moving fingers in his hair. With a scream he fell to the floor. He had shut his eyes in horror, but he felt compelled to open them again to see what this thing was that clung to him, writhing and panting. A little spurt of flame had shot up, and showed him the face. Its eyes were blinking and rolling. Its mouth moved horribly and convulsively, and there was foam on the white lips. The face was close to his own; it drew nearer; it touched him. It was wet.

Bill suddenly woke up and sprang to his feet, shivering and maddened with terror. The green was dark and deserted. A cold, strong wind had sprung up, and he heard it howling dismally. An impulse seized him to run—to run for his life. For a moment he hesitated; and then, under the shadow of the wall, slinking along in the darkness, he saw something white coming towards him, and with a quick gasp he turned and ran. He paid no heed to the direction in which he was going; he dared not look behind, for he felt sure that the nameless horror was behind him; he ran until he was breathless, and then walked a few paces, and ran again. As he crossed the road, at the outer edge of the green, a policeman stopped and looked at him suspiciously. Bill did not even see the policeman. His one idea was escape.

It happened that he ran in the direction of the river. He had left the road now, and was following a muddy track that led through some grimy, desolate market-gardens. All around him there was horror. It screamed in the screaming wind with a voice that was half human; it took shape in the darkness, and lean, white arms, convulsively active, seemed to be snatching at him as he passed; the pattering of blown leaves was changed by it into the pattering of something ghastly, coming very quickly after him. For one second he paused on the river's brink; and then, pressing both his hands tightly over his eyes, he flung himself into the water.

And the river went on unconcerned, and the laws of Nature did not deviate from their regular course. So the boy was drowned. It was a pity, for he was in some ways a lovable boy, and there were possibilities in him.

Bill's aunt was putting the untidy bedroom straight when his mother, opening her eyes and turning a little in the bed, said, in a low, tired voice—

"I want Bill. Wheere's Bill?"

"I sent 'im out, dearie; 'e'll be back d'rectly. Don't you worry yourself about Bill. Why, that drattid lamp's a-shinin' strite onto your eyes. I'll turn it down."

There was a moment's pause, while the vehement woman—quiet enough now—arranged the lamp and took her place by the bedside. She smoothed the young mother's faded hair with one hand. "Go to sleep, dearie," she said.

Then she began to sing in a hushed, quavering voice. It was a favourite hymn, and for devotional purposes she rarely used more than one vowel sound—

"Urbud wuth me! Fust-fulls the uvven-tud!"

The Glass of Supreme Moments

Lucas Morne sat in his college rooms, when the winter afternoon met the evening, depressed and dull. There were various reasons for his depression. He was beginning to be a little nervous about his health. A week before he had run second in a mile race, the finish of which had been a terrible struggle; ever since then any violent exertion or excitement had brought on symptoms which were painful, and to one who had always been strong, astonishing. He had felt them early that afternoon, on coming from the river. Besides, he was discontented with himself. He had had several men in his rooms that afternoon, who were better than he was, men who had enthusiasms and had had found them satisfying. Lucas had a moderate devotion to athletics, but no great enthusiasm. Neither had he the finer perceptions. Neither was he a scholar. He was an ordinary man, and reputed to be a good fellow.

His visitors had drunk his tea, talked of their own enthusiasms, and were now gone. Nothing is so unclean as a used tea-cup; nothing is so cold as toast which has once been hot, and the concrete expression of dejection is crumbs. Even Lucas Morne, who had not the finer perceptions, was dimly conscious that his room had become horrible, and now flung open the window. One of the men—a large, clumsy man—had been smoking mitigated Latakia; and Latakia has a way of rolling itself all round the atmosphere and kicking. Lucas seated himself in his easiest chair.

His rooms were near the chapel, and he could hear the organ. The music and the soft fall of the darkness were soothing; he could hardly see the used tea-cups now; the light from the gas-lamp outside came just a little way into the room, shyly and obliquely.

Well, he had not noticed it before, but the fireplace had become a staircase. He felt too lazy to wonder much at this. He would, he thought, have the things all altered back again on the morrow. It would be worth while to sell the staircase, seeing that its steps were fashioned of silver and crystal. Unfortunately he could not see how much there was of it, or whither it led. The first five steps were clear enough; he felt convinced that the workmanship of them was Japanese. But the rest of the staircase was hidden from his sight by a gray veil of mist. He found himself a little angry, in a severe and strictly logical way, that in these days of boasted science we could not prevent a piece of fog, measuring ten feet by seven, from coming in at an open window and sitting down on a staircase which had only just begun to exist, and blotting out all but five steps of it in its very earliest moments. He allowed that it was a beautiful mist; its colour changed slowly from gray to rose, and then back again from rose to gray; fire-flies of silver and gold shot through it at intervals; but it was a nuisance, because he wanted to see the rest of the staircase, and it prevented him. Every moment the desire to see more grew stronger. At last he determined to shake off his laziness, and go up the staircase and through the mist into the something beyond. He felt sure that the something beyond would be beautiful—sure with the certainty which has nothing to do with logical conviction.

It seemed to him that it was with an effort that he brought himself to rise from the chair and walk to the foot of that lovely staircase. He hesitated there for a moment or two, and as he did so he heard the sound of footsteps high up, far away, yet coming nearer and nearer, with light music in the sound of them. Some one was coming down the staircase. He listened eagerly and excitedly. Then through the gray mist came a figure robed in gray.

It was the figure of a woman—young, with wonderful grace in her movements. Her face was veiled, and all that could be seen of her as she paused on the fifth step was the soft dark hair that reached to her waist, and her arms—white wonders of beauty. The rest was hidden by the gray veil and the long gray robe, that left, however, their suggestion of classical grace and slenderness. Lucas Morne stood looking at her tremulously. He felt sure, too, that she was looking at him, and that she could see through the folds of the thin gray veil that hid her face. She was the first to speak. Her voice in its gentleness and delicacy was like the voice of a child; it was only afterwards that he heard in it the under-thrill which told of more than childhood.

"Why have you not come? I have been waiting for you, you know, up there. And this is the only time," she added.

"I am very sorry," he stammered. "You see—I never knew the staircase was there until to-day. In fact—it seems very stupid of me—but I always thought it was a fire-place. I must have been dreaming, of course. And then this afternoon I thought, or dreamed, that a lot of men came in to see me. Perhaps they really did come; and we got talking, you know—"

"Yes," she said, with the gentlest possible interruption. "I *do* know.

There was one man, Fynsale, large, ugly, clumsy, a year your senior. He sat in that chair over there, and sulked, and smoked Latakia. I rather like the smell of Latakia. He especially loves to write or to say some good thing; and at times he can do it. Therefore you envy him. Then there was Blake. Blake is an athlete, like yourself, but is just a little more successful. Yes, I know you are good, but Blake is very good. You were tried for the 'Varsity—Blake was selected. He and Fynsale both have delight in ability, and you envy both. There was that dissenting little Paul Reece. He is not exactly in your set, but you were at school with him, and so you tolerate him. How good he is, for all his insignificance and social defects! Blake knows that, and kept a guard on his talk this afternoon. He would not offend Paul Reece for worlds. Paul's belief gives him earnestness, his earnestness leads him to self-sacrifice, and self-sacrifice is deep delight to him. You have more ability than Paul Reece, but you cannot reach that kind of enthusiastic happiness, and therefore you envy him. I could say similar things of the other men. It was because they made you vaguely dissatisfied with yourself that they bored you. You take pleasure—a certain pleasure—in athletics, and that pleasure would become an enthusiastic delight if you were a little better at them. Some men could get the enthusiastic delight out of as much as you can do, but your temperament is different. I know you well. You are not easily satisfied. You are not clever, but you are—" She paused, but without any sign of embarrassment.

"What am I?" he asked eagerly. He felt sure that it would be something good, and he was not less vain than other men.

"I do not think I will say—not now."

"But who are you?" His diffidence and stammering had vanished beneath her calm, quiet talk. "You must let me at least ask that. Who are you? And how do you know all this?"

"I am a woman, but not an earth-woman. And the chief difference between us is that I know nearly all the things you do not know, and you do not know nearly all the things that I know. Sometimes I forget your ignorance—do not be angry for a word; there is no other for it, and it is not your fault. I forgot it just now when I asked you why you had not come to me up the staircase of silver and crystal, through the gray veil where the fire-flies live, and into that quiet room beyond. This is the only time; tomorrow it will not be possible. And I have—" Once more she paused. There was a charm for Lucas Morne in the things which she did not say. "Your room is dark," she continued, "and I can hardly see you."

"I will light the lamp," said Lucas hurriedly, "and—and won't you let me get you some tea?" He saw, as soon as he had said it, how unspeakably ludicrous this proffer of hospitality was. He almost fancied a smile, a moment's shimmer of little white teeth, beneath the long gray veil. "Or shall I come now—at once," he added.

"Come now; I will show you the mirror."

"What is that?"

"You will understand when you see it. It is the glass of supreme moments. I shall tell you about it. But come."

She looked graceful, and she suggested the most perfect beauty as she stood there, a slight figure against the background of gray mist, which had grown luminous as the room below grew darker. Lucas Morne went carefully up the five steps, and together they passed through the gray, misty curtain. He was wondering what the face was like which was hidden beneath that veil; would it be possible to induce her to remove the veil? He might, perhaps, lead the conversation thither—delicately and subtly.

"A cousin of mine," he began, "who has travelled a good deal, once told me that the women of the East—"

"Yes," she said, and her voice and way were so gentle that it hardly seemed like an interruption; "and so do I."

He felt very much anticipated; for a moment he was driven back into the shy and stammering state. There were only a few more steps now, and then they entered through a rosy curtain into a room, which he supposed to be "that quiet room beyond," of which she had spoken.

It was a large room, square in shape. The floor was covered with black and white tiles, with the exception of a small square space in the centre, which looked like silver, and over which a ripple seemed occasionally to pass. She pointed it out to him. "That," she said, "is the glass of supreme moments." There were no windows, and the soft light that filled the room seemed to come from that liquid silver mirror in the centre of the floor. The walls, which were lofty, were hung with curtains of different colours, all subdued, dreamy, reposeful. These colours were repeated in the painting of the ceiling. In a recess at the further end of the room there were seats, low seats on which one could sleep. There was a faint smell of syringa in the air, making it heavy and drowsy. Now and then one heard faintly, as if afar off, the great music of an organ. Could it, he found himself wondering, be the organ of the college chapel? It was restful and pleasant to hear. She drew him to one of the seats in the recess, and once more pointed to the mirror.

"All the ecstasy in the world lies reflected there. The supreme moments of each man's life—the scene, the spoken words—all lie there. Past and present, and future—all are there."

"Shall I be able to see them?"

"If you will."

"And how?"

"Bend over the mirror, and say the name of the man or woman into whose life you wish to see. You only have to want it, and it will appear before your eyes. But there are some lives which have no supreme moments."

"Commonplace lives?"

"Yes."

Lucas Morne walked to the edge of the mirror and knelt down, looking into it. The ripple passed to and fro over the surface. For a moment he hesitated, doubting for whom he should ask; and then he said in a low voice: "Are there supreme moments in the life of Blake—Vincent Blake, the athlete?" The surface of the mirror suddenly grew still, and in it rose what seemed a living picture.

He could see once more the mile race in which he had been defeated by Blake. It was the third and last lap; and he himself was leading by some twenty yards, for Blake was waiting. There was a vast crowd of spectators, and he could hear every now and then the dull sound of their voices. He saw Vincent Blake slightly quicken his pace, and marked his own plucky attempt to answer it; he saw, too, that he had very little left in him. Gradually Blake drew up, until at a hundred yards from the finish there were not more than five yards between the two runners. Then he noticed his own fresh attempt. There were some fifty yards of desperate fighting, in which neither seemed to gain or lose an inch on the other. The voices of the excited crowd rose to a roar. And then—then Blake had it his own way. He saw himself passed a yard from the tape.

"Blake has always just beaten me," he said savagely as he turned from the mirror.

He went back to his seat. "Tell me," he said: "Does that picture really represent the supreme moments of Blake's life?"

"Yes," answered the veiled woman, "he will have nothing quite like the ecstasy which he felt at winning that race. He will marry, and have children, and his married life will be happy, but the happiness will not be so intense. There is an emotion-meter outside this room, you know, which measures such things."

"Now if one wanted to bet on a race," he began. Then he stopped short. He had none of the finer perceptions, but it did not take these to show him that he was becoming a little inappropriate. "I will look again at the mirror," he added after a pause. "I am afraid, though, that all this will make me more discontented with myself."

Once more he looked into the glass of supreme moments. He murmured the name of Paul Reece, the good little dissenter, his old schoolfellow. It was not in the power of accomplishment that Paul Reece excelled Lucas Morne, but only in the goodness and spirituality of his nature. As he looked, once more a picture formed on the surface of the mirror. It was of the future this time.

It was a sombre picture of the interior of a church. Through the open door one saw the snow falling slowly into the dusk of a winter afternoon. Within, before the richly decorated altar, flickered the little ruby flames of hanging lamps. On the walls, dim in the dying light, were painted the stations of the Cross. The fragrance of the incense smoke still lingered in the air. He could see but one figure, bowed, black-robed, before the altar. "And is this Paul Reece—who was a dissenter?" he asked himself, knowing that it was he. Some one was seated at the organ, and the cry of the music was full of appeal, and yet full of peace; *"Agnus Dei, qui tollis peccata mundi!"*

Then the picture died away, and once more the little ripple moved to and fro over the surface of the liquid silver mirror. Lucas went back again to his place. The veiled woman was leaning backward, her small white hands linked together. She did not speak, but he was sure that she was looking at him—looking at him intently. Slowly it came to him that there was in this woman a subtle, mastering attraction which he had never known before. And side by side with this thought there still remained the feeling which had filled him as he witnessed the supreme moments of Paul Reece, a paradoxical feeling which was half restlessness and half peace.

"I do not know if I envy Paul," he said, "but if so, it is not the envy which hurts. I shall never be like him. I can't feel as he does. It's not in me. But this picture did not make me angry as the other did." He looked steadfastly at the graceful, veiled figure, and added in a lower tone: "When I spoke of the travels of my cousin a little while ago—over Palestine, and Turkey, and thereabouts, you know—I had meant to lead up to a question, as you saw. I had meant to ask you if you would put away your veil and let me see your face. And there are many things which I want to know about you. May I not stay here by your side and talk?"

"Soon, very soon, I will talk with you, and after that you shall see me.

What do you think, then, of the glass of supreme moments?"

"It is wonderful. I only feared the sight of exquisite happiness in others would make me more discontented. At first you seemed to think that I was too dissatisfied."

"Do not be deceived. Do not think that these supreme moments are everything; for that life is easiest which is gentle, level, placid, and has no supreme moments. There is a picture in the life, of your friend Fynsale which I wish you to see. Look at it in the mirror, and then I shall have something to tell you."

Lucas did as he was bidden. The mirror showed him a wretched, dingy room—sitting-room and bedroom combined—in a lodging-house. At a little rickety table, pushed in front of a very small fire, Fynsale sat writing by lamp-light. The lamp was out of order apparently. The combined smell of lamp and Latakia was poignant. There was a pile of manuscript before him, and on the top of it he was placing the sheet he had just written. Then he rose from his chair, folded his arms on the mantel-piece, and bent down, with his head on his hands, looking into the fire. It was an uncouth attitude of which, Lucas remembered, Fynsale had been particularly fond when he was at college.

When the picture had passed, Lucas looked round, and saw that the veiled woman had left the recess, and was now standing by his side. "I do not understand this," he said. "How can those be the supreme moments in Fynsale's life? He looked poor and shabby, and the room was positively wretched. Where does the ecstasy come in?"

"He has just finished his novel; and he is quite madly in love with it. Some of it is very good, and some of it—from merely physical reasons—is very bad; he was half-starved when he was writing it, and it is not possible to write very well when one is half-starved. But he loves it. I am speaking of all this as if, like the picture of it, it was present; although, of course, it has not happened yet. But I will tell you more. I will show you, in this case at least, what these moments of ecstasy are worth. Some of Fynsale's book, I have said, is very good, and some of it is very bad; but none of it is what people want. He will take it to publisher after publisher, and they will refuse it. After three years it will at last be published, and it will not succeed in the least. And all through these years of failure he will recall from time to time the splendid joy he felt at finishing that book, and how glad he was that he had made it. The thought of that past ecstasy will make the torture all the worse."

"Perhaps, then, after all, I should be glad that I am commonplace?" said Lucas.

"It does not always follow, though, that the commonplace people have commonplace lives. There have been men who have been so ordinary that it hurt one to have anything to do with them, and yet the gods have made them come into poetry."

Once more Lucas fancied that a smile with magic in it might be flutter-ing under that gray veil. Every moment the fascination of this woman, whose face he had not seen, and with whom he had spoken for so short a time, grew stronger on him. He did not know from whence it came, whether it lay in the grace of her figure and her movements, or in the beauty of her long, dark hair, or in the music of her voice, or in that sub-tle, indefinable way in which she seemed to show him that she cared for him deeply. The room itself, quiet, mystical, restful, dedicated to the ec-stasy of the world, had its effect upon his senses. More than ever before he felt himself impressed, tremulous with emotion. He knew that she saw how, in spite of himself, the look of adoration would come into his eyes.

And suddenly, she, whom but a moment before he had imagined to be smiling at her own light thoughts, seemed swayed by a more serious im-pulse.

"You must be comforted, though, and be angry with yourself no long-er. For you are not commonplace, because you know that you are com-monplace. It is something to have wanted the right things, although the gods have given you no power to attain them, nor even the wit and words to make your want eloquent." Her voice was deeper, touched with the un-der-thrill.

"This," he said, "is the second time you have spoken of the gods—and yet we are in the nineteenth century."

"Are we? I am very old and very young. Time is nothing to me; it does not change me. Yesterday in Italy each grave and stream spoke of divinity: *'Non omnis moriar,'* sang one in confidence, *'Non omnis moriar!'* I heard his voice, and now he is passed and gone from the world."

"We read him still," said Lucas Morne, with a little pride. He was not intending to take the classical tripos, but he had with the help of a transla-tion read that ode from which she was quoting. She did not heed his inter-ruption in the least. She went on speaking:

"And to-day in England there is but little which is sacred; yet here, too, my work is seen; and here, too, as they die, they cry: 'I shall not die, but live!'"

"You will think me stupid," said Lucas Morne, a little bewildered, "but I really do not understand you. I do not follow you. I cannot see to what you refer."

"That is because you do not know who I am. Before the end of to-day I think we shall understand each other well."

There was a moment's pause, and then Lucas Morne spoke again.

"You have told me that even in the lives of commonplace people there are sometimes supreme moments. I had scarcely hoped for them, and you have bidden me not to desire them. Shall I—even I—know what ecstasy means?"

"Yes, yes; I think so."

"Then let me see it, as I saw the rest pictured in the mirror." He spoke with some hesitation, his eyes fixed on the tiled floor of the room.

"That need not be," she answered, and she hardly seemed to have perfect control over the tones of her voice now. "That need not be, Lucas Morne, for the supreme moments of your life are here, here and now."

He looked up, suddenly and excitedly. She had flung back the gray veil over her long, dark hair, and stood revealed before him, looking ardently into his eyes. Her face was paler than that of average beauty; the lips, shapely and scarlet, were just parted; but the eyes gave the most wonderful charm. They were like flames at midnight—not the soft, gray eyes that make men better, but the passionate eyes that make men forget honour, and reason, and everything. She stretched out both hands towards him, impulsively, appealingly. He grasped them in his own. His own hands were hot, burning; every nerve in them tingled with excitement. For a moment he held her at arm's-length, looking at her, and said nothing. At last he found words:

"I knew that you would be like this. I think that I have loved you all my life. I wish that I might be with you for ever."

There was a strange expression on her face. She did not speak, but she drew him nearer to her.

"Tell me your name," he said.

"Yesterday, where that poet lived—that confident poet—they called me Libitina; and here, to-day, they call me Death. My name matters not, if you love me. For to you alone have I come thus. For the rest, I have done my work unseen. Only in this hour—only in this hour—was it possible."

He had hardly heeded what she said. He bent down over her face.

"Stay!" she said in a hurried whisper, "if you kiss me you will die."

He smiled triumphantly. "But I shall die kissing you," he said. And so their lips met. Her lips were scarlet, but they were icy cold.

The captain of the football team had just come out of evening chapel, his gown slung over his arm, his cap pulled over his eyes, looking good-tempered, and strong, and jolly, but hardly devotional. He saw the window of Morne's rooms open—they were on the ground floor—and looked in. By the glow of the failing fire he saw what he thought was Lucas Morne seated in a lounge chair. He called to him, but there was no answer. "The old idiot's asleep," he said to himself, as he climbed in at the window. "Wake up, old man," he cried, as he put his hand on the shoulder of Lucas Morne's body, and swung it forward; "wake up, old man."

The body rolled forward and fell sideways to the ground heavily and clumsily. It lay there motionless.

Exchange

I
DORIS

There was once a girl-child named Doris who went out skating with her bigger brothers one afternoon over flooded fields in the Fen country. But her brothers played hockey with schoolfellows, and Doris skated contentedly enough by herself. She was wearing Bob's skates, which she liked better than her own, and the man had put them on very well indeed. She went from one field through a gap in the hedge into the next, and then on into a third field. There were very few people here, and most of the ice was not swept; all of this was very pleasant to Doris, and made her feel adventurous. It was beautiful, too; and even children unconsciously understand a sunset with those old thin trees trembling black against the crimson disc, and everywhere bits of white brightness on a gray sea of fog. She skated as fast as she could, the wind helping her, feeling strangely and splendidly animated, when quite suddenly . . .

But this was not the Fen country. This was the north of Yorkshire. She had been here before on a visit to her cousins. Yonder was the top of Winder; she had climbed it on clear days and seen Morecambe Bay flashing in the distance. But it was night now, almost a black night, and it was very cold for Doris to be wandering over those hills alone. She had an irritating sensation that she had to go somewhere before the dawn came, and that she did not know where or why. It was lonely and awesome. "If I only had somebody to speak to, I shouldn't mind it so much," she said to herself. At once she heard a low voice saying "Doris! Doris!" and she looked round.

In a recess of the ravine which a ghyll had made for itself as it leapt from the cold purity of a hill-top to the warm humanity of a village in the valley—a village no better than it should have been—a small fire of sticks was smouldering. Doris could just see that the person crouched in front of the fire—the person who had called her by her name—was an old, haggard woman, with her chin resting on her knees.

"Tell me, old woman," Doris said, almost angrily, "what does this all mean? I was at Lingay Fen skating, and now I am wandering over the Yorkshire hills. It has changed from afternoon to night—"

"It generally does," said the old woman in a chilly, unemphatic way. Doris stamped her foot impatiently: "I mean that it has changed quite suddenly. Just a moment ago, too, I felt quite certain that I had to go somewhere, and I had forgotten where. Now I don't think I have to go anywhere."

"No—you have arrived," said the old woman softly.

At that moment a dry twig burst into flame, and lit up the old woman's face and figure for a second. She was hideous enough; her face was thin and yellow; her cavernous eyes sparkled to the momentary flicker. Her dress and cloak were torn and faded, but they had been bright scarlet.

"You naturally ask why," she continued, "because you are young and have not yet learned the uselessness of it. What has just happened to you seems very meaningless and foolish, but it is not more meaningless and foolish than the rest of things. It is all a poor sort of game, you know. Explain? No, I shall not explain; but it was I who brought you here. Sit down by me under the night sky, and watch."

"No, I will not," said Doris, and walked away. She took about ten paces away, and then came back again and did the very thing which she said she would not do. She sat down by the old woman, and was a little angry because she could not help doing it. Then she began to grumble at the fire. "That's not half a fire," she said; "it just smoulders and makes smoke. I will show you what you ought to do. You put on some fresh sticks—so. Then you put your mouth quite close to the embers, and blow and keep—on—blowing. There!" She had fitted her actions to her words, and now a bright flame leaped out. It shone all over, on her dark hair and dark bright eyes, and on the gray furs of her dress. It shone, too, on the old woman, who was smiling an ugly, half-suppressed smile.

"Doris," said the old woman, "leave the fire alone. I do not want flame. I only want it to stream forth smoke."

"But why?"

"See now—there." The old woman made a downward gesture with both hands, and the flame sank obediently down again, giving place to a quick yield of black smoke. "Look at the smoke, Doris. That is what you have to watch." There was a little more energy in the old, quavering voice now.

Doris did as she was told; but suddenly she stopped and cried, half-frightened: "There are faces in it!"

"Yes, yes," said the old woman almost eagerly; "and there are pictures of the future in it—of the future as it will be unless I alter it this night. I alone can alter it, you know. Are you not glad now that you came?"

"It is something like fortune-telling: did you ever have your fortune told?"

"No, I never did," replied the old woman. Her smile was very ugly indeed.

"But how shall I know that it's true?"

"Why, you *do* know."

That was the strangest part of it. Doris felt certain without having a reason that she could give for it. "Show me my future," she said breathlessly.

"Watch the smoke, then."

So she watched, and picture followed picture. At the first of them she made some little exclamation. "Ah!" she cried, "that is a splendid dress; and I *do* like those shoes. I wish I might have long dresses now—I'm sure I'm old enough; and I want to have my hair done up the proper way, but—." She stopped suddenly, because the picture had changed. "I look much prettier in this one," she said. "I have been dancing, I think, from the dress, and because I seem a little out of breath. There is a man with me and now he— no, no! I would *not*. I should hate it. That picture cannot be right!" The third picture represented her marriage with great splendour. "Well," she said, "I do not mind that so much—just standing up and wearing a beautiful veil. But I don't want to be married at all. I like skating ever so much better."

There was a faint sound of laughter, muffled and bitter, from the old woman. "You like skating?" she said. "Where are your skates, then, Doris?" Doris looked for them, but could not find them, and this distressed her. "Oh, what *shall* I do? They were not my skates: they were Bob's."

"Who is Bob?"

"Bob is my smallest brother—ever so much younger than I am; he's my favourite brother, too. He's got red hair, but he's a pretty boy."

"He must be a milksop if he can't skate."

"He *can* skate. He can do the outside edge backwards; he skates better than any of my three big brothers."

"Well, well—it's a pity that he's stupid though."

"Stupid. Do you know why he lent me his skates? Because he was going to write a story this afternoon, and he's going to put me in it. Bob can do almost anything. He's wonderful. When he grows up he'll very likely write a whole book, he says."

"Look at his future—Bob's future—in the smoke," said the old woman grimly, heaping on more sticks.

Doris looked reluctantly. The pictures came flashing past one after the other. Some she could not altogether understand, for she knew nothing of the vices of young men; but they were vaguely terrible. But even a child could understand the last picture of all. It was awful and vivid. She almost fancied that she could hear the report of the pistol, and the dim thud as the body fell awkwardly on the floor.

"You needn't cry," said the old woman, as Doris burst into tears.

"Oh—Bob is so splendid!" sobbed Doris. "Don't let it be like that. Do alter it. You don't know him, or you would change it. You said you could. I'll give you everything I've got if you'll stop it somehow."

"Will you give me your beauty—your youth—your life?"

"Oh, willingly—everything!"

"I want none of them—none of them," said the old woman fiercely and quickly. "But I want something else. Give it me, and I will alter it, as you wish." She stretched out a lean finger and tapped Doris's forehead, and whispered a few words in her ear.

Doris turned white enough, but she nodded assent. "Then it will alter my future too," she said with a little gasp.

"It will alter the future of everybody in the world—indirectly and in some cases very slightly. But you will give it me?"

"Yes, yes." She paused a moment, and then added a torrent of questions: "Old woman, who are you? Why are you dressed in scarlet, why did you have me brought here? I should like it to turn out to be a dream. Oh! why do you want it? Why are you so horribly—horribly cruel?"

But the old woman, and the fire, and the great dark hills grew dim and indistinct; and there was no answer.

The two old men—one with a medical, the other with a military air— came slowly down the broad staircase from the bedrooms without speaking. The little red-headed boy was waiting for them as usual. "Is Doris any better, papa?" he asked eagerly. "Will she live?"

It was no good to keep it from him; he would have to know sooner or later.

"Yes, Bob," said the Colonel, "she will live. But the—the injury to her head has—" He stopped with a gulping sound in his voice. The boy looked up at him wistfully with a scared face.

"Don't, Colonel," said the doctor; "you'd better leave it to me. I will tell the boy."

II
MAJOR GUNNICAL

Nobody ever denied in my presence that Major Gunnical was a capital shot and a good fellow. He went straight, and it was always imputed to him for righteousness. But the other day the only man of the world with whom I am acquainted accused the Major of want of taste, and based his accusation on the fact that he took the liberty of dying in the country-house of a friend, not having been invited for that purpose. I might have pointed out that Major Gunnical knew Sir Charles quite well enough to take a liberty which would have been unpardonable in a casual guest; I might have added that it was one of those accidents which may happen to any man, and that it was unintentional and unforeseen on the Major's part. But I prefer to give the facts of the case, which seem to me to explain everything.

On the evening which opened the night of his death, Major Gunnical had gone upstairs to dress sooner than the rest of them. He stood in his bedroom with his back to the fire, well knowing that if the back be warm the whole body is warm also. He was half afraid that he had caught a chill, and chills affected him. There was nothing in his appearance to tell you that his heart was wrong. His body was large and muscular, and he looked a strong man. His hair had only just begun to get a little gray. His complexion was pale, but it had been tanned by hot suns and seemed clear and healthy. His eyes were thoughtful gray eyes—quite out of keeping with the active look of the man. His best point was his simple directness: he could do right things, even when they were not easy, without thinking of them at the time or afterwards. His worst point was his temper, which broke loose occasionally. At the present moment he was thinking about himself, which was not a usual occurrence with Major Gunnical, and his thoughts were depressing; so he tried to dismiss them. "It's all nervousness and too much tobacco," he thought to himself; "but I will go up to town to-morrow and let old Peterson prescribe for me. I shall be all right in a day—probably only liver—no exercise, thanks to this cursed frost. Oh yes, it's just liver—nothing else."

He paused once when he was fastening his collar, and said slowly and distinctly, "Damn presentiments." But he was not able to shake off a feeling of quietness: a desire to be at peace with men, and a tendency to look at the sad side of things. When he got downstairs he found only one man already in the drawing-room: a man called Kenneth, who wrote. Now there was a certain disagreement between Kenneth and the Major. In the smoking-room the night before, the Major had expressed his sincere admiration for a certain story of soldier-life by a new writer, and Kenneth had explained to him that this admiration was wrong, because the story was not at all well constructed.

"I own," he had said, "that it takes a critic to see the faults of the technique." This was a little vain of Kenneth. "Yes," said the Major hotly, "and it takes a *man* to feel the merits of the story." This was a little rude of the Major, for Kenneth was obviously an effeminate person. Kenneth put up his eyeglasses and looked at the Major curiously. "Don't be so damnably affected," said the Major. Then Sir Charles had interposed lazily.

Consequently, when the Major entered the drawing-room Kenneth at once began to assume more dignity than Providence had made him able to carry easily. The Major walked up to him and held out one hand. "Look here, Kenneth," he said, "I'm an old fool, and always thinking I know another man's business as well as my own. I'd no right to question your opinion last night and make an angry ass of myself. I'm sorry." Kenneth's dignity came down heavily, and he took the Major's hand at once. For a fortnight he loved him, and then he told publicly the story of how he had gone to the Major and forced him to apologize. For there is a combination of imagination and vanity which nothing—not even kindness—can kill.

The Major was very dull at dinner, but when his host's two children came in afterwards they seemed to find him very satisfactory. The Major loved children. He did not stop very long in the smoking-room that night. He wanted badly to be alone.

For some time after he had gone to bed he lay awake thinking. Maude, his host's elder daughter, reminded him in appearance of his own niece Doris. It seemed hard that Maude should be so bright and happy, and that Doris—owing to a skating accident—should be condemned to lose all her brightness, and her flow of talk, and her power to understand. Yet Doris never seemed actually unhappy; her eyes were vacant, as if the light behind them had gone out, but she did not seem to be suffering. During the first part of her illness she had babbled about some woman, an old woman dressed in scarlet, who frightened her.

Thus thinking, the Major fell asleep. It was long past midnight when he opened his eyes and saw a figure of a woman standing on the hearthrug, and stretching yellow hands like claws towards the remnant of the fire. It startled him, but he did not want to wake up the rest of the house.

"What are you doing in my room?" he said in a rapid whisper.

The old woman turned round. He could hardly see her face, but the flicker of the fire showed him that she was dressed in rags of faded scarlet.

Her voice was very gentle and low.

"Awake? Are you awake? I made a little noise to wake you on purpose. But generally they go on sleeping when I come. I am the scarlet woman of whom Doris spoke. She has been taken."

"Dead? A merciful deliverance."

"No, she is not delivered yet. She has to go through life again in a lower form before she is delivered. I hate her. I will see that she is unhappy again before she is delivered."

"Why does this all seem real, instead of seeming fantastic and absurd—as t ought to?"

"Because it *is* real: but they always ask me that, all those who see me. Doris shall become a caged bird, I think—one of those who are driven nearly mad by captivity, and yet are so strong that they die slowly."

"You can't do that," said the Major quickly.

"You know I can, and you know I shall," replied the old woman in the same soft whisper. "I need not argue, or prove, or do anything of that kind. When I speak men *know* that all is as I say; but they do not often hear me, because they are nearly always asleep when I come."

"Where is Doris now?"

"She waits in dreamland, where nothing is real, until I get my opportunity, and she is born once more, and caught, and caged, and tortured."

As she said this she seemed to grow a little more excited; and, as if in sympathy with her, the fire suddenly burned up more brightly, and showed her horrible, lean face and deep, leering eyes.

"That's cruel," said the Major. "And what shall I be when I die?"

"You will not have a bad time," she said, grinning. "You shall be a dear little white lamb that lives an hour and then is delivered. You will die to-night, by-the-way. But Doris shall beat her heart out against bars, because I hate her. You will see one another in dreamland, while you are waiting until I get the two right opportunities."

An idea occurred to the Major. "Change us, Doris and myself."

The old woman trembled with agitation, and her voice rose shrilly. "I will not! I will not!" she cried.

But something bright and sure, like a steady light, seemed to fill the man's mind. "But you will—you cannot help it," he answered very quietly.

The old woman strode quickly across the room, her face aflame with rage, and touched him on the heart. He fell backward, and did not speak any more.

"I must always come when they are asleep in future," said the old woman, as she went back to the fire. "It is too much to risk—I have lost by Doris and this man." There was a long pause. "But I will torture him even more than I would have tortured Doris," she whispered gently to the fire.

Two months afterwards a white lamb was born, in a sheltered place, on a grassy fell. And in an hour it died.

And on the same day a certain bird-catcher, resident in Whitechapel, went out early and had luck.

III
DORIS IN THE HEREAFTER

The release had come at last. To Doris it was an exquisite release; the years spent in darkness were over; the short, mystical period which followed her death was over; her spirit went out into the moonlit night—white, naked, beautiful. She could remember but little consciously of her earth-life. She had suffered—she could recollect that, and she had spoken with a grim woman: an old woman dressed in rags of faded scarlet. She did not recollect what had been said, but she knew that it had been the beginning of the darkness which had fallen on her mind. Of her death she knew nothing; of a short strange time after her death she knew little, dimly and vaguely.

She was free, and it was enough for her. It seemed to her that she still kept the body which had been called Doris during its earth-life, but that now it was light as the air, stronger than before, and far more beautiful. She stood, a childish figure, graceful and erect, on a shred of dark cloud which a steady night-wind blew past the hill-tops and over the valley. Below her she could see the flooded river, angry with its old stone bridges, crying itself to sleep in long, still reaches, with the mists rising white all about it. She saw, too, much that the living do not see. In a lonely cottage, low and roughly built, some young Spring flowers had just died: she saw their souls—their fragrance, as she had been used to call it—pass upwards; and as they passed they changed, and became a handful of ghost-lilies in the garden-land of dreams. And all night long she went on her way, seeing beautiful things. She could never be tired any more; and the rain and the dew did not hurt her; and the cold wind did not seem cold to her.

And when the morning came, a little baby breeze came up to her with a message. It was so young and forgetful that it had not got the exact words of the message. But it remembered the drift of it. "He said you were to go and look for sorrows," it whispered in her ear. It lingered for a moment, playing with her hair, and then it went down below and tried to blow a dandelion clock. And not being strong enough, it sat down and sulked; for it had not yet learnt that the only things worth doing are the things one cannot do.

Then Doris went on about her work, very happy, singing little songs that she remembered. And first of all she went to a great house where a proud and beautiful lady lived. But the proud lady sat huddled up and quite undignified in her own room, crying till her nose was red and she was not pleasant to see. And all because some one or other—I think it was her husband—was dead, and was going to be for ever happy! Doris laughed contemptuously, and passed on.

She next went to a nursery where there was a little freckled girl with sandy hair. And the little girl was unhappy because of a bad accident to a ninepenny doll, which was her most intimate friend. There was a small hole in the doll's neck and a possible escape of sawdust. It was only by holding the doll wrong way up and shaking it that you could make the sawdust come out; and the little girl did not want the sawdust to come out at all, for it caused her agony when it came out; and yet she held the doll upside down and shook it. For this was the kind of girl that, when she grows up, becomes a woman. Doris was sorry for her, and whispered in her ear: "You had better get a little piece of stamp-paper and stick it over the hole in the doll's neck—but it won't last long." The child thought Doris was a beautiful idea, and went radiantly to the study and opened the dispatch-box. There was no stamp paper. There was one penny stamp, and she knew that it was wicked to take it. So she compromised—which was feminine of her—and tore the stamp in two and only took half of it. Then she went back to the nursery, and fixed the half-stamp as Doris had suggested. Doris, who had watched her, was horrified. "You ought not to have taken that stamp," she said to her. "You had better confess what you have done, and say that you do not wish to tell a lie." Then the little girl supposed Doris was conscience—for, of course, Doris was invisible—and did not think quite so much of her. Neither did she confess. Doris was not very unhappy about it, knowing that children are always forgiven and occasionally forgotten.

She saw many other sorrows, and she thought very little of them. People, she perceived, always exaggerated the importance of death, of money, and love. Yet she saw a wind—a venomous wind—snap the stalk of the very loveliest daffodil, and nobody wore black clothes for it, or had sherry-and-biscuits, or showed any of the signs of sorrow. She had only been for a few hours in the Hereafter, and yet she already felt herself to be out of touch with humanity.

And it happened that she came to a great dirty city, and she stopped where a cage of wicker-work was hung outside a grimy shop in a grimy street. There were several things in the cage: a yellow glass for water, with no water in it; a blue glass for seed, with no seed in it; something which had once been a turf and now looked like a badly cooked brick; and something which panted on the floor of the cage in the corner—it was all that was left of a bird, a soaring bird that loved the upper air and the sunlight, but was now reduced to plain dying and high thinking. Now none of the other sorrowful persons had seen Doris; but the bird saw her and called to her, but she did not understand the language. She went into the shop and whispered to the man in charge: "Your bird outside wants attention; it's ill."

"Bless my soul! and I gave a shilling for it!" So he took the bird some water and something to eat which was not good for it. The bird chirped. "It knows me, and loves me already," said the man. It was really saying, "Would you kindly wring my neck, and end this?"

"I am sorry for it," said Doris, as she passed on. "I am glad I was never a pet." She would have been more sorry if she had known all the history of that bird.

The Diary of a God

During the week there had been several thunderstorms. It was after the last of these, on a cool Saturday evening, that he was found at the top of the hill by a shepherd. His speech was incoherent and disconnected; he gave his name correctly, but could or would add no account of himself. He was wet through, and sat there pulling a sprig of heather to pieces. The shepherd afterwards said that he had great difficulty in persuading him to come down, and that he talked much nonsense. In the path at the foot of the hill he was recognised by some people from the farmhouse where he was lodging, and was taken back there. They had, indeed, gone out to look for him. He was subsequently removed to an asylum, and died insane a few months later.

Two years afterwards, when the furniture of the farmhouse came to be sold by auction, there was found in a little cupboard in the bedroom which he had occupied an ordinary penny exercise-book. This was partly filled, in a beautiful and very regular handwriting, with what seems to have been something in the nature of a diary, and the following are extracts from it:

June 1st.—It is absolutely essential to be quiet. I am beginning life again, and in quite a different way, and on quite a different scale, and I cannot make the break suddenly. I must have a pause of a few weeks in between the two different lives. I saw the advertisement of the lodgings in this farmhouse in an evening paper that somebody had left at the restaurant. That was when I was trying to make the change abruptly, and I may as well make a note of what happened.

After attending the funeral (which seemed to me an act of hypocrisy, as I hardly knew the man, but it was expected of me), I came back to my Charlotte Street rooms and had tea. I slept well that night. Then next morning I went to the office at the usual hour, in my best clothes, and with a deep band still on my hat. I went to Mr. Toller's room and knocked. He said, "Come in," and after I had entered: "Can I do anything for you? What do you want?"

Then I explained to him that I wished to leave at once. He said:

"This seems sudden, after thirty years' service."

"Yes," I replied. "I have served you faithfully for thirty years, but things have changed, and I have now three hundred a year of my own. I will pay something in lieu of notice, if you like, but I cannot go on being a clerk any more. I hope, Mr. Toller, you will not think that I speak with any impertinence to yourself, or any immodesty, but I am really in the position of a private gentleman."

He looked at me curiously, and as he did not say anything I repeated:

"I think I am in the position of a private gentleman."

In the end he let me go, and said very politely he was sorry to lose me. I said good-bye to the other clerks, even to those who had sometimes laughed at what they imagined to be my peculiarities. I gave the better of the two office-boys a small present in money.

I went back to the Charlotte Street rooms, but there was nothing to do there. There were figures going on in my head, and my fingers seemed to be running up and down columns. I had a stupid idea that I should be in trouble if Mr. Toller were to come in and catch me like that. I went out and had a capital lunch, and then I went to the theatre. I took a stall right in the front row, and sat there all by myself. Then I had a cab to the restaurant. It was too soon for dinner, so I ordered a whisky-and-soda, and smoked a few cigarettes. The man at the table next me left the evening paper in which I saw the advertisement of these farmhouse lodgings. I read the whole of the paper, but I have forgotten it all except that advertisement, and I could say it by heart now—all about bracing air and perfect quiet and the rest of it. For dinner I had a bottle of champagne. The waiter handed me a list, and asked which I would prefer. I waved the list away and said:

"Give me the best."

He smiled. He kept on smiling all through dinner until the end; then he looked serious. He kept getting more serious. Then he brought two other men to look at me. They spoke to me, but I did not want to talk. I think I fell asleep. I found myself in my rooms in Charlotte Street next morning, and my landlady gave me notice because, she said, I had come home beastly drunk. Then that advertisement flashed into my mind about the bracing air. I said:

"I should have given you notice in any case; this is not a suitable place for a gentleman."

June 3rd.—I am rather sorry that I wrote down the above. It seems so degrading. However, it was merely an act of ignorance and carelessness on my part, and, besides, I am writing solely for myself. To myself I may own freely that I made a mistake, that I was not used to the wine, and that I had not fully gauged what the effects would be. The incident is disgusting, but I simply put it behind me, and think no more about it. I pay here two pounds ten shillings a week for my two rooms and board. I take my meals, of course, by myself in the sitting-room. It would be rather cheaper if I took them with the family, but I do not care about that. After all, what is two pounds ten shillings a week? Roughly speaking, a hundred and thirty pounds a year.

June 17th.—I have made no entry in my diary for some days. For a certain period I have had no heart for that or for anything else. I had told the people here that I was a private gentleman (which is strictly true), and that I was engaged in literary pursuits. By the latter I meant to imply no more than that I am fond of reading, and that it is my intention to jot down from time to time my sensations and experiences in the new life which has burst upon me. At the same time I have been greatly depressed. Why, I can hardly explain. I have been furious with myself. Sitting in my own sitting-room, with a gold-tipped cigarette between my fingers, I have been possessed (even though I recognised it as an absurdity) by a feeling that if Mr. Toller were to come in suddenly I should get up and apologize. But the thing which depressed me most was the open country. I have read, of course, those penny stories about the poor little ragged boys who never see the green leaf in their lives, and I always thought them exaggerated. So they are exaggerated: there are the Embankment Gardens with the Press Band playing; there are parks; there are Sunday-school treats. All these little ragged boys see the green leaf, and to say they do not is an exaggeration—I am afraid a wilful exaggeration. But to see the open country is quite a different thing. Yesterday was a fine day, and I was out all day in a place called Wensley Dale. On one spot where I stood I could see for miles all round. There was not a single house, or tree, or human being in sight. There was just myself on the top of a moor; the bigness of it gave me a regular scare. I suppose I had got used to walls: I had got used to feeling that if I went straight ahead without stopping I should knock against something. That somehow made me feel safe. Out on that great moor—just as if I were the last man left alive in the world—I do not feel safe. I find the track and get home again, and I tremble like a half-drowned kitten until I see a wall again, or somebody with a surly face who does not answer civilly when I speak to him. All these feelings will wear off, no doubt, and I shall be able to enter upon the new phase of my existence without any discomfort. But I was quite right to take a few months' quiet retirement. One must get used to things gradually. It was the same with the champagne—to which, by the way, I had not meant to allude any further.

June 20th.—It is remarkable what a fascination these very large moors have for me. It is not exactly fear any more—indeed, it must be the reverse. I do not care to be anywhere else. Instead of making this a mere pause between two different existences, I shall continue it. To that I have quite made up my mind. When I am out there in a place where I cannot see any trees, or houses, or living things, I am the last person left alive in the world. I am a kind of a god. There is nobody to think anything at all about me, and it does not matter if my clothes are not right, or if I drop an " h"—which I rarely do except when speaking very quickly. I never knew what real independence was before. There have been too many houses around, and too many people looking on. It seems to me now such a common and despicable thing to live among people, and to have one's character and one's ways altered by what they are going to think. I know now that when I ordered that bottle of champagne I did it far more to please the waiter and to make him think well of me than to please myself. I pity the kind of creature that I was then, but I had not known the open country at that time. It is a grand education. If Toller were to come in now I should say, "Go away. Go back to your bricks and mortar, and account-books, and swell friends, and white waistcoats, and rubbish of that kind. You cannot possibly understand me, and your presence irritates me. If you do not go at once I will have the dog let loose upon you." By the way, that was a curious thing which happened the other day. I feed the dog, a mastiff, regularly, and it goes out with me. We had walked some way, and had reached that spot where a man becomes the last man alive in the world. Suddenly the dog began to howl, and ran off home with its tail between its legs, as if it were frightened of something. What was it that the dog had seen and I had not seen? A ghost? In broad daylight? Well, if the dead come back they might walk here without contamination. A few sheep, a sweep of heather, a gray sky, but nothing that a living man planted or built. They could be alone here. If it were not that it would seem a kind of blasphemy, I would buy a piece of land in the very middle of the loneliest moor and build myself a cottage there.

June 23rd.—I received a letter to-day from Julia. Of course she does not understand the change which has taken place in me. She writes as she always used to write, and I find it very hard to remember and realize that I liked it once, and was glad when I got a letter from her. That was before I got into the habit of going into empty places alone. The old clerking, account-book life has become too small to care about. The swell life of the private gentleman, to which I looked forward, is also not worth considering. As for Julia, I was to have married her; I used to kiss her. She wrote to say that she thought a great deal of me; she still writes. I don't want her. I don't want anything. I have become the last man alive in the world. I shall leave this farmhouse very soon. The people are all right, but they are *people*, and therefore insufferable. I can no longer live or breathe in a place where I see people, or trees which people have planted, or houses which people have built. It is an ugly word—people.

July 7th.—I was wrong in saying that I was the last man alive in the world. I believe I am dead. I know now why the mastiff howled and ran away. The whole moor is full of them; one sees them after a time when one has got used to the open country—or perhaps it is because one is dead. Now I see them by moonlight and sunlight, and I am not frightened at all. I think I must be dead, because there seems to be a line ruled straight through my life, and the things which happened on the further side of the line are not real. I look over this diary, and see some references to a Mr. Toller, and to some champagne, and coming into money. I cannot for the life of me think what it is all about. I suppose the incidents described really happened, unless I was mad when I wrote about them. I suppose that I am not dead, since I can write in a book, and eat food, and walk, and sleep and wake again. But since I see them now—these people that fill up the lonely places—I must be quite different to ordinary human beings. If I am not dead, then what am I? To-day I came across an old letter signed "Julia Jarvis"; the envelope was addressed to me. I wonder who on earth she was?

July 9th.—A man in a frock-coat came to see me, and talked about my best interest. He wanted me, so far as I could gather, to come away with him somewhere. He said I was all right, or, at any rate, would become all right, with a little care. He would not go away until I said that I would kill him. Then the woman at the farmhouse came up with a white face, and I said I would kill her too. I positively cannot endure people. I am something apart, something different. I am not alive, and I am not dead. I cannot imagine what I am.

July 16th.—I have settled the whole thing to my complete satisfaction. I can without doubt believe the evidence of my own senses. I have seen, and I have heard. I know now that I am a god. I had almost thought before that this might be. What was the matter was that I was too diffident: I had no self-confidence; I had never heard before of any man, even a clerk in an old-established firm, who had become a god. I therefore supposed it was impossible until it was distinctly proved to be.

I had often made up my mind to go to that range of hills that lies to the north. They are purple when one sees them far off. At nearer view they are gray, then they become green, then one sees a silver network over the green. The silver network is made by streams descending in the sunlight. I climbed the hill slowly; the air was still, and the heat was terrible. Even the water which I drank from the running stream seemed flat and warm. As I climbed, the storm broke. I took but little notice of it, for the dead that I had met below on the moor had told me that lightning could not touch me. At the top of the hill I turned, and saw the storm raging beneath my feet. It is the greatest of mercies that I went there, for that is where the other gods gather, at such times as the lightning plays between them and the earth, and the black thunder-clouds, hanging low, shut them out from the sight of men.

Some of the gods were rather like the big pictures that I have seen on the hoardings, advertising plays at the theatre, or some food which is supposed to give great strength and muscular development. They were handsome in face, and without any expression. They never seemed to be angry or pleased, or hurt. They sat there in great long rows, resting, with the storm raging in between them and the earth. One of them was a woman. I spoke to her, and she told me that she was older than this earth; yet she had the face of a young girl, and her eyes were like eyes that I have seen before somewhere. I cannot think where I saw the eyes like those of the goddess, but perhaps it was in that part of my life which is forgotten and ruled off with a line. It gave one the greatest and most majestic feelings to stand there with the gods, and to know that one was a god one's self, and that lightning did not hurt one, and that one would live for ever.

July 18th.—This afternoon the storm returned, and I hurried to the meeting-place, but it is far away to the hills, and though I climbed as quickly as I could the storm was almost passed, and they had gone.

August 1st.—I was told in my sleep that to-morrow I was to go back to the hill again, and that once more the gods would be there, and that the storm would gather round us, and would shut us from profane sight, and the steely lightnings would blind any eye that tried to look upon us. For this reason I have refused now to eat or drink anything; I am a god and have no need of such things. It is strange that now when I see all real things so clearly and easily—the ghosts of the dead that walk across the moors in the sunlight and the concourse of the gods on the hill-top above the storm—men and women with whom I once moved before I became a god are no more to me than so many black shadows. I scarcely know one from the other, only that the presence of a black shadow anywhere near me makes me angry, and I desire to kill it. That will pass away; it is probably some faint relic of the thing that I once was in the other side of my life on the other side of the line which has been ruled across it. Seeing that I am a god it is not natural that I can feel anger or joy any more. Already all feeling of joy has gone from me, for to-morrow, so I was told in my sleep, I am to be betrothed to the beautiful goddess that is older than the world, and yet looks like a young girl, and she is to give me a sprig of heather as a token and—

It was on the evening of August 1 he was found.

This Is All

It was a very hot summer day. The doctor's brougham had been waiting in the shade of the chestnut avenue leading to the big white house. Then a servant brought out a message.

"Morning, Jameson"—he knew the coachman. "Stopping to luncheon—you're to go round to the stables."

"I guessed as much. What—is he worse this morning?"

"No, not a bit of it." Then, confidentially: "Between ourselves, there's no more the matter with Mr. Wyatt nor there is with you nor me."

"So I've always supposed." If you can be surprised at anything you will not make a good coachman. "Well—see you again later." And the wheels crunched slowly along the gravel.

In the meantime Mr. Alexander Wyatt paced the entire length of his great library. He was lean, tall, bent in the shoulders. His hair was gray and rather too long; his face was clean-shaven and ashy in colour. He looked worried—hunted.

Dr. Holling watched him narrowly. The doctor was no younger, but his hair was black. He was a giant—his chest was broad and deep, and he stood six foot three in his socks. His face was slightly florid, and his figure showed some tendency towards corpulence. But he looked like a man of the world, and not like a mere sensualist—there was that distinction. Under the heavy brows were the eyes of a man who knows what he wants to know and is quite sure that he knows it. He looked confident and clever.

"My dear fellow," said the doctor, "the long and short of it is that you ought to have come to me long ago. I don't mean in Harley Street—I mean here at home. Of course, I wouldn't see any ordinary patient here; but an old friend like you—yes, really you ought to have come to me."

"I might have gone up to Harley Street. It's only an hour away. You go there and back most days in the year, and I might have taken the journey for once. I don't know why I didn't—I had thought of it—but you're always so busy."

"Busy? Well, yes. But I don't let myself be so busy that I can't see a friend who's ill."

Wyatt sighed heavily.

"And now you're spoiling one of your rare holidays for my sake. I say, old man, do take a fee—a proper fee—something in proportion."

"Now, don't talk like that. If fees had had anything to do with it, could I have come to you and suggested that it might be as well if I just went over you? Besides, I wouldn't give up a day of my holiday for any fee. Why should I? I've already made more money than I shall ever spend. I'm not stopping because I've got a patient. I'm stopping because an old friend is ill."

"It's very good of you—very, very good."

"Come back to the point. Why didn't you send for me before—you must have known that you were ill?"

"I had my suspicions. I—I didn't want to think about it."

"And so you waited until, from mere casual observation, I also had my suspicions, and told you so. I think you were foolish. Come now: what were you afraid of? I haven't hurt you."

"No, no," said Wyatt. "Of course not. But I didn't want to know that I was going to die." There was a longish pause, and Wyatt's eyes grew rounder and stared. "O, my God! O, my God!" he muttered to himself.

"Well?" said Dr. Holling.

He hated these exhibitions, but he spoke sympathetically.

"I can't die!" stammered Wyatt. "It—it—it mustn't be—"

"You will find ultimately that you can die," said Dr. Holling. "We all shall. If you will persist in working yourself up into this condition of shivering cowar—of nervous panic, you will die rather sooner, or possibly very much sooner, than you otherwise would. Come, man, you may have another ten or a dozen years, if you'll avoid every kind of stress. You're wealthy, have no ambitions, have no hard work, are not passionately attached to anybody. It is highly unlikely that the stress will come upon you from the outside—take care that it does not come from yourself."

"You're right, you're right. I shall pull myself together," he said; but he still spoke excitedly. "I—I only gave way for the moment. Ten or a dozen years at the least; with absolute moderation, quiet living, self-restraint, and so on, who knows that it might not be a score of years?"

The doctor looked at him curiously and said nothing.

"There, you see—I'm all right. I've faced the situation. And now tell me exactly what's the matter with me."

"Heart," said the doctor laconically.

"I know that," Wyatt said irritably. "I want to know the name of the disease, and if there's any complication."

"Well, I shan't tell you. You'd try to look yourself up in your old edition of Roberts's 'Theory and Practice of Medicine,' and you'd find something more or less like yourself, and it wouldn't do you any good."

"Some doctors would have told me."

"Hang it! then, go and ask them," said Dr. Holling quite quietly. "Whomever else I meet in consultation, it's quite certain I won't meet my own patient."

"Of course not. I only mentioned it. I'm not silly enough to go to any other doctor—never dreamed of it. Of course, I know very well that you're the first man on heart. I'm not so ignorant of medicine as you suppose."

"Ah!" said the doctor cheerfully, "I wish you were twice as ignorant, or else knew a thousand times as much as you do."

Luncheon was announced. The doctor rose smiling. Poor Wyatt did what he could during luncheon to shake off the heavy depression that weighed on him, but he did not make much of a host. He could only talk of his own illness, and speculate on what death really was. On these subjects Dr. Holling had little to say, but he spoke of the rising value of land in the neighbourhood; and Wyatt was a landlord. Wyatt heard with a wretchedly simulated cheerfulness on his sad-eyed, sallow face. What would it profit him though he gained the whole world?

Wyatt had been in his day the brightest and best of companions; but when a man's material heart within him has taken on autumnal tints the man's spirits droop also. Both, the doctor knew, were symptomatic.

And he who knew this, and had known the old Wyatt, was patient; but when he was being driven away from the great white house he became very sad.

That afternoon Wyatt sat crouching in a big easy-chair in his library, alone. It was a hot day, but he had a shawl wrapped round his feet: latterly his feet had been always cold, as though already they felt the chill of wet earth. There was a pile of books on the table beside him, and on the floor. He turned avidly and restlessly from one to the other. There were comforting books of religion; there were terrifying books of religion; there were works of metaphysics; there were blasphemous diatribes; there was science conscious of its limitations. Now he would take for company some drunken tinker jeering at the notion of a hereafter, repelling by its brutal ignorance but appealing by its complete self-confidence. And now again he would hear the calm voice of science: "There are beautiful stories, but I dare not tell you that they are true. In some places, where it has been possible to test them, I have tested and found they were not true. As to the rest, those stories seem more beautiful than probable. I still wait for verification or disproof—not with folded hands, but working at other things."

He had always feared death and now for many long days and nights he had busied himself in this futile search for something certain about it. He heard a hundred voices all crying differently, and knew not to which he should listen.

He used to make attempts, from time to time, to pull himself together; he made one now.

"What does all this concern me?" he said aloud. "I'm not going to die. Holling said so. Holling gave me twenty years, with reasonable care, and he knows what he is talking about." He pushed the books aside contemptuously. "Pack of nonsense!" He picked up instead a catalogue that his wine merchant had sent him. There was some port of a fairly recent vintage that he wished to put down. "That's it," he said, marking the catalogue with pencil, "we'll say fifty dozen." He rubbed his chilly hands together, and hummed a light tune.

At five his man Jackson brought him in a glass of whisky-and-water, carefully measured. Wyatt had got into the habit of drinking a good deal of strong tea in the afternoon while he pottered over his collections—one philatelic, the other eighteenth-century autographs. The doctor had forbidden tea, and Wyatt, even when he was pulling himself together, obeyed the doctor.

Holling had forbidden late hours also. Wyatt had induced—actually induced—the habit of insomnia. Before the doctor's interference he would never go to bed before two or three in the morning. After one of his own delightful dinners, or if he had been dining out, he would still sit up. He professed that these hours were of incalculable value—that he could not live in society unless for a little time each day he lived absolutely alone. All the lights were put out except in the library; the rest of the house went to sleep. Wyatt smoked, read, thought about things. At intervals he sipped strong coffee. It was only when he found himself unable to keep awake that he lit his candle and went upstairs. Every night, or early morning, as his candle lit the long mirror on the landing, he saw himself reflected, and the reflection always came as a surprise. He never looked as he supposed that he looked; sometimes the reflection seemed almost unrecognisable.

"I can't sleep before three in the morning," Wyatt had maintained to the doctor.

"Then it must be morphia," said Holling.

He called that night with a hypodermic syringe, and that night Wyatt went up to bed at ten o'clock and slept at once.

"But I mustn't go on with morphia, of course," said Wyatt knowingly.

"It won't be necessary," said Holling. "You see, after I've given it you for three nights, I shall have broken through your habit. Then you at once return to the normal state, and go to sleep at the ordinary time."

The doctor reeled off this absolute nonsense with an air of the utmost gravity and conviction. He knew his patient. He had never given him any morphia at all—he had punctured the skin, but injected nothing. Wyatt's insomnia yielded completely to discreet and masterly humbug and the abolition of his after-dinner coffee.

Strong tea and late hours were quite given up now. Wyatt was positively anxious to give things up; in his mad terror of death he had grown to regard it as a monster to be appeased by sacrifice. He had a notion—vague but deeply rooted—that the more he gave up the longer he would live. He was almost disappointed that the doctor did not forbid stimulants.

Jackson, Wyatt's servant, had been with him for twenty years. When Wyatt was alone it was Jackson himself who made the after-dinner coffee—for on this point Wyatt mistrusted women. Jackson was a creature of habit. For over a week he had diligently remembered that coffee was forbidden. To-night he forgot it; habit asserted itself, and twenty minutes after Wyatt had left the dining-room for the library, Jackson entered the library with the coffee. He was considerably startled at his reception.

Fits of deep depression sometimes alternate with fits of extreme irritation. Wyatt flew into a mad rage. He swore the wretched man was trying to kill him, ordered him out of the house, and abused him virulently, loudly, and at length. "Go, go!" he shrieked finally.

Jackson conveyed the news to the kitchen that there was only one thing the matter with Mr. Wyatt—he was clean off his head, that was all.

As Jackson left the library Wyatt dropped into a chair, his face contorted, covered with sweat, bending forward, his hands tightly fixed against his chest. That awful anginal pain! No, it had never been like that before. It must mean death. Ah, if he could only get to that bell! He tried to call. The words, "Dr. Holling . . . at once," came out in a whisper.

The pain ceased, almost suddenly. A strange calm came over him, and for the first time in many days he thought of other people. Dr. Holling? Of course he would not send for him. It would be too bad, at that time of

night—altogether too bad. Besides, it was his own fault. He had given way
to temper, and had been punished for it. Why, he might have died. Upon
his word, it would have served him right if he *had* died. Poor Jackson! It
was the first time in his life he had spoken to Jackson like that. Well, when
he came to die Jackson was remembered in his will, and would forgive
him. After all, why live so long, at such care, with such trouble? Nature
calls—obey cheerfully.

And the calm became drowsiness, and the drowsiness became sleep all
very quickly. It was a lovely sleep, with a consciousness of well-being per-
meating its faintly-sketched dreams.

Jackson looked in at ten o'clock, at a quarter-past, at twenty-five minutes past, and at half-past.

Then he sought Mrs. Palfrey, the housekeeper.

"He's still asleep," said Jackson.

"You're sure it's sleep?" said Mrs. Palfrey gloomily.

"Oh, I leave to-morrow, anyhow, whatever he says," said Jackson. "It's
the responsibility I can't stand. It's wearing me. But come and see for
yourself."

They opened the library door cautiously and peered in.

"The top of his shirt-front's moving," said Mrs. Palfrey in an under-
tone. "He's asleep."

"Don't he look awful? I 'on't wake him. I swear I 'on't wake him."

"Better not. Put his candle on the table, by the lamp; cough, as if accidental, as you go out. Then if he wakes, so much the better. If not, we'll all
go to bed, and you'll put the lights out, same as in the old days."

Jackson shivered, and followed this advice carefully. The cough (as if
accidental) was unavailing, and the lights were put out. Only in the library
the lamplight fell on the gleaming shirt-front, still moving. And on the
landing the full-length mirror waited, its eyes closed in the darkness, but
ready to wake as the lighted candle came slowly up the staircase, and to
reflect in a moment the figure of the master of the house, dishevelled, late,
on his way to bed.

He was awake. The lamp had burned itself out; the dawn, the early
midsummer dawn, was already advanced; its light came, tempered yet sufficient, through the ugly Venetian blinds. From the garden and the country
beyond came the shrill concert of innumerable birds. A heavy cart jolted
and bumped to early work on some distant road. No, there was no need
of the candle; he would go to bed by daylight, with that delightful sense of

well-being, that firm conviction that there was no good in worry or argument, still comforting him.

Ah! how often at this hour he had trod the stairs, with a fantastic curiosity to see what he looked like in the tall mirror. By this time his head should have appeared in it, coming close to the Japanese cabinet. There in the mirror gleamed the pale gold of the cabinet, and there was the blue-and-white of the tall Oriental vase, and there were the masses of dark shadow beyond. Alexander Wyatt found all there but himself. Him only the mirror gave back no more.

Back! back to the library as in a panic. Something has happened!

And there in the library the spirit of Alexander Wyatt, that the mirror saw not, found in the easy-chair the huddled body, dressed in clothes that no longer moved to the breathing.

"I am dead," said Alexander Wyatt, "and this—this—this is all."

The Moon-Slave

The Princess Viola had, even in her childhood, an inevitable submission to the dance; a rhythmical madness in her blood answered hotly to the dance music, swaying her, as the wind sways trees, to movements of perfect sympathy and grace.

For the rest, she had her beauty and her long hair, that reached to her knees, and was thought lovable; but she was never very fervent and vivid unless she was dancing; at other times there almost seemed to be a touch of lethargy upon her. Now, when she was sixteen years old, she was betrothed to the Prince Hugo. With others the betrothal was merely a question of state. With her it was merely a question of obedience to the wishes of authority; it had been arranged; Hugo was *comme ci, comme ça*—no god in her eyes; it did not matter. But with Hugo it was quite different—he loved her.

The betrothal was celebrated by a banquet, and afterwards by a dance in the great hall of the palace. From this dance the Princess soon made her escape, quite discontented, and went to the furthest part of the palace gardens, where she could no longer hear the music calling her.

"They are all right," she said to herself as she thought of the men she had left, "but they cannot dance. Mechanically they are all right; they have learned it and don't make childish mistakes; but they are only one—two—three machines. They haven't the inspiration of dancing. It is so different when I dance alone."

She wandered on until she reached an old forsaken maze. It had been planned by a former king. All round it was a high crumbling wall with foxgloves growing on it. The maze itself had all its paths bordered with high opaque hedges; in the very centre was a circular open space with tall pinetrees growing round it. Many years ago the clue to the maze had been lost; it was but rarely now that anyone entered it. Its gravel paths were green with weeds, and in some places the hedges, spreading beyond their borders, had made the way almost impassable.

For a moment or two Viola stood peering in at the gate—a narrow gate with curiously twisted bars of wrought iron surmounted by a heraldic device. Then the whim seized her to enter the maze and try to find the space in the centre. She opened the gate and went in.

Outside everything was uncannily visible in the light of the full moon, but here in the dark shaded alleys the night was conscious of itself. She soon forgot her purpose, and wandered about quite aimlessly, sometimes forcing her way where the brambles had flung a laced barrier across her path, and a dragging mass of convolvulus struck wet and cool upon her cheek. As chance would have it she suddenly found herself standing under the tall pines, and looking at the open space that formed the goal of the maze. She was pleased that she had got there. Here the ground was carpeted with sand, fine and, as it seemed, beaten hard. From the summer night sky immediately above, the moonlight, unobstructed here, streamed straight down upon the scene.

Viola began to think about dancing. Over the dry, smooth sand her little satin shoes moved easily, stepping and gliding, circling and stepping, as she hummed the tune to which they moved. In the centre of the space she paused, looked at the wall of dark trees all round, at the shining stretches of silvery sand and at the moon above.

"My beautiful, moonlit, lonely, old dancing-room, why did I never find you before?" she cried; "but," she added, "you need music—there must be music here."

In her fantastic mood she stretched her soft, clasped hands upwards towards the moon.

"Sweet moon," she said in a kind of mock prayer, "make your white light come down in music into my dancing-room here, and I will dance most deliciously for you to see." She flung her head backward and let her hands fall; her eyes were half closed, and her mouth was a kissing mouth. "Ah! sweet moon," she whispered, "do this for me, and I will be your slave; I will be what you will."

Quite suddenly the air was filled with the sound of a grand invisible orchestra. Viola did not stop to wonder. To the music of a slow saraband she swayed and postured. In the music there was the regular beat of small drums and a perpetual drone. The air seemed to be filled with the perfume of some bitter spice. Viola could fancy almost that she saw a smouldering campfire and heard far off the roar of some desolate wild beast. She let her long hair fall, raising the heavy strands of it in either hand as she moved slowly to the laden music. Slowly her body swayed with drowsy grace, slowly her satin shoes slid over the silver sand.

The music ceased with a clash of cymbals. Viola rubbed her eyes. She fastened her hair up carefully again. Suddenly she looked up, almost imperiously.

"Music! more music!" she cried.

Once more the music came. This time it was a dance of caprice, pelting along over the violin-strings, leaping, laughing, wanton. Again an illusion seemed to cross her eyes. An old king was watching her, a king with the sordid history of the exhaustion of pleasure written on his flaccid face. A hook-nosed courtier by his side settled the ruffles at his wrists and mumbled, "Ravissant! Quel malheur que la vieillesse!" It was a strange illusion. Faster and faster she sped to the music, stepping, spinning, pirouetting; the dance was light as thistle-down, fierce as fire, smooth as a rapid stream.

The moment that the music ceased Viola became horribly afraid. She turned and fled away from the moonlit space, through the trees, down the dark alleys of the maze, not heeding in the least which turn she took, and yet she found herself soon at the outside iron gate. From thence she ran through the palace garden, hardly ever pausing to take breath, until she reached the palace itself. In the eastern sky the first signs of dawn were showing; in the palace the festivities were drawing to an end. As she stood alone in the outer ball Prince Hugo came towards her.

"Where have you been, Viola?" he said sternly. "What have you been doing?"

She stamped her little foot.

"I will not be questioned," she replied angrily.

"I have some right to question," he said.

She laughed a little.

"For the first time in my life," she said, "I have been dancing."

He turned away in hopeless silence.

The months passed away. Slowly a great fear came over Viola, a fear that would hardly ever leave her. For every month at the full moon, whether she would or no, she found herself driven to the maze, through its mysterious walks into that strange dancing-room. And when she was there the music began once more, and once more she danced most deliciously for the moon to see. The second time that this happened she had merely thought that it was a recurrence of her own whim, and that the music was but a trick that the imagination had chosen to repeat. The third time frightened her, and she knew that the force that sways the tides had strange power over her. The fear grew as the year fell, for each month the music went on for a longer time—each month some of the pleasure had gone from the dance. On bitter nights in winter the moon called her and she came, when the breath was vapour, and the trees that circled her dancing-room were black bare skeletons, and the frost was cruel. She dared not tell anyone, and yet it was with difficulty that she kept her secret. Somehow chance seemed to favour her, and she always found a way to return from her midnight dance to her own room without being observed. Each month the summons seemed to be more imperious and urgent. Once when she was alone on her knees before the lighted altar in the private chapel of the palace she suddenly felt that the words of the familiar Latin prayer had gone from her memory. She rose to her feet, she sobbed bitterly, but the call had come and she could not resist it. She passed out of the chapel and down the palace-gardens. How madly she danced that night!

She was to be married in the spring. She began to be more gentle with Hugo now. She had a blind hope that when they were married she might be able to tell him about it, and he might be able to protect her, for she had always known him to be fearless. She could not love him, but she tried to be good to him. One day he mentioned to her that he had tried to find his way to the centre of the maze, and had failed. She smiled faintly. If only she could fail! But she never did.

On the night before the wedding-day she had gone to bed and slept peacefully, thinking with her last waking moments of Hugo. Overhead the full moon came up the sky. Quite suddenly Viola was wakened with the impulse to fly to the dancing-room. It seemed to bid her hasten with breathless speed. She flung a cloak around her, slipped her naked feet into her dancing-shoes, and hurried forth. No one saw her or heard her—on the marble staircase of the palace, on down the terraces of the garden, she ran as fast as she could. A thorn-plant caught in her cloak, but she sped on, tearing it free; a sharp stone cut through the satin of one shoe, and her foot was wounded and bleeding, but she sped on. As the pebble that is flung from the cliff must fall until it reaches the sea, as the white ghost-moth must come in from cool hedges and scented darkness to a burning death in the lamp by which you sit so late—so Viola had no choice. The moon called her. The moon drew her to that circle of hard, bright sand and the pitiless music.

It was brilliant, rapid music to-night. Viola threw off her cloak and danced. As she did so, she saw that a shadow lay over a fragment of the moon's edge. It was the night of a total eclipse. She heeded it not. The intoxication of the dance was on her. She was all in white; even her face was pale in the moonlight. Every movement was full of poetry and grace.

The music would not stop. She had grown deathly weary. It seemed to her that she had been dancing for hours, and the shadow had nearly covered the moon's face, so that it was almost dark. She could hardly see the trees around her. She went on dancing, stepping, spinning, pirouetting, held by the merciless music.

It stopped at last, just when the shadow had quite covered the moon's face, and all was dark. But it stopped only for a moment, and then began again. This time it was a slow, passionate waltz. It was useless to resist; she began to dance once more. As she did so she uttered a sudden shrill scream of horror, for in the dead darkness a hot hand had caught her own and whirled her round, *and she was no longer dancing alone.*

The search for the missing Princess lasted during the whole of the following day. In the evening Prince Hugo, his face anxious and firmly set, passed in his search the iron gate of the maze, and noticed on the stones beside it the stain of a drop of blood. Within the gate was another stain. He followed this clue, which had been left by Viola's wounded foot, until he reached that open space in the centre that had served Viola for her dancing-room. It was quite empty. He noticed that the sand round the edges was all worn down, as though someone had danced there, round and round, for a long time. But no separate footprint was distinguishable there. Just outside this track, however, he saw two footprints clearly defined close together: one was the print of a tiny satin shoe; the other was the print of a large naked foot—a cloven foot.

The Green Light

The man looked down at the figure of the woman on the couch. The little silver clock on the mantelpiece began to chime; he could not bear the sound of it. He flew at the clock like a madman, and dashed it on the ground, and stamped on it. Then he drew down the blind, and opened the door and listened; there was no one on the staircase. Silence seemed now as intolerable to him as sound had been a moment before. He tried to whistle, but his lips were too dry and made only a ridiculous hissing sound. Closing the door behind him, he ran down the staircase and out into the street. The woman on the couch never moved or spoke. It was late in the afternoon; the light from the low sun penetrated the green blind and took from it a horrible colour that seemed to tint the face of the woman on the couch. Flies came out of the dark corners of the room, sulkily busy, crawling and buzzing. One very little fly passed backwards and forwards over the woman's white ringed hand; it moved rapidly, a black speck.

Outside in the street, the man stepped from the pavement into the roadway; a cabman shouted and swore at him, and someone dragged him back by the arm, and told him roughly to look where he was going. He stood still for a minute, and rubbed his forehead with his hand. This would not do. The critical moment had come, the moment when, above all things, it was necessary that his nerve should be perfect and his thoughts clear; and now, when he tried to think, a picture came before the thought and filled his mind—the picture of the white face with the green light upon it. And his heart was beating too fast, and, it seemed to him, almost audibly. He began to feel his pulse, counting the strokes out loud as he stood on the kerb; then he was conscious that two or three boys and loafers were standing in a little group watching him and laughing at him. One of the loafers handed him his hat; it had fallen off when he dodged back on to the pavement, and he had not noticed it. He took the hat, and felt for some coins to give the man. He found a half-crown and a half-penny; he held them in his hand, and stared at them, and forgot why he had wanted them. Then he suddenly remembered and gave them. There was a loud yell of laughter; the boys and loafers were running away, and he heard one of them shouting, "Let the old stinker out a bit too soon, ain't they?" and another, "Garn! 'E's tight—that's all's wrong with 'im."

Again he told himself that this would not do. He must not think of the past—the awful past. He must not think of the future—of his schemes for escape. He must concentrate his thoughts on the present moment, until he could get to some place where he could be alone. Yes, Regent's Park would do well, and it was near. He brushed his hat with his coat-sleeve, put it on, and walked. He thought about the movement of his feet, and the best way to cross the road, and how to avoid running into people, and how to behave as other people in the street behaved. All the things that one generally does unconsciously and automatically required now for their conduct a distinct mental effort.

As he walked on, his mind seemed to clear a little. He reached a spot in Regent's Park where he could lie down in the grass with no one near him, out of sight. "Now," he said to himself, "I need concentrate my thoughts no longer—I can let them go." In a second he had gone rapidly through the past—the jealousy that had burned in his heart, and the way that he had quieted himself and made his scheme, and carried it out slowly. It had been finished that afternoon, when he had lost control over himself, and—

Through the transparent leaves of the tree near him the sun came with a greenish glare. He shuddered and turned away, so that he could not see it.

Yes, he was to escape—he had made all the arrangements for that. He drew from his side-pocket a roll of notes, and counted them, and entered the numbers in his pocketbook. He had changed a cheque for fifty pounds at the bank that morning. The police would find that out, and endeavour to trace him by discovering where the notes with those numbers were changed. That was one of his means of escape. He would see to it that the notes were never changed by himself, or in any town where he had been or was likely to be. He was going to sacrifice those ten bank-notes to put the police on a wrong scent. He had plenty of money ready in gold—in gold that could not be traced—for his own needs. He chuckled to himself. It was brilliant, this scheme for providing a wrong scent, for making the very carefulness and astuteness of the detectives the stumbling-block in their way; and it would be so easy to get the notes changed by others—the dishonesty of ordinary human beings would serve his purpose.

His mood had changed now to one of exultation. He told himself time after time that he was right. The law would condemn him, but morally he was right, and had only punished the woman as she deserved to be punished. Only, he must escape. And—yes—he must not forget.

He looked round. There was still no one near; but his position did not satisfy him. Not a person must see what he was going to do next. He went on, and found a spot near the canal, where he seemed to be out of sight, and more secure from interruption. Then he took from his pocket a little looking-glass and a pair of scissors. Very carefully he cut away his beard and moustache, that hid the thin-lipped, wide mouth, and the small weak chin. He cut as close as he could, and when he had finished he looked like a man who had neglected to shave for a day or two. A barber would shave him now without suspicion. He was satisfied with the operation. The glass showed him a face so changed that it startled him to look at it. He glanced at his watch—it was time to start for the station, where his luggage had been waiting since the day before, if he meant to get shaved on the way there.

He walked a little way, and sat down again. "How well everything has been thought out!" he said to himself. All would succeed. With a new name, and in another country, without that drunken, faithless, beautiful woman, he would grow happy again. He had only meant to sit down for a minute or two, but his thoughts rambled and became nonsense, and suddenly he fell into a deep sleep. He had been overtaxed.

An hour passed. The train that he had intended to take steamed out of the station, and still he slept. It grew dusk, and still he slept. When the park-keeper touched him on the shoulder, he half woke, and spoke querulously. Then consciousness came back, and slowly he realized what had happened.

As he walked slowly out of the park, his mind refreshed with sleep, he for the first time realized something else. In the awful moment when he had left the woman, he had broken down, and forgotten everything. The bag of gold was still lying on the table of the room with the green blind. He must go back and get it. It would be horrible to re-enter that room, but it could not be helped. He dared not change the notes himself, and in any case that amount would be insufficient. He must have the gold.

It added, he told himself, slightly to the risk of discovery, but only slightly. His servants had all been sent out and were not to return until half-past nine. No one else could have entered the house. He would find everything as he left it—the gold on the table and the figure of the woman on the couch. He would let himself in with his latch-key. No passer-by would take any notice of so ordinary an incident. He had no occasion to hurry now, and he turned into the first barber's shop that he saw. His mind was as alert now as it had been when he first formed his scheme.

"Let me have your best razor," he said; "my skin's tender; in fact, for the last two or three days I haven't been able to shave at all."

He chatted with the barber about horse-racing, and said that he himself had a couple of horses in training. Then he inquired the way to Piccadilly, saying that he was a stranger in London, and seemed to take careful note of the barber's directions.

He walked briskly away from the shop towards his own house. A comfortable-looking, ruddy-faced woman was coming towards him. A shaft of green light from a chemist's shop-window fell full on her face as she passed, and the horror came back upon him. It was with difficulty that he checked himself from crying out. He hurried on, but that hideous light seemed to linger in his eyes and to haunt him.

"Keep quiet!" he kept saying to himself under his breath. "Steady yourself; don't be a fool!"

There was an Italian restaurant near, and he went in and drank a couple of glasses of cognac. Then only was he able to go on.

As he turned the corner where his house came into sight he looked up. All the house was dark but for one great green eye in the centre that looked at him. There were lights in that room.

He stood still close to a lamp-post, just touching it to keep his balance. He spoke to himself aloud:

"It's green . . . it's green . . . someone's there!"

A workingman passed him, heard him mumbling, looked at him curiously, and went on.

The great green eye stared at him and fascinated him. Then other lights darted about, red lights, white lights. Someone must be going up and down the staircase and passages. Had she got off the couch? Was the dead woman walking? How his head throbbed! There were two nerves that seemed to sound like two consecutive notes on a piano, struck in slow alternation, then quickening to a rapid shake—whirr! whirr! Now the two notes were struck together, a repeated discord, thumped out—clatter! clatter! No, the sound was outside in the street, and it was the sound of people running. There were boys with excited eyes and white faces, and blowsy, laughing women, and a little old ferret-faced man who coughed as he ran. A police-whistle screamed.

In front of the door of the house a black mass grew up, getting quickly bigger and bigger. It was a crowd of people swaying backwards and forwards, kept back by the police.

The police! He was discovered, then. He must get away at once, not wait another moment. Only the green light was looking at him.

"Stop that light!" he called.

No one noticed him. The green light went on glimmering, and drew him nearer. He had to get there. He was on the outskirts of the crowd now.

Why would not the crowd let him pass? Could not they hear that he was being called? He pushed his way, struggling, dragging people on one side. There were angry voices, a hum growing louder and louder. He caught a woman by the neck and flung her aside. She screamed. Someone struck him in the face, and he tried to strike back. Down! He was down on the road. The air was stifling and stinking there. He tried to get up, and was forced back. Ah! now he was up again, his coat torn off his back, muddy, bleeding, fighting, spitting, howling like a madman.

"Damn you! damn you all!"

The crowd was a storm all round him, tossing him here and there. Again and again he was struck. There was blood streaming over his eyes, and through the blood and mingled with blood he saw the green light looking.

There came a sudden lull. A couple of policemen stood by him, and one of them had him by the arm, and asked him what he was doing. He began to cry, sobbing like a child.

"Take me up there," he said, panting, "where the green light is; it's the dead woman calling."

The policeman stood for a moment hesitating. For a moment the crowd was motionless and silent. Then one of those white-faced boys shrank further back whispering:

"It's the man!"

The Magnet

[Subsequent to the inquest on the body of the Rev. Ingram Shallow, who shot himself in the churchyard of St. John's, Ilworthy, Bedfordshire, on the evening of October 14, the following paper was found at his lodgings in the village and is here published for the first time. It will be remembered that at the inquest the usual verdict of temporary insanity was returned.]

Thursday, October 6.—The world is still ringing with the news of the ghastly accident to the express the night before last. The *Times* has a column and a half. Nothing else is spoken of in the village. Yesterday afternoon I went over on my bicycle to witness the scene of the accident. Of course, the more horrible traces of it had already been removed; the screams of the injured and dying and the sight of mangled bodies, about which we read in the papers, would have been too much for me. The up line was already clear, and it was expected the down line would also be clear in the course of a couple of hours. There was a perfect army of men at work, with every kind of ingenious contrivance for removing the heavy obstacles. All along the embankment fragments of the débris are still strewn. At a distance of at least forty yards from the point where the accident actually happened I found, among some wet grass and fern, a part of one of those plates they have up in the carriages, giving the number that the carriage is intended to carry. I have often noticed, when standing in the station, the appearance of strength which locomotives and carriages on the fast trains always have. Yet here one saw all this strength of no avail. The engine and the carriages were broken up just like a child's toys. I do most sincerely hope and believe that it was nobody in Ilworthy who was responsible for the disaster. Whoever it is, I do trust and pray that he may be discovered, and that he may pay with his own life for the lives of those hundreds his fiendish action has sent, without a moment of warning, into eternity.

Friday, October 7.—The Vicar came back with me to breakfast this morning after the early service. After some talk about the accident, I asked him if he intended to touch upon it on Sunday morning. He said that he would if I thought it necessary, but that his sermon was already written, being one of a series on the Gospels for the day, which he prepared some time ago. I said that undoubtedly the accident was a terrible event, and one which had sunk very deeply into the minds of everybody in Ilworthy. It was an event which might give point and weight to many a lesson, and it had been my view that Christianity was a practical religion, and the priest should, wherever possible, bring it to bear upon the events of the day. At the same time I did not insist; it was not for me to instruct him, the contrary was rather the case. He smiled good-temperedly, and said that since I seemed to be so full of the accident, and had taken such an absorbing interest in it, I could probably preach a better sermon on it myself, and I might use that as my subject for Sunday evening. I thanked him, and said that I would do so. I have spent the whole day over this sermon. I do not, like the Vicar, read my sermons, but I have written this out in full, and shall commit it to memory. I have given what I think is really a somewhat vivid and impressive picture of the great express rushing at headlong speed to ruin; the obstacle just seen by the driver one moment before his engine crashed into it; the sudden darkness of the train through the extinction of the lights; the screams for help; the sight of the dead bodies laid out on the embankment. . . . I have worked myself up so much about this sermon, that I have only to shut my eyes actually to witness the scene myself. I seem to be standing by the obstruction, and to see the long train crashing down upon me when it is too late to do anything. I hope I am not exciting myself too much about it. It is already past ten, and I think I shall have a cup of hot cocoa quietly and go to bed. I notice that one of the illustrated papers in the reading-room has a magnificent full-page illustration of the accident. I have often thought, by the way, of writing a little for the papers myself. I know I have some taste for the work, and I am inclined to think I have some little gift also. The supplement to one's income would be useful.

Sunday, October 9.—I have just returned from church, exhausted. I preached over forty minutes, without the least sign of impatience from any of the congregation. No coughing or shuffling of the feet, or anything of the kind. In the vestry afterwards, Mr. Johnson, our senior churchwarden, took me aside, and told me that it was one of the strongest and most impressive addresses he had ever heard delivered from that pulpit. I hope I did not appear to be unduly pleased at this; one must not think of self in these matters, and I strive against it. I was a little surprised that after this special effort of mine the Vicar should have said nothing at all. He is not a small-minded man, and I cannot believe him to be actuated by jealousy.

He spoke of the accident again, and said in what seemed to be rather a patronizing way that he was afraid I was letting it prey too much on my mind. I tried to be humble, and I think I can submit to a rebuke when it is deserved. But, really, this is nonsense. I still picture to myself at times the man standing by the obstruction and watching the express coming towards him. But for the awful wickedness of it, it would be, in a way, a magnificent moment. He would have the thought that he, a weak man, could at his will check the rush of a train, hurl it over, twist and break the strong iron as if it were cardboard, and avenge himself on hundreds of people; and then have all the police in the country hunting for him—and in vain. Exhausted though I am, I am afraid that I shall get no sleep to-night until I have been out in the fresh air a little. The church was crowded, and oppressively hot. The whole village is asleep, and no one will be any the wiser. I think I will get on my bicycle and ride down again to the place where the accident happened. It is within a quarter of an hour to midnight, and so Sunday is practically over. Besides, there are many very good men who do not consider that cycling on Sunday is wrong.

Monday, October 10.—To-day I have been beset by a terrible and most extraordinary temptation. I thank God that I have wrestled against it successfully; but the fact that such a temptation could even occur to me appalls me.

Tuesday, October 11.—The Vicar called this morning. He will take both sermons next Sunday. He said that I looked ill, and that he thought I had been overdoing it, and was in want of a holiday. I think he is right. He is really a very kind man. I shall go away next week. Again, all day long, I have been subject to the same diabolical impulse. I was half tempted to speak to the Vicar about it, but shame prevented me. I get but little sleep now at nights, and if I do sleep I am always haunted by the same dream. I see the lights of the express coming nearer and nearer. . . .

Wednesday, October 12.—It is done now. It had to be done, and it was no good to contend against it. I believe that it must have been the will of God that I should do it, for ever since the burden has been lifted from my mind, and I have been quite myself again. Late last night, or rather very early this morning, finding myself unable to sleep, I got up and went out. I did not take my bicycle. I ran all the way to that point on the line that I have always been thinking about. There is a stack of heavy sleepers there. It is at the bottom of a deep cutting, and you can see the train coming for some distance. I knew by the tables that I had not much time to spare. I had got six of the heavy sleepers across the rails, when I thought I heard it coming, but I was mistaken. I dragged on another, and then I heard the roar; there was no mistake about it. I could see the lights flashing as I saw them in my dream. I am ashamed that I had not the strength of mind to wait until the last moment. I tried to, but I could not. I ran away up the embankment and crossed some fields. I saw some men coming and hid behind a hedge. I knew that detectives were about. I lay there panting, and was afraid they would hear me, but they passed on. I got back to my lodgings while it was still dark; nobody had heard me go out, and nobody heard me come back. That is all right.

Since writing the above I have been to the Wednesday evening service. The Vicar was to deliver an address. At the last moment I felt that I wished to preach on this awful accident and the lessons it must have for every one of us. I crossed over to the Vicar and asked permission to preach. He refused. I warned him that I intended to preach, and that if he attempted to occupy the pulpit he would do so at his peril. Then I suddenly seemed to see the matter in a different light and apologized to him. However, I wish very much to address the village on the subject, and as I am not allowed to preach in church I shall call a public meeting on the recreation-ground. I must remember to get arrangements made as to the printing and posting of bills to-morrow.

The Case of Vincent Pyrwhit

The death of Vincent Pyrwhit, J.P., of Ellerdon House, Ellerdon, in the county of Buckingham, would in the ordinary way have received no more attention than the death of any other simple country gentleman. The circumstances of his death, however, though now long since forgotten, were sensational, and attracted some notice at the time. It was one of those cases which is easily forgotten within a year, except just in the locality where it occurred. The most sensational circumstances of the case never came before the public at all. I give them here simply and plainly. The psychical people may make what they like of them.

Pyrwhit himself was a very ordinary country gentleman, a good fellow, but in no way brilliant. He was devoted to his wife, who was some fifteen years younger than himself, and remarkably beautiful. She was quite a good woman, but she had her faults. She was fond of admiration, and she was an abominable flirt. She misled men very cleverly, and was then sincerely angry with them for having been misled. Her husband never troubled his head about these flirtations, being assured quite rightly that she was a good woman. He was not jealous; she, on the other hand, was possessed of a jealousy amounting almost to insanity. This might have caused trouble if he had ever provided her with the slightest basis on which her jealousy could work, but he never did. With the exception of his wife, women bored him. I believe she did once or twice try to make a scene for some preposterous reason which was no reason at all; but nothing serious came of it, and there was never a real quarrel between them.

On the death of his wife, after a prolonged illness, Pyrwhit wrote and asked me to come down to Ellerdon for the funeral, and to remain at least a few days with him. He would be quite alone, and I was his oldest friend. I hate attending funerals, but I *was* his oldest friend, and I was, moreover, a distant relation of his wife. I had no choice and I went down.

There were many visitors in the house for the funeral, which took place in the village churchyard, but they left immediately afterwards. The air of heavy gloom which had hung over the house seemed to lift a little. The servants (servants are always very emotional) continued to break down at intervals, noticeably Pyrwhit's man, Williams, but Pyrwhit himself was self-possessed. He spoke of his wife with great affection and regret, but still he could speak of her and not unsteadily. At dinner he also spoke of one or two other subjects, of politics and of his duties as a magistrate, and of course he made the requisite fuss about his gratitude to me for coming down to Ellerdon at that time. After dinner we sat in the library, a room well and expensively furnished, but without the least attempt at taste. There were a few oil paintings on the walls, a presentation portrait of himself, and a landscape or two—all more or less bad, as far as I remember. He had eaten next to nothing at dinner, but he had drunk a good deal; the wine, however, did not seem to have the least effect upon him. I had got the conversation definitely off the subject of his wife when I made a blunder. I noticed an Erichsen's extension standing on his writing-table. I said:

"I didn't know that telephones had penetrated into the villages yet."

"Yes," he said, "I believe they are common enough now. I had that one fitted up during my wife's illness to communicate with her bedroom on the floor above us on the other side of the house."

At that moment the bell of the telephone rang sharply.

We both looked at each other. I said with the stupid affectation of calmness one always puts on when one is a little bit frightened:

"Probably a servant in that room wishes to speak to you."

He got up, walked over to the machine, and swung the green cord towards me. The end of it was loose.

"I had it disconnected this morning," he said; "also the door of that room is locked, and no one can possibly be in it."

He had turned the colour of gray blotting-paper; so probably had I.

The bell rang again—a prolonged, rattling ring.

"Are you going to answer it?" I said.

"I am not," he answered firmly.

"Then," I said, "I shall answer it myself. It is some stupid trick, a joke not in the best of taste, for which you will probably have to sack one or other of your domestics."

"My servants," he answered, "would not have done that. Besides, don't you see it is impossible? The instrument is disconnected."

"The bell rang all the same. I shall try it."

I picked up the receiver.

"Are you there?" I called.

The voice which answered me was unmistakably the rather high staccato voice of Mrs. Pyrwhit.

"I want you," it said, "to tell my husband that he will be with me to-morrow."

I still listened. Nothing more was said.

I repeated, "Are you there?" and still there was no answer.

I turned to Pyrwhit.

"There is no one there," I said. "Possibly there is thunder in the air affecting the bell in some mysterious way. There must be some simple explanation, and I'll find it all out to-morrow."

He went to bed early that night. All the following day I was with him. We rode together, and I expected an accident every minute, but none happened. All the evening I expected him to turn suddenly faint and ill, but that also did not happen. When at about ten o'clock he excused himself and said goodnight I felt distinctly relieved. He went up to his room and rang for Williams.

The rest is, of course, well known. The servant's reason had broken down, possibly the immediate cause being the death of Mrs. Pyrwhit. On entering his master's room, without the least hesitation, he raised a loaded revolver which he carried in his hand, and shot Pyrwhit through the heart. I believe the case is mentioned in some of the textbooks on homicidal mania.

The Bottom of the Gulf

Three hundred and sixty-two years before Christ a chasm opened in the Roman Forum, and the soothsayers declared that it would never close until the most precious treasure of Rome had been thrown into it. It is said that a youth named Mettus (or Mettius) Curtius appeared on horseback in full armour, and before a very fair audience, exclaiming that Rome had no dearer possession than arms and courage, leaped down into the gulf, which thereupon closed over him. This incident, like most of the legendary history of Rome, has been subjected to severe criticism. Those who too hastily disbelieve in it will reconsider their opinion on reading the account, not previously published, of what took place at the bottom of the gulf.

Curtius and the horse fell in the order in which they had started, with the horse underneath. After a few minutes' rapid passage the horse stopped falling somewhat suddenly, broke most of itself, and died. Curtius, who, though a little shaken, was uninjured, sat up on his dead horse and looked round to see if he could discover the nearest way back. As he looked upward he saw the top edges of the cavern close together, and the daylight shut out. But a curious greenish light still lingered in the cavern in which he found himself, and from one of its recesses came a voice which startled Mettus considerably. It said interrogatively:

"Did you hurt yourself?"

"Not much," replied Curtius. "I didn't know there was anybody down here. You quite startled me. Do come out and let me see you."

"No, thanks," said the voice. "Did you really believe that you would die when you jumped down the gulf?"

"Certainly I did."

The voice laughed, a mean little snigger.

"So you will, too. You'll die of suffocation, slowly, when the air in this cavern is exhausted."

"Then we'd better get to work at once," said Curtius. "I have an excellent sword here and a couple of daggers. I put them on for the occasion. I didn't fall so far as I expected, and if we both of us work hard we shall be able to cut our way out."

"Thanks," said the voice, "but I'm not going to do any work. I'm not of the same kind as yourself. I don't need the air of the outer world. In fact, I don't think much of the outer world, even its best specimens. That's why I live down here. You've got to die. Sorry, but there's no help for it. I've set my trap, and I caught you, and if you're the best specimen they can provide on top, my low opinion of them is confirmed."

"What do you mean by the 'trap'?" asked Curtius.

"Well, it was I who caused the chasm to open, knowing the kind of tomfool thing your soothsayers would remark about it. I sat here wondering what I should get. Shouldn't have been surprised at a brace of vestal virgins. They would have exclaimed, 'Purity and devotion,' instead of 'Courage and arms,' amid loud applause, of course, Or it might have been an elderly matron, with a good old tag that Rome held nothing more precious than the tender love of her mothers. It might have been a soothsayer, it might have been anything. As it is, it's you, and I think very little of you. Arms? Of what use do you think all those tin-pot arrangements which you have hung about you are likely to be? Courage? Why, man alive! you've got no courage at all."

"I have," said Curtius stolidly; "I fully expected to die, and I was willing to die."

"Just for one moment," said the voice, "when you had got all that mob of howling fools around applauding you. Applause is an intoxicant, and you got drunk on it. Now you are sober again, and you don't want to die at all. The man who can die alone, slowly and terribly, is courageous. But you've got no more courage in you than a piece of chewed string. You're as white as chalk."

"That's the effect of the green light," interposed Curtius.

"Rubbish!" replied the voice, "green light doesn't make a man shake all over, does it?"

"That's just the shock from the fall," said Curtius. "But I can't stop here arguing with you; I'm off to explore the cavern. There must be a way out somewhere."

"There isn't," said the voice; "but you can explore."

"I can't die like a rat in a trap," said Curtius, whimpering.

And off he went on his exploration. He looked in at the recess from which the voice had proceeded and found nothing. The cave was enormous. For many hours he tramped on and on, and never through one tiny chink in the roof did he see the light of day. Exhausted and ravenous, at last he flung himself down on the floor of the cave, and almost immediately the voice, which had been silent all this time, began again. First of all came that faint, mean little snigger; then it said:

"Hungry?"

"Worn out with hunger," sobbed Curtius; "I'm thirsty, too. My mouth is so parched that I can hardly speak, and there doesn't seem to be one drop of moisture in this damned cavern."

"There isn't," said the voice, "nor one crumb of food either, with the exception of your horse, and I don't think you will be able to find that again. You can try back if you like. Now I come to think of it, you won't die of suffocation, but of starvation. Cuts my entertainment rather shorter than I had hoped, but I must put up with that."

"I can't die like this," sobbed Curtius.

"Courage and arms," replied the voice, "are the things which Rome holds most precious. Go on, my boy; you'll last some time yet."

Then Curtius drew his sword, and went to look for the proprietor of the voice in order to slay him. But he didn't find him. He resumed his explorations.

In a few hours he was too weak to walk any further. He fell into a kind of doze, and when he woke again his arms had been taken from him.

"Where is my sword?" he exclaimed.

"I've got it," replied the voice, this time from the roof of the cavern; "what do you want it for?"

"Want to kill myself," said Curtius.

"If I give you your sword, will you own that you were merely a drunken theatrical impostor?"

"Yes."

"And that you are a coward, and are dying the death of a coward?"

"Yes."

The sword clattered down from the roof on to the floor of the cavern at the feet of the hero.

He picked it up and set his teeth.

The End of a Show

It was a little village in the extreme north of Yorkshire, three miles from a railway-station on a small branch line. It was not a progressive village; it just kept still and respected itself. The hills lay all round it, and seemed to shut it out from the rest of the world. Yet folks were born, and lived, and died, much as in the more important centres; and there were intervals which required to be filled with amusement. Entertainments were given by amateurs from time to time in the schoolroom; sometimes hand-bell ringers or a conjurer would visit the place, but their reception was not always encouraging. "Conjurers is nowt, an' ringers is nowt," said the sad native judiciously; "ar dornt regard 'em." But the native brightened up when in the summer months a few caravans found their way to a piece of waste land adjoining the churchyard. They formed the village fair, and for two days they were a popular resort. But it was understood that the fair had not the glories of old days; it had dwindled. Most things in connection with this village dwindled.

The first day of the fair was drawing to a close. It was half-past ten at night, and at eleven the fair would close until the following morning. This last half-hour was fruitful in business. The steam roundabout was crowded, the proprietor of the peep-show was taking pennies very fast, although not so fast as the proprietor of another, somewhat repulsive, show. A fair number patronized a canvas booth which bore the following inscription:

POPULAR SCIENCE LECTURES.
Admission Free.

At one end of this tent was a table covered with red baize; on it were bottles and boxes, a human skull, a retort, a large book, and some bundles of dried herbs. Behind it was the lecturer, an old man, gray and thin, wearing a bright-coloured dressing-gown. He lectured volubly and enthusiastically; his energy and the atmosphere of the tent made him very hot, and occasionally he mopped his forehead.

"I am about to exhibit to you," he said, speaking clearly and correctly, "a secret known to few, and believed to have come originally from those wise men of the East referred to in Holy Writ." Here he filled two test-tubes with water, and placed some bluish-green crystals in one and some yellow crystals in the other. He went on talking, quoting scraps of Latin, telling stories, making local and personal allusions, finally coming back again to his two test-tubes, both of which now contained almost colour-less solutions. He poured them both together into a flat glass vessel, and the mixture at once turned to a deep brownish purple. He threw a frag-ment of something on to the surface of the mixture, and that fragment at once caught fire. This favourite trick succeeded; the audience were un-doubtedly impressed, and before they quite realized by what logical con-nection the old man had arrived at the subject, he was talking to them about the abdomen. He seemed to know the most unspeakable and inti-mate things about the abdomen. He had made pills which suited its pecu-liar needs, which he could and would sell in boxes at sixpence and one shilling, according to size. He sold four boxes at once, and was back in his classical and anecdotal stage, when a woman pressed forward. She was a very poor woman. Could she have a box of these pills at half-price? Her son was bad, very bad. It would be a kindness.

He interrupted her in a dry, distinct voice:

"Woman, I never yet did anyone a kindness, not even myself."

However, a friend pushed some money into her hand, and she bought two boxes.

It was past twelve o'clock now. The flaring lights were out in the little group of caravans on the waste ground. The tired proprietors of the shows were asleep. The gravestones in the churchyard were glimmering white in the bright moonlight. But at the entrance to that little canvas booth the quack doctor sat on one of his boxes, smoking a clay pipe. He had taken off the dressing-gown, and was in his shirt-sleeves; his clothes were black, much worn. His attention was arrested—he thought that he heard the sound of sobbing.

"It's a God-forsaken world," he said aloud. After a second's silence he spoke again. "No, I never did a kindness even to myself, though I thought I did, or I shouldn't have come to this."

He took his pipe from his mouth and spat. Once more he heard that strange wailing sound; this time he arose, and walked in the direction of it.

Yes, that was it. It came from that caravan standing alone where the trees made a dark spot. The caravan was gaudily painted, and there were steps from the door to the ground. He remembered having noticed it once during the day. It was evident that someone inside was in trouble—great trouble. The old man knocked gently at the door.

"Who's there? What's the matter?"

"Nothing," said a broken voice from within.

"Are you a woman?"

There was a fearful laugh.

"Neither man nor woman—a show."

"What do you mean?"

"Go round to the side, and you'll see."

The old man went round, and by the light of two wax matches caught a glimpse of part of the rough painting on the side of the caravan. The matches dropped from his hand. He came back, and sat down on the steps of the caravan.

"You are not like that," he said.

"No, worse. I'm not dressed in pretty clothes, and lying on a crimson velvet couch. I'm half naked, in a corner of this cursed box, and crying because my owner beat me. Now go, or I'll open the door and show myself to you as I am now. It would frighten you; it would haunt your sleep."

"Nothing frightens me. I was a fool once, but I have never been frightened. What right has this owner over you?"

"He is my father," the voice screamed loudly; then there was more weeping; then it spoke again: "It's awful; I could bear anything now—anything—if I thought it would ever be any better; but it won't. My mind's a woman's and my wants are a woman's, but I am not a woman. I am a show. The brutes stand round me, talk to me, touch me!"

"There's a way out," said the old man quietly, after a pause.

An idea had occurred to him.

"I know—and I daren't take it—I've got a thing here, but I daren't use it."

"You could drink something—something that wouldn't hurt?"

"Yes."

"You are quite alone?"

"Yes; my owner is in the village, at the inn."

"Then wait a minute."

The old man hastened back to the canvas booth, and fumbled about with his chemicals. He murmured something about doing someone a kindness at last. Then he returned to the caravan with a glass of colourless liquid in his hand.

"Open the door and take it," he said.

The door was opened a very little way. A thin hand was thrust out and took the glass eagerly. The door closed, and the voice spoke again.

"It will be easy?"

"Yes."

"Good-bye, then. To your health—"

The old man heard the glass crash on the wooden floor, then he went back to his seat in front of the booth, and carefully lit another pipe.

"I will not go," he said aloud. "I fear nothing—not even the results of my best action."

He listened attentively.

No sound whatever came from the caravan. All was still. Far away the sky was growing lighter with the dawn of a fine summer day.

The Undying Thing

Up and down the oak-panelled dining-hall of Mansteth the master of the house walked restlessly. At formal intervals down the long severe table were placed four silver candlesticks, but the light from these did not serve to illuminate the whole of the surroundings. It just touched the portrait of a fair-haired boy with a sad and wistful expression that hung at one end of the room; it sparkled on the lid of a silver tankard. As Sir Edric passed to and fro it lit up his face and figure. It was a bold and resolute face with a firm chin and passionate, dominant eyes. A bad past was written in the lines of it. And yet every now and then there came over it a strange look of very anxious gentleness that gave it some resemblance to the portrait of the fair-haired boy. Sir Edric paused a moment before the portrait and surveyed it carefully, his strong brown hands locked behind him, his gigantic shoulders thrust a little forward.

"Ah, what I was!" he murmured to himself—"what I was!"

Once more he commenced pacing up and down. The candles, mirrored in the polished wood of the table, had burnt low. For hours Sir Edric had been waiting, listening intently for some sound from the room above or from the broad staircase outside. There had been sounds—the wailing of a woman, a quick abrupt voice, the moving of rapid feet. But for the last hour he had heard nothing. Quite suddenly he stopped and dropped on his knees against the table:

"God, I have never thought of Thee. Thou knowest that— Thou knowest that by my devilish behaviour and cruelty I did veritably murder Alice, my first wife, albeit the physicians did maintain that she died of a decline—a wasting sickness. Thou knowest that all here in Mansteth do hate me, and that rightly. They say, too, that I am mad; but that they say not rightly, seeing that I know how wicked I am. I always knew it, but I never cared until I loved—oh, God, I never cared!"

His fierce eyes opened for a minute, glared round the room, and closed again tightly. He went on:

"God, for myself I ask nothing; I make no bargaining with Thee. Whatsoever punishment Thou givest me to bear I will bear it; whatsoever Thou givest me to do I will do it. Whether Thou killest Eve or whether Thou keepest her in life—and never have I loved but her—I will from this night be good. In due penitence will I receive the holy Sacrament of Thy Body and Blood. And my son, the one child that I had by Alice, I will fetch back again from Challonsea, where I kept him in order that I might not look upon him, and I will be to him a father in deed and very truth. And in all things, so far as in me lieth, I will make restitution and atonement. Whether Thou hearest me or whether Thou hearest me not, these things shall be. And for my prayer it is but this: of Thy loving kindness, most merciful God, be Thou with Eve and make her happy; and after these great pains and perils of childbirth send her Thy peace. Of Thy loving-kindness, Thy merciful loving-kindness, O God!"

Perhaps the prayer that is offered when the time for praying is over is more terribly pathetic than any other. Yet one might hesitate to say that this prayer was unanswered.

Sir Edric rose to his feet. Once more he paced the room. There was a strange simplicity about him, the simplicity that scorns an incongruity. He felt that his lips and throat were parched and dry. He lifted the heavy silver tankard from the table and raised the lid; there was still a good draught of mulled wine in it with the burnt toast, cut heart-shape, floating on the top.

"To the health of Eve and her child," he said aloud, and drained it to the last drop.

Click, click! As he put the tankard down he heard distinctly two doors opened and shut quickly, one after the other. And then slowly down the stairs came a hesitating step. Sir Edric could bear the suspense no longer. He opened the dining-room door, and the dim light strayed out into the dark hall beyond.

"Dennison," he said, in a low, sharp whisper, "is that you?"

"Yes, yes. I am coming, Sir Edric."

A moment afterwards Dr. Dennison entered the room. He was very pale; perspiration streamed from his forehead; his cravat was disarranged. He was an old man, thin, with the air of proud humility. Sir Edric watched him narrowly.

"Then she is dead," he said, with a quiet that Dr. Dennison had not expected.

"Twenty physicians—a hundred physicians could not have saved her, Sir Edric. She was—" He gave some details of medical interest.

"Dennison," said Sir Edric, still speaking with calm and restraint, "why do you seem thus indisposed and panic-stricken? You are a physician; have you never looked upon the face of death before? The soul of my wife is with God—"

"Yes," murmured Dennison, "a good woman, a perfect, saintly woman."

"And," Sir Edric went on, raising his eyes to the ceiling as though he could see through it, "her body lies in great dignity and beauty upon the bed, and there is no horror in it. Why are you afraid?"

"I do not fear death, Sir Edric."

"But your hands—they are not steady. You are evidently overcome. Does the child live?"

"Yes, it lives."

"Another boy—a brother for young Edric, the child that Alice bore me?"

"There—there is something wrong. I do not know what to do. I want you to come upstairs. And, Sir Edric, I must tell you, you will need your self-command."

"Dennison, the hand of God is heavy upon me; but from this time forth until the day of my death I am submissive to it, and God send that that day may come quickly! I will follow you and I will endure."

He took one of the high silver candlesticks from the table and stepped towards the door. He strode quickly up the staircase, Dr. Dennison following a little way behind him.

As Sir Edric waited at the top of the staircase he heard suddenly from the room before him a low cry. He put down the candlestick on the floor and leaned back against the wall listening. The cry came again, a vibrating monotone ending in a growl.

"Dennison, Dennison!"

His voice choked; he could not go on.

"Yes," said the doctor, "it is in there. I had the two women out of the room, and got it here. No one but myself has seen it. But you must see it, too."

He raised the candle and the two men entered the room—one of the spare bedrooms. On the bed there was something moving under cover of a blanket. Dr. Dennison paused for a moment and then flung the blanket partially back.

They did not remain in the room for more than a few seconds. The moment they got outside, Dr. Dennison began to speak.

"Sir Edric, I would fain suggest somewhat to you. There is no evil, as

Sophocles hath it in his 'Antigone,' for which man hath not found a remedy, except it be death, and here—"

Sir Edric interrupted him in a husky voice.

"Downstairs, Dennison. This is too near."

It was, indeed, passing strange. When once the novelty of this—this occurrence had worn off, Dr. Dennison seemed no longer frightened. He was calm, academic, interested in an unusual phenomenon. But Sir Edric, who was said in the village to fear nothing in earth, or heaven, or hell, was obviously much moved.

When they had got back to the dining-room, Sir Edric motioned the doctor to a seat.

"Now, then," he said, "I will hear you. Something must be done—and to-night."

"Exceptional cases," said Dr. Dennison, "demand exceptional remedies. Well, it lies there upstairs and is at our mercy. We can let it live, or, placing one hand over the mouth and nostrils, we can—"

"Stop," said Sir Edric. "This thing has so crushed and humiliated me that I can scarcely think. But I recall that while I waited for you I fell upon my knees and prayed that God would save Eve. And, as I confessed unto Him more than I will ever confess unto man, it seemed to me that it were ignoble to offer a price for His favour. And I said that whatsoever punishment I had to bear, I would bear it; and whatsoever He called upon me to do, I would do it; and I made no conditions."

"Well?"

"Now my punishment is of two kinds. Firstly, my wife, Eve, is dead. And this I bear more easily because I know that now she is numbered with the company of God's saints, and with them her pure spirit finds happier communion than with me; I was not worthy of her. And yet she would call my roughness by gentle, pretty names. She gloried, Dennison, in the mere strength of my body, and in the greatness of my stature. And I am thankful that she never saw this—this shame that has come upon the house. For she was a proud woman, with all her gentleness, even as I was proud and bad until it pleased God this night to break me even to the dust. And for my second punishment, that, too, I must bear. This thing that lies upstairs, I will take and rear; it is bone of my bone and flesh of my flesh; only, if it be possible, I will hide my shame so that no man but you shall know of it."

"This is not possible. You cannot keep a living being in this house unless it be known. Will not these women say, 'Where is the child?'"

Sir Edric stood upright, his powerful hands linked before him, his face working in agony; but he was still resolute.

"Then if it must be known, it shall be known. The fault is mine. If I had but done sooner what Eve asked, this would not have happened. I will bear it."

"Sir Edric, do not be angry with me, for if I did not say this, then I should be but an ill counsellor. And, firstly, do not use the word shame. The ways of nature are past all explaining; if a woman be frail and easily impressed, and other circumstances concur, then in some few rare cases a thing of this sort does happen. If there be shame, it is not upon you but upon nature—to whom one would not lightly impute shame. Yet it is true that common and uninformed people might think that this shame was yours. And herein lies the great trouble—the shame would rest also on her memory."

"Then," said Sir Edric, in a low, unfaltering voice, "this night for the sake of Eve I will break my word, and lose my own soul eternally."

About an hour afterwards Sir Edric and Dr. Dennison left the house together. The doctor carried a stable lantern in his hand. Sir Edric bore in his arms something wrapped in a blanket. They went through the long garden, out into the orchard that skirts the north side of the park, and then across a field to a small dark plantation known as Hal's Planting. In the very heart of Hal's Planting there are some curious caves: access to the innermost chamber of them is exceedingly difficult and dangerous, and only possible to a climber of exceptional skill and courage. As they returned from these caves, Sir Edric no longer carried his burden. The dawn was breaking and the birds began to sing.

"Could not they be quiet just for this morning?" said Sir Edric wearily.

There were but few people who were asked to attend the funeral of Lady Vanquerest and of the baby which, it was said, had only survived her by a few hours. There were but three people who knew that only one body—the body of Lady Vanquerest—was really interred on that occasion. These three were Sir Edric Vanquerest, Dr. Dennison, and a nurse whom it had been found expedient to take into their confidence.

During the next six years Sir Edric lived, almost in solitude, a life of great sanctity, devoting much of his time to the education of the younger Edric, the child that he had by his first wife. In the course of this time some strange stories began to be told and believed in the neighbourhood with reference to Hal's Planting, and the place was generally avoided.

When Sir Edric lay on his deathbed the windows of the chamber were open, and suddenly through them came a low cry. The doctor in attendance hardly regarded it, supposing that it came from one of the owls in the trees outside. But Sir Edric, at the sound of it, rose right up in bed before anyone could stay him, and flinging up his arms cried, "Wolves! wolves! wolves!" Then he fell forward on his face, dead.

And four generations passed away.

II

Towards the latter end of the nineteenth century, John Marsh, who was the oldest man in the village of Mansteth, could be prevailed upon to state what he recollected. His two sons supported him in his old age; he never felt the pinch of poverty, and he always had money in his pocket; but it was a settled principle with him that he would not pay for the pint of beer which he drank occasionally in the parlour of The Stag. Sometimes Farmer Wynthwaite paid for the beer; sometimes it was Mr. Spicer from the post-office; sometimes the landlord of The Stag himself would finance the old man's evening dissipation. In return, John Marsh was prevailed upon to state what he recollected; this he would do with great heartiness and strict impartiality, recalling the intemperance of a former Wynthwaite and the dishonesty of some ancestral Spicer while he drank the beer of their direct descendants. He would tell you, with two tough old fingers crooked round the handle of the pewter that you had provided, how your grandfather was a poor thing "fit for nowt but to brak steeans by ta rord-side." He was so disrespectful that it was believed that he spoke truth. He was particularly disrespectful when he spoke of that most devilish family, the Vanquerests; and he never tired of recounting the stories that from generation to generation had grown up about them. It would be objected, sometimes, that the present Sir Edric, the last surviving member of the race, was a pleasant-spoken young man, with none of the family wildness and hot temper. It was for no sin of his that Hal's Planting was haunted—a thing which every one in Mansteth, and many beyond it, most devoutly believed. John Marsh would hear no apology for him, nor for any of his ancestors; he recounted the prophecy that an old mad woman had made of the family before her strange death, and hoped, fervently, that he might live to see it fulfilled.

The third baronet, as has already been told, had lived the latter part of his life, after his second wife's death, in peace and quietness. Of him John Marsh remembered nothing, of course, and could only recall the few fragments of information that had been handed down to him. He had been told that this Sir Edric, who had travelled a good deal, at one time kept wolves, intending to train them to serve as dogs; these wolves were not kept under proper restraint, and became a kind of terror to the neighbourhood. Lady Vanquerest, his second wife, had asked him frequently to destroy these beasts; but Sir Edric, although it was said that he loved his second wife even more than he hated the first, was obstinate when any of his whims were crossed, and put her off with promises. Then one day Lady Vanquerest herself was attacked by the wolves; she was not bitten, but she was badly frightened. That filled Sir Edric with remorse, and, when it was too late, he went out into the yard where the wolves were kept and shot them all. A few months afterwards Lady Vanquerest died in childbirth. It was a queer thing, John Marsh noted, that it was just at this time that Hal's Planting began to get such a bad name. The fourth baronet was, John Marsh considered, the worst of the race; it was to him that the old mad woman had made her prophecy, an incident that Marsh himself had witnessed in his childhood and still vividly remembered.

The baronet, in his old age, had been cast up by his vices on the shores of melancholy; heavy-eyed, gray-haired, bent, he seemed to pass through life as in a dream. Every day he would go out on horseback, always at a walking pace, as though he were following the funeral of his past self. One night he was riding up the village street as this old woman came down it. Her name was Ann Ruthers; she had a kind of reputation in the village, and although all said that she was mad, many of her utterances were remembered, and she was treated with respect. It was growing dark, and the village street was almost empty; but just at the lower end was the usual group of men by the door of The Stag, dimly illuminated by the light that came through the quaint windows of the old inn. They glanced at Sir Edric as he rode slowly past them, taking no notice of their respectful salutes. At the upper end of the street there were two persons. One was Ann Ruthers, a tall, gaunt old woman, her head wrapped in a shawl; the other was John Marsh. He was then a boy of eight, and he was feeling somewhat frightened. He had been on an expedition to a distant and fœtid pond, and in the black mud and clay about its borders he had discovered live newts; he had three of them in his pocket, and this was to some extent a joy to him, but his joy was damped by his knowledge that he was coming home much too late, and would probably be chastised in consequence. He was unable to walk fast or to run, because Ann Ruthers was immediately in front of him, and he dared not pass her, especially at night. She walked on until she met Sir Edric, and then, standing still, she called him by name.

He pulled in his horse and raised his heavy eyes to look at her. Then in loud clear tones she spoke to him, and John Marsh heard and remembered every word that she said; it was her prophecy of the end of the Vanquerests. Sir Edric never answered a word. When she had finished, he rode on, while she remained standing there, her eyes fixed on the stars above her. John Marsh dared not pass the mad woman; he turned round and walked back, keeping close to Sir Edric's horse. Quite suddenly, without a word of warning, as if in a moment of ungovernable irritation, Sir Edric wheeled his horse round and struck the boy across the face with his switch.

On the following morning John Marsh—or rather, his parents—received a handsome solatium in coin of the realm; but sixty-five years afterwards he had not forgiven that blow, and still spoke of the Vanquerests as a most devilish family, still hoped and prayed that he might see the prophecy fulfilled. He would relate, too, the death of Ann Ruthers, which occurred either later on the night of her prophecy or early on the following day. She would often roam about the country all night, and on this particular night she left the main road to wander over the Vanquerest lands, where trespassers, especially at night, were not welcomed. But no one saw her, and it seemed that she had made her way to a part where no one was likely to see her; for none of the keepers would have entered Hal's Planting by night. Her body was found there at noon on the following day, lying under the tall bracken, dead, but without any mark of violence upon it. It was considered that she had died in a fit. This naturally added to the ill-repute of Hal's Planting. The woman's death caused considerable sensation in the village. Sir Edric sent a messenger to the married sister with whom she had lived, saying that he wished to pay all the funeral expenses. This offer, as John Marsh recalled with satisfaction, was refused.

Of the last two baronets he had but little to tell. The fifth baronet was credited with the family temper, but he conducted himself in a perfectly conventional way, and did not seem in the least to belong to romance. He was a good man of business, and devoted himself to making up, as far as he could, for the very extravagant expenditure of his predecessors. His son, the present Sir Edric, was a fine young fellow and popular in the village. Even John Marsh could find nothing to say against him; other people in the village were interested in him. It was said that he had chosen a wife in London—a Miss Guerdon—and would shortly be back to see that Mansteth Hall was put in proper order for her before his marriage at the close of the season. Modernity kills ghostly romance. It was difficult to associate this modern and handsome Sir Edric, bright and spirited, a good sportsman and a good fellow, with the doom that had been foretold for the Vanquerest family. He himself knew the tradition and laughed at it. He wore clothes made by a London tailor, looked healthy, smiled cheerfully, and, in a vain attempt to shame his own headkeeper, had himself spent a night alone in Hal's Planting. This last was used by Mr. Spicer in argument, who would ask John Marsh what he made of it. John Marsh replied contemptuously that it was "nowt." It was not so that the Vanquerest family was to end; but when the thing, whatever it was, that lived in Hal's Planting, left it and came up to the house, to Mansteth Hall itself, then one would see the end of the Vanquerests. So Ann Ruthers had prophesied. Sometimes Mr. Spicer would ask the pertinent question, how did John Marsh know that there really was anything in Hal's Planting? This he asked, less because he disbelieved, than because he wished to draw forth an account of John's personal experiences. These were given in great detail, but they did not amount to very much. One night John Marsh had been taken by business—Sir Edric's keepers would have called the business by hard names—into the neighbourhood of Hal's Planting. He had there been suddenly startled by a cry, and had run away as though he were running for his life. That was all he could tell about the cry—it was the kind of cry to make a man lose his head and run. And then it always happened that John Marsh was urged by his companions to enter Hal's Planting himself, and discover what was there. John pursed his thin lips together, and hinted that that also might be done one of these days. Whereupon Mr. Spicer looked across his pipe to Farmer Wynthwaite and smiled significantly.

Shortly before Sir Edric's return from London, the attention of Mansteth was once more directed to Hal's Planting, but not by any supernatural occurrence. Quite suddenly, on a calm day, two trees there fell with a crash; there were caves in the centre of the plantation, and it seemed as if the roof of some big chamber in these caves had given way.

They talked it over one night in the parlour of The Stag. There was water in these caves, Farmer Wynthwaite knew it; and he expected a further subsidence. If the whole thing collapsed, what then?

"Ay," said John Marsh. He rose from his chair, and pointed in the direction of the Hall with his thumb. "What then?"

He walked across to the fire, looked at it meditatively for a moment, and then spat in it.

"A trewly wun'ful owd mon," said Farmer Wynthwaite as he watched him.

III

In the smoking-room at Mansteth Hall sat Sir Edric with his friend and intended brother-in-law, Dr. Andrew Guerdon. Both men were on the verge of middle-age; there was hardly a year's difference between them. Yet Guerdon looked much the older man; that was, perhaps, because he wore a short, black beard, while Sir Edric was clean shaven. Guerdon was thought to be an enviable man. His father had made a fortune in the firm of Guerdon, Guerdon and Bird; the old style was still retained at the bank, although there was no longer a Guerdon in the firm. Andrew Guerdon had a handsome allowance from his father, and had also inherited money through his mother. He had taken the degree of Doctor of Medicine; he did not practise, but he was still interested in science, especially in out-of-the-way science. He was unmarried, gifted with perpetually good health, interested in life, popular. His friendship with Sir Edric dated from their college days. It had for some years been almost certain that Sir Edric would marry his friend's sister, Ray Guerdon, although the actual betrothal had only been announced that season.

On a bureau in one corner of the room were spread a couple of plans and various slips of paper. Sir Edric was wrinkling his brows over them, dropping cigar-ash over them, and finally getting angry over them. He pushed back his chair irritably, and turned towards Guerdon.

"Look here, old man" he said. "I desire to curse the original architect of this house—to curse him in his down-sitting and his uprising."

"Seeing that the original architect has gone to where beyond these voices there is peace, he won't be offended. Neither shall I. But why worry yourself? You've been rooted to that blessed bureau all day, and now, after dinner, when every self-respecting man chucks business, you return to it again—even as a sow returns to her wallowing in the mire."

"Now, my good Andrew, do be reasonable. How on earth can I bring Ray to such a place as this? And it's built with such ingrained malice and vexatiousness that one can't live in it as it is, and can't alter it without having the whole shanty tumble down about one's ears. Look at this plan now. That thing's what they're pleased to call a morning room. If the window had been *here* there would have been an uninterrupted view of open country. So what does this forsaken fool of an architect do? He sticks it *there*, where you see it on the plan, looking straight on to a blank wall with a stable yard on the other side of it. But that's a trifle. Look here again—"

"I won't look any more. This place is all right. It was good enough for your father and mother and several generations before them until you arose to improve the world; it was good enough for you until you started to get married. It's a picturesque place, and if you begin to alter it you'll spoil it." Guerdon looked round the room critically. "Upon my word," he said, "I don't know of any house where I like the smoking-room as well as I like this. It's not too big, and yet it's fairly lofty; it's got those comfortable-looking oak-panelled walls. That's the right kind of fireplace, too, and these corner cupboards are handy."

"Of course this won't *remain* the smoking-room. It has the morning sun, and Ray likes that, so I shall make it into her boudoir. It *is* a nice room, as you say."

"That's it, Ted, my boy," said Guerdon bitterly; "take a room which is designed by nature and art to be a smoking-room and turn it into a boudoir. Turn it into the very deuce of a boudoir with the morning sun laid on for ever and ever. Waste the twelfth of August by getting married on it. Spend the winter in foreign parts, and write letters that you can breakfast out of doors, just as if you'd created the mildness of the climate yourself. Come back in the spring and spend the London season in the country in order to avoid seeing anybody who wants to see you. That's the way to do it; that's the way to get yourself generally loved and admired!"

"That's chiefly imagination," said Sir Edric. "I'm blest if I can see why I should not make this house fit for Ray to live in."

"It's a queer thing: Ray was a good girl, and you weren't a bad sort yourself. You prepare to go into partnership, and you both straightway turn into despicable lunatics. I'll have a word or two with Ray. But I'm serious about this house. Don't go tinkering it; it's got a character of its own, and you'd better leave it. Turn half Tottenham Court Road and the culture thereof—Heaven help it!—into your town house if you like, but leave this alone."

"Haven't got a town house—yet. Anyway I'm not going to be unsuitable; I'm not going to feel myself at the mercy of a big firm. I shall supervise the whole thing myself. I shall drive over to Challonsea to-morrow afternoon and see if I can't find some intelligent and fairly conscientious workmen."

"That's all right; you supervise them and I'll supervise you. You'll be much too new if I don't look after you. You've got an old legend, I believe, that the family's coming to a bad end; you must be consistent with it. As you are bad, be beautiful. By the way, what do you yourself think of the legend?"

"It's nothing," said Sir Edric, speaking, however, rather seriously.

"They say that Hal's Planting is haunted by something that will not die. Certainly an old woman, who for some godless reason of her own made her way there by night, was found there dead on the following morning; but her death could be, and was, accounted for by natural causes. Certainly, too, I haven't a man in my employ who'll go there by night now."

"Why not?"

"How should I know? I fancy that a few of the villagers sit boozing at The Stag in the evening, and like to scare themselves by swopping lies about Hal's Planting. I've done my best to stop it. I once, as you know, took a rug, a revolver and a flask of whisky and spent the night there myself. But even that didn't convince them."

"Yes, you told me. By the way, did you hear or see anything?"

Sir Edric hesitated before he answered. Finally he said:

"Look here, old man I wouldn't tell this to anyone but yourself. I did think that I heard something. About the middle of the night I was awakened by a cry; I can only say that it was the kind of cry that frightened me. I sat up, and at that moment I heard some great, heavy thing go swishing through the bracken behind me at a great rate. Then all was still; I looked about, but I could find nothing. At last I argued as I would argue now that a man who is just awake is only half awake, and that his powers of observation, by hearing or any other sense, are not to be trusted. I even persuaded myself to go to sleep again, and there was no more disturbance. However, there's a real danger there now. In the heart of the plantation there are some caves and a subterranean spring; lately there has been some slight subsidence there, and the same sort of thing will happen again in all probability. I wired to-day to an expert to come and look at the place; he has replied that he will come on Monday. The legend says that when the thing that lives in Hal's Planting comes up to the hall the Vanquerests will be ended. If I cut down the trees and then break up the place with a charge of dynamite I shouldn't wonder if I spoiled that legend."

Guerdon smiled.

"I'm inclined to agree with you all through. It's absurd to trust the immediate impressions of a man just awakened; what you heard was probably a stray cow."

"No cow," said Sir Edric impartially. "There's a low wall all round the place—not much of a wall, but too much for a cow."

"Well, something else—some equally obvious explanation. In dealing with such questions, never forget that you're in the nineteenth century. By the way, your man's coming on Monday. That reminds me to-day's Friday, and as an indisputable consequence to-morrow's Saturday, therefore, if you want to find your intelligent workmen it will be, of no use to go in the afternoon."

"True," said Sir Edric, "I'll go in the morning." He walked to a tray on a side table and poured a little whisky into a tumbler. "They don't seem to have brought any seltzer water," he remarked in a grumbling voice.

He rang the bell impatiently.

"Now why don't you use those corner cupboards for that kind of thing? If you kept a supply there, it would be handy in case of accidents."

"They're full up already."

He opened one of them and showed that it was filled with old account-books and yellow documents tied up in bundles. The servant entered.

"Oh, I say, there isn't any seltzer. Bring it, please."

He turned again to Guerdon.

"You might do me a favour when I'm away to-morrow, if there's nothing else that you want to do. I wish you'd look through all these papers for me. They're all old. Possibly some of them ought to go to my solicitor, and I know that a lot of them ought to be destroyed. Some few may be of family interest. It's not the kind of thing that I could ask a stranger or a servant to do for me, and I've so much on hand just now before my marriage—"

"But of course, my dear fellow, I'll do it with pleasure."

"I'm ashamed to give you all this bother. However, you said that you were coming here to help me, and I take you at your word. By the way, I think you'd better not say anything to Ray about the Hal's Planting story."

"I may be some of the things that you take me for, but really I am not a common ass. Of course I shouldn't tell her."

"I'll tell her myself, and I'd sooner do it when I've got the whole thing cleared up. Well, I'm really obliged to you."

"I needn't remind you that I hope to receive as much again. I believe in compensation. Nature always gives it and always requires it. One finds it everywhere, in philology and onwards."

"I could mention omissions."

"They are few, and make a belief in a hereafter to supply them logical."

"Lunatics, for instance?"

"Their delusions are often their compensation. They argue correctly from false premises. A lunatic believing himself to be a millionaire has as much delight as money can give."

"How about deformities or monstrosities?"

"The principle is there, although I don't pretend that the compensation is always adequate. A man who is deprived of one sense generally has another developed with unusual acuteness. As for monstrosities of at all a human type one sees, none; the things exhibited in fairs are, almost without exception, frauds. They occur rarely, and one does not know enough about them. A really good text-book on the subject would be interesting. Still, such stories as I have heard would bear out my theory—stories of their superhuman strength and cunning, and of the extraordinary prolongation of life that has been noted, or is said to have been noted, in them. But it is hardly fair to test my principle by exceptional cases. Besides, any-one can prove anything except that anything's worth proving."

"That's a cheerful thing to say. I wouldn't like to swear that I could prove how the Hal's Planting legend started; but I fancy, do you know, that I could make a very good shot at it."

"Well?"

"My great-grandfather kept wolves—I can't say why. Do you remember the portrait of him?—not the one when he was a boy, the other. It hangs on the staircase. There's now a group of wolves in one corner of the picture. I was looking carefully at the picture one day and thought that I detected some over-painting in that corner; indeed, it was done so roughly that a child would have noticed it if the picture had been hung in a better light. I had the over-painting removed by a good man, and underneath there was that group of wolves depicted. Well, one of these wolves must have escaped, got into Hal's Planting, and scared an old woman or two; that would start a story, and human mendacity would do the rest."

"Yes," said Guerdon meditatively, "that doesn't sound improbable. But why did your great-grandfather have the wolves painted out?"

IV

Saturday morning was fine, but very hot and sultry. After breakfast, when Sir Edric had driven off to Challonsea, Andrew Guerdon settled himself in a comfortable chair in the smoking-room. The contents of the corner cupboard were piled up on a table by his side. He lit his pipe and began to go through the papers and put them in order. He had been at work about a quarter of an hour when the butler entered rather abruptly, looking pale and disturbed.

"In Sir Edric's absence, sir, it was thought that I had better come to you for advice. There's been an awful thing happened."

"Well?"

"They've found a corpse in Hal's Planting about half an hour ago. It's the body of an old man, John Marsh, who used to live in the village. He seems to have died in some kind of a fit. They were bringing it here, but I had it taken down to the village where his cottage is. Then I sent to the police and to a doctor."

There was a moment or two's silence before Guerdon answered.

"This is a terrible thing. I don't know of anything else that you could do. Stop; if the police want to see the spot where the body was found, I think that Sir Edric would like them to have every facility."

"Quite so, sir."

"And no one else must be allowed there."

"No, sir. Thank you."

The butler withdrew.

Guerdon arose from his chair and began to pace up and down the room.

"What an impressive thing a coincidence is!" he thought to himself. "Last night the whole of the Hal's Planting story seemed to me not worth consideration. But this second death there—it can be only coincidence. What else could it be?"

The question would not leave him. What else could it be? Had that dead man seen something there and died in sheer terror of it? Had Sir Edric really heard something when he spent that night there alone? He returned to his work, but he found that he got on with it but slowly. Every now and then his mind wandered back to the subject of Hal's Planting. His doubts annoyed him. It was unscientific and unmodern of him to feel any perplexity because a natural and rational explanation was possible; he was annoyed with himself for being perplexed.

After luncheon he strolled round the grounds and smoked a cigar. He noticed that a thick bank of dark, slate-coloured clouds was gathering in the west. The air was very still. In a remote corner of the garden a big heap of weeds was burning; the smoke went up perfectly straight. On the top of the heap light flames danced; they were like the ghosts of flames in the strange light. A few big drops of rain fell. The small shower did not last for five seconds. Guerdon glanced at his watch. Sir Edric would be back in an hour, and he wanted to finish his work with the papers before Sir Edric's return, so he went back into the house once more.

He picked up the first document that came to hand. As he did so, another, smaller, and written on parchment, which had been folded in with it, dropped out. He began to read the parchment; it was written in faded ink, and the parchment itself was yellow and in many places stained. It was the confession of the third baronet—he could tell that by the date upon it. It told the story of that night when he and Dr. Dennison went together carrying a burden through the long garden out into the orchard that skirts the north side of the park, and then across a field to a small, dark plantation. It told how he made a vow to God and did not keep it. These were the last words of the confession:

"Already upon me has the punishment fallen, and the devil's wolves do seem to hunt me in my sleep nightly. But I know that there is worse to come. The thing that I took to Hal's Planting is dead. Yet will it come back again to the Hall, and then will the Vanquerests be at an end. This writing I have committed to chance, neither showing it nor hiding it, and leaving it to chance if any man shall read it."

Underneath there was a line written in darker ink, and in quite a different handwriting. It was dated fifteen years later, and the initials R. D. were appended to it:

"It is not dead. I do not think that it will ever die."

When Andrew Guerdon had finished reading this document, he looked slowly round the room. The subject had got on his nerves, and he was almost expecting to see something. Then he did his best to pull himself together. The first question he put to himself was this: "Has Ted ever seen this?" Obviously he had not. If he had, he could not have taken the tradition of Hal's Planting so lightly, nor have spoken of it so freely. Besides, he would either have mentioned the document to Guerdon, or he would have kept it carefully concealed. He would not have allowed him to come across it casually in that way. "Ted must never see it," thought Guerdon to himself. He then remembered the pile of weeds he had seen burning in the garden. He put the parchment in his pocket, and hurried out. There was no one about. He spread the parchment on the top of the pile, and waited until it was entirely consumed. Then he went back to the smoking-room; he felt easier now.

"Yes," thought Guerdon, "if Ted had first of all heard of the finding of that body, and then had read that document, I believe that he would have gone mad. Things that come near us affect us deeply."

Guerdon himself was much moved. He clung steadily to reason; he felt himself able to give a natural explanation all through, and yet he was nervous. The net of coincidence had closed in around him; the mention in Sir Edric's confession of the prophecy which had subsequently become traditional in the village alarmed him. And what did that last line mean? He supposed that R. D. must be the initials of Dr. Dennison. What did he mean by saying that the thing was not dead? Did he mean that it had not really been killed, that it had been gifted with some preternatural strength and vitality and had survived, though Sir Edric did not know it? He recalled what he had said about the prolongation of the lives of such things. If it still survived, why had it never been seen? Had it joined to the wild hardiness of the beast a cunning that was human—or more than human? How could it have lived? There was water in the caves, he reflected, and food could have been secured—a wild beast's food. Or did Dr. Dennison mean that though the thing itself was dead, its wraith survived and haunted the place? He wondered how the doctor had found Sir Edric's confession, and why he had written that line at the end of it. As he sat thinking, a low rumble of thunder in the distance startled him. He felt a touch of panic—a sudden impulse to leave Mansteth at once and, if possible, to take Ted with him. Ray could never live there. He went over the whole thing in his mind again and again, at one time calm and argumentative about it, and at another shaken by blind horror.

Sir Edric, on his return from Challonsea a few minutes afterwards, came straight to the smoking-room where Guerdon was. He looked tired and depressed. He began to speak at once:

"You needn't tell me about it—about John Marsh. I heard about it in the village."

"Did you? It's a painful occurrence, although, of course—"

"Stop. Don't go into it. Anything can be explained—I know that."

"I went through those papers and account-books while you were away. Most of them may just as well be destroyed; but there are a few—I put them aside there—which might be kept. There was nothing of any interest."

"Thanks; I'm much obliged to you."

"Oh, and look here, I've got an idea. I've been examining the plans of the house, and I'm coming round to your opinion. There are some alterations which should be made, and yet I'm afraid that they'd make the place look patched and renovated. It wouldn't be a bad thing to know what Ray thought about it."

"That's impossible. The workmen come on Monday, and we can't consult her before then. Besides, I have a general notion what she would like."

"We could catch the night express to town at Challonsea, and—"

Sir Edric rose from his seat angrily and hit the table.

"Good God! don't sit there hunting up excuses to cover my cowardice, and making it easy for me to bolt. What do you suppose the villagers would say, and what would my own servants say, if I ran away to-night? I am a coward—I know it. I'm horribly afraid. But I'm not going to act like a coward if I can help it."

"Now, my dear chap, don't excite yourself. If you are going to care at all—to care as much as the conventional damn—for what people say, you'll have no peace in life. And I don't believe you're afraid. What are you afraid of?"

Sir Edric paced once or twice up and down the room, and then sat down again before replying.

"Look here, Andrew, I'll make a clean breast of it. I've always laughed at the tradition; I forced myself, as it seemed at least, to disprove it by spending a night in Hal's Planting; I took the pains even to make a theory which would account for its origin. All the time I had a sneaking, stifled belief in it. With the help of my reason I crushed that; but now my reason has thrown up the job, and I'm afraid. I'm afraid of the Undying Thing that is in Hal's Planting. I heard it that night. John Marsh saw it last night—they took me to see the body, and the face was awful; and I believe that one day it will come from Hal's Planting—"

"Yes," interrupted Guerdon, "I know. And at present I believe as much. Last night we laughed at the whole thing, and we shall live to laugh at it again, and be ashamed of ourselves for a couple of superstitious old women. I fancy that beliefs are affected by weather—there's thunder in the air."

"No," said Sir Edric, "my belief has come to stay."

"And what are you going to do?"

"I'm going to test it. On Monday I can begin to get to work, and then I'll blow up Hal's Planting with dynamite. After that we shan't need to believe—we shall *know*. And now let's dismiss the subject. Come down into the billiard-room and have a game. Until Monday I won't think of the thing again."

Long before dinner, Sir Edric's depression seemed to have completely vanished. At dinner he was boisterous and amused. Afterwards he told stories and was interesting.

It was late at night; the terrific storm that was raging outside had wakened Guerdon from sleep. Hopeless of getting to sleep again, he had arisen and dressed, and now sat in the window-seat watching the storm. He had never seen anything like it before; and every now and then the sky seemed to be torn across as if by hands of white fire. Suddenly he heard a tap at his door, and looked round. Sir Edric had already entered; he also had dressed. He spoke in a curious subdued voice.

"I thought you wouldn't be able to sleep through this. Do you remember that I shut and fastened the dining-room window?"

"Yes, I remember it."

"Well, come in here."

Sir Edric led the way to his room, which was immediately over the dining-room. By leaning out of window they could see that the dining-room window was open wide.

"Burglar," said Guerdon meditatively.

"No," Sir Edric answered, still speaking in a hushed voice. "It is the Undying Thing—it has come for me."

He snatched up the candle, and made towards the staircase; Guerdon caught up the loaded revolver which always lay on the table beside Sir Edric's bed and followed him. Both men ran down the staircase as though there were not another moment to lose. Sir Edric rushed at the dining-room door, opened it a little, and looked in. Then he turned to Guerdon, who was just behind him.

"Go back to your room," he said authoritatively.

"I won't," said Guerdon. "Why? What is it?"

Suddenly the corners of Sir Edric's mouth shot outward into the hideous grin of terror.

"It's there! It's there!" he gasped.

"Then I come in with you."

"Go back!"

With a sudden movement, Sir Edric thrust Guerdon away from the door, and then, quick as light, darted in, and locked the door behind him.

Guerdon bent down and listened. He heard Sir Edric say in a firm voice:

"Who are you? What are you?"

Then followed a heavy, snorting breathing, a low, vibrating growl, an awful cry, a scuffle.

Then Guerdon flung himself at the door. He kicked at the lock, but it would not give way. At last he fired his revolver at it. Then he managed to force his way into the room. It was perfectly empty. Overhead he could hear footsteps; the noise had awakened the servants; they were standing, tremulous, on the upper landing.

Through the open window access to the garden was easy. Guerdon did not wait to get help; and in all probability none of the servants could have been persuaded to come with him. He climbed out alone, and, as if by some blind impulse, started to run as hard as he could in the direction of Hal's Planting. He knew that Sir Edric would be found there.

But when he got within a hundred yards of the plantation, he stopped. There had been a great flash of lightning, and he saw that it had struck one of the trees. Flames darted about the plantation as the dry bracken caught. Suddenly, in the light of another flash, he saw the whole of the trees fling their heads upwards; then came a deafening crash, and the ground slipped under him, and he was flung forward on his face. The plantation had collapsed, fallen through into the caves beneath it. Guerdon slowly regained his feet; he was surprised to find that he was unhurt. He walked on a few steps, and then fell again; this time he had fainted away.

The Gray Cat

I heard this story from Archdeacon M——. I should imagine that it would not be very difficult, by trimming it a little and altering the facts here and there, to make it capable of some simple explanation; but I have preferred to tell it as it was told to me.

After all, there is some explanation possible, even if there is not one definite and simple explanation clearly indicated. It must rest with the reader whether he will prefer to believe that some of the so-called uncivilized races may possess occult powers transcending anything of which the so-called civilized are capable, or whether he will consider that a series of coincidences is sufficient to account for the extraordinary incidents which, in a plain brief way, I am about to relate. It does not seem to me essential to state which view I hold myself, or if I hold neither, and have reasons for not stating a third possible explanation.

I must add a word or two with regard to Archdeacon M——. At the time of this story he was in his fiftieth year. He was a fine scholar, a man of considerable learning. His religious views were remarkably broad; his enemies said remarkably thin. In his younger days he had been something of an athlete, but owing to age, sedentary habits, and some amount of self-indulgence, he had grown stout, and no longer took exercise in any form. He had no nervous trouble of any kind. His death, from heart disease, took place about three years ago. He told me the story twice, at my request; there was an interval of about six weeks between the two narrations; some of the details were elicited by questions of my own. With this preliminary note, we may proceed to the story.

In January, 1881, Archdeacon M——, who was a great admirer of Tennyson's poetry, came up to London for a few days, chiefly in order to witness the performance of "The Cup," at the Lyceum. He was not present on the first night (Monday, January 3), but on a later night in the same week. At that time, of course, the poet had not received his peerage, nor the actor his knighthood.

On leaving the theatre, less satisfied with the play than with the magnificence of the setting, the Archdeacon found some slight difficulty in getting a cab. He walked a little way down the Strand to find one, when he encountered unexpectedly his old friend, Guy Breddon.

Breddon (that was not his real name) was a man of considerable fortune, a member of the learned societies, and devoted to Central African exploration. He was two or three years younger than the Archdeacon, and a man of tremendous physique.

Breddon was surprised to find the Archdeacon in London, and the Archdeacon was equally surprised to find Breddon in England at all. Breddon carried off the Archdeacon with him to his rooms, and sent a servant in a cab to the Langham to pay the Archdeacon's bill and fetch his luggage. The Archdeacon protested, but faintly, and Breddon would not hear of his hospitality being refused.

Breddon's rooms were an expensive suite immediately over a ruinous upholsterer's in a street off Berkeley Square. There was a private street-door, and from it a private staircase to the first and second floors.

The suite of rooms on the first floor, occupied by Breddon, was entirely shut off from the staircase by a door. The second floor suite, tenanted by an Irish M.P., was similarly shut off, and at that time was unoccupied.

Breddon and the Archdeacon passed through the street-door and up the stairs to the first landing, from whence, by the staircase-door, they entered the flat. Breddon had only recently taken the flat, and the Archdeacon had never been there before. It consisted of a broad L-shaped passage with rooms opening into it. There were many trophies on the walls. Horned heads glared at them; stealthy but stuffed beasts watched them furtively from under tables. There was a perfect arsenal of murderous weapons gleaming brightly under the shaded gaslights.

Breddon's servant prepared supper for them before leaving for the Langham, and soon the two men were discussing Mr. Tennyson, Mr. Irving, and a parody of the "Queen of the May" which had recently appeared in *Punch*, and doing justice to some oysters, a cold pheasant with an excellent salad, and a bottle of '74 Pornmery. It was characteristic of the Archdeacon that he remembered exactly the items of the supper, and that Breddon rather neglected the wine.

After supper they passed into the library, where a bright fire was burning. The Archdeacon walked towards the fire, rubbing his plump hands together. As he did so, a portion of the great rug of gray fur on which he was standing seemed to rise up. It was a gray cat of enormous size, larger than any that the Archdeacon had ever seen before, and of the same colour as the rug on which it had been sleeping. It rubbed itself affectionately against the Archdeacon's leg, and purred as he bent down to stroke it.

"What an extraordinary animal!" said the Archdeacon. "I had no idea cats could grow to this size. Its head's queer, too—so much too small for the body."

"Yes," said Breddon, "and his feet are just as much too big."

The gray cat stretched himself voluptuously under the Archdeacon's caressing hand, and the feet could be seen plainly. They were very broad, and the claws, which shot out, seemed unusually powerful and well developed. The beast's coat was short, thick, and wiry.

"Most extraordinary!" the Archdeacon repeated.

He lowered himself into a comfortable chair by the fire. He was still bending over the cat and playing with it when a slight chink made him look up. Breddon was putting something down on the table behind the liquor decanters.

"Any particular breed?" the Archdeacon asked.

"Not that I know of. Freakish, I should say. We found him on board the boat when I left for home—may have come there after mice. He'd have been thrown overboard but for me. I got rather interested in him. Smoke?"

"Oh, thank you."

Outside a cold north wind screamed in quick gusts. Within came the sharp scratch of the match on the ribbed glass as the Archdeacon lit his cigar, the bubble of the rose-water in Breddon's hookah, the soft step of Breddon's man carrying the Archdeacon's luggage into the bedroom at the end of the L-shaped passage, and the constant purring of the big gray cat.

"And what's the cat's name?" the Archdeacon asked.

Breddon laughed.

"Well, if you must have the plain truth, he's called Gray Devil—or, more frequently, Devil *tout court*."

"Really, now, really, you can't expect an Archdeacon to use such abominable language. I shall call him Gray—or perhaps Mr. Gray would be more respectful, seeing the shortness of our acquaintance. Do you object to the smell of smoke, Mr. Gray? The intelligent beast does not object. Probably you've accustomed him to it."

"Well, seeing what his name is, he could hardly object to smoke, could he?"

Breddon's servant entered. As the door opened and shut, one heard for a moment the crackle of the newly-lit fire in the room that awaited the

Archdeacon. The servant swept up the hearth, and, under Archidiaconal direction, mixed a lengthy brandy-and-soda. He retired with the information that he would not be wanted again that night.

"Did you notice," asked the Archdeacon, "the way Mr. Gray followed your man about? I never saw a more affectionate cat."

"Think so?" said Breddon. "Watch this time."

For the first time he approached the gray cat, and stretched out his hand as if to pet him. In an instant the cat seemed to have gone mad. Its claws shot out, its back hooped, its coat bristled, its tail stood erect; it cursed and spat, and its small green eyes glared. But a close observer would have noticed that all the time it watched not only Breddon, but also that object which had chinked as Breddon had put it down behind the decanters.

The Archdeacon lay back in his chair and laughed heartily.

"What funny creatures they are, and never so funny as when they lose their tempers! Really, Mr. Gray, out of respect to my cloth, you might have refrained from swearing like that. Poor Mr. Gray! Poor puss!"

Breddon resumed his seat with a grim smile. The gray cat slowly subsided, and then thrust its head, as though demanding sympathy, into the fat palm of the Archdeacon's dependent hand.

Suddenly the Archdeacon's eye lighted on the object which the cat had been watching, visible now that the servant had displaced the decanters.

"Goodness me!" he exclaimed, "you've got a revolver there."

"That is so," said Breddon.

"Not loaded, I trust?"

"Oh yes, fully loaded."

"But isn't that very dangerous?"

"Well, no; I'm used to these things, and I'm not careless with them. I should have thought it more dangerous to have introduced Gray Devil to you without it. He's much more powerful than an ordinary cat, and I fancy there's something beside cat in his pedigree. When I bring a stranger to see him I keep the cat covered with the revolver until I see how the land lies. To do the brute justice, he has always been most friendly with everybody except myself. I'm his only antipathy. He'd have gone for me just now but that he's smart enough to be afraid of this."

He tapped the revolver.

"I see," said the Archdeacon seriously, "and can guess how it happened. You scared him one day by firing the revolver for joke; the report frightened him, and he's never forgiven you or forgotten the revolver.

Wonderful memory some of these animals have!"

"Yes," said Breddon, "but that guess won't do. I have never, intentionally or by chance, given the 'Devil' any reason for his enmity. So far as I know he has never heard a firearm, and certainly he has never heard one since I made his acquaintance. Somebody may have scared him before, and I'm inclined to think that somebody did, for there can be no doubt that the brute knows all that a cat need know about a revolver, and that he's scared of it.

"The first time we met was almost in darkness. I'd got some cases that I was particular about, and the captain had said I could go down to look after them. Well, this beast suddenly came out of a lump of black and flew at me. I didn't even recognise that it was a cat, because he's so mighty big. I fetched him a clip on the side of the head that knocked him off, and whipped out my iron. He was away in a streak. He knew. And I've had plenty of proof since that he knows. He'd bite me now if he had the chance, but he understands that he hasn't got the chance. I'm often half inclined to take him on plain—shooting barred—and to feel my own hands breaking his damned neck!"

"Really, old man, really!" said the Archdeacon in perfunctory protest, as he rose and mixed himself another drink.

"Sorry to use strong language, but I don't love that cat, you know."

The Archdeacon expressed his surprise that in that case Breddon did not get rid of the brute.

"You come across him on board ship and he flies at you. You save his life, give him board and lodging, and he still hates you so much that he won't let you touch him, and you are no fonder of him than he is of you. Why don't you part company?"

"As for his board, I've rarely known him to eat anything except his own kill. He goes out hunting every night. I keep him simply and solely because I'm afraid of him. As long as I can keep him I know my nerves are all right. If I let my funk of him make any difference—well, I shouldn't be much good in a Central African forest. At first I had some idea of taming him—and, besides, there was a queer coincidence."

He rose and opened the window, and Gray Devil slowly slunk up to it. He paused a few moments on the window-sill and then suddenly sprang and vanished.

"What was the coincidence?"

"What do you think of that?"

Breddon handed the Archdeacon a figure of a cat which he had taken from the mantelpiece. It was a little thing about three inches high. In colour, in the small head, enormous feet, and curiously human eyes, it seemed an exact reproduction of Gray Devil.

"A perfect likeness. How did you get it made?"

"I got the likeness before I got the original. A little Jew dealer sold it me the night before I left for England. He thought it was Egyptian, and described it as an idol. Anyhow, it was a niceish piece of jade."

"I always thought jade was bright green."

"It may be—or white—or brown. It varies. I don't think there can be any doubt that this little figure is old, though I doubt if it's Egyptian."

Breddon put it back in its place.

"By the way, that same night the little Jew came to try and buy it back again. He offered me twice what I had given for it. I said he must have found somebody who was pretty keen on it. I asked if it was a collector. The Jew thought not; said it was a coloured gentleman. Well, that finished it. I wasn't going to do anything to oblige a nigger. The Jew pleaded that it was a particularly fine buck-nigger, with mountains of money, who'd been tracking the thing for years, and hinted at all manner of mumbo-jumbo business—to scare me, I suppose. However, I wouldn't listen, and kicked him out. Then came the coincidence. Having bought the likeness, next day I found the living original. Rum, wasn't it?"

At this moment the clock struck, and the Archdeacon recognised with horror that it was very, very much past the time when respectable Archdeacons should be in bed and asleep. He rose and said good-night, observing that he'd like to hear more about it on the morrow.

This was extremely unfortunate, for it will be seen it is just at this part of the story that one wants full details and on the morrow it became impossible to elicit them.

Before leaving the library Breddon closed the window, and the Archdeacon asked how "Mr. Gray," as he called him, would get back.

"Very likely he's back already. He's got a special window in the kitchen, made on purpose, just big enough to let him get in and out as he likes."

"But don't other cats get in, too?"

"No," said Breddon. "Other cats avoid Gray Devil."

The Archdeacon found himself unaccountably nervous when he got to his room. He owned to me that he had to satisfy himself that there was no one concealed under the bed or in the wardrobe. However, he got into bed, and after a little while fell into a deep sleep; his fire was burning brightly, and the room was quite light.

Shortly after four he was awakened by a loud scream. Still sleepy, he did not for the moment locate the sound, thinking that it must have come from the street outside. But almost immediately afterwards he heard the report of a revolver fired twice in quick succession, and then, after a short pause, a third time.

The Archdeacon was terribly frightened. He did not know what had happened, and thought of armed burglars. For a time—he did not think it could have been more than a minute—fear held him motionless. Then with an effort he rose, lit the gas, and hurried on his clothes. As he was dressing, he heard a step down the passage and a knock at his door.

He opened it, and found Breddon's servant. The man had put on a blue overcoat over his night-things, and wore slippers. He was shivering with cold and terror.

"Oh, my God, sir!" he exclaimed, "Mr. Breddon's shot himself. Would you come, sir?"

The Archdeacon followed the man to Breddon's bedroom. The smoke still hung thickly in the room. A mirror had been smashed, and lay in fragments on the floor. On the bed, with his back to the Archdeacon, lay Breddon, dead. His right hand still grasped the revolver, and there was a blackened wound behind the right ear.

When the Archdeacon came round to look at the face he turned faint, and the servant took him out into the library and gave him brandy, the glasses and decanters still standing there. Breddon's face certainly had looked very ghastly; it had been scratched, torn and bitten; one eye was gone, and the whole face was covered with blood.

"Do you think it was that brute did it?"

"Sure of it, sir; sprang on his face while he was asleep. I knew it would happen one of these nights. He knew it too; always slept with the revolver by his side. He fired twice at the brute, but couldn't see for the blood. Then he killed himself."

It seemed likely enough, with his eyesight gone, horribly mauled, in an agony of pain, possibly believing that he was saving himself from a death still more horrible, Breddon might very well have turned the weapon on himself.

"What do we do now?" the man asked.

"We must get a doctor and fetch the police at once. Come on."

As they turned the corner of the passage, they saw that the door communicating with the staircase was open.

"Did you open that door?" asked the Archdeacon.

"No," said the man, aghast.

"Then who did?"

"Don't know, sir. Looks as if we weren't at the end of this yet."

They passed down the stairs together, and found the street-door also ajar. On the pavement outside lay a policeman slowly recovering consciousness. Breddon's man took the policeman's whistle and blew it. A passing hansom, going back to the mews, slowed up; the cab was sent to fetch a doctor, and communication with the police-station rapidly followed.

The injured policeman told a curious story. He was passing the house when he heard shots fired. Almost immediately afterwards he heard the bolts of the front-door being drawn, and stepped back into the neighbouring doorway. The front-door opened, and a negro emerged clad in a gray tweed suit with a gray overcoat. The policeman jumped out, and without a second's hesitation the black man felled him. "It was all done before you could think," was the policeman's phrase.

"What kind of negro?" asked the Archdeacon.

"A big man—stood over six foot, and black as coal. He never waited to be challenged; the moment he knew that he was seen he hit out."

The policeman was not a very intelligent fellow, and there was little more to be got out of him. He had heard the shots, seen the street-door open and the man in gray appear, and had been felled by a lightning blow before he had time to do anything.

The doctor, a plain, matter-of-fact little man, had no hesitation in saying that Breddon was dead, and must have died almost immediately. After the injuries received, respiration and heart-action must have ceased at once. He was explaining something which oozed from the dead man's ear, when the Archdeacon could stand it no longer, and staggered out into the library. There he found Breddon's servant, still in the blue overcoat, explaining to a policeman with a notebook that as far as he knew nothing was missing except a jade image or idol of a cat which formerly stood on the mantelpiece.

The cat known as "Gray Devil" was also missing, and, although a description of it was circulated in the public press, nothing was ever heard of it again. But gray fur was found in the clenched left hand of the dead man.

The inquest resulted in the customary verdict, and brought to light no new facts. But it may be as well to give what the police theory of the case was. According to the police the suicide took place much as Breddon's servant had supposed. Mad with pain and unable to bear the thought of his awful mutilation, Breddon had shot himself.

The story of the jade image, as far as it was known, was told at the inquest. The police held that this image was an idol, that some uncivilized tribe was much perturbed by the theft of it, and was ready to pay an enormously high price for its recovery. The negro was assumed to be aware of this, and to have determined to obtain possession of the idol by fair means or foul. Fair means failing, it was suggested that the negro followed Breddon to England, tracked him out, and on the night in question found some means to conceal himself in Breddon's flat. There it was assumed that he fell asleep, was awakened by the screams and the sound of the firing, and, being scared, caught up the jade image and made off. Realizing that the shots would have been heard outside, and that his departure at that moment would be considered extremely suspicious, he was ready as he opened the street-door to fell the first man that he saw. The temporary unconsciousness of the policeman gave him time to get away.

The theory sounds at first sight like the only possible theory. When the Archdeacon first told me the story I tried to find out indirectly whether he accepted it. Finding him rather disposed to fence with my hints and suggestions, I put the question to him plainly and bluntly:

"Do you believe in the police theory?"

He hesitated, and then answered with complete frankness:

"No, most emphatically not."

"Why?" I asked; and he went over the evidence with me.

"In the first place, I do not believe that Breddon, in the ordinary sense, committed suicide. No amount of physical pain would have made him even think of it. He had unending pluck. He would have taken the facial disfigurement and loss of sight as the chances of war, and would have done the best that could be done by a man with such awful disabilities. One must admit that he fired the fatal shot—the medical evidence on that point is too strong to be gainsaid—but he fired it under circumstances of supernatural horror of which we, thank God! know nothing."

"I'm naturally slow to admit supernatural explanation."

"Well, let's go on. What's this mysterious tribe the police talk about? I want to know where it lives and what its name is. It's wealthy enough to offer a huge reward; it must be of some importance. The negro managed to get in and secrete himself. How? Where? I know the flat, and that theory won't do. We don't even know that it was the negro who took that little image, though I believe it was. Anyhow, how did the negro get away at that hour of the morning absolutely unobserved? Negroes are not so common in London that they can walk about without being noticed; yet not one trace of him was ever found, and equally mysterious is the disappearance of the Gray Cat. It was such an extraordinary brute, and the description of it was so widely circulated that it would have seemed almost certain we should hear of it again. Well, we've not heard."

We discussed the police theory for some little time, and something which he happened to say led me to exclaim:

"Really! Do you mean to say that the Gray Cat actually was the negro?"

"No," he replied, "not exactly that, but something near it. Cats are strange animals, anyhow. I needn't remind you of their connection with certain old religions or with that witchcraft in which till even in England to-day some still believe, and not so long ago almost all believed. I have never, by the way, seen a good explanation of the fact that there are people who cannot bear to be in a room with a cat, and are aware of its presence as if by some mysterious extra sense. Let me remind you of the belief which undoubtedly exists both in China and Japan, that evil spirits may enter into certain of the lower animals, the fox and badger especially. Every student of demonology knows about these things."

"But that idea of evil spirits taking possession of cats or foxes is surely a heathen superstition which you cannot hold."

"Well, I have read of the evil spirits that entered into the swine. Think it over, and keep an open mind."

The Four-Fingered Hand

Charles Yarrow held fours, but as he had come up against Brackley's straight flush they only did him harm, leading him to remark—by no means for the first time—that it did not matter what cards one held, but only when one held them. "I get out here," he remarked, with resignation. No one else seemed to care for further play. The two other men left at once, and shortly afterwards Yarrow and Brackley sauntered out of the club together.

"The night's young," said Brackley; "if you're doing nothing you may as well come round to me."

"Thanks, I will. I'll talk, or smoke, or go so far as to drink; but I don't play poker. It's not my night."

"I didn't know," said Brackley, "that you had any superstitions."

"Haven't. I've only noticed that, as a rule, my luck goes in runs, and that a good run or a bad run usually lasts the length of a night's play. There is probably some simple reason for it, if I were enough of a mathematician to worry it out. In luck as distinct from arithmetic I have no belief at all."

"I wish you could bring me to that happy condition. The hard-headed man of the world, without a superstition or a belief of any kind, has the best time of it."

They reached Brackley's chambers, lit pipes, and mixed drinks. Yarrow stretched himself in a lounge chair, and took up the subject again, speaking lazily and meditatively. He was a man of thirty-eight, with a clean-shaven face; he looked, as indeed he was, travelled and experienced.

"I don't read any books," he remarked, "but I've been twice round the world, and am just about to leave England again. I've been alive for thirty-eight years and during most of them I have been living. Consequently, I've formed opinions, and one of my opinions is that it is better to dispense with superfluous luggage. Prejudices, superstitions, beliefs of any kind that are not capable of easy and immediate proof are superfluous luggage; one goes more easily without them. You implied just now that you had a certain amount of this superfluous luggage, Brackley. What form does it take? Do you turn your chair—are you afraid of thirteen at dinner?"

"No, nothing of that sort. I'll tell you about it. You've heard of my grandfather—who made the money?"

"Heard of him? Had him rubbed into me in my childhood. He's in *Smiles* or one of those books, isn't he? Started life as a navvy, educated himself, invented things, made a fortune, gave vast sums in charity."

"That is the man. Well, he lived to be a fair age, but he was dead before I was born. What I know of him I know from my father, and some of it is not included in those improving books for the young. For instance, there is no mention in the printed biography of his curious belief in the four-fingered hand. His belief was that from time to time he saw a phantom hand. Sometimes it appeared to him in the daytime, and sometimes at night. It was a right hand with the second finger missing. He always regarded the appearance of the hand as a warning. It meant, he supposed, that he was to stop anything on which he was engaged; if he was about to let a house, buy a horse, go on a journey, or whatever it was, he stopped if he saw the four-fingered hand."

"Now, look here," said Yarrow, "we'll examine this thing rationally. Can you quote one special instance in which your grandfather saw this maimed hand, broke off a particular project, and found himself benefited?"

"No. In telling my father about it he spoke quite generally."

"Oh, yes," said Yarrow, drily. "The people who see these things do speak quite generally as a rule."

"But wait a moment. This vision of the four-fingered hand appears to have been hereditary. My father also saw it from time to time. And here I can give you the special circumstances. Do you remember the Crewe disaster some years ago? Well, my father had intended to travel by the train that was wrecked. Just as he was getting into the carriage he saw the four-fingered hand. He at once got out and postponed his journey until later in the day. Another occasion was two months before the failure of Varings'. My father banked there. As a rule he kept a comparatively small balance at the bank, but on this occasion he had just realized an investment, and was about to place the result—six thousand pounds—in the bank, pending reinvestment. He was on the point of sending off his confidential clerk with the money, when once more he saw the four-fingered hand. Now at that time Varings' was considered to be as safe as a church. Possibly a few people with special means of information may have had some slight suspicion at the time, but my father certainly had none. He had always banked with Varings', as his father had done before him. However, his faith in the warning hand was so great that instead of paying in the six thousand he withdrew his balance that day. Is that good enough for you?"

"Not entirely. Mind, I don't dispute your facts, but I doubt if it requires the supernatural to explain them. You say that the vision appears to be hereditary. Does that mean that you yourself have ever seen it?"

"I have seen it once."

"When?"

"I saw it tonight." Brackley spoke like a man suppressing some strong excitement. "It was just as you got up from the card-table after losing on your fours. I was on the point of urging you and the other two men to go on playing. I saw the hand distinctly. It seemed to be floating in the air about a couple of yards away from me. It was a small white hand, like a lady's hand, cut short off at the wrist. For a second it moved slowly towards me, and then vanished. Nothing would have induced me to go on playing poker tonight."

"You are—excuse me for mentioning it—not in the least degree under the influence of drink. Further, you are by habit an almost absurdly temperate man. I mention these things because they have to be taken into consideration. They show that you were not at any rate the victim of a common and disreputable form of illusion. But what service has the hand done you? We play a regular point at the club. We are not the excited gamblers of fiction. We don't increase the points, and we never play after one in the morning. At the moment when the hand appeared to you, how much had you won?"

"Twenty-five pounds—an exceptionally large amount."

"Very well. You're a careful player. You play best when your luck's worst. We stopped play at half-past eleven. If we had gone on playing till one, and your luck had been of the worst possible description all the time, we will say that you might have lost that twenty-five and twenty-five more. To me it is inconceivable, but with the worst luck and the worst play it is perhaps possible. Now then, do you mean to tell me that the loss of twenty-five pounds is a matter of such importance to a man with your income as to require a supernatural intervention to prevent you from losing it?"

"Of course it isn't."

"Well, then, the four-fingered hand has not accomplished its mission. It has not saved you from anything. It might even have been inconvenient. If you had been playing with strangers and winning, and they had wished to go on playing, you could hardly have refused. Of course, it did not matter with us—we play with you constantly, and can have our revenge at any time. The four-fingered hand is proved in this instance to have been useless and inept. Therefore, I am inclined to believe that the appearances when it really did some good were coincidences. Doubtless your grandfather and father and yourself have seen the hand, but surely that may be due to some slight hereditary defect in the seeing apparatus, which, under certain conditions, say, of the light and of your own health creates the illusion. The four-fingered hand is natural and not supernatural, subjective and not objective."

"It sounds plausible," remarked Brackley. He got up, crossed the room, and began to open the card-table. "Practical tests are always the most satisfactory, and we can soon have a practical test." As he put the candles on the table he started a little and nearly dropped one of them. He laughed drily. "I saw the four-fingered hand again just then," he said. "But no matter—come—let us play."

"Oh, the two game isn't funny enough."

"Then I'll fetch up Blake from downstairs; you know him. He never goes to bed, and he plays the game."

Blake, who was a youngish man, had chambers downstairs. Brackley easily persuaded him to join the party. It was decided that they should play for exactly an hour. It was a poor game; the cards ran low, and there was very little betting. At the end of the hour Brackley had lost a sovereign, and Yarrow had lost five pounds.

"I don't like to get up a winner, like this," said Blake. "Let's go on."

But Yarrow was not to be persuaded. He said that he was going off to bed. No allusion to the four-fingered hand was made in speaking in the presence of Blake, but Yarrow's smile of conscious superiority had its meaning for Brackley. It meant that Yarrow had overthrown a superstition, and was consequently pleased with himself. After a few minutes' chat Yarrow and Blake said good-night to Brackley, and went downstairs together.

Just as they reached the ground floor they heard, from far up the staircase, a short cry, followed a moment afterwards by the sound of a heavy fall.

"What's that?" Blake exclaimed.

"I'm just going to see," said Yarrow, quietly. "It seemed to me to come from Brackley's rooms. Let's go up again."

They hurried up the staircase and knocked at Brackley's door. There was no answer. The whole place was absolutely silent. The door was ajar; Yarrow pushed it open, and the two men went in.

The candles on the card-table were still burning. At some distance from them, in a dark corner of the room, lay Brackley, face downwards, with one arm folded under him and the other stretched wide.

Blake stood in the doorway. Yarrow went quickly over to Brackley, and turned the body partially over.

"What is it?" asked Blake, excitedly. "Is the man ill? Has he fainted?"

"Run downstairs," said Yarrow, curtly. "Rouse the porter and get a doctor at once."

The moment Blake had gone, Yarrow took a candle from the card-table, and by the light of it examined once more the body of the dead man. On the throat there was the imprint of a hand—a right hand with the second finger missing. The marks, which were crimson at first, grew gradually fainter.

Some years afterwards, in Yarrow's presence, a man happened to tell some story of a warning apparition that he himself had investigated.

"And do you believe that?" Yarrow asked.

"The evidence that the apparition was seen—and seen by more than one person—seems to me fairly conclusive in this case."

"That is all very well. I will grant you the apparition if you like. But why speak of it as a warning? If such appearances take place, it still seems to me absurd and disproportionate to suppose that they do so in order to warn us, or help us, or hinder us, or anything of the kind. They appear for their own unfathomable reasons only. If they seem to forbid one thing or command another, that also is for their own purpose. I have an experience of my own which would tend to show that."

The Tower

In the billiard-room of the Cabinet Club, shortly after midnight, two men had just finished a game. A third had been watching it from the lounge at the end of the room. The winner put up his cue, slipped on his coat, and with a brief "Good-night" passed out of the room. He was tall, dark, clean-shaven and foreign in appearance. It would not have been easy to guess his nationality, but he did not look English.

The loser, a fair-haired boy of twenty-five, came over to the lounge and dropped down by the side of the elderly man who had been watching the billiards.

"Silly game, ain't it, doctor?" he said cheerfully. The doctor smiled.

"Yes," he said, "Vyse is a bit too hot for you, Bill."

"A bit too hot for anything," said the boy. "He never takes any trouble; he never hesitates; he never thinks; he never takes an easy shot when there's a brilliant one to be pulled off. It's almost uncanny."

"Ah," said the doctor, reflectively, "it's a queer thing. You're the third man whom I have heard say that about Vyse within the last week."

"I believe he's quite all right—good sort of chap, you know. He's frightfully clever too—speaks a lot of beastly difficult Oriental languages—does well at any game he takes up."

"Yes," said the doctor, "he is clever; and he is also a fool."

"What do you mean? He's eccentric, of course. Fancy his buying that rotten tower—a sweet place to spend Christmas in all alone, I don't think."

"Why does he say he's going there?"

"Says he hates the conventional Christmas, and wants to be out of it; says also that he wants to shoot duck."

"That won't do," said the doctor. "He may hate the conventional Christmas. He may, and he probably will, shoot duck. But that's not his reason for going there."

"Then what is it?" asked the boy.

"Nothing that would interest you much, Bill. Vyse is one of the chaps that want to know too much. He's playing about in a way that every medical man knows to be a rotten, dangerous way. Mind, he may get at something; if the stories are true he has already got at a good deal. I believe it is possible for a man to develop in himself certain powers at a certain price."

"What's the price?"

"Insanity, as often as not. Here, let's talk about something pleasanter. Where are you yourself going this Christmas, by the way?"

"My sister has taken compassion upon this lone bachelor. And you?"

"I shall be out of England," said the doctor. "Cairo, probably."

The two men passed out into the hall of the club.

"Has Mr. Vyse gone yet?" the boy asked the porter.

"Not yet, Sir William. Mr. Vyse is changing in one of the dressing-rooms. His car is outside."

The two men passed the car in the street, and noticed the luggage in the tonneau. The driver, in his long leather coat, stood motionless beside it, waiting for his master. The powerful headlight raked the dusk of the street; you could see the paint on a tired woman's cheek as she passed through it on her way home at last.

"See his game?" said Bill.

"Of course," said the doctor. "He's off to the marshes and that blessed tower of his tonight."

"Well, I don't envy him—holy sort of amusement it must be driving all that way on a cold night like this. I wonder if the beggar ever goes to sleep at all?"

They had reached Bill's chambers in Jermyn Street.

"You must come in and have a drink," said Bill.

"Don't think so, thanks," said the doctor; "it's late, you know."

"You'd better," said Bill, and the doctor followed him in.

A letter and a telegram were lying on the table in the diminutive hall. The letter had been sent by messenger, and was addressed to Sir William Orlsey, Bart., in a remarkably small handwriting. Bill picked it up, and thrust it into his pocket at once, unopened. He took the telegram with him into the room where the drinks had been put out, and opened it as he sipped his whisky-and-soda.

"Great Scot!" he exclaimed.

"Nothing serious, I hope," said the doctor.

"I hope not. I suppose all children have got to have the measles some time or another; but it's a bit unlucky that my sister's three should all go down with it just now. That does for her house-party at Christmas, of course."

A few minutes later, when the doctor had gone, Bill took the letter from his pocket and tore it open. A cheque fell from the envelope and fluttered to the ground. The letter ran as follows:

"Dear Bill,—I could not talk to you tonight, as the doctor, who happens to disapprove of me, was in the billiard-room. Of course, I can let you have the hundred you want, and enclose it herewith with the utmost pleasure. The time you mention for repayment would suit me all right, and so would any other time. Suit your own convenience entirely.

"I have a favour to ask of you. I know you are intending to go down to the Leylands' for Christmas. I think you will be prevented from doing so. If that is the case, and you have no better engagement, would you hold yourself at my disposal for a week? It is just possible that I may want a man like you pretty badly. There ought to be plenty of duck this weather, but I don't know that I can offer any other attraction—Very sincerely yours,

"Edward Vyse."

Bill picked up the cheque, and thrust it into the drawer with a feeling of relief. It was a queer invitation, he thought—funnily worded, with the usual intimations of time and place missing. He switched off the electric lights and went into his bedroom. As he was undressing a thought struck him suddenly.

"How the deuce," he said aloud, "did he know that I should be prevented from going to Polly's place?" Then he looked round quickly. He thought that he had heard a faint laugh just behind him. No one was there, and Bill's nerves were good enough. In twenty minutes he was fast asleep.

The cottage, built of gray stone, stood some thirty yards back from the road, from which it was screened by a shrubbery. It was an ordinary eight-roomed cottage, and it did well enough for Vyse and his servants and one guest—if Vyse happened to want a guest. There was a pleasant little walled garden of a couple of acres behind the cottage. Through a doorway in the further wall one passed into a stunted and dismal plantation, and in the middle of this rose the tower, far higher than any of the trees that surrounded it.

Sir William Orlsey had arrived just in time to change before dinner. Talk at dinner had been of indifferent subjects—the queer characters of the village and the chances of sport on the morrow. Bill had mentioned the tower, and his host had hastened to talk of other things. But now that dinner was over, and the man who had waited on them had left the room, Vyse of his own accord returned to the subject.

"Danvers is a superstitious ass," he observed, "and he's in quite enough of a funk about that tower as it is; that's why I wouldn't give you the story of it while he was in the room. According to the village tradition, a witch was burned on the site where the tower now stands, and she declared that where she burned the devil should have his house. The lord of the manor at that time, hearing what the old lady had said, and wishing to discourage house-building on that particular site, had it covered with a plantation, and made it a condition of his will that this plantation should be kept up."

Bill lit a cigar. "Looks like checkmate," he said. "However, seeing that the tower is actually there—"

"Quite so. This man's son came no end of a cropper, and the property changed hands several times. It was divided and sub-divided. I, for instance, only own about twenty acres of it. Presently there came along a scientific old gentleman and bought the piece that I now have. Whether he knew of the story, or whether he didn't, I cannot say, but he set to work to build the tower that is now standing in the middle of the plantation. He may have intended it as an observatory. He got the stone for it on the spot from his own quarry, but he had to import his labour, as the people in these parts didn't think the work healthy. Then one fine morning before the tower was finished they found the old gentleman at the bottom of his quarry with his neck broken."

"So," said Bill, "they say of course that the tower is haunted. What is it that they think they see?"

"Nothing. You can't see it. But there are people who think they have touched it and have heard it."

"Rot, ain't it?"

"I don't know exactly. You see, I happen to be one of those people."

"Then, if you think so, there's something in it. This is interesting. I say, can't we go across there now?"

"Certainly, if you like. Sure you won't have any more wine? Come along, then."

The two men slipped on their coats and caps. Vyse carried a lighted stable-lantern. It was a frosty moonlit night, and the path was crisp and hard beneath their feet. As Vyse slid back the bolts of the gate in the garden wall, Bill said suddenly, "By the way, Vyse, how did you know that I shouldn't be at the Leylands' this Christmas? I told you I was going there."

"I don't know. I had a feeling that you were going to be with me. It might have been wrong. Anyhow, I'm very glad you're here. You are just exactly the man I want. We've only a few steps to go now. This path is ours. That cart-track leads away to the quarry where the scientific gentleman took the short cut to further knowledge. And here is the door of the tower."

They walked round the tower before entering. The night was so still that, unconsciously, they spoke in lowered voices and trod as softly as possible. The lock of the heavy door groaned and screeched as the key turned. The light of the lantern fell now on the white sand of the floor and on a broken spiral staircase on the further side. Far up above one saw a tangle of beams and the stars beyond them. Bill heard Vyse saying that it was left like that after the death in the quarry.

"It's a good solid bit of masonry," said Bill, "but it ain't a cheerful spot exactly. And, by Jove! it smells like a menagerie."

"It does," said Vyse, who was examining the sand on the floor.

Bill also looked down at the prints in the sand. "Some dog's been in here."

"No," said Vyse, thoughtfully. "Dogs won't come in here, and you can't make them. Also, there were no marks on the sand when I left the place and locked the door this afternoon. Queer, isn't it?"

"But the thing's a blank impossibility. Unless, of course, we are to suppose that—"

He did not finish his sentence, and, if he had finished it, it would not have been audible. A chorus of grunting, growling and squealing broke out almost from under his feet, and he sprang backwards. It lasted for a few seconds, and then died slowly away.

"Did you hear that?" Vyse asked quietly.

"I should rather think so."

"Good; then it was not subjective. What was it?"

"Only one kind of beast makes that row. Pigs, of course—a whole drove of them. It sounded as if they were in here, close to us. But as they obviously are not, they must be outside."

"But they are not outside," said Vyse. "Come and see."

They hunted the plantation through and through with no result, and then locked the tower door and went back to the cottage. Bill said very little. He was not capable of much self-analysis, but he was conscious of a sudden dislike of Vyse. He was angry that he had ever put himself under an obligation to this man. He had wanted the money for a gambling debt, and he had already repaid it. Now he saw Vyse in the light of a man with whom one should have no dealings, and the last man from whom one should accept a kindness. The strange experience that he had just been through filled him with loathing far more than with fear or wonder. There was something unclean and diabolical about the whole thing that made a decent man reluctant to question or to investigate. The filthy smell of the brutes seemed still to linger in his nostrils. He was determined that on no account would he enter the tower again, and that as soon as he could find a decent excuse he would leave the place altogether.

A little later, as he sat before the log fire and filled his pipe, he turned to his host with a sudden question: "I say, Vyse, why did you want me to come down here? What's the meaning of it all?"

"My dear fellow," said Vyse, "I wanted you for the pleasure of your society. Now, don't get impatient. I also wanted you because you are the most normal man I know. Your confirmation of my experiences in the tower is most valuable to me. Also, you have good nerves, and, if you will forgive me for saying so, no imagination. I may want help that only a man with good nerves would be able to give."

"Why don't you leave the thing alone? It's too beastly."

Vyse laughed. "I'm afraid my hobby bores you. We won't talk about it. After all, there's no reason why you should help me?"

"Tell me just what it is that you wanted."

"I wanted you if you heard this whistle"—he took an ordinary police whistle down from the mantelpiece—"any time tonight or tomorrow night, to come over to the tower at once and bring a revolver with you. The whistle would be a sign that I was in a tight place—that my life, in fact, was in danger. You see, we are dealing here with something preternatural, but it is also something material; in addition to other risks, one risks ordinary physical destruction. However, I could see that you were repelled by the sight and the sound of those beasts, whatever they may be; and I can tell you from my own experience that the touch of them is even worse. There is no reason why you should bother yourself any further about the thing."

"You can take the whistle with you," said Bill. "If I hear it I will come."

"Thanks," said Vyse, and immediately changed the subject. He did not say why he was spending the night in the tower, or what it was he proposed to do there.

It was three in the morning when Bill was suddenly startled out of his sleep. He heard the whistle being blown repeatedly. He hurried on some clothes and dashed down into the hall, where his lantern lay all ready for him. He ran along the garden path and through the door in the wall until he got to the tower. The sound of the whistle had ceased now, and everything was horribly still. The door of the tower stood wide open, and without hesitation Bill entered, holding his lantern high.

The tower was absolutely empty. Not a sound was to be heard. Bill called Vyse by name twice loudly, and then again the awful silence spread over the place.

Then, as if guided by some unseen hand, he took the track that led to the quarry, well knowing what he would find at the bottom of it.

The jury assigned the death of Vyse as an accident, and said that the quarry should be fenced in. They had no explanation to offer of the mutilation of the face, as if by the teeth of some savage beast.

The Unfinished Game

At Tanslowe, which is on the Thames, I found just the place that I wanted. I had been born in the hotel business, brought up in it, and made my living at it for thirty years. For the last twenty I had been both proprietor and manager, and had worked uncommonly hard, for it is personal attention and plenty of it which makes a hotel pay. I might have retired altogether, for I was a bachelor with no claims on me and had made more money than enough; but that was not what I wanted. I wanted a nice, old-fashioned house, not too big, in a nice place with a longish slack season. I cared very little whether I made it pay or not. The Regency Hotel at Tanslowe was just the thing for me. It would give me a little to do and not too much. Tanslowe was a village, and though there were two or three public houses, there was no other hotel in the place, nor was any competition likely to come along. I was particular about that, because my nature is such that competition always sets me fighting, and I cannot rest until the other shop goes down. I had reached a time of life when I did want to rest and did not want any more fighting. It was a free house, and I have always had a partiality for being my own master. It had just the class of trade that I liked—principally gentlefolk taking their pleasure in a holiday on the river. It was very cheap, and I like value for money. The house was comfortable, and had a beautiful garden sloping down to the river. I meant to put in some time in that garden—I have a taste that way.

The place was so cheap that I had my doubts. I wondered if it was flooded when the river rose, if it was dropping to pieces with dry-rot, if the drainage had been condemned, if they were going to start a lunatic asylum next door, or what it was. I went into all these points and a hundred more. I found one or two trifling drawbacks, and one expects them in any house, however good—especially when it is an old place like the Regency. I found nothing whatever to stop me from taking the place.

I bought the whole thing, furniture and all, lock, stock and barrel, and moved in. I brought with me my own head-waiter and my man-cook, Englishmen both of them. I knew they would set the thing in the right key. The head-waiter, Silas Goodheart, was just over sixty, with gray hair and a wrinkled face. He was worth more to me than two younger men would have been. He was very precise and rather slow in his movements. He liked bright silver, clean table-linen, and polished glass. Artificial flowers in the vases on his tables would have given him a fit. He handled a decanter of old port as if he loved it—which, as a matter of fact, he did. His manner to visitors was a perfect mixture of dignity, respect and friendliness. If a man did not quite know what he wanted for dinner, Silas had sympathetic and very useful suggestions. He took, I am sure, a real pleasure in seeing people enjoy their luncheon or dinner. Americans loved him, and tipped him out of all proportion. I let him have his own way, even when he gave the thing away.

"Is the coffee all right here?" a customer asked after a good dinner.

"I cannot recommend it," said Silas. "If I might suggest, sir, we have the Chartreuse of the old French shipping."

I overheard that, but I said nothing. The coffee was extract, for there was more work than profit in making it good. As it was, that customer went away pleased, and came back again and again, and brought his friends too. Silas was really the only permanent waiter. When we were busy I got one or two foreigners from London temporarily. Silas soon educated them. My cook, Timbs, was an honest chap, and understood English fare. He seemed hardly ever to eat, and never sat down to a meal; he lived principally on beer, drank enough of it to frighten you, and was apparently never the worse for it. And a butcher who tried to send him second-quality meat was certain of finding out his mistake.

The only other man I brought with me was young Harry Bryden. He always called me uncle, but as a matter of fact he was no relation of mine. He was the son of an old friend. His parents died when he was seven years old and left him to me. It was about all they had to leave. At this time he was twenty-two, and was making himself useful. There was nothing which he was not willing to do, and he could do most things. He would mark at billiards, and played a good game himself. He had run the kitchen when the cook was away on his holiday. He had driven the station-omnibus when the driver was drunk one night. He understood book-keeping, and when I got a clerk who was a wrong 'un, he was on to him at once and saved me money. It was my intention to make him take his proper place when I got to the Regency; for he was to succeed me when I died. He was clever, and not bad-looking in a gipsy-faced kind of way. Nobody is perfect, and Harry was a cigarette maniac. He began when he was a boy, and I didn't spare the stick when I caught him at it. But nothing I could say or do made any difference; at twenty-two he was old enough and big enough to have his own way, and his own way was to smoke cigarettes eternally. He was a bundle of nerves, and got so jumpy sometimes that some people thought he drank, though he had never in his life tasted liquor. He inherited his nerves from his mother, but I daresay the cigarettes made them worse.

I took Harry down with me when I first thought of taking the place. He went over it with me and made a lot of useful suggestions. The old proprietor had died eighteen months before, and the widow had tried to run it for herself and made a mess of it. She had just sense enough to clear out before things got any worse. She was very anxious to go, and I thought that might have been the reason why the price was so low.

The billiard-room was an annexe to the house, with no rooms over it. We were told that it wasn't used once in a twelvemonth, but we took a look at it—we took a look at everything. The room had got a very neglected look about it. I sat down on the platform—tired with so much walking and standing—and Harry whipped the cover off the table. "This was the one they had in the Ark," he said.

There was not a straight cue in the rack, the balls were worn and untrue, the jigger was broken. Harry pointed to the board. "Look at that, uncle," he said. "Noah had made forty-eight; Ham was doing nicely at sixty-six; and then the Flood came and they never finished." From neatness and force of habit he moved over and turned the score back. "You'll have to spend some money here. My word, if they put the whole lot in at a florin we're swindled." As we came out Harry gave a shiver. "I wouldn't spend a night in there," he said, "not for a five-pound note."

His nerves always made me angry. "That's a very silly thing to say," I told him. "Who's going to ask you to sleep in a billiard-room?"

Then he got a bit more practical, and began to calculate how much I should have to spend to make a bright, up-to-date billiard-room of it. But I was still angry.

"You needn't waste your time on that," I said, "because the place will stop as it is. You heard what Mrs. Parker said—that it wasn't used once in a twelvemonth. I don't want to attract all the loafers in Tanslowe into my house. Their custom's worth nothing, and I'd sooner be without it. Time enough to put that room right if I find my staying visitors want it, and people who've been on the river all day are mostly too tired for a game after dinner."

Harry pointed out that it sometimes rained, and there was the winter to think about. He had always got plenty to say, and what he said now had sense in it. But I never go chopping and changing about, and I had made my mind up. So I told him he had got to learn how to manage the house, and not waste half his time over the billiard-table. I had a good deal done to the rest of the house in the way of redecorating and improvements, but I never touched the annexe.

The next time I saw the room was the day after we moved in. I was alone, and I thought it certainly did look a dingy hole as compared with the rest of the house. Then my eye happened to fall on the board and it still showed sixty-six–forty-eight, as it had done when I entered the room with Harry three months before. I altered the board myself this time. To me it was only a funny coincidence; another game had been played there and had stopped exactly at the same point. But I was glad Harry was not with me, for it was the kind of thing that would have made him jumpier than ever.

It was the summer time and we soon had something to do. I had been told that motor-cars had cut into the river trade a good deal; so I laid myself out for the motorist. Tanslowe was just a nice distance for a run from town before lunch. It was all in the old-fashioned style, but there was plenty of choice and the stuff was good; and my wine-list was worth consideration. Prices were high, but people will pay when they are pleased with the way they are treated. Motorists who had been once came again and sent their friends. Saturday to Monday we had as much as ever we could do, and more than I had ever meant to do. But I am built like that— once I am in a shop I have got to run it for all it's worth.

I had been there about a month, and it was about the height of our season, when one night, for no reason that I could make out, I couldn't get to sleep. I had turned in, tired enough, at half-past ten, leaving Harry to shut up and see the lights out, and at a quarter past twelve I was still awake. I thought to myself that a pint of stout and a biscuit might be the cure for that. So I lit my candle and went down to the bar. The gas was out on the staircase and in the passages, and all was quiet. The door into the bar was locked, but I had thought to bring my pass-key with me. I had just drawn my tankard of stout when I heard a sound that made me put the tankard down and listen again.

The billiard-room door was just outside in the passage, and there could not be the least doubt that a game was going on. I could hear the click-click of the balls as plainly as possible. It surprised me a little, but it did not startle me. We had several staying in the house, and I supposed two of them had fancied a game. All the time that I was drinking the stout and munching my biscuit the game went on—click, click-click, click. Everybody has heard the sound hundreds of times standing outside the glass-panelled door of a billiard-room and waiting for the stroke before entering. No other sound is quite like it.

Suddenly the sound ceased. The game was over. I had nothing on but my pyjamas and a pair of slippers, and I thought I would get upstairs again before the players came out. I did not want to stand there shivering and listening to complaints about the table. I locked the bar, and took a glance at the billiard-room door as I was about to pass it. What I saw made me stop short. The glass panels of the door were as black as my Sunday hat, except where they reflected the light of my candle. The room, then, was not lit up, and people do not play billiards in the dark. After a second or two I tried the handle. The door was locked. It was the only door to the room.

I said to myself: "I'll go on back to bed. It must have been my fancy, and there was nobody playing billiards at all." I moved a step away, and then I said to myself again: "I know perfectly well that a game was being played. I'm only making excuses because I'm in a funk."

That settled it. Having driven myself to it, I moved pretty quickly. I shoved in my pass-key, opened the door, and said "Anybody there?" in a moderately loud voice that sounded somehow like another man's. I am very much afraid that I should have jumped if there had come any answer to my challenge, but all was silent. I took a look round. The cover was on the table. An old screen was leaning against it; it had been put there to be out of the way. As I moved my candle the shadows of things slithered across the floor and crept up the walls. I noticed that the windows were properly fastened, and then, as I held my candle high, the marking-board seemed to jump out of the darkness. The score recorded was sixty-six–forty-eight.

I shut the door, locked it again, and went up to my room. I did these things slowly and deliberately, but I was frightened and I was puzzled. One is not at one's best in the small hours.

The next morning I tackled Silas.

"Silas," I said, "what do you do when gentlemen ask for the billiard-room?"

"Well, sir," said Silas, "I put them off if I can. Mr. Harry directed me to, the place being so much out of order."

"Quite so," I said. "And when you can't put them off?"

"Then they just try it, sir, and the table puts them off. It's very bad. There's been no game played there since we came."

"Curious," I said. "I thought I heard a game going on last night."

"I've heard it myself, sir, several times. There being no light in the

room, I've put it down to a loose ventilator. The wind moves it and it
clicks."

"That'll be it," I said. Five minutes later I had made sure that there was
no loose ventilator in the billiard-room. Besides, the sound of one ball
striking another is not quite like any other sound. I also went up to the
board and turned the score back, which I had omitted to do the night before. Just then Harry passed the door on his way from the bar, with a cigarette in his mouth as usual. I called him in.

"Harry," I said, "give me thirty, and I'll play you a hundred up for a
sovereign. You can tell one of the girls to fetch our cues from upstairs."

Harry took his cigarette out of his mouth and whistled. "What, uncle!"
he said. "Well, you're going it, I don't think. What would you have said to
me if I'd asked you for a game at ten in the morning?"

"Ah!" I said, "but this is all in the way of business. I can't see much
wrong with the table, and if I can play on it, then other people may.
There's a chance to make a sovereign for you anyhow. You've given me
forty-five and a beating before now."

"No, uncle," he said, "I wouldn't give you thirty. I wouldn't give you
one. The table's not playable. Luck would win against Roberts on it."

He showed me the faults of the thing and said he was busy. So I told
him if he liked to lose the chance of making a sovereign he could.

"I hate that room," he said, as we came out. "It's not too clean, and it
smells like a vault."

"It smells a lot better than your cigarettes," I said. For the next six
weeks we were all busy, and I gave little thought to the billiard-room.
Once or twice I heard old Silas telling a customer that he could not recommend the table, and that the whole room was to be redecorated and
refitted as soon as we got the estimates. "You see, sir, we've only been
here a little while, and there hasn't been time to get everything as we
should like it quite yet."

One day Mrs. Parker, the woman who had the Regency before me,
came down from town to see how we were getting on. I showed the old
lady round, pointed out my improvements, and gave her a bit of lunch in
my office.

"Well, now," I said, as she sipped her glass of port afterwards, "I'm not
complaining of my bargain, but isn't the billiard-room a bit queer?"

"It surprises me," she said, "that you've left it as it is. Especially with
everything going ahead, and the yard half full of motors. I should have
taken it all down myself if I'd stopped. That iron roof's nothing but an

eyesore, and you might have a couple of beds of geraniums there and improve the look of your front."

"Let's see," I said. "What was the story about that billiard-room?"

"What story do you mean?" she said, looking at me suspiciously.

"The same one you're thinking of," I said.

"About that man, Josiah Ham?"

"That's it."

"Well, I shouldn't worry about that if I were you. That was all thirty years ago, and I doubt if there's a soul in Tanslowe knows it now. Best forgotten, I say. Talk of that kind doesn't do a hotel any good. Why, how did you come to hear of it?"

"That's just it," I said. "The man who told me was none too clear. He gave me a hint of it. He was an old commercial passing through, and had known the place in the old days. Let's hear your story and see if it agrees with his."

But I had told my fibs to no purpose. The old lady seemed a bit flustered. "If you don't mind, Mr. Sanderson, I'd rather not speak of it."

I thought I knew what was troubling her. I filled her glass and my own. "Look here," I said. "When you sold the place to me it was a fair deal. You weren't called upon to go thirty years back, and no reasonable man would expect it. I'm satisfied. Here I am, and here I mean to stop, and twenty billiard-rooms wouldn't drive me away. I'm not complaining. But just as a matter of curiosity, I'd like to hear your story."

"What's your trouble with the room?"

"Nothing to signify. But there's a game played there and marked there—and I can't find the players, and I think it's never finished. It stops always at sixty-six–forty-eight."

She gave a glance over her shoulder. "Pull the place down," she said. "You can afford to do it, and I couldn't." She finished her port. "I must be going, Mr. Sanderson. There's rain coming on, and I don't want to sit in the train in my wet things. I thought I would just run down to see how you were getting on, and I'm sure I'm glad to see the old place looking up again."

I tried again to get the story out of her, but she ran away from it. She had not got the time, and it was better not to speak of such things. I did not worry her about it much, as she seemed upset over it.

I saw her across to the station, and just got back in time. The rain came down in torrents. I stood there and watched it, and thought it would do my garden a bit of good. I heard a step behind me and looked round. A fat chap with a surly face stood there, as if he had just come out of the coffee-room. He was the sort that might be a gentleman and might not.

"Afternoon, sir," I said. "Nasty weather for motoring."

"It is," he said. "Not that I came in a motor. You the proprietor, Mr. Sanderson?"

"I am," I said. "Came here recently."

"I wonder if there's any chance of a game of billiards."

"I'm afraid not," I said. "Table's shocking. I'm having it all done up afresh, and then—"

"What's it matter?" said he. "I don't care. It's something to do, and one can't go out."

"Well," I said, "if that's the case, I'll give you a game, sir. But I'm no flyer at it at the best of times, and I'm all out of practice now."

"I'm no good myself. No good at all. And I'd be glad of the game."

At the billiard-room door I told him I'd fetch a couple of decent cues. He nodded and went in.

When I came back with my cue and Harry's, I found the gas lit and the blinds drawn, and he was already knocking the balls about.

"You've been quick, sir," I said, and offered him Harry's cue. But he refused and said he would keep the one he had taken from the rack. Harry would have sworn if he had found that I had lent his cue to a stranger, so I thought that was just as well. Still, it seemed to me that a man who took a twisted cue by preference was not likely to be an expert.

The table was bad, but not so bad as Harry had made out. The luck was all my side. I was fairly ashamed of the flukes I made, one after the other. He said nothing, but gave a short, loud laugh once or twice—it was a nasty-sounding laugh. I was at thirty-seven when he was nine, and I put on eleven more at my next visit and thought I had left him nothing.

Then the fat man woke up. He got out of his first difficulty, and after that the balls ran right for him. He was a player, too, with plenty of variety and resource, and I could see that I was going to take a licking. When he had reached fifty-one, an unlucky kiss left him in an impossible position. But I miscued, and he got going again. He played very, very carefully now, taking a lot more time for consideration than he had done in his previous break. He seemed to have got excited over it, and breathed hard, as fat men do when they are worked up. He had kept his coat on, and his face shone with perspiration.

At sixty-six he was in trouble again; he walked round to see the exact position, and chalked his cue. I watched him rather eagerly, for I did not like the score. I hoped he would go on. His cue slid back to strike, and then dropped with a clatter from his hand. The fat man was gone—gone, as I looked at him, like a flame blown out, vanished into nothing.

I staggered away from the table. I began to back slowly towards the door, meaning to make a bolt for it. There was a click from the scoring-board, and I saw the thing marked up. And then—I am thankful to say—the billiard-room door opened, and I saw Harry standing there. He was very white and shaky. Somehow, the fact that he was frightened helped to steady me.

"Good heavens, uncle!" he gasped. "I've been standing outside. What's the matter? What's happened?"

"Nothing's the matter," I said sharply. "What are you shivering about?" I swished back the curtain, and sent up the blind with a snap. The rain was over now, and the sun shone in through the wet glass—I was glad of it.

"I thought I heard voices—laughing—somebody called the score."

I turned out the gas. "Well," I said, "this table's enough to make any man laugh, when it don't make him swear. I've been trying your game of one hand against the other, and I daresay I called the score out loud. It's no catch—not even for a wet afternoon. I'm not both-handed, like the apes and Harry Bryden."

Harry is as good with the left hand as the right, and a bit proud of it. I slid my own cue back into its case. Then, whistling a bit of a tune, I picked up the stranger's cue, which I did not like to touch. I nearly dropped it again when I saw the initials "J. H." on the butt. "Been trying the cues," I said, as I put it in the rack. He looked at me as if he were going to ask more questions. So I put him on to something else. "We've not got enough cover for those motor-cars," I said. "Lucky we hadn't got many here in this rain. There's plenty of room for another shed, and it needn't cost much. Go and see what you can make of it. I'll come out directly, but I've got to talk to that girl in the bar first."

He went off, looking rather ashamed of his tremors.

I had not really very much to say to Miss Hesketh in the bar. I put three fingers of whisky in a glass and told her to put a dash of soda on top of it. That was all. It was a full-sized drink and did me good.

Then I found Harry in the yard. He was figuring with pencil on the back of an envelope. He was always pretty smart where there was anything practical to deal with. He had spotted where the shed was to go, and was finding what it would cost at a rough estimate.

"Well," I said, "if I went on with that idea of mine about the flower-beds it needn't cost much beyond the labour."

"What idea?"

"You've got a head like a sieve. Why, carrying on the flower-beds round the front where the billiard-room now stands. If we pulled that down it would give us all the materials we want for the new motor shed. The roofing's sound enough, for I was up yesterday looking into it."

"Well, I don't think you mentioned it to me, but it's a rare good idea."

"I'll think about it," I said.

That evening my cook, Timbs, told me he'd be sorry to leave me, but he was afraid he'd find the place too slow for him—not enough doing. Then old Silas informed me that he hadn't meant to retire so early, but he wasn't sure—the place was livelier than he had expected, and there would be more work than he could get through. I asked no questions. I knew the billiard-room was somehow or other at the bottom of it, and so it turned out. In three days' time the workmen were in the house and bricking up the billiard-room door; and after that Timbs and old Silas found the Regency suited them very well after all. And it was not just to oblige Harry, or Timbs, or Silas that I had the alteration made. That unfinished game was in my mind; I had played it, and wanted never to play it again. It was of no use for me to tell myself that it had all been a delusion, for I knew better. My health was good, and I had no delusions. I had played it with Josiah Ham—with the lost soul of Josiah Ham—and that thought filled me not with fear, but with a feeling of sickness and disgust.

It was two years later that I heard the story of Josiah Ham, and it was not from old Mrs. Parker. An old tramp came into the saloon bar begging, and Miss Hesketh was giving him the rough side of her tongue.

"Nice treatment!" said the old chap. "Thirty years ago I worked here, and made good money, and was respected, and now it's insults."

And then I struck in. "What did you do here?" I asked.

"Waited at table and marked at billiards."

"Till you took to drink?" I said.

"Till I resigned from a strange circumstance."

I sent him out of the bar, and took him down the garden, saying I'd find him an hour or two's work. "Now, then," I said, as soon as I had got him alone, "what made you leave?"

He looked at me curiously. "I expect you know, sir," he said. "Sixty-six. Unfinished."

And then he told me of a game played in that old billiard-room on a wet summer afternoon thirty years before. He, the marker, was one of the players. The other man was a commercial traveller, who used the house pretty regularly. "A fat man, ugly-looking, with a nasty laugh. Josiah Ham his name was. He was sixty-six when he got himself into a tight place. He moved his ball—did it when he thought I wasn't looking. But I saw it in the glass, and I told him of it. He got very angry. He said he wished he might be struck dead if he ever touched the ball."

The old tramp stopped. "I see," I said.

"They said it was apoplexy. It's known to be dangerous for fat men to get very angry. But I'd had enough of it before long. I cleared out, and so did the rest of the servants."

"Well," I said, "we're not so superstitious nowadays. And what brought you down in the world?"

"It would have driven any man to it," he said. "And once the habit is formed—well, it's there."

"If you keep off it I can give you a job weeding for three days."

He did not want the work. He wanted a shilling and he got it; and I saw to it that he did not spend it in my house.

We have got a very nice billiard-room upstairs now. Two new tables and everything ship-shape. You may find Harry there most evenings. It is all right. But I have never taken to billiards again myself.

And where the old billiard-room was there are flower-beds. The pansies that grow there have got funny markings—like figures.

The Unseen Power

Winter walked restlessly about the room as he told his story. He was a slender young man, with very smooth hair worn rather too long, a gold-mounted pince-nez, and an expression which showed that vanity was not wholly absent from his composition. It was the story of a haunted house. The man who owned it, and was now unable to let it, had asked Winter to investigate.

"And the whole point of it is that you've got to come along and help me," he concluded.

"Thank you," said Mr. Arden, "but I will not go."

Arden was a man of fifty, white-haired, thin, heavily lined.

"Well, why not?" said Winter, peevishly. "I want to know why not. It seems to me it would be rather interesting. You can choose any night you like, and—"

Arden waved the subject away with one hand. "It's useless to talk about it," he said, "I'm not going."

"But what do you mean?" said Winter. "You are not going to tell me that you're superstitious or afraid?"

"I should say," said Arden, "that I am what you would call superstitious. You, I presume, are not."

"Emphatically not," said Winter.

"Nor afraid?"

"Nor afraid," Winter echoed.

"Then why don't you go alone?" said Arden.

Winter murmured of sociability; it was no great fun to sit up all night by one's self. Besides, in the detection of a practical joke, which was probably all that it was, two would be better than one. Arden must see for himself that—

Arden broke in impetuously. "Look here," he said. "Stop wandering about the room and sit down. I'll tell you why I won't come. Did you ever hear of Minnerton Priory?"

"Of course I've heard about it. I don't know the whole story, and I don't suppose anybody does. A man lost his life over it, didn't he?"

"Two men lost their lives. I was the third man. Now, you know why I won't play with these things any more."

"Tell me about it," said Winter. "I've only heard scraps here and there, and reports are always inaccurate. So you were actually one of them. I should never have guessed it."

"I will tell you the story if you wish. Will you have it now, or will you wait till you have finished your investigation of the house at Falmouth?"

"I will hear it now," said Winter.

This is the story that Arden told.

In 1871 my aunt, Lady Wytham, bought Minnerton Priory. The place had been uninhabited for the best part of half a century, and was in very bad repair. It was cheap and it was picturesque, and both cheapness and picturesqueness appealed to Lady Wytham. Of the original Priory there was very little left standing. Frequent additions had been made to it at different periods, and the general effect of the place when I first saw it was rather grim and queer. Lady Wytham was very energetic, had the place surveyed, and in a few months had got her workmen down there. In one wing of the house a secret chamber had been found. It was on the ground floor, and it was a small room of perhaps twelve feet square. There was one window to it, placed very high up, and this window had been built up on the outside. Opposite to the window was a small fireplace, and the only entrance to the room was from the big dining-hall. The hall was panelled, and one of the panels formed the door into the secret chamber. I believe this kind of thing is fairly common in old houses dating back to the times of religious and political trouble, when hiding-places were constantly wanted.

The builders had not been at work many months at the Priory before there was trouble. I cannot say exactly what it was. It began with the un-bricking of the little window in the secret chamber. I know that the men refused point-blank to do any work whatever in the great dining-hall. Many were dismissed and new hands were taken on, but the trouble still persisted, till finally Lady Wytham herself went down to interview the clerk of works and a foreman or two. On the following day she wrote to me. She said that an idiotic story was being told with reference to the newly-discovered chamber of Minnerton Priory, and she was anxious to have it satisfactorily knocked on the head. Would I, and any friends that I might care to bring down, spend a few nights in the secret chamber? It would probably be very uncomfortable, but she would send over furniture and a servant to wait on us. The postscript explained that the servant would not sleep in the house.

The idea rather appealed to me, but being, unlike yourself, a little nervous over the business, I determined to take a couple of men down with me. One of them was an intimate friend of mine, Charles Stavold, a good-natured giant, but a useful man in a row. He and I talked it over together, and finally selected as the third man a young doctor, Bernard Ash. Ash was a remarkably brilliant young man, and we looked to him to supply the brains of the trio. If any practical joke were attempted he would be quite certain to find it out, and both Stavold and myself were quite sure that some practical joke would be attempted. Minnerton Priory lies in a very conservative county. The rustics of the village were quite capable of resenting Lady Wytham's intrusion into the Priory. It had always been uninhabited in their father's time, and that would be quite reason enough to determine them that it should not be inhabited now. There were some objections to our choice. Ash led an extremely dissipated life, and Stavold and myself were a little inclined to doubt his nerves. This doubt, by the way, was not justified by results.

We reached Minnerton in the afternoon. A large staff of men was busy at work at the place, but the only person in or anywhere near the great dining-hall was Lady Wytham's servant, Rudd. She could not have sent us a better man. He could turn his hand to anything. He had already unpacked the beds and other furniture that had been sent and put them in place, and was at present engaged on getting dinner for us. We went through the dining-hall and into the secret chamber.

"This won't do," said Ash at once.

"What don't do?" asked Stavold.

"Why, there's no furniture in here of any kind. One can't sleep on these stone flags."

"Are we going to sleep in here?" I asked.

"One of us is," he said.

I called up Rudd and gave my directions. He brought mattresses and made up a bed on the floor. Then we went round and examined the walls carefully, for, as Ash observed, where there is one trick panel there may be another. But we could find nothing that seemed in any way suspicious.

We came back into the great hall, and sat down there and talked the thing over. It was now growing dusk. Already the tapping and hammering of the workmen had ceased, and we had heard them laughing as they passed the window on their way home. Right away at the other end of the hall came the chink of plates and the hiss of a frying-pan where Rudd was busy with his preparations. He had brought four big lamps with him, and these he now lit, but there seemed to be something impenetrable about the darkness of this vast room. The light was still dim, with masses of dark shadow waving in the far corners and in the vaulted roof above us.

"Who's going to sleep in the haunted chamber?" Stavold asked.

"I am," said Ash.

We squabbled about it, and finally decided to toss for it. Ash had his own way. He was to sleep there that night, Stavold was to sleep there the second night, and I myself was left the third night. By this time we had little doubt that we should be at the bottom of the mystery.

Rudd gave us an excellent dinner, and had shown wisdom in his choice of the wine which he had brought with him. The wine made glad the heart of man, and before dinner was over we were treating the whole thing more as an amusing kind of spree than as a serious investigation. At ten o'clock Rudd inquired at what hour we should like breakfast in the morning, and asked if there was anything further he could do for us that night.

"Aren't you going to stop and see the ghost, Rudd?" I asked.

"I think not, sir," he said quietly. "Her ladyship had arranged, sir, that I should sleep at the inn."

So we let him go, and I had a curious feeling that with him went the most competent man of the four. Perhaps the same idea had occurred to Ash.

"He's a perfect wonder," said Ash. "Fancy being able to turn out a dinner like that here, with no proper appliances of any kind. I don't call it cooking; I call it conjuring tricks."

"Perhaps you'll see some more conjuring tricks a little later," said Stavold, grimly.

After dinner we played poker for an hour or so and then turned in. One of the lamps was left burning in the big hall, and Ash took a candle with him into the secret chamber. But he did not propose to leave it lighted. It wouldn't be playing the game, he said.

Some time after I had got into bed I could hear Ash tapping on the panels and trying them again, and I could see the light under the door. Stavold was already heavily sleeping. I knew nothing more till I was awakened by him early on the following morning. Rudd had already returned, and was preparing breakfast. Naturally our first move was to the secret chamber. We opened the panel door and went in. Ash's clothes were lying on the only chair in the room. The bed had been slept in, but there was no one there now. I noticed that the two candlesticks had also vanished. For a moment or two neither of us spoke, and then I asked my companion what he made of it.

"That's all right," he said, "Ash woke early, and has slipped down to the river in his pyjamas to get a swim. It's ten to one we find him there."

It was not impossible, but I was surprised that he had not awakened either of us in passing through the hall. We picked up our towels and went down to the river. We called and got no answer, but we had not at this time begun to be anxious. Possibly after his bath he had gone off for a stroll through the plantations. We took a long swim, lit our pipes, and walked up to the house. The workmen were busy now on the new part far away from the big hall. In the hall itself we found breakfast laid for three.

"Dr. Ash has come back then?" I said to Rudd.

Rudd looked puzzled. "I have not seen him this morning, sir."

"Drowned himself?" I suggested to Stavold.

"Not a bit of it. Why should he? This is a little practical joke of Ash's. We'll see if he doesn't get tired of it before we do. Hunger will bring him back at lunch-time."

Late in the afternoon he had not returned, and we sent word up to the police-station. The police-station sent us the usual idiot, who made his notes and did his best to look as if he knew what to do. We spent the rest of the day in searching for Ash with no success. At ten o'clock we gave it up, and Rudd went back to the inn. We did very little talking, and I had some curious and inexplicable feelings as I sat there in the silence. My tobacco pouch lay on the table at arm's length, and I found myself thinking that I might have an impulse to take it up in my hand but that as I did not want the pouch at the moment I should resist the impulse. Then my hand shot right out to the pouch, gripped it, and shook it.

"What the devil are you doing?" said Stavold.

I flung the pouch down and got up from my chair. "Dropping off to sleep, I fancy," I said.

"You didn't look it."

"Well, I ought to know, oughtn't I? Help me to drag another bed into that chamber there. We'll see it through together to-night."

"Oh, no, we won't," said my companion. "If we did that we should leave this hall here for the use of the practical jokers, if there are any. You will sleep here to-night. I shall take my turn in the secret chamber; only, if I can help it, I shan't sleep."

"I wonder where on earth Ash is," I said.

"We don't know and it won't improve our nerves to imagine. Yours seem a bit jumpy anyhow. We've done all we can to find him. Leave it at that."

I did not expect to sleep that night, yet sleep came to me in fits. I had wakened many times, and at last I determined that I might as well get up. In half an hour the gray dawn would be beginning. I remembered that Stavold had told me that he did not mean to go to sleep. I whistled softly as I slipped on my clothes, so that he might hear that I was moving about and join me. As he did not come I listened at the door of the chamber and heard no sound. In a moment I was standing inside it with the lamp shaking in my hand. The room was exactly as we had found it the morning before. There was nobody there. The bed had been slept in, and was now empty. The clothes lay on the chair. The candlestick had gone. I was horribly frightened.

I did not wait for Rudd to come back. I went on to the village police-station at once and told my story. There was no doubt that this was a serious matter, and before breakfast-time an inspector had arrived from Saltham. Accompanied by a serjeant and myself he came over to the Priory and into the dining-hall.

"I think I'll take a look round by myself first," he said. "You can wait here." He went into the chamber, and I could hear his heavy boots on the flags and the useless tapping on the walls. I was confident that nothing could be found there. There were a few minutes of silence, and he opened the door and said, "Will you come in here, Mr. Arden?"

I went in and saw that the bed had been pulled out from its usual place in the corner. He pointed to a large flagstone which the bed had covered.

"I should like to show you, sir, a curious optical effect there is in this room. Would you mind standing on that flagstone there?"

I came round the bed to it, and my foot had just touched it when I was jerked backwards and fell to the floor.

"Beg your pardon, sir," said the inspector behind me. "I had to satisfy myself that you didn't know of the trap. See here."

He knelt down beside the big flagstone and touched it lightly with his fingers. It was exactly balanced by a big iron pin through the centre, and it now swung open, showing a dark shaft going far down into the earth.

"You mean that they are down there?" I said.

"Not a doubt. Each of them, as is only natural, tried the floor as well as the walls, and moved the bed for the purpose. That finished them. It's the merest chance that I didn't go down the shaft myself."

"Well," I said, "the sooner we go down there the better. Where can we get a rope?"

The inspector picked up a small tin match-box and emptied out the matches into the palm of his hand. "Listen," he said. He flung the box down the shaft. We listened, and listened, but heard no sound. "See?" he said. "That's deep. No use to get a rope there. Anyone who fell down there is dead. That's been a well, I should say."

I was angry with the man's cock-surety, and said that I was going down in any case. A rope was brought and attached to a lighted lantern. The lantern was lowered, and in a few yards went out. The experiment was tried again and again, and each time the lantern was extinguished by the foul air. It was hopeless. No human being could have lived for five minutes down there.

I rose from the floor, put on my coat, and turned to the inspector. "This explains nothing," I said. "On the morning that Dr. Ash was missed I went in here with Mr. Stavold, and we found the bed placed as it had been the night before, immediately over this trap. If Dr. Ash fell down it how did he put the bed back after him? The same thing applies to Mr. Stavold; again the bed was left over the trap."

"They did not move the bed back again, but somebody else did."

"Who?"

"That is what I hope to find out to-night. Are you yourself willing to sleep to-night in the big hall alone?"

"Certainly. I don't exactly see what the idea is."

"Never mind about that. It may come to nothing. One can but try. You say that Rudd locked the door to this hall when he went out at night?"

"Yes. A modern lock had been fitted, and the door locked itself as soon as it was shut. It could only be opened from the outside with a latch-key."

"And no one but yourself, that you know of, had a key?"

"No one that I know of."

"Very well. I have a few things to see after. I must speak to this man Rudd. I shall see you again before nightfall."

I spent a horribly long day. I had to telegraph to the relatives of my two friends. I sent Rudd for books, and tried in vain to read. Rudd was aware that the police had a suspicious eye upon him and was in a state of suppressed fury. While Rudd was away I again examined the inner chamber. The window was too high up to be reached by anyone within the room, and too closely barred to admit of anyone passing through it. The chimney was equally impassable. No vestige of hope was left to me. At ten o'clock the inspector came in and told me that he had given up for the night. He looked thoughtfully towards the whisky decanter. I gave him a drink and mixed one for myself. Then he said good-night and went off.

I had not expected to sleep, but an insurmountable drowsiness came over me. I flung myself down on the bed as I was, without undressing, hoping that in this way I should wake again in an hour or so.

When I woke the room was brightly lighted. The inspector, two of his men, and Rudd himself were all there. I was startled.

"What's the matter? What's up?" I said.

"Nothing much," said the inspector, "but I know who put the bed back in its place."

"Who was it?"

"It was yourself, sir. You did it in your sleep. It had occurred to me that this was just possible, and I had a man watching through the window of the room."

"It is impossible," I said. "I should know something of it. I am sure I have been here ever since you left me. Your man must have made a mistake."

"My man made no mistake," said the inspector, drily, "for my man happened to be myself. You came in, set the lamp down, pushed the bed over to one corner, and then went to the chair, where you seemed to be folding up imaginary clothes."

The bodies were recovered two days later, and the whole story of course got into the papers. I was away from England for some years after that. It was one of the things that one wishes to forget. You ask me to take part in another of these investigations. In all probability there is nothing to investigate but a practical joke, or a chance noise, or something equally explicable, but you will understand that I will not take the risk that there may be something else.

"But, my dear Arden," said Winter, balancing the pince-nez in his hand, "there is nothing whatever in the story that you have told me. What could be more natural than that your two friends should examine the floor, should do so with too little care, and should reap the consequences? The repeated dream is itself quite natural; I should imagine there are few people who have not had it. At the most it is a coincidence that the dream, accompanied by somnambulism, should have come three nights in succession, but there is nothing supernatural there."

"Never mind that word supernatural. Do you think there is anything inexplicable? You are forgetting that the bed in that chamber had been slept in both nights. The sleeper had been awakened by some sound. What was it? What drew him to the trap-door? What was it that took possession of my will and my body so that my own personality was as blotted out as if I had been dead? But," he added, impatiently, "I do not want to convince you. When you are brought in touch, as I have been, with the unseen power you will be convinced. As your friend, I hope you never will be."

The Widower

The decision of Edward Morris to marry again was one of the few practical things of his record. He had married first at the age of eighteen without the knowledge of his parents. His wife died two years later. He had no children by her. At her death he was desolate.

He was as desolate, that is, as one can be at twenty. He was free from the annoying minor-poet habit of advertising his afflictions, but it was quite clear to himself that there was nothing more left. Yet it is idle for a man to say he will stop when Nature, his proprietor, says that he will go on. There is no comedy at ninety, and there is no tragedy at twenty. After he had deposited the remains of his wife in Brompton cemetery—she had a strong aversion to cremation and inwardly believed that it destroyed the immortal soul—he went off into the country, selecting a village where he knew nobody. Here he learned by heart considerable portions of the poems of Heine, neglected to return the call of the rector, and bored himself profusely. It must not be understood that he resented the boredom. That was what life was to be in future, a continuous dreariness. After a brief stay in the village he went off to Paris to study art. At the time when he thought of giving himself to music all noticed his ability in painting. When he took to art they remembered that he had musical talent. A year later, when he returned to England to live the life of a hermit, to teach in song what he had learned in sorrow, some said that he was a lost artist, and some that he was a lost musician, and others that he was a well-defined case of dilettantism. It is, however, difficult to be a hermit in London. London has many tentacles; it puts them out and draws you into the liveliest part of itself. A claim of relationship, an old friendship, a piece of medical advice, a chance meeting—anything may become a tentacle. Almost before he knows it the misanthropical hermit is dragged from his shell and is writing that he has much pleasure in accepting her very kind invitation for the thirteenth, and wonders if that man in Sackville Street will be able to make him some evening clothes in time, his others being not so much clothes as a relic of those pre-hermit days when his wife, his only love, still lived and took him out to dinners, and would have the glass down in the hansoms. The thought that he resented this last action at the time saddens him, but the acceptance is posted. He is drawn into the vortex.

Once in, Edward Morris had to explain to himself how he got there. Nobody else wanted any explanation. Nobody else knew that the first time he took his hostess in to dinner he looked down the long table towards his host's right hand and remembered. His explanation to himself was that he did it to avoid comment. One could not wear one's heart on one's coat sleeve. One must go somewhere and must do something. One must unfortunately live, even when the savour of life has gone. So he lived, and in living the savour of life came back again.

It was on a muggy December evening that he accompanied Lady Marchsea and her eminent husband to a first-night performance. When the eminent man was grumbling at the draught, and Lady Marchsea was, with justification, admiring herself, her dress, and everything that was hers, Edward Morris looked up. Out of the gloom of the box above him a brown-faced girl with dark eyes, her chin leaning on her white gloves, bent forward and looked down.

Yet it was not till the end of the first act that he asked who she was and was told that she was nobody, but was apparently with the Martins, who were very, very dear friends, and would Mr. Morris take her round? That was the beginning of it, and the end of it was his engagement to Adela Constantia Graham, who was nobody. Everybody who knew Adela Constantia knew that it was an excellent thing for her—a much wealthier man than she had any reason to expect. Everyone who knew Edward Morris knew that it was the best thing for him. "Ballast," said Lady Marchsea, emphatically, "that is what marriage means to a man like Edward Morris. He needs ballast; something to make him concentrate himself and trust himself; something to encourage him and urge him on."

Her notions of the general uses of ballast were vague, but her conviction was sincere that Edward Morris, happily re-married, would achieve something in one, or possibly in all, of the arts. Her eminent husband said: "Nice sort of man, but no good really." But still he paid for the dinner-service with the sanctifying mark on the bottom of all the plates, which they forwarded to Edward Morris a short time before the wedding—the wedding which never took place.

About a week before the date fixed for that wedding it occurred to Edward Morris in a moment of leisure—he was naturally very busy at the time—that his first wife had been a jealous woman, and he wondered what she would have thought and said if she had been alive. He could laugh at the illogicality. If she had been alive there would have been nothing to think or to say. The haunting face with the chin pressed on the white gloves against the darkness at the back of the box would have been merely a face and nothing more, and would not have haunted. He collected his old love-letters and burned them. Other little relics of his first wife he gathered together, had them placed in a box and deposited at his bankers. The old life was done; the new life was beginning. Yet one night as he stood in a darkened room with Adela Constantia in his arms the door opened with a little quick click some few inches. She stepped back from him, thinking it was a servant, and he turned white, thinking, in a moment of madness, that it was someone else; then he went to the door and opened it wider. No one was there.

The position of the widower who marries again is irritating to him if he be, as Edward Morris was, a man of nice feeling. He has to say, and to believe, that he loves as he never loved in his life before. Scraps of used romance must be whipped up out of his respectable past to set against the virginal fervour of the young woman who has just begun to love him. Yet he feels that all this is an insult to the dead—to the woman who loved him before. A man of the world has a happy habit of forgetting and of ignoring. He may marry for the second or third time quite easily. He takes nothing too seriously. He may order a new overcoat, but he does not feel that the coat will be worthless unless he swears and tries to believe that he never wore a coat like that before. Morris, however, was a sentimentalist, and so he became irritated with himself. The next step inevitably followed. He became irritated with his dead wife. She had got her cold arms round his neck and was dragging him down and holding him back from the joyful development of his life.

When in London it was his custom to visit her grave in Brompton cemetery at regular intervals, once every month. During his engagement to Adela Constantia he made up his mind that this regular visit must be dropped. Some arrangement could be made to have the grave kept in decent order, but he could not go near it again. He remembered having been told a story of a widower who married again and went hand-in-hand with his second wife to stand by the grave of the first. It had been told him as something pathetic. He had never been able to see in it anything but a subject for a humorous paper; Guy de Maupassant would have done wonders with it. He settled the day when the last visit should be made. He selected an appropriate wreath, in which everlastings and dead leaves were symbolically interwoven. But that afternoon more than ever before his hatred to his dead wife grew within him. He recollected her strange belief with regard to cremation. Fire destroyed everything, even the immortal soul, and it seemed as if fire destroyed love too. He remembered that he had burnt her letters. As he drove down Regent Street an old friend, a man whom he had not seen for some time, recognised him. He stopped the cab and his friend came up.

"Why do I never see you now?" said the friend. "But of course I know. Very much engaged, aren't you? (That's not bad for an impromptu, by the way.) I suppose you are going there now?"

"No," said Morris, "as a matter of fact I am not."

"Well, you are evidently going somewhere, and you carry a big box with you with a florist's label on it, so all I can say is that if you are not going there you ought to be."

Edward Morris laughed, and to laugh was the last touch of horror.

"Well," the friend said, "if you are really not going to see Miss Graham I have no scruples in annexing you. Come round to the club for a game of billiards."

"Thanks," said Morris, "I am afraid I am very busy this afternoon."

However, he let himself be persuaded. The box containing the wreath was left in the charge of the hall-porter at the club. On the following day Morris despatched the wreath to Brompton cemetery by a messenger-boy, where the symbolical offering was deposited on the grave of Charles Ernest Jessop, who died at the age of two and a half, and of whose death or previous existence Morris was unaware. Messenger-boys are so careless. Morris never even attempted to visit the cemetery again. It was not only anger, it was not only hatred; it was also fear that kept him away. He was assured in his own mind that the dead woman was awake again and was watching him jealously.

The moment when he had just awoken from sleep was always a horrible one for him. The fear of the dead woman was in his mind then and nothing else was very clear. He left the electric light on all night and, as a rule, slept fairly well and without any haunting or painful dreams. But the moment of waking was always a trial. He kept on expecting to see something that he never did see. He would not have wondered if, as he awoke, someone had touched his hand, or the electric light had been suddenly switched off.

Of course everybody noticed that he looked wretchedly ill. Adela Constantia was in despair about his health. There were things about him which were very queer; that he did not like dark rooms. That when he was talking to her he would suddenly look over his shoulder—at nothing. The comforting doctor told her that Morris has been very busy indeed with the preparation for his married life and, the doctor added, a lot of worry upsets the nerves. This is quite true.

On his wedding morning he certainly looked much fitter to be buried than to be married. His best man gave him champagne and told him to hold his head up more. The bride made an adorable and pathetic figure; a beautiful young girl is always a pathetic figure on her wedding-morning. Her sisters fluttered around her, ready to cry at the right moments. Her father looked a little nervous and elated. He had had quite a long talk with Lady Marchsea, whose husband was kept away by the toothache. The ceremony went with its customary brilliance until that point when the bridegroom was required to say: "I, Edward, take thee, Adela Constantia." He said this in a loud voice, but he did not say "Adela Constantia"; he gave another name. There was a moment's pause, and while everybody was looking at everybody he fainted and fell.

At the inquest it was found that the blow on the head from the sharp edge of the stone step satisfactorily accounted for the death. All the evening papers had readable paragraphs headed "Tragic End to a Fashionable Wedding Ceremony."

And Adela Constantia married somebody else.

And the dead woman went to sleep again.

Smeath

I

Percy Bellowes was not actually idle, had a good deal of ability, and wished to make money. But at the age of thirty-five he had not made it. He had been articled to a solicitor, and, in his own phrase, had turned it down. He had neglected the regular channels of education which were open to him. He could give a conjuring entertainment for an hour, and though his tricks were stock tricks, they were done in the neat professional manner.

He could play the cornet and the violin, neither of them very well. He could dance a breakdown. He had made himself useful in a touring theatrical company. But he could not spell correctly, and his grammar was not always beyond reproach. He disliked regularity. He could not go to the same office at the same time every morning. He was thriftless, and he had been, but was no longer, intemperate. He was a big man, with smooth black hair, and a heavy moustache, and he had the manners of a bully.

At the age of thirty-five he considered his position. He was at that time travelling the country as a hypnotic entertainer, under the name of Dr. Sanders-Bell. At each of his entertainments he issued a Ten Thousand Pound Challenge, not having at the time ten thousand pence in the world.

He employed confederates, and he had to pay them. It was not a good business at all. His gains in one town were always being swallowed up in his losses in another. His confederates gave him constant trouble.

But though he turned things over for long in his mind, he could see nothing else to take up. There is no money nowadays for a conjurer without originality, an indifferent musician, or passable actor. His hypnotic entertainment would have been no good in London, but it did earn just enough to keep him going in the provinces.

Also, Percy Bellowes had an ordinary human weakness; he liked to be regarded with awe as a man of mystery. Even off the stage he acted his part. He had talked delirious science to agitated landladies in cheap lodgings in many towns.

Teston was a small place, and Percy Bellowes thought that he had done very well, after a one-night show, to cover his expenses and put four pounds in his pocket. He remained in the town on the following day, because he wished to see a man who had answered his advertisement for a confederate. "Assistant to a Hypnotic Entertainer" was the phrase Mr. Bellowes had used for it.

He was stopping at the Victoria Hotel. It was the only hotel in the place, and it was quite bad. But Percy Bellowes was used to that. A long course of touring had habituated him to doubtful eggs and indistinguishable coffee. This morning he faced a singularly repulsive breakfast without quailing. He was even cheerful and conversational with a slatternly maid who waited on him.

"So you saw the show last night," he said.

"Yes, sir, I did. And very wonderful it was. There has never been anything like it in Teston, not in my memory."

"Ah, my dear. Well, you watch this."

He picked up the two boiled eggs which had been placed before him. He hurled one in the air, where it vanished. He swallowed the other one whole. He then produced them both from a vase on the mantelpiece.

"Well, I never!" said the maid. "I wonder if there's anything you can't do, sir?"

"Just one or two things," said Mr. Bellowes, sardonically. "By the way, my dear, if a man comes here this morning and asks for me, I want to see him." He consulted a soiled letter which he had taken from his pocket. "The name's Smeath."

Mr. Smeath arrived, in fact, before Bellowes had finished his breakfast, and was told he could come in. He was a man of extraordinary appearance.

He was a dwarf, with a slightly hunched back. His hands were a size too large for him, and were always restless. His expression was one of snarling subservience. At first Bellowes was inclined to reject him, for a confederate should not be a man of unusual appearance, and easily recognizable. Then it struck him that, after all, this would be a very weird and impressive figure on the stage.

"Ever do anything of this kind before?" he asked.

"No, sir," said Smeath. "But I've seen it done and can pick it up. I think I could give you satisfaction. You see, it's not very easy for a man like me to find work."

All the time that he was speaking, his hands were busy.

"When you've finished tearing up my newspaper," said Bellowes.

"Sorry, sir," said the man. He pushed the newspaper away from him, but caught up a corner of the tablecloth. It was frayed, and he began to pull the threads out of it, quickly and eagerly.

"Ever been hypnotized?" Bellowes asked.

"No, sir," said Smeath, with a cunning smile. "But that doesn't matter, does it? I can act the part all right."

"It matters a devilish lot, as it happens. And you can't act the part all right, either. My assistants are always genuinely hypnotized. I employ them to save time on the stage. After I have hypnotized you a few times, I shall be able to put you into the hypnotic state in a minute or less, and to do it with certainty. I can't depend on chance people from the audience. Many of them cannot be hypnotized at all, and with most of the others it takes far too long. There are exceptional cases—I had one at my show only last night—but I don't often come across them. Come on up with me to my room."

"You want to see if you can hypnotize me?"

"No, I don't. I know I can. I simply want to do it."

Upstairs in the dingy bedroom Bellowes made Smeath sit down. He held the bright lid of a cigarette-tin between Smeath's eyes and slightly above the level of them.

"Look at that," he said. "Keep on looking at it. Keep on!"

In a few minutes Bellowes put the tin down, put his fingers on Smeath's eyes, and closed them. The eyes remained closed. The little hunchback sat tense and rigid.

An hour later, in the coffee-room downstairs, Bellowes made his definite agreement with Smeath.

"You understand?" said Bellowes. "You'll be at the town hall at Warlow tomorrow night at seven. When I invite people to come up on the platform, you will come up. That's all you've got to do. Got any money?"

"Enough for the present." Smeath began to pull matches from a box on the table. He broke each match into four pieces. "But suppose that tomorrow night you can't do it?"

"There'll never be a day or night I can't do it with you now. That's definite. Now, then, leave those matches alone. I might be wanting one of them directly."

After Smeath's departure, Percy Bellowes sat for a few minutes deep in thought. In that dingy room upstairs he had seen something of which he thought that various uses might be made. He picked up the newspaper, and was pleased to find that Smeath's busy fingers had spared the racing intelligence. Then he sought out the landlord.

"I say," he said, "I've got a fancy to put a few shillings on a horse. Do you know anybody here it would be safe to do it with?"

"Well," said the landlord, "as a matter of fact you can do it with me, if you like. I do a little in that way on the quiet."

"The police don't bother you?"

"No; they're not a very bright lot, the police here. Besides, they're pretty busy just now. We had a murder in Teston the day before you came."

"Who was that?"

"A Miss Samuel, daughter of some very well-to-do people here. They think it was a tramp. See that plantation up on the hill there? That was where they found her—her head all beaten to pulp and her money gone."

"Nice set of blackguards you've got in Teston, I don't think. Well now, about this race today."

When Percy Bellowes left the Victoria Hotel on the following morning he was not required to pay a bill. On the contrary, he had a small balance to receive from the landlord.

"Bless you, I don't mind," said the landlord, as he paid him. "Pretty well all my crowd were on the favourite. Queer thing that horse should have fallen."

II

At Warlow the entertainment went very well. When it was over, Bellowes asked Smeath to come round to the hotel. They had the little smoking-room to themselves.

"You remember when I hypnotized you yesterday?"

"Yes, sir. Yes, Mr. Bellowes."

"Do you remember what you did, or said?"

Smeath shook his head.

"I went to sleep, the same as I did tonight. That was all."

"Know anything about horse-racing?"

"Nothing. Never touched it."

"You mean to say you've never seen a horse-race?"

"Never."

"What did you do before you came to see me?"

"I had not been in any employment for some time. I was once in business as a bird-fancier. I had bad luck and made no money in it. You ask me a great many questions, sir."

"I do. That's because I've been turning things over in my mind. I want you to put your name to an agreement with me for three years. A pound a week. That's a good offer. A man who's been in business, and failed, ought to appreciate an absolute certainty like that."

"It would be the same kind of work?" Smeath asked.

"Pretty much the same. When I've finished this tour I am thinking of settling down in London. I should employ you there."

"No, thank you, Mr. Bellowes," said Smeath. "I would rather not."

"Oh, all right," said Bellowes. "Make an idiot of yourself, if you like. It doesn't make a pin's head of difference to me. I can easily find plenty of other men who would grab at it. I thought I was doing you a kindness. As you said yourself, chaps of your build don't find it any too easy to get work."

"I will work for you for six months—possibly a month or two longer than that. But, afterwards, well, I wish to return to the bird-fancying again."

"No, you don't," said Bellowes, savagely. "If you can't take my terms, you're not going to make your own. If you won't sign for three years, out you get! You're talking like a fool, too. How can you go back to this rotten business in six months? D'you think you're going to save the capital for it out of a pound a week?"

"I have friends who might help me."

"Who are they?"

"They are—well, they're friends of mine. You will perhaps give me till tomorrow morning to think it over."

"Very well. If you're not here by ten tomorrow morning to go round to the solicitor's office with me, I've finished with you. Now then, I'm going to hypnotize you again."

"What for?"

"Practice. Now then, look at me."

In a few moments Smeath sat with his eyes open but fixed.

"Tell me what you see?" asked Bellowes.

"Nothing," said Smeath. "I see nothing."

"Yes, you do," said Bellowes. "There are horses with jockeys on them. They are racing, see? They get near the winning-post."

"Yes," said Smeath, dully. "I see them, but it is through a mist and a long way off. Now they're gone."

"Yesterday when I hypnotized you, you saw clearly. You actually described a race which afterwards took place. You gave me the colours. You gave me the names that the crowd shouted. You described how the favourite crossed his legs and fell. Can you do nothing of the kind today?"

"No, not today. Today I see other things."

"What?"

"I see a street in London. There is a long row of sandwichmen. My name is on their boards. There are many fashionable people in the street. Expensive shops. Jewellers' shops, picture galleries. I can see you, too. You have just come into the street."

"Where have I come from?"

"How can I tell? It may be your own house or offices. Your name is on a very small brass plate by the side of the door. You have got a fur coat on, and you are wearing a diamond pin. You get into a car. It is your own car, and you tell the man who opens the door for you to drive to the bank. You look very pleased and prosperous. Now the car starts. That is all. I can see no more."

Bellowes leaned forward and blew lightly on Smeath's eyes. The tenseness of his muscles relaxed. He rubbed his eyes and stood up.

"Do you know what you've been saying?" Bellowes asked.

"I've been saying nothing," said Smeath. "I have been asleep, as you know. You made me go to sleep."

Bellowes looked round the room. His eye fell on an empty cigarette-box, lying in the fender.

"Pick that up, and hold it in your hands," he said.

Smeath looked surprised, but he did as he was told. There was a loose label on the box, and his fingers began to tear it off in small pieces.

"Now then," said Bellowes, "can you tell me anything about the man who had that box, and threw it down there?"

"Of course I can't. How should I be able to do that? It's not possible."

"Very well," said Bellowes. "I'm going to put you to sleep once more."

"I don't like this," whined Smeath. "There's too much of it. It's bad for one's health."

"Nonsense! Look here, Smeath. I want you for three years, don't I? Then I'm not likely to do anything that will injure your health. You'll be all right."

When Bellowes had hypnotized Smeath, he again put the cigarette-box in his hands.

"And now what do you see?" he asked.

"This is quite clear. It is a short, thick-set man who takes the last cigarette out of the box and throws it down. As he smokes it, he walks up and down the room, frowning. He is puzzled about something. He takes out his pocket-book, and as he opens it a card drops to the floor."

"Can you see what's on the card?"

"Yes. It lies face upwards. The name is 'Mr. Vincent'. And in the left-hand corner are the words 'Criminal Investigation Department, Scotland Yard'. Now he closes his note-book."

"What was written in it?"

"I only saw one word—the name 'Samuel'. Now a waiter comes into the room, and the man asks for a timetable."

Once more Bellowes restored Smeath to his normal state.

"That'll do," he said. "That's all for tonight. You can be off now, and think over that offer of mine."

At ten on the following morning Smeath kept his appointment. He said he would sign an agreement for two years only, and that he would want thirty shillings a week.

"What makes you suddenly think you're worth thirty shillings a week?"

"I have no idea at all, but I know you need me very much. I have that feeling."

"It was three years I said, not two. If I pay you thirty shillings a week you can sign for three years."

"I cannot. I want to get back to my birds. I will sight for thirty shillings a week for two years, or I will go away."

"Oh, very well," growled Bellowes. "You're an obstinate little devil. Have it your own way. I hope to goodness I'm not going to lose money over you. I've never paid more than a pound to an assistant before. By the way, Smeath, were you ever in London?"

"Yes; several times."

"Do you know Piccadilly, or Bond Street, or Regent Street?"

Smeath shook his head.

"I have only passed through in going from one place to another. I know the names of those streets, but I've never been in them."

"Very well," said Bellowes. "Come along with me, and we'll fix up the agreement."

III

About a month later Mr. Bellowes, who had come up to London for the purpose, called at the office of Mr. Tangent's agency in Sussex Street.

"Appointment," said Mr. Bellowes, as he handed in his card, and was taken immediately into the inner office. Mr. Tangent, a florid and slightly overdressed man of fifty, rose from his American desk to shake hands with him.

"Well, my dear old boy," said Tangent, "and how are you?"

"Fit," said Bellowes. "Remarkably fit."

"And what can I do for you? I had an enquiry the other day that brought you to my mind. It's not much. A week, with a chance of an engagement if you catch on."

"Thanks, old man, but I don't want it. I've got on to something a bit better. What I want from you is a hundred and fifty pounds."

Tangent laughed genially.

"Long time since I've seen so much money as that. Well, well! What's it for? Tell us the story."

"I've had a bit of luck, Tangent. I've got a man booked up to me for the next two years who is simply the most marvellous clairvoyant the world has ever seen."

"Clairvoyants aren't going well," said Tangent. "Most of them don't make enough to pay for their rent and their ads in the Sunday papers. The fact is there are too many of them. I don't care what the line is—palmistry, crystal-gazing, psychometry, or what you like. There's no money in it."

"Let's talk sense. You say there's no money in it? Do you remember when Merion fell, and a ten-to-one chance romped home?"

"Remember it? I've got good reason to. I'd backed Merion both ways, and didn't see how I was going to lose."

"Well, I backed the winner. Not being a Croesus like yourself, I only had five bob on. I backed him, because my clairvoyant saw the whole thing, and described it to me before the race was run."

"Can he do it again?"

"He has not been able to do it again yet. He has seen what happened in the past many times, and he has never been wrong. He is exceptional. He is only clairvoyant when he is hypnotized. In the normal state he sees nothing. He's an ugly little devil, a dwarf, and if I bring him to London he'll make a sensation. What's more, he'll make money. Pots of money. I know the crowd you've been talking about. They are a hit-or-miss lot. They're no good. This is something quite different. We shall have all the Society women paying any fee I like to consult him. There's a fortune in it."

Tangent lit a cigarette, and pushed the box across to Bellowes. "What is it you propose to do?" he asked.

"Rooms in Bond Street. Good furniture. Uniformed servant. Sandwichmen at first. Once the thing gets started, it will go by itself. Any woman who has consulted him once is absolutely bound to tell all her friends. The man's a miracle. I'll tell you another thing I'm going to do. When the next sensational murder turns up, and Scotland Yard can't put their hands on the man who did it, I'm going to turn my chap on to the job. I'll bet all I've got to sixpence that we find the man."

"There was the case of that girl—Esther Samuel."

"Yes, I remember that. But by this time most of the public have forgotten it. A better chance is bound to turn up soon."

"I don't see how you're going to start on a hundred and fifty."

"I'm not, my boy. I've got money of my own that I'm putting into it as well."

"Let's see," said Tangent, picking up a pencil. "What did you say was this man's name and address?"

Bellowes laughed. "Oh, no you don't," he said. "At present that's my business. Make it your own business as well and you shall be told everything."

"I don't know why you should call it business at all. You ask me to lend you a hundred and fifty. You offer no security. All I've got is your story that you've found a clairvoyant who's really good."

"Very well. If you satisfied yourself that the man was really good, would you lend the money then?"

"On terms, yes. But they'd have to be satisfactory terms."

"They would be. Well, you shall see for yourself. The man's waiting in a cab downstairs."

"You might have said that before."

"Why? Anyhow, I'll go and bring him up now."

It was a chilly morning, and Smeath shivered in a thick overcoat, which he refused to remove. No time was wasted on preliminaries. Bellowes hypnotized him at once.

"Now then, my boy," said Bellowes. "You shall see for yourself. Give me any article which you or someone else has worn, or has frequently handled."

Tangent opened a drawer in his desk, and produced a lady's glove. "That," he said, "was left in my office a week ago. Let's see what he makes out of it."

Bellowes put the glove in Smeath's hands. Smeath began to pull the buttons off it. He dragged and tore at the glove like a wild animal at its prey. Then suddenly he began to speak.

"I see a handsome woman with bright golden hair. I think the hair has been dyed. It has that appearance. She is talking with Mr. What's-his-name in this room. Each is angry with the other. She is accusing him of something. Suddenly—yes—she picks up an ink-bottle and throws it at him. Ink all over the place. He bangs on a little bell, and a man comes in who looks like a clerk. That is all. I cannot see any more."

"Wake him up and send him down to the cab again," said Tangent. "Then we can talk."

"Now," said Bellowes, when they were alone together. "Had he got that right?"

"Absolutely. The woman was Cora Vendall. She wanted a particular berth, and thought I ought to have got it for her. She's fifty-six if she's a day, and not in any way suitable for it. If I had proposed it, the people would simply have laughed at me. She did get into a blind fury with me, and she did throw the ink at me. She's been made to pay for that, and she's been told not to show her powdered nose inside my office again. Your man is remarkable, Bellowes. There can be no two opinions about it. There is certainly money in him."

"You will find the hundred and fifty then?"

"Yes, I'll do that. Mind, I must have a word to say in the management. The right sort of people will have to be got to see that man. Once that has been done, I do believe you're right, and the thing will go by itself."

"What interest do you want?"

"I don't want interest. What I do is buy for a hundred and fifty pounds a share in your profits from your agreement with the clairvoyant."

"You shall have it. It's a jolly good thing I'm putting into your way, Tangent. I had never meant to part with a share, and I'd sooner pay you fifteen per cent on your money. However, if you insist, you can take a sixteenth."

"Rats!" said Mr. Tangent, impolitely. "This is not everybody's business. Step across to the Bank of England, and see how much they'll advance you on it. There are three of us in it. Him and you and me. I'm going to take a third. Do just as you like about it. If I go into it I can make it a certainty. I can get the right people to see the man."

"A third's too much. You must be reasonable, Tangent. I discovered him.'"

"A man once discovered a gold-mine. He had no means of getting the gold out. He was a thousand miles from anywhere, and he was all alone.

He died on the top of his blessed gold-mine. However, I'm not arguing. I'm simply telling you. Give me a third, and my cheque and the agreement will be ready this time tomorrow morning. Otherwise, no business."

Mr. Bellowes hesitated, and then gave in.

IV

At six o'clock on a summer evening, in a well-furnished room that overlooked the traffic of Bond Street, Smeath and his employer sat and quarrelled together. Both of them wore new clothes, but Bellowes had the air of prosperity, and Smeath had not.

"It's no good to talk to me," whined Smeath. "I know what I'm saying. Where an essential consideration has been intentionally concealed, an agreement cannot stand. You never told me I was a clairvoyant."

"No," said Bellowes, "I did not. And I don't tell a man what the colour of his hair is, either. Why? Because he knows it already. You knew that you were a clairvoyant."

"I did not. I swear I did not!" said Smeath, raising his voice.

"Now, don't get excited. Don't squeal."

"I'm not squealing. Do you think that if I'd known, I would ever have come to you for a wage like that? We've had fourteen people here today. What did they pay?"

"Mind your own business!"

"But it is my business. And as you wouldn't tell me, I've taken my own steps to find out. Not one of them paid less than a guinea. You had as much as five guineas from some. And here am I with thirty shillings a week. I can get that agreement set aside. I can prove what I'm saying. I had never been hypnotized until I met you."

"Look here," said Bellowes. "Let us get this fixed up once and for all. I don't know who's been cramming you up with these fairy-tales about my fees, but I don't get what you think, or anything like it. I get so little, that I don't want to waste any of it on lawyers. Besides, it would do the business no good, and it would do you no good. I should leave you, and then where would you be? Remember that you are no clairvoyant until I make you clairvoyant."

"You think, perhaps, I have not read what the newspapers say about me? I can find a hundred hypnotists very easily. But there is no other man who's clairvoyant as I am."

"And there is no other man who can run a show as I can. Who

brought the newspaper men here? Who paid for the advertisements? Who did pretty well everything? However, I'm not going to argue. If you want more money, you can have it. Name your figure. If it is in any way reasonable, you shall have it, on the understanding that this is the last advance you get. If it is undesirable, you'll get nothing. You can take the thing into the courts, and I'll fight it. And, mark my words, Smeath. If I do, you might get a surprise. You know nothing at all about hypnotism. You may find yourself in the witness-box saying things that you did not intend to say. Now, then, name your figure."

The little man took time to think it over. He rubbed his chin with his fingers reflectively. He seemed on the point of speaking, and then stopped. Suddenly he snapped out:

"I want four pounds a week!"

"It's simply bare-faced robbery," said Bellowes. "But you shall have it. Mind you, you will have to sign another paper tomorrow, and this time there shall be no doubt about it."

"If you pay me that, I'll sign anything. With four pounds a week I can keep some very good birds again. But you are right that it is bare-faced robbery, and I am the man who is being robbed."

There had been many disputes between the two men during the six weeks that they had been associated. It was by Tangent's directions that Bellowes acted in the present quarrel.

"It would be better to pay the little devil twenty pounds a week, and keep him, than to refuse and lose him," said Tangent. "I believe he's right, and that your precious agreement isn't worth the paper it's written on. Anyhow, I'll get a new agreement ready. Pay him what he wants, and he'll sign it."

"Well," said Bellowes, doubtfully, "if you say so you're probably right. But in that case we ought to get an extension of time out of him."

"No," said Tangent, "the chap's suspicious of you. He hates you. If you try any sort of monkeying, he'll be off. Besides, with the fees you're charging, two years will about see it through. There are not such a vast number of people who can afford the game."

"As things go at present, it looks as though it might last for ever. You should see the engagement-book. We've got appointments booked for two months ahead. It isn't only a game, you see. It's not just a pastime for fashionable women. We get men from the Stock Exchange, business men of all sorts, racing-men. Yesterday morning we had the Prime Minister's private secretary. He didn't give his right name, but Smeath was on to it, and then he admitted it."

"Hot stuff, Smeath. Do you get much out of him in the way of prophecy? Foretelling the future?"

"Not very often. He has done some wonderful things that way, but more usually he deals with something that is past."

"Why don't you get him to foretell your own future, Percy?"

Bellowes shook his head.

"Not taking any," he said. "He shall have a shot with you if you like."

But Tangent also refused.

Their business had certainly progressed very rapidly. Tangent arranged a report in a newspaper. He communicated with one or two doctors whom he knew to be interested in the subject. He sent a couple of popular actresses to Smeath. He arranged a special séance for a Cabinet Minister, whose principal interest was psychology. After the first week they no longer employed sandwichmen and advertisements. The ball had begun to roll. Everybody who came to Smeath sent somebody else. Everybody in Society was talking about the hideous little dwarf and his marvellous powers. Bellowes was regarded as a showman and a charlatan, but Smeath was clearly the genuine thing.

Despite their mutual dislike, Bellowes and Smeath both lived in the same house—the Bloomsbury lodging-house. It was Bellowes who had insisted on this. He had never felt quite safe about Smeath, and even after the new agreement had been signed he had his suspicions. He was afraid that Smeath would run away. Bellowes occupied fairly good rooms on the first floor. Smeath had one room at the top of the house, but this happened to suit him. Through his windows he could get on to a flat, leaded roof. There he made friends with the pigeons and sparrows. The maid-servant at the house, who one day saw him out on the roof with the birds all round him, said that it was witchcraft.

"They were 'opping about all over 'im. Sometimes he put one down and called another up. I never saw anything like it in my life before."

She had the hatred of the unusual which is prevalent among domestic servants, and gave notice at once. But before the month was up she had grown quite accustomed to seeing Smeath playing with the birds, and the notice was revoked.

V

Bellowes still used for business purposes the name of Sanders-Bell, but he no longer called himself a doctor. He was meeting too many real doctors, and Tangent had advised against it. The room in Bond Street was divided in two by a curtain. The outer part served as a waiting-room, and here, too, Bellowes had his bureau. In the inner part of the room the actual interview between the client and the clairvoyant took place. Their usual hours were only from eleven to one and two to four, but Bellowes would sometimes arrange for a special interview at an unusual hour and an increased price. On these occasions he always took care to pacify Smeath. Sometimes he gave him money, and sometimes other presents; on one occasion he gave him a big book about birds, with coloured illustrations, and Smeath remained docile and in a good temper for days afterwards.

"Yes," said Bellowes. "You have complained once that I was robbing you. You can't say that now. You have fixed your own salary. If there is the least little bit of extra work to be done, you always get something for it. You are not as grateful as you ought to be, Smeath. Where would you have been without me? What were you doing before you came to me?"

"Nothing. For some weeks I had been very hungry. I make no complaint against you, but when my time's up I shall stay no longer. I go back to the birds again."

"It would be more sensible of you," said Bellowes, "if you banked your money. What did you want to buy that great owl for? He makes the devil of a row at night. We shall have people complaining about it."

"She is a very good friend to me, that owl," said Smeath. "I am teaching her much. She will be valuable."

At this moment there was the sound of a footstep on the stairs, and Smeath stepped behind his curtain.

The man who entered was not at all the type of client that Bellowes generally received. He was a thick-set man of common appearance, and he was unfashionably dressed. He did not look in the least as if he could afford the fee. Bellowes saluted him somewhat curtly.

"It is ten minutes to eleven, sir, and our hour for beginning is eleven. However, as you have called, if you like to pay the fee now—two guineas—I will make an appointment for you, but I'm afraid it will have to be in nine weeks' time."

The visitor looked reflective, turning his seedy bowler hat round in his hands.

"Don't think that would do," he said. "Nine weeks—that's a very long time. Couldn't Mr. Smeath see me today? Couldn't he make an exception?"

"Only by giving you a special appointment. And for that a very much higher fee is charged."

"How much?" asked the man.

"He could give you ten minutes at one o'clock today. But the charge for that would be six guineas. You see, Mr. Smeath is only clairvoyant while in the hypnotic state, and that cannot be repeated indefinitely."

The visitor took an old-fashioned purse from his hip-pocket. He pulled out a five-pound note, a sovereign, and six shillings.

"There you are," he said. "Please book me ten minutes with Mr. Smeath at one o'clock today."

"Very good," said Bellowes, opening the engagement-book. He looked up, with his pen in his hand. "What name shall I put down?"

"I am Mr. Vincent."

"You'll be careful to be punctual, of course. Mr. Smeath will be ready exactly at one o'clock."

"I shall be here," said the man.

He had no sooner gone than Smeath emerged from behind the curtain again. "What on earth did you do that for?" he asked excitedly.

"Keep your hair on, Smeath. It's all right. I'm going to buy you a big cage for that owl of yours."

"I do not want any cage. My birds are not kept in cages. It is not the extra work that I mind. It is that I cannot do anything for that man. I tell you he is dangerous."

"In what way dangerous?"

"I don't know. He is dangerous to me."

"He looked to me an honest man enough. He had the appearance of a chap up from the country. Probably wants to know what his best girl is doing. I shouldn't worry about it if I were you. Don't stand in the way of business, Smeath. You don't know what the expenses are here. I've got to pay the rent next week, and if I told you what that was, you wouldn't believe it. If you don't want the bird-cage, you shall have something else."

But it was necessary to show Smeath a sovereign, and to present him with it before he would consent. Even then, he did so with great reluctance.

Clients with appointments came in, and the ordinary business of the morning began. Smeath no longer spoke when in the clairvoyant state, for he was often consulted upon matters requiring secrecy, and what he said might have been heard by other clients in waiting. He had a writing-block, and scribbled down on it in pencil what he saw.

At one o'clock precisely Mr. Vincent returned, and was at once brought behind the curtain. Smeath sat there motionless. His eyes were open, but he did not look up at Mr. Vincent.

"Now then, sir," said Bellowes. "What is it you want?"

Mr. Vincent drew from his pocket a comb wrapped in paper. It was of the kind that women wear in their hair, and it had been broken.

"I want him to tell me about the girl who wore this at the time when it was broken."

Bellowes placed the comb in Smeath's hands. Smeath held it for a moment, and then the fingers relaxed, and it dropped to the floor.

Bellowes again placed it in his hand, and this time Smeath flung it from him. But immediately he began to write, Mr. Vincent watching him narrowly as he did so. He wrote with an extraordinary rapidity. Presently Bellowes, who had been standing behind him, and reading what he wrote, asked Mr. Vincent to wait in the outer part of the room. As soon as he was alone with Smeath, he took the writing-block out of his hands, tore the sheet from it, folded it and put it in his pocket. Then he rejoined Vincent.

"I am extremely sorry, sir," said Bellowes, "that the experiment has failed completely. There is perhaps some kind of antipathy between Mr. Smeath and yourself. These things do occasionally happen. I find that he can tell you nothing at all, and under the circumstances, I should perhaps return your fee."

Vincent did not seem particularly surprised.

"Very well," he said. "I had hardly expected to get what I wanted, but I thought I might as well try. I paid you six guineas, I think. You seem to be treating me fairly, and I have given you a certain amount of trouble. Supposing you return me five of them."

The money was handed over, and Vincent departed. Bellowes went back to Smeath and brought him out of the trance. Smeath shivered.

"Is he here still?"

"No. Gone."

"Was it all right?"

"It was quite all right."

"I'm glad he's gone," said Smeath. "I was horribly afraid of something. Now I can go out and get my lunch, and I have to buy food for the birds too."

"I shouldn't spend too much money on it if I were you," said Bellowes.

Smeath laughed.

"It is not very expensive," he said. "And I have made one extra sovereign. Why not?"

"Because in future, Smeath, you are going to work for me for much less money—for a pound a week, to be precise."

"I shall not," said Smeath, loudly.

"I told you once before not to squeal. I don't like it. You will do exactly as I say, and for a very good reason. If you don't you will be taken to prison, and you will be tried before a judge, and you will be hanged, Smeath. Hanged for the murder of Esther Samuel in the woods at Teston."

VI

"What makes you say that? How do you know it?" asked Smeath. The fingers of his big hands locked and separated and locked again. His eyes were fixed intently on Bellowes. He looked excited again, but not frightened.

"How do I know it?" echoed Bellowes. "I have it here in your own handwriting." He tapped his breast-pocket. "You do not remember what happened when you were hypnotized. I put a broken comb into your hands. It was a comb which the murdered woman had worn. You began to write at once. You've put the rope around your neck, Smeath."

"And that man—the man that I knew to be dangerous?"

"Mr. Vincent? I told him that the experiment had failed, and returned his fee. He knows nothing. So long as you do exactly what I tell you, you are quite safe."

"Who was he, this Vincent?"

Bellowes shrugged his shoulders.

"How should I know? Possibly one of the Samuel family. Possibly a 'tec. If I had given him what he had paid for, we should have had the police in here by now. I have saved your skin for you, Smeath. Don't forget it."

"Will you read it out to me, the thing I wrote down?"

"No. It tells one everything, except the motive."

"The motive was obvious enough. I was hungry and had no money. I had tramped to Teston and reached there two days too soon. I had nowhere to go, and I lived and slept in the woods. I begged from the girl at first, and if she had given me a few pence she might have been alive now. She was not in the least bit afraid of me. Why should she have been? I was small, misshapen, and looked weak. She was tall and strong. As she turned away from me, she said the tramps in the neighbourhood were becoming a nuisance, and she would send the police after me. Even then I only meant to hit her once, but that is a queer thing—you cannot hit a human being once. You see the body lying at your feet, and you have to go on striking and striking. When I knew she must be dead, I flung the stick down. I took nothing but the money, nothing which could be traced. Even the money made me so nervous that I hid most of it—buried it in a place where I could find it again. If the police found me, there would only have been a few coppers in my possession, and I did not look like a man who could have done it. But they never did find me."

"I see. That was why, when I offered to advance your railway fare, you told me you had money. You had a pair of new boots on when you turned up at Warlow. I remember what an infernal squeaking row they made on the platform. Well, you've done for yourself, Smeath. You've got to work for me on very different terms now."

"No," said Smeath. "That is not so."

"Very good. I'll write my note to Mr. Vincent now. He'll do the rest."

"No you won't, and I'll tell you why. You can destroy me very likely, but if you do, you'll destroy your own livelihood. And you always take very good care for yourself, Mr. Bellowes."

"Destroy my livelihood?" said Bellowes, thumping on the table with his fist. "That's where you make your mistake, you little devil! Because you're useful, you think you're indispensable. You're not. There's a reward of two hundred pounds out for anyone who finds the murderer of Esther Samuel. I'm a born showman. With two hundred pounds capital I can chuck this and start something else that will pay me just as well."

"It looks as if I shall have to give in. Well, there's no help for it. I must get a much cheaper room, of course."

"No, you won't. You'll stop in the same house as me. D'you think I haven't worked it all out? After you've paid your rent, you've a shilling a day for food, and better men have lived on less. I'm not going to give you a chance to bolt. And mark my words, Smeath, if you do bolt, the very moment I find you've gone I give you up. Don't imagine you can get away. There are not many men of your build. The police would have you for a certainty within twenty-four hours."

"Then I become a slave; I can do nothing. There were other birds that I meant to buy. And in time I could have started a business again. That must all go."

"Quite so. That must all go. In fact, before a fortnight is out I expect you'll sell that big white owl of yours. You'll grudge him his keep."

"It is a she-owl, and I shall not let her go. She can do things that would surprise you."

"Can she?" said Bellowes. "It might be rather effective if you brought her down here. She would impress the clients."

"I shall not. I keep her for myself!"

"Don't talk like a fool! You are forgetting that I hold you between my thumb and finger. If I tell you to wring that bird's neck you will have to do it."

Smeath rose to his feet in fury.

"Where's my hat?" he said. "Give me my hat!"

Bellowes stood in front of the door.

"What's the matter with you? Where are you off to?"

"Checkmate for you, Mr. Bellowes. I am going now to give myself up. Where is your two hundred pounds reward, eh? Where is the money that you make out of the clairvoyant?"

"Sit down, and don't talk in that silly way. I never told you to kill the bird. I was only speaking in your interests when I said I doubted if you could afford to keep it. As a matter of fact, I don't care a pin's head about it either way. If you set so much store by it, keep it by all means."

"In that case," said Smeath, "I will go on working for you and on the terms that you have said."

"That's all right; and now you can go out to lunch. Remember that you have to be back at two o'clock. If you are not here by ten minutes past two, I shall send the police to look for you."

"I shall be here, Mr. Bellowes."

Every Saturday morning at half-past nine Tangent called on Bellowes in Bond Street, to look over the books and to collect his share of the profits. Tangent had no great faith in Mr. Bellowes. Smeath was never allowed to be present on these occasions.

On the Saturday after Mr. Vincent's visit, Tangent was well pleased with the results.

"Mind you," he said, "the little dwarf isn't doing so badly out of it either. He gets his regular four pounds a week. This week I see he's had one pound ten in cash for extra work, and you're charging twelve-and-six for a present for him. What was the present?"

"Oh, a bird of sorts. The little beggar's simply mad about birds. That did more good than if I'd given him the actual cash."

"Oh, I'm not grumbling, Bellowes," said Tangent, surveying with complacency the diamond ring on his finger. "If, by giving him a trifle extra now and then, you can keep his goodwill, it's quite worth our while to do it. No man will work for nothing, and I suppose he finds this clairvoyant game rather exhausting. Not over and above good for the health, eh?"

"He says it's exhausting. He seems to me well enough."

When Tangent had gone Bellowes smiled. To swindle Tangent was a real pleasure to him, even apart from the profit he made for himself. He remembered the terms which Tangent had forced him to accept for the provision of capital for the enterprise.

The introduction of a large white owl into the Bloomsbury lodging-house could have but one effect. The maidservant gave notice at once on general principles. It was Smeath this time who persuaded her to remain.

"You must not be afraid of the white owl," he said. "Owls are wise birds. She knows who my friends are, and who my enemies are. You are my friend, and she will never hurt you. She will let you feed her and stroke her feathers. They are very, very soft, the feathers of an owl."

In a week's time Jane was neglecting her work to play with the white owl out on the leads.

VII

For several weeks no change took place. Smeath did his work with patience and docility. He addressed Mr. Bellowes with respect. He made very little objection to private engagements. As a munificent reward, on two occasions Bellowes took him out to luncheon, and once presented him with some Sunday tickets for the Zoo, which he himself did not want. Every Saturday Tangent inspected, with satisfaction, some purely fantastic accounts. Bellowes was specially careful that Smeath and Tangent should never meet, lest the discrepancy between the statements in the books and the actual facts should be discovered.

And then business began to fall off. There was no excessive drop, but the previous standard was not quite maintained. That astute showman, Mr. Bellowes, decided that something would have to be done. Some new feature would have to be introduced, to set people talking again.

"Smeath," he said one day, "didn't you tell me something once about a white owl?"

"Yes," said Smeath, "I have one."

"It does tricks, don't it?"

"It does a few things," said Smeath, grudgingly. "You do not want it. You said that you would leave me my owl."

"You needn't get into a stew about it, and do for goodness sake keep those great hands of yours still. They get on my nerves. Nobody wants to take your blessed owl away from you. The only thing that I was wondering about was whether it might not be worthwhile to keep the bird here, instead of at your lodgings."

"No, sir! No, Mr. Bellowes! It is in my leisure time that I want my owl."

"Well, I was talking to Mr. Tangent about it, and he thought it was a good idea; in fact, he said I ought to have done it before. We must think about it. I have been pretty easy with you, Smeath."

"Also, I've worked very hard for you."

"You've done what you were told, and of late you've given me no trouble. You might let Tangent and myself have a look at the bird, anyhow. It would be effective, you know—the dwarf clairvoyant and the great white owl on the back of his chair. Tangent spoke of a poster. I'll tell him to give us a call in Bloomsbury on Sunday morning."

"I do not want my owl to be taken away. It lives there on the leads outside my window. Here it would be unhappy. How could I leave it here all night alone?"

"Don't be unreasonable, Smeath. You will see more of the bird than you do now."

"No," said Smeath. "The greater part of the time when I'm here I'm like a dead man, and know nothing."

Bellowes had quite realized that this was the point on which Smeath would have to be handled carefully.

"Look here," he said, "I wouldn't do anything to hurt the bird. At any rate, let Mr. Tangent and myself see it. Let us see if it can really do the things that that girl Jane jabbers so much about. If Tangent and I think it would be an asset to the show, I am prepared to go quite beyond our agreement. I'll give you two or three shillings for yourself, Smeath. You can give yourself a treat. You've not been having many treats lately; in fact, you look just about half starved."

It was true. The little dwarf had grown very thin. His eyes seemed to have got bigger and brighter. There was a look in them now which would have made Bellowes suspicious if he had noticed it.

"Jane," said Smeath, as he met her on the stairs that night, "they are coming on Sunday morning to see my owl."

"Then they'll see miracles," said Jane, with confidence.

"And they're going to take it away."

"If that bird goes, I goes!"

Smeath burst into a peal of mirthless laughter.

Mr. Tangent arrived in a taxi-cab at the Bloomsbury lodgings at eleven on the following Sunday morning. He was in a bad temper, and swore and grumbled profusely.

"So I've got to turn out on a Sunday morning and work seven days a week, just because you're such a damn bad showman, Bellowes? You've let the thing down. The books on Saturday were perfectly awful."

"I'm not a bad showman, and it's not my fault. The weather's been against us, for one thing. And, besides, no novelty lasts for ever. We must put something else into it to buck it up, and we must get that poster out."

"That means more expense. I don't see why we should keep on paying Smeath four pounds a week if business is falling off. And as for that rotten old owl of his, I'm no great believer in it. It will look all right on the poster, but it will do no good in your Bond Street rooms. I know those tricks. The bird picks out cards from a pack, or shams dead, or some other nursery foolery. Stale, my boy, hopelessly stale."

"According to what I hear, the bird does none of those things. It's a new line."

"Is it? I'll bet a dollar it ain't. However, tell Smeath to bring it down, and let's get it over."

"Smeath won't bring it down. We shall have to go up to it. He makes a great favour of showing it to us at all. And, if you will take my tip, you'll say nothing to Smeath beyond a good morning. I can tell you he wants devilish careful handling about this bird of his. If you interfere, you'll spoil it. All you've got to do, if you think it at all remarkable, is to say to me that it might possibly do. I shall understand. Now then, come along up!"

"All those stairs!" groaned Tangent. He was a heavy and plethoric man. When they reached Smeath's room he stood for a minute, panting.

The room was ordinarily dingy enough. It was a fine morning and the sun streamed in through the window. On the leads outside they could see the great white owl perched on the bough of a tree which had been fixed there. Smeath, with his hat off, stood beside it, and seemed to be talking to it. Around his feet were a flock of pigeons and sparrows. He nodded to the two men and then gave one wave of his hands. The pigeons and sparrows flew off and left him alone with the white owl.

"Funny sight!" grunted Tangent. "Devilish funny sight!"

Smeath opened the window and called into the room:

"Good morning, gentlemen! Will you come out?"

"Don't much like it," said Tangent. "I've no head for this kind of thing."

"Oh, you're all right!" said Bellowes. "You needn't go anywhere near the edge."

He placed a chair for him, and Tangent climbed out onto the roof, followed by Bellowes.

"I will leave you to look at the bird by yourselves, gentlemen," said Smeath, and stepped down into the room.

"Then who's going to make the bird do its tricks?" asked Tangent. "It's a fine-looking beggar, anyhow. Seems about half asleep. Tame enough." He passed his jewelled hand over the snowy plumage on the bird's breast. "There's a feather-bed for you," he said, laughing.

The bird opened its eyes, and leaped straight into the face of Bellowes. Its plumage half stifled him, its sharp claws tore his eyes. He screamed for help.

Tangent, in horror, had flung himself down flat on the leads, covering his face. Within the room Smeath stood with folded arms, watching the scene with the utmost calmness.

Bellowes tore at the bird with his hands, but step by step it forced him back. There came one final scream from him, and then two seconds of silence, and then the thud as his body struck the stones below. Up above, the white owl flew swiftly away.

The dwarf rubbed his hands and laughed. And then, changing his expression to one of extreme dismay, went to the help of the prostrate Tangent.

Linda

My elder brother, Lorrimer, married ten years ago the daughter of a tenant farmer. I was at that time a boy at school, already interested in the work which has since made me fairly well known, and I took very little interest in Lorrimer or my sister-in-law. From time to time I saw her, of course, when I paid brief visits to their farm in Dorset during the holidays. But I did not greatly enjoy these visits. Lorrimer seemed to me to become daily more morose and taciturn. His wife had the mind of a heavy peasant, deeply interested in her farm and in little else, and only redeemed from the commonplace by her face. I have heard men speak of her as being very beautiful and as being hideous. Already an artist, I saw the point of it all at once: her eyes were not quite human. Sometimes when she was angry with a servant over some trivial piece of neglect, they looked like the eyes of a devil. She was exceedingly superstitious and had little education.

Our guardian had the good sense to send me to Paris to complete my art education, and one snowy March I was recalled suddenly from Paris to his death-bed. I was at this time twenty-two years of age, and of course the technical guardianship had ceased. Accounts had been rendered, Lorrimer had taken his share of my father's small fortune and I had taken mine. But we both felt a great regard for this uncle who, during so many years, had been in the place of a father to us. I found Lorrimer at the house when I arrived, and learned then, for the first time, that our uncle had strongly dis-approved of his marriage. He spoke of it in the partially conscious moments which preceded his end, and he said some queer things. I heard little, be-cause Lorrimer asked me to go out. After my guardian's death Lorrimer re-turned to his farm and I to my studies in Paris. A few months later I had a brief letter from Lorrimer announcing the death of his wife. He asked me, and, indeed, urged me not to return to England for her funeral, and he added that she would not be buried in consecrated ground. Of the details of her death he said nothing, and I have heard nothing to this day. That was five years ago, and from that time until this last winter I saw nothing of my brother. Our tastes were widely different—we drifted apart.

During those five years I made great progress and a considerable sum of money. After my first Academy success I never wanted commissions. I had sitters all the year round all the day while the light lasted. I worked very hard, and, possibly, a little too hard. Of my engagement with Lady Adela I will say nothing, except that it came about while I was painting her portrait, and that the engagement was broken off in consequence of the circumstances I am about to relate.

It was then one day last winter that a letter was brought to me in my studio in Tite Street from my brother Lorrimer. He complained slightly of his health, and said that his nerves had gone all wrong. He complained that there some curious matters on which he wished to take advice, and that he had no one to whom he could speak on those subjects. He urged me to come down and stay for some time. If there were no room in the farmhouse that suited me for painting he would have a studio built for me. This was put in his usual formal and business-like language, but there was a brief postscript—"For Heaven's sake come soon!" The letter puzzled me. Lorrimer, as I knew him, had always been a remarkably independent man, reserved, taking no one into his confidence, resenting interference. His manner towards me had been slightly patronizing, and his attitude toward my painting frankly contemptuous. This letter was of a man disturbed, seeking help, ready to make any concessions.

As I have already said, I had been working far too hard, and wanted a rest. During the last year I had made twenty times the sum that I had spent. There was no reason why I should not take a holiday. The country around my brother's place is very beautiful. If I did work there at all, I thought it might amuse me to drop portraits for a while and to take up with my first love—landscape. There had never been any affection between Lorrimer and myself, but neither had there been any quarrel; there was just the steady and unsentimental family tie. I wrote to him briefly that I would come on the following day, and I hoped he had, or could get, some shooting for me. I told him that I should do little or no work, and he need not bother about a studio for me. I added: "Your letter leaves me quite in the dark, and I can't make out what the deuce is the matter with you. Why don't you see a doctor if you're ill?"

It was a tedious journey down. One gets off the main line onto an insignificant local branch. People on the platform stare at the stranger and know when he comes from London. In order to be certain where he is going, they read with great care and no sense of shame the labels on his luggage. There are frowsy little refreshment rooms, tended by frowsy old women, who could never at any period of their past have been barmaids, and you can never get anything that you want. If you turn in despair from these homes of the fly-blown bun and the doubtful milk, to the platforms, you may amuse yourself by noting that the farther one gets from civilization, the greater is the importance of the railway porter. Some of them quite resent being sworn at. I got out at the least important station on this unimportant line, and as I gave up my ticket, asked the man if Mr. Estcourt was waiting for me.

"If," said the man slowly, "you mean Mr. Lorrimer Estcourt, of the Dyke Farm, he is outside in his dogcart."

"What's the sense of talking like that, you fool?" I asked. "Have you got twenty different Estcourts about here?"

"No," he replied gravely, "we have not, and I don't know that we want them."

I explained to him that I was not interested in what he wanted or didn't want, and that he could go to the devil. He mumbled some angry reply as I went out of the station. Lorrimer leant down from the dog-cart and shook hands with me impassively. He is a big man, with a stern, thin-lipped, clean-shaven face. I noted that his hair had gone very gray, though at this time he was not more than thirty-six years of age. He shouted a direction that my luggage was to come up in the farm cart that stood just behind, bade me rather impatiently to climb up, and brought his whip sharply across his mare's shoulder. There was no necessity to have touched her at all, and, as she happened to be a good one, she resented it. Once outside the station yard, we went like the wind. So far as driving was concerned, his nerves seemed to me to be right enough. The road got worse and worse, and the cart jolted and swayed.

"Steady, you idiot!" I shouted to him. "I don't want my neck broken."

"All right," he said. He pulled the mare in, spoke to her and quieted her. Then he turned to me. "If this makes you nervous," he said, "I'd better turn round and drive you back. A man who is easily frightened wouldn't be of much use to me at Dyke Farm just now."

"When a man drives like a fool, I suppose it's always a consolation to call the man a funk who tells him so. You can go on to your farm, and I'll promise you one thing—when I am frightened I will tell you."

He became more civil at once. He said that was better. As for the driving, he had merely amused himself by trying to take a rise out of a Londoner. His house was six miles from the station, and for the rest of the way we chatted amicably enough. He told me that he was his own bailiff and his own housekeeper—managed the farm like a man and the house like a woman. He said that hard work suited him.

"You must find it pretty lonely," I said.

"I do," he answered. "Lately I have been wishing that I could find it still lonelier."

"Look here," I said, "do you mind telling me plainly what on earth is the matter?"

"You shall see for yourself," he said.

The farmhouse had begun by being a couple of cottages and two or three considerable additions had been made to it at different times; consequently, the internal architecture was somewhat puzzling. The hall and two of the living-rooms were fairly large, but the rooms upstairs were small and detestably arranged. Often one room opened into another and sometimes into two or three others. The floor was of different heights, and one was always going up or down a step or two. Three staircases in different parts of the house led from the ground floor to the upper storey. The old moss-grown tiles of the roof were pleasing, and the whole place was rather a picturesque jumble. But we only stopped in the house for the time of a whisky-and-soda. Lorrimer took me round the garden almost immediately. It was a walled garden and good as only an old garden can be. Lorrimer was fond of it. His spirits seemed to improve, and at the moment I could find nothing abnormal in him. The farm cart, with my luggage, lumbered slowly up, and presently a gong inside the house rang loudly.

"Ah!" said Lorrimer, pulling out his watch, "time to dress. I'll show you your room if you like."

My room consisted really of two rooms, opening into one another. They seemed comfortable enough, and there were beautiful views from the windows of both of them. Lorrimer left me, and I began, in a leisurely way, to dress for dinner. As I was dressing I heard a queer little laugh coming apparently from one of the upper rooms in the passage. I took little notice of it at first; I supposed it was due to one of the neat and rosy-cheeked maids who were busy about the house. Then I heard it again, and this time it puzzled me. I knew that laugh, knew it perfectly well, but could not place it. Then, suddenly, it came to me. It was exactly like the laugh of my sister-in-law who had died in this house. It struck me as a queer coincidence.

Naturally enough, I blundered on coming downstairs and first opened the door of the dining-room. I noticed that the table was laid for three people, and supposed that Lorrimer had asked some neighbour to meet me, possibly a man over whose land I was to shoot. One of the maids directed me to the drawing-room, and I went in. At one end of the room a log fire flickered and hissed, and the smell of the wood was pleasant. The room was lit by two large ground-glass lamps, relics of my dead sister-in-law's execrable taste. I had at once the feeling that I was not alone in the room, and almost instantly a girl who had been kneeling on the rug in front of the fire got up and came towards me with hands outstretched.

Her age seemed to be about sixteen or seventeen. She had red hair, perhaps the most perfect red that I have ever seen. Her face was beautiful. Her eyes were large and gray, but there was something queer about those eyes. I noticed it immediately. She was dressed in the simplest manner in white. As she came towards me she gave that little laugh which I had heard upstairs. And then I knew what was strange in her eyes. They also at moments did not look quite human.

"You look surprised," she said. "Did not Mr. Estcourt tell you that I should be here? I am Linda, you know." Linda was the name of my dead sister-in-law. The name, the laugh, the eyes—all suggested that this was the daughter of Linda Estcourt. But this was a girl of sixteen or seventeen, and my brother's marriage had taken place only nine years before. Besides, she spoke of him as "Mr. Estcourt". I was making some amiable and some more or less confused reply when Lorrimer entered.

"Ah!" he said, "I see you have already made Miss Marston's acquaintance. I had hoped to be in time to introduce you."

We began to chat about my journey down, the beauty of the country, all sorts of commonplace things. I was struck greatly by her air, at once mysterious and contemptuous. It irritated, and yet it fascinated me. At dinner she said laughingly that it would really be rather confusing now; there would be two Mr. Estcourts—Mr. Lorrimer Estcourt and Mr. Hubert Estcourt. She would have to think of some way of making a distinction.

"I think," she said, turning to my brother, "I shall go on calling you Mr. Estcourt, and I shall call your brother Hubert."

I said that I should be greatly flattered, and her gray eyes showed me that I had no need to be. From this time onward she called me Hubert, as though she had known me and despised me all my life. I noticed that two or three times at dinner she seemed to fall into fits of abstraction, in which she was hardly conscious that one had spoken to her; I noticed, moreover, that these fits of abstraction irritated my brother immensely. She rose at the end of dinner, and said she would see if the billiard-room was lit up. We could come and smoke in there as soon as we liked. I gave a sigh of relief as I closed the door behind her.

"At last!" I said. "Now, then, Lorrimer, perhaps you will tell me who this Miss Marston is?"

"Tell me who you think she is—no, don't. She is my dead wife's younger sister, younger by many years. Her father took the name of Marston shortly before his death. I am her guardian. My wife's dying words were occupied entirely with this sister, about whom she told much that would seem to you strange beyond belief; and at that time she gave me injunctions, wrested promises from me which, under certain conditions, I shall have to carry out. The conditions may arise; I think they will. I don't mind saying that I'm afraid they will."

"Why does she bear her sister's name? Why does she address you as 'Mr. Estcourt'? And why do you address her as 'Miss Marston,' when she introduces herself to me simply as 'Linda'?"

"Her mother had three daughters. The eldest was called Linda. When she died, the second, who was my wife, took that name. When my wife died the name descended to the third of them. There has always been a Linda in the family. The rest is simply Miss Marston's own whim. She has several."

"Who chaperones her here?" I asked.

He smiled. "That question is typical of you. She is little more than a child, and she has an almost excessively respectable governess living here to look after her. Only I can't be bothered with the governess at dinner quite every night. Does that satisfy you?"

"No; well, perhaps yes. I suppose so."

"It may make your rigid mind a little easier if I tell you—and it is the truth—that if I had my own way I would turn Miss Marston out of this house tomorrow, and I would never set eyes on her again; that I have a horror of her, and she has a contempt of me."

"And of most other people, I fancy. Well, anyhow, what's the trouble?"

"I haven't the time to tell you a long story now; she will be waiting for us. Besides, you would merely laugh at me. You have not yet seen for yourself. What would you say if I told you of a compact made years and years ago with some power of evil, and that this girl was concerned in the fulfilment of it?"

"What should I say? Very little. I should get a couple of doctors to sign you up at once."

"Naturally. You would think me mad. Well, wait here for a few weeks, and see what you make of things. In the meantime, come along to the billiard-room."

The billiard-room was an addition that Lorrimer himself had made to the house. We found Linda crouched on the rug in front of the blazing fire; I soon found that this was a favourite attitude with her. Her coffee cup was balanced on her knees. Her eyes stared into the flames. She did not seem to notice our entrance.

"Miss Marston," said my brother. There was a shade of annoyance in his voice. She looked up at him with a disdainful smile. "Do you care to give Hubert a game?" he asked.

"Not yet. I want to watch a game first. You two play, and I'll mark."

"What am I to give you, Lorrimer?" I asked. "Thirty?" He was not even a moderate player. I had always been able to give him at least that.

"You had better play even," said Linda. "And I think you will be beaten, Hubert."

I looked at Lorrimer in astonishment. "Very well, Miss Marston," he said, as he took down his cue. I could only suppose that during the last few years his play had improved considerably. And even then I did not see why Linda had interfered. How on earth could she know what my game was like?

"This is your evening," I said to Lorrimer after his first outrageous fluke.

"It would seem so," he answered, and fluked again. And this went on. His game had not improved; he did the wrong things and did them badly, and they turned out all right. Now and again, I heard Linda's brief laugh, and looked up at her. Her eyes seemed to have power to coax a lagging ball into a pocket; one had a curious feeling that she was controlling the game. I did my best with all the luck dead against me. It was a close finish, but I was beaten, as Linda said I should be.

Linda would not play. She said she was too tired, and suddenly she looked tired. The light went out of her eyes. She lit a cigarette, and went back to her place on the rug before the fire. Lorrimer talked about his farm with me. The quiet of the place seemed almost ghastly to a man who was used to London. Presently Linda got up to go to bed. "Good-night, Mr. Estcourt," she said, as she shook hands with my brother. Then she turned to me: "Good-night, Hubert. You shouldn't quarrel with ticket-collectors about nothing. It's silly, isn't it?" She kissed me on the cheek, and ran off laughing. She left me astounded by her words and insulted by her kiss.

Lorrimer turned out the lights over the billiard-table, and we sat down again by the fire.

"What did you think of that game?" he asked.

"It was remarkable."

"Nothing more?"

"I never saw a game like it before. But there was nothing impossible about it."

"Very well. And did you have a row with that ticket-collector?"

"Not a row exactly. He annoyed me, and I may have called him a fool. I suppose you overheard and told her about it."

"I could not have overheard. I was outside the station buildings and you were on the farther platform."

"Yes, that's true. It's a queer coincidence."

"I tried that, too, at first—the belief that things were remarkable, but not impossible, and that queer coincidences happen. Personally I can't keep it up any more."

"Look here," I said. "We may as well go to the point at once. Why do you want me here? Why did you send for me?"

"Suppose I said that I wanted you to marry Miss Marston?"

"I thought at the time of my engagement with Adela I wrote and gave you the news."

"You did. The artistic temperament does sometimes do a brilliant business thing for itself. Lady Adela Marys—"

"We won't discuss her."

"Then suppose we discuss you. You are half in love with Linda already."

"Very well," I said, "let us carry the supposition a little further. Suppose that I or anybody else was entirely in love with her, what on earth would be the use? The one thing that one can feel absolutely certain about in her is that she has amused contempt for the rest of her species, male or female. It's not affected, it's perfectly genuine. Even if I wished to marry her, she would not look at me."

"Really?" said Lorrimer, with a sneer. "She seemed fond enough of you when she said good-night."

"That," I said meditatively, "was the cleverest kiss that ever was kissed. It finished what the interchange of Christian names began. It settled the situation exactly—that I was the fool of a brother, and she the good-natured, though contemptuous sister."

"You needn't look at it like that. It is important, exceedingly important that she should be married."

"Marry her yourself—it won't be legal in this country, but it will in others, and I don't know that it matters."

"No, I don't know that it matters. On the day I wrote to you I did ask her to be my wife. She replied that it was disagreeable to have to speak of such things, and that they need not be allowed to come to the surface again, but that, as a matter of fact, *au fond* we hated one another. It was true. I do hate her. What I do for her is for my dead wife's sake, for the promises I made, and perhaps, a little for common humanity. There are others who would marry her. The man whose pheasants you will be shooting next week would give his soul for her cheerfully, and it's no use. Very likely it will be of no use in your case."

"What was the story that you had not time to tell me after dinner?"

The door opened, and a servant brought in the decanters and soda-water and arranged them on the table by Lorrimer's side. He did not speak until the servant had gone out of the room, and then he seemed to be talking almost more to himself than to me.

"At night, when one wakes up in the small hours, after a bad dream or hearing some sudden noise in the house, one believes things of which one is a little ashamed next morning."

He paused, and then leant forward, addressing me directly. "Look here; I'll say it in a few words. You won't believe it, and that doesn't matter a tinker's curse to me. You'll believe it a little later if you stop here. Generations ago, in the time of witches, a woman who was to have been burned as a witch escaped miraculously from the hands of the officers. It was said that she had a compact with the devil; that at some future time he should take a living maiden of her line. Death and marriage are the two ways of safety for any woman of that family. The compact has not yet been carried out, and Linda is the last of the line. She bears the signs of which my wife told me. One by one I watch them coming out in her. Her power over inanimate objects, her mysterious knowledge of things which have happened elsewhere, the terror which all animals have of her. A year or two ago she was always about the farm on the best of terms with every dog and horse in the place. Now they will not let her come near them. Well, it is my business to save Linda. I have given my promise. I wish her to be married. If that is not possible, and the moment arrives, I must kill her."

"Why talk like a fool?" I said. "Come and live in London for a week. It strikes me that both Linda and yourself might perhaps be benefited by being put into the hands of a specialist. In any case, don't tell these fairy stories to a sane man like myself."

"Very well," he said, getting up. "I must be going to bed. I am out on the farm before six every morning, and I shall probably have breakfasted before you are up. Miss Marston and Mrs. Dennison—that's her old governess—breakfast at nine. You can join them if you like, or breakfast by yourself later."

Long after my brother had gone to bed I sat in the billiard-room thinking the thing over, angry with myself, and, indeed, ashamed, that I could not disbelieve quite as certainly as I wished. At breakfast next morning I asked Linda to sit to me for her portrait, and she consented. We found a room with a good light. Mrs. Dennison remained with us during the sitting.

This went on for days. The portrait was a failure. I have the best of several attempts that I made still. The painting's all right. But the likeness is not there; there is something missing in the eyes. I saw a great deal of Linda, and I came at last to this conclusion, that I had no explanation whatever of the powers which she undoubtedly possessed. I also learned that she herself was well acquainted with the story of her house. She alluded to the fact that neither of her sisters was buried in consecrated ground; no woman of her family would ever be.

"And you?" I asked.

"I am not sure that I shall be buried at all. To me strange things will happen."

I had letters occasionally from Lady Adela. I was glad to see that she was getting tired of the whole thing. My conduct had not been so calculating and ignoble as Lorrimer had supposed. She was a very beautiful woman. It was easy enough to suppose that one was in love with her—until one happened to fall in love. I determined to go to London to see Lady Adela, and to give her the chance, which I was sure she wanted, to throw me over. I promised Lorrimer that I would only be away for one night. Lady Adela missed her appointment with me at her mother's house, and left a note of excuse. Something serious had happened, I believe, with regard to a dress that she was going to wear that night. But, really, I do not remember what her excuse was. I went back to my rooms in Tite Street, and there I found a telegram from Mrs. Dennison. It told me in plain language, and with due regard to the fact that each word cost a halfpenny, that my brother, in a fit of madness, had murdered Linda Marston and taken his own life. I got back to my brother's farm late that night.

The evidence at the inquest was simple enough. Linda had three rooms, opening into one another, the one farthest from the passage being her bedroom. At the time of the murder Mrs. Dennison was in the second room, reading, and Linda was playing the piano in the room which opened into the passage. Mrs. Dennison heard the music stop suddenly. Linda was whimsical in her playing, as in everything else. There was a pause, during

which the governess was absorbed in her book. Then she heard in the
next room Lorrimer say distinctly: "It is all right, Linda. I have come to
save you." This was followed by three shots in succession. Mrs. Dennison
rushed in and found the two lying dead. She was greatly affected at the inquest, and as few questions as possible were put to her.

Some time afterwards Mrs. Dennison told me a thing which she did
not mention at the inquest. Shortly after the music had stopped, and before Lorrimer entered the room, she had heard another voice, as though
someone were speaking with Linda. This third voice, and Linda's own,
were in low tones, and no words could be heard. I thought this over, and I
remembered that Lorrimer fired three times, and that the third bullet was
found in another part of the room.

Lady Adela was certainly quite right to give me up, which she did in a
most tactful and sympathetic letter.

Celia and the Ghost

Through half-closed eyes that were still heavy with sleep, Celia saw that the dawn had come—the early dawn of a summer morning. The decision to which she had come the night before floated vaguely on the surface of her mind. She could see the letter that she had written and addressed to her mother; she had put it on the mantelpiece under the spotted engraving of some tiresome cathedral. She could hear the footsteps of the bored policeman passing slowly in the street below.

The letter was as follows:—

"DEAREST MOTHER,—I love you and father, and my brother. That love comes of nature, and nothing could ever alter it. But I am going away. Early in the morning, before anybody else in the house is awake, I shall start. Don't be angry or frightened. I am not going to commit suicide, or do anything disgraceful. I can take care of myself, and I have with me five pounds that I have saved. I shall write to you, too, so that you will know I am well and safe. But I am going, because I must.

"I wonder if you will understand. I don't think a girl of seventeen ought to be sick of life as I am. I am sick of the quarrels and sordid economies of home. I am sick of the drudgery of the office, and the tea-shop luncheons, and everything. I have no liberty. I do not live—I only execute orders.

"So I am going, without any very definite plans, to see if the world has anything better for me. Perhaps it has not, and then no doubt I shall return, when my memory is spent, and father will have the pleasure of calling me a fool and an idiot, as he does most days. But I shall have been alive for a little while. Your loving and unhappy CELIA."

No, she did not repent of the decision. Soon she would get up, but there was plenty of time; nobody in the house would be moving for hours yet. Her body was suffused with a pleasant and equable warmth. Her mind tasted already the strong joy of freedom.

And on no account, she told herself firmly, must she go to sleep again.

Bright sunlight, and London all behind her. She must have been walking for hours, and her sensible shoes were white with dust. But she did not feel tired; she was filled with a sense of exhilaration, almost of triumph. Sitting on the stile that led to the field-path she ate hungrily the apples and biscuits that she had bought. Not for years, she thought, had she breakfasted so deliciously. And where she was she neither knew nor cared. At the next village she would make discreet inquiries, and if there were a railway-station and a train that went seaward she would take a ticket. She had been too wise to take a ticket at any London station, lest capture should follow.

She glanced at a diminutive, thoroughly inexpensive, gun-metal watch. In about one hour and a half, she calculated, Mr. Abrahams, portly and white-whiskered, would be demanding the stenographic services of Miss Melrose, and he would be informed that Miss Melrose had not arrived at the office. Whereupon Mr. Abrahams would request that his soul might be blessed and become apoplectic. His sweet son, Mr. Sam Abrahams, aged twenty-two, would also be disappointed. Celia recalled with disgust that Mr. Sam Abrahams distinctly leered, and that he had once put his grimy hand on her shoulder. Ugh!

And at that moment another hand touched her shoulder, ever so lightly. Celia sprang to her feet, thus dropping an apple and the greater part of a biscuit.

"So you've run away, little girl, have you?" said a man's voice. Well, yes, Celia admitted, it was a pleasant voice. And she liked the looks of the young man who stood on the other side of the stile. Not handsome, perhaps, but interesting—which, in Celia's view, was so much better. Yet it was necessary to show that Miss Melrose knew how to take care of herself.

"How dare you speak to me?" she said, with breathless firmness. "If you don't go away at once I'll—"

"Useless for two reasons. Firstly, there is no policeman for you to call. Secondly, there is no necessity to call him. Unconventional I may be, but I would not dream of hurting or offending you in any way, little runaway."

He knew that she had run away? He might take steps to send her back again. Clearly this man must be managed.

"Why do you say that?" she asked, shyly. "What makes you think that I have run away?"

"The satchel on your back, the dust on your shoes, but above all the ecstasy in your eyes. May I have this?" He picked up the biscuit.

"But I've bitten it!" exclaimed Celia.

"That's why," said the young man, calmly. "I'll give you the apple, though I am not the serpent nor even Paris."

"Don't understand," said. Celia, as she took the proffered apple.

"No? Did you never hear of the prize of beauty?"

"But I'm not," said Celia, blushing.

"After you had gone to bed last night," said the young man, "your father and mother were speaking of you, and they agreed that you were a dangerously pretty girl. Of course, their devotion to you may prejudice them in your favour, but I must say that I agree with them."

"You were not there last night. You can't have been. I don't know you. In fact," she added, a little feebly, "I ought not to be speaking to you."

"No," he said, "you don't know me. But all the same I am a friend of the family. Also—as I should, possibly have explained before—I am a ghost."

At this surprising statement Celia was compelled to laugh.

"A ghost?" she said. "You're a very substantial ghost. Do ghosts wear flannel suits and straw hats, and appear at nine in the morning, and eat what's left of my biscuit, and then smoke a Russian cigarette, as you're doing? A ghost, indeed! Whatever do you mean?"

"I am a ghost," he repeated, "just as surely as you are Celia Melrose." She was a little startled to find that he knew her name. "It is as easy for a ghost to be solid and opaque as it is for it to be vaporous and transparent. It is as easy for it to appear at nine in the morning as at midnight. Also there are two kinds of ghosts. The story-tellers speak only of one kind of ghost—the ghost of what has been. That's ignorance. I belong to the other kind. I am the ghost of what will be. Coming events cast their shadows before. It is true that I am solid, but I am also just such a shadow."

"A shadow of what?" said Celia, almost in a whisper. For she loved no man and yet longed to love, and this type of man—if he had not been only a ghost—appealed.

"The shadow," he said, gravely, "of your lover, your husband, the father of your children. You will love me as I shall love you—and what more has the earth for anybody? I will tell you more. In a year's time you and I will be standing here by this stile. The man that I shall then be will have forgotten, and you also will have forgotten—"

"Never!" exclaimed Celia. "It's far too extraordinary. I shall remember this to my dying day." But even as she said it she looked at the man, and commonplace clothes could not prevent her conviction that she was indeed speaking to a being of another world.

"You also will have forgotten," the man repeated calmly. "Why do you doubt me?"

"Oh, I don't know," said Celia. "You knew that I had run away. You know my name. That was all right. But then you went on to speak of the devotion of my father and mother. Mummy's fond of me, though she's sometimes cross. Matter of fact, when I ran away I made my letter to her just as nice as I possibly could. But my father's temper's awful. You don't know the things he says to me. I simply couldn't stand it any longer. Why, if I'd thought they both cared for me very much I wouldn't have dreamed of running away."

"There is a saying, Celia, that to know everything is to forgive everything. Your father teaches music, I think."

"Yes—it's his profession."

"And the poor man's a real musician. He has not been successful as a composer so far, and he does not know—as I do—that success will come to him before very long. Meanwhile, he teaches the piano to duffers. Think what that means. Every day, on the average, his true and sensitive ear is tortured with seven hundred and eighty-six wrong notes. I include Sundays, when he does not give lessons, or the average would be much higher. And he goes through this continuous martyrdom for the sake of those he loves—your mother, your brothers at school, and you, Celia. Then he is a poor man. He is bothered always with debts and money troubles. He had to pawn his watch to buy your last birthday present. He just manages to keep on the right side of bankruptcy. The wonder is that he has not been driven into raving lunacy. As it is, his temper and language are frequently deplorable—but his whole life speaks more loudly than his language and contradicts it."

Celia's pretty mouth twitched a little, and there were tears in her eyes, but she controlled herself.

"Oh, dear!" she said. "I didn't know. I wish you hadn't told me about the watch. What a beast I've been! And it's not true that he's always in a temper. Often he says things in his grim sort of way that make us laugh. Ghost, you seem to know everything—tell me what I can do."

The ghost smiled an enigmatic smile. "All that a runaway can do," he said, "is to enjoy the perfect sense of freedom—the escape from drudgery and routine—so long as the money lasts. I think you have five pounds and some small change. Up to that point you can live your own life, develop your individuality, assert your claim to put yourself outside the circle of—"

Celia stamped her foot. "Stop talking that nonsense!" she said, angrily. Perhaps she had just a touch of hr father's temper.

And still the ghost smiled enigmatically.

"You must admit," he said, "that it would have been easier to tell you what you might have done if you had not run away."

"What?"

"One thing has already occurred to your mind, I think. You make thirty shillings a week, you know, at the office. But I will tell you of another thing. Bad temper is infectious. When your father is furious your mother is cross and you are sulky. Good temper is infectious, but not so instantaneously. Still in three days an invincibly equable temper will make its effect. One more point—it is just as easy to talk, to be entertaining, to take a little trouble, in the home circle as it is when other people are present. Believe me, Celia, it is vulgar to have 'company manners.'"

"Yes, you may call me vulgar," said Celia, mournfully. "I'm such a lot of worse things as well that it doesn't matter much. But I never meant any harm. Really, I didn't. It was only that I didn't think, or didn't know, or looked at things the wrong way."

"That is quite true," said the ghost, gravely.

"Good-bye, ghost. I'm going home now—at once. They'll be angry with me, and I'll endure it. I suppose I've lost my job in the City, haven't I?"

"I think Mr. Abrahams generally sacks people who absent themselves without good reasons. But in your case the son, Mr. Sam Abrahams, might intercede with success. He is sometimes kind to pretty girls, you know, and he always expects them to—to pay for it."

"Then I will get work elsewhere. And now I must telegraph home so that they won't be anxious. Can you tell me where the nearest telegraph office is?"

"I could, but I can give you better help than that. All ghosts—the ghosts of the future just as much as the ghosts of the past—have strange powers. I will give to you a power that no human being has had yet, though at some point in their lives every man and every woman would give all they possess—and many would even give their lives—to have that power."

Celia looked at him with big eyes, spellbound.

"What is that power?" she asked.

"Simply," he said, in his ordinary voice—and perhaps he was the more impressive because he was never for a moment histrionic—"simply the power to put back the time of the whole world for a few hours, so that the things which happened in these hours will not have happened at all."

"Yes, I see," said Celia, excitedly. "But it's impossible. How do I do it?"

"Move back the hands of your little watch. I promise you that the time of the whole world shall move backward with them."

"I've been told," said Celia, "that it's bad for a watch to move the hands backwards. But I don't care; I don't care if it breaks. I believe in you. I'm going to do it."

And she did. Perhaps it was really bad for the watch, for it made a knocking sound. It knocked louder. It knocked as the engine of a motor-car knocks just before it sends in its resignation. And then—

And then Celia, with slowly-opening eyes, recognized that it was only a knock at her bedroom door. She heard her mother's plaintive voice.

"Celia, you've already been called once. Why don't you get up? The bathroom's ready for you. And you don't want to be late at the office."

"So sorry, mummy," Celia called, cheerfully. "I'll get up at once and hurry like anything."

There had been times when she had met such appeals with a certain acerbity.

She sprang from her bed and stretched her arms wide, her head thrown backward. What a blessed sense of relief! So she had not really run away. She had not really hurt really the people she really loved. She had fallen asleep again after all, and had dreamed the most delightful dream that she had ever known.

The letter she had written to her mother was still on the mantelpiece under the spotted engraving. Celia took it down, and spoke to it as if it had been a living being.

"Do you know what I'm going to do with you, you, silly piece of iniquity?" said Celia. "I'm going to put you in prison—in my despatch-case. And in the luncheon hour I'm going to tear you to pieces and throw you over Blackfriars Bridge into the dirty Thames. There!"

She opened her despatch-case. It was rather a good one; it had been a birthday present to her from her father, as Celia remembered. It was at present the guardian of, amongst other things, five one-pound notes, and these Celia took out and placed under a hair-brush on her dressing-table. Then she threw her letter into the despatch-case and shut and locked it.

Then followed a swirl of blue dressing-gown and a dash for the bathroom.

She dressed, her gun-metal watch assured her, in very good time, considering what a lot of hair she had to brush. Just before she went she took the one-pound notes from the table and put them in a very pretty hiding-place.

As she entered the breakfast-room she heard her father's voice.

"I don't believe they'll cut the light off. I shall get Levison's cheque at the end of this week, and then I can pay. However, I'll go and see them about it."

Celia greeted her parents with more cheerful warmth than usual, helped herself to quite a good deal of porridge, and sat down. Her mother looked at her curiously.

"You're looking very pleased at something or other, Celia," said Mrs. Melrose.

"I know," said Celia. "I had a simply lovely dream last night."

"Good," said her father. "Lovely dreams and Mr. Melrose's fees for tuition are about the only two things that have not gone up in price lately."

"And the dream was partly about you, father. Listen. You're going to have a great success as a composer. It's certain."

"A long time ago," said Mr. Melrose, "I dreamt that I saw a red and blue monkey playing the flute part from the 'William Tell' overture on the E-flat clarionet. It hasn't come true yet, but it may. So may the success."

"It's quite certain," said Celia, "and it's to come before very long. The ghost said so."

"A ghost?" said her mother. "Why, that sounds more like a nightmare."

"But it wasn't. He wasn't a bit like any other ghost."

"And possibly," said Mr. Melrose, "the success won't be like any other success. How goes the time?" His hand went instinctively to an empty watch-pocket and dropped. He glanced at the clock on the mantelpiece. "Twenty minutes, and then I start teaching the 'Moonlight Sonata' to the younger Miss Levison." As he went out he put his hand for a moment on his daughter's head. "Never mind, Celia," he said, "you're a good girl to dream nice things about me."

"Your father seems in much better spirits this morning," said Mrs. Melrose.

Celia assented. She could not remember that he had said anything particularly sunny, but his manner had been more cheerful than usual.

"He had a good night," Mrs. Melrose went on, "and that makes all the difference. It rests the nerves. It's all a question of the nerves. That's how it is that sometimes in the evening, when his nerves have been on the rack all day, he seems—well, almost irritable."

This was a mild but beautiful understatement.

"I know—I understand," said Celia. "And all the pupils will learn that 'Moonlight Sonata,' or at any rate part of it. The last movement exceeds the speed limit, I fancy, though I've forgotten the old thing. By the way, I've got five pounds towards the housekeeping." Her right hand dived into her blouse and produced the notes. "I've got everything I want for myself, and this is left over. It's been gradually accumulating."

"Oh, Celia! This is very good and kind of you. But I don't think your father will ever—"

"He must. If he won't let me pay even a little bit of my own expenses here, I'll go and live somewhere else and break my heart."

"I think, then, I'll just run up and give your father this before he goes out. It might rather—er—alter his plans for the day. But, Celia, why don't you give it to him yourself?"

"Couldn't," said Celia, and looked suddenly mournful. "I couldn't explain, and I might begin to cry."

"But that's silly, child. Why, what on earth could there be to—"

But Celia had already escaped from the room.

At the office later that morning Sam Abrahams, who was not averse to a speculative investment, informed Celia that he intended to take her out to luncheon that day.

Celia did not even take the trouble to make a polite excuse.

"No, thank you," she said, glacially.

"All right," said Sam; "don't get cross. No one's bitten you."

Having thrown the shreds of her runaway letter into the Thames, Celia lunched alone in the Embankment Gardens. And for lunch she had biscuits and apples, but there are no ghosts in the Embankment Gardens.

If you ever meet the famous composer, Mr. Hubert Melrose, do not speak to him of the song with which he first achieved popularity. He may tell you that the song was muck, or he may express himself more strongly, but in any case he will be annoyed with you.

And this is a little ungrateful of him. The song, which was published a fortnight after Celia's dream, had a good melody, dignified and a little ecclesiastical. The words were suitable for singers of either sex, and the accompaniment was within the reach of the vicar's daughter. Its success was instantaneous. In a fortnight the publishers ceased to waste money on advertising it, as the song went by itself; only by the most strenuous efforts could they produce it as fast as they could sell it. And they became most polite and friendly to Mr. Hubert Melrose, and said that they had always been confident of his ultimate success—a fact they had previously forgotten to mention.

And then other compositions by Mr. Melrose, which had been published and had died years before, walked out of their tombs and followed in the song's triumphal procession. These were for the most part more ambitious and important work, and when the critics said that it was a pity that a composer with the genius of Hubert Melrose should waste his time in writing popular ballads, Mr. Melrose smiled with a malicious joy. Prosperity and a tactful daughter had improved his temper.

By Christmas he had given up tuition altogether, and was devoting himself solely to composition. And since he required a secretary who understood business and had a fair knowledge of music as well, Celia worked for him and abandoned Mr. Abrahams. "And a good thing too," said Sam Abrahams. "There never was any spirit of give-and-take about that girl."

One day Celia's father said to her: "It's just come back to my mind that a week or so before I published that putrescent song of mine you barged into breakfast one morning with a prophecy that I was to have a big success. You dreamed it, you said. It would interest me to have an account of that dream. I wish you'd just sit down and type it out."

"I'll try," said Celia, doubtfully. She put a sheet of paper into the machine, and for a few minutes stared at it blankly. Then she got up. "It's no good," she said. "I've forgotten absolutely every single thing about it. And I wish I hadn't."

Later in the evening she tried again, but in vain, to recall her dream. The ghost had told her the truth.

So when, a few evenings afterwards, she met at a dance the young man whose ghost she had seen in that dream, she did not recognize him. Nor did he recognize her. They had to be introduced in the usual way. They danced every dance together that they did not sit out together, and he took her down to supper, otherwise neither showed any special mark of preference for the other. Celia went home in a taxi-cab, which seemed to have touches of the seventh heaven about it.

And after that events moved rapidly.

In the following summer, on a sunny morning, Celia walked in the country on the outskirts of London with the young man whom she was very shortly to marry. She had been engaged to him for countless ages, she said, but it can only have been a few months, since he was the same young man that she met at that dance. When they reached the stile at the footpath across the fields Celia sat down to rest and to eat biscuits from a paper bag.

"I think I'm a greedy pig," said Celia, seriously.

"I'm sure of it," said the young man, with equal gravity.

And then they laughed at their own folly, as very happy people often do, and Celia dropped the greater part of the biscuit which was then in action. In an absent-minded way the young man picked it up and finished it.

Suddenly Celia sprang to her feet. "This has all happened before," she exclaimed. "I feel absolutely sure of it."

The young man smiled enigmatically.

"Quite likely," he said. "Perhaps we met long ago, some time when I wasn't here."

"No, I think you were there and I wasn't. But I wish I had been."

And as she said this she looked so perfectly adorable that it became imperative for the young man to kiss her.

"Oh!" said Celia. "You're terrible; suppose somebody had come past just then."

"Somebody didn't," the young man said, philosophically, and lit a Russian cigarette.

The Tree of Death

I

In the cool of the evening I always saw her. She came up from the river with the other women. That was a great moment when she, who all the day had been in my heart, came at last into the sight of my eyes. Sometimes she would be soon lost to me, going into her father's house. Sometimes she would crouch with the others on the steps by the wall of a brown hut listening to the old story-teller, and it was wonderful to see that story reflected in her eyes as she heard it, like the image of the palm-tree in the deep river. Sometimes even she would walk by my side and speak with me, and those were evenings to be long remembered for rapture and for sorrow.

And one day I went to the story-teller. He was black-skinned and not of our race, and he had come from a far country, travelling for many months alongside the river. Some said that he had fled for his life.

"This evening," I said to him, "I beg that you will come out and tell your stories to us."

He waved his hand at me in refusal, saying that he would not. But when I showed him the gift I had brought for him, then he consented. And I did this because my eyes ached for the sight of her, and I could not bear that this evening she should pass quickly by me.

And when the black man began to draw with his stick in the sand, and tell stories of that distant country from which he had come, she was among those that gathered round to listen. And I gazed at her as one tortured with thirst who sees far off the water he would drink.

He told us of a tree that is called the tree of death. He said that the seed was like bright silver to look at and of the size of a man's fist. If you set that seed in the ground, for two years nothing would appear, and then came the miracle, for betwixt sunrise and sunset the tree came to full maturity, growing with incredible rapidity to twice the height of a man, and died again. And in those short hours of life that tree sought to drink the blood of a man, sending out a heavy fragrance that brought sleep and death, and lashing its victim with long, writhing tendrils. And each tendril was covered with sucking mouths like the mouth of a leech.

And thereon he told us a story of a faithless woman and of a man's deferred vengeance. Secretly, by night, the man planted the seed of the tree of death in the garden of his wife's lover. But when in two years the tree came to being, it slew the woman for whom the lover had deserted the wife. They found her white body in the morning, buried beneath the dead and decaying ruin of the tree, and they found, moreover, the three silver seeds that the tree had produced.

"And in the whole earth," said the black man, "there are but those three seeds left, and because the tree is so evil, those seeds have not yet been planted." Twice he stretched out the fingers of both hands and closed them again. "Yes, twenty times since then the river as risen and fallen. And for five years more the silver seed must be kept and guarded. And then the power of life, which is the power of evil, will have left those seeds and they will be harmless toys, and never any more will man or woman behold the great magic of the tree of death."

I give his story in a few words. He told it in many words, making it a living picture, so that we seemed to see all as it happened and to hear the very words that were spoken. And all the while my eyes were fixed upon the woman whom I loved in vain. She was as one entranced, breathing deeply, and her fingers tore to pieces the flowers of scarlet hibiscus that she carried, the petals dropping on the sand as drops of blood. The sunset, too, was blood-red that evening.

As he finished speaking we heard a jackal far away in the desert. And then a boy, laughing, said that the black man told many lies.

"Son of a dog, I lie not," said the black man, with sudden fury. "I tell you what I have seen and known. In this hand—this very hand—I have held the silver seed of the tree of death. Yes, yes." He rose and stood erect, and his voice dropped to a whisper. "Was it not I, myself," he said, "who planted that seed in the garden of my wife's lover?"

We were all silent, and he turned and left us. And then for the first time that evening the woman looked at me and her hand made a little sign. So I followed her down to the river bank, and there for a while we sat and talked in the light of a great burnished moon.

II

"You praise me and say that I am very beautiful," she said. "It may be and it may not be, but it is pleasant to hear. You bring many gifts to my father's house, and again, it is pleasant to receive gifts. I think you paid the old story-teller, for clearly he showed more deference to you than to others. And that is the best of all, for one day is as another, and we go the same round continuously, like the ox with bandaged eyes that draws up the water for the garden; but in the hearing of stories we live many lives and are ever changing. But then—then—you pour out your love to me, and would have me give you mine. How can one give who has it not? Others also speak of love to me and have the same answer. It may be that I am still too young, for I am very young, and that one day the fire will burn up in me. But now, when you speak of love, it is as though I gazed at the writing of a scribe having no skill to read it. And yet—and yet—there was something I would say."

"Speak on. Your voice is sweet to hear."

"It is of the story that we have heard. I think there is truth in it, even if it be not all true. I will tell you why, and I have told no other of this. Two years ago an old woman lay dying in her house, and those that should have tended her had fled in fear. And I brought up water for her from the river. She drank eagerly of it, for the fever was on her. And then she bade me pour a little of the water in the hollowed palm of my left hand and hold it so that she might gaze into it. She looked long into it, so that my little hand shook. And then she said words that I have never forgotten and never yet told. These are the words: 'The eyes of the dying have seen beyond, and as I say it shall be. The man of your love shall come to you holding in his hand a ball that is not of silver but of the colour of silver, and in that ball there shall be life and death.'

"To-night I knew that the ball must be the seed of the tree of death. I know not where the seed is. The old man said it was guarded. It may be that one must go a long and perilous journey, and that blood must be shed, and that a great price must be paid. But this I know—on the day that you come to me holding in your hand a seed of the tree of death, I shall be so filled with love for you that my head will droop and my eyes will faint, and my body and my soul will be yours."

And in a voice that had become suddenly hoarse I said: "And you have told no other of this?"

"Have I not said it? Also, if you swear that you will get for me the silver seed, I shall tell no other until it is clear that you have failed. I chose you for many reasons. You are gentle, and when my beauty is gone and you cease to love me you will not then begin to beat me. You are not so wealthy as some of those that seek me, but neither do you hold your wealth with so hard a grip as they do. Did you not also pay the story-teller for my delight?"

"For your delight and for the delight of my eyes in you."

"It is as I thought. And without that I might never have heard of the tree of death or understood the secret of my future. And though I do not now love you—not in the very least—yet I come to you first. But if you think it too hard and hazardous for you, then—"

"Ah, wait!" I said. "Believe me that not for a moment has there been a doubt in my mind. If anywhere on earth there be that silver seed, I swear that I will find it, and bring it to you, and nothing save death shall stay me."

"It is enough," she said. "And when will you bring it?"

"I do not yet know how long it will be. Will you wait for me for a year if need be?"

"Yes, for a year. But I have seen love run away as water. If, when you hold the seed in your hand, you no longer love me, then bring it not to me, lest you bring sorrow with it."

I pointed to the river at our feet. "The river runs for ever," I said, "but the river is ever there. So is my love for you."

And as we parted I said to her: "Then you wish to have this seed of the tree?"

"To me," she said, "it is no more than a sign of destiny. If you bring it, then I shall love you. But if you are not destined, then another will bring it, and I shall love him. But for the seed itself, since it is evil, it shall be fuel for the fire. Or haply"—she looked at me with steady eyes—"I may keep it till it has no more power to harm, and then it may serve as a toy for the children that I bear."

That night I slept ill, my thoughts going backward and forward between joy and sorrow like a ball that is struck by the hands of the players. It was joy that she had spoken to me seated close by my side, that she had trusted me with a secret, that of her own will she had given me the chance to gain her love.

It was sorrow that she loved me not yet, and that if I failed in the adventure she would never love me and would love another. Nay, the black man had said that there were three seeds of the tree of death. It might be that if I found one of them, another man also might find one, and he, going more swiftly or by a shorter road, might take from me my beloved.

Moreover, though in this adventure I might risk all, yet if I were not destined I should fail; and if I were destined, then, though I sat quietly in my house and risked nothing, the unseen hand would place in mine the silver seed of the tree. And so I came back to the wisdom that is old and strong and cruel as the granite rock—that which is written, is written, and that which will be, will be.

And yet what pleasure could I have of gold dust and gems, of herds and fertile land, if I had not this woman? Without her, life itself was worthless. So I was determined to risk all. Had I not seen this myself, and had I not heard of it in many stories—that he who of his own will makes a great sacrifice shall in the end have his reward?

III

I found the old black man, as I had expected, stretched upon his bed, though for some hours the sun had been up. He was ever idle, though he still had strength to work. Those that by chance listened to his stories would bring him small gifts. But if one would command a story, as I had done, then the gift was greater; and so he lived.

And at first, as I came in from the bright sunlight, the hut seemed dark, But presently I saw him well, and I knew who had given him the robe that he wore and who had given him the loose slippers that lay on the ground beside him.

And after our words of salutation I said to him: "I have in my mind a great matter of which I would speak with you, desiring your help. If you can help me, then in return I will give many and very rich presents. Come into my garden, where we may talk quietly, and there is pleasant shade, and the fruit of last year still hangs upon my orange-tree."

So he said courteously that I was without doubt of divine descent and that he was my servant. And, rising from the bed, he thrust his feet into his slippers and came shuffling after me.

Seated under the orange-tree, he sipped the coffee that was brought out to him, but the oranges that I gave him he wrapped in a fold of his robe for another time.

"Last night," I said, "you told us of the tree of death."

"And for that reason," he said, "a woman brought me this morning bread and coffee, but the coffee was less good than this."

"She was beautiful?"

"She was a song of love, but unfortunately I am now old. When I had eaten and drunk, I went out and found that son of a dog who said that I lied, and beat him with my slipper until he howled. For I had told of things that have been and still are. True, I have also stories of things that might be, and these are more beautiful. What of it? Shall the young insult the old? But this matter in which you need my help, I beg you to tell me of it."

"I go to seek one of the three silver seeds of the tree of death. As beside that, my life and such wealth as I have are nothing. I must have that seed. You can tell me whither I must go and what I must do to attain it."

"If a man travel with the utmost rapidity and sparing nothing, he may make the journey in four months."

"Then in four months I will accomplish it."

"There are perils of the road—robbers and dangerous beasts."

"I fear them not." And I showed him the dagger that I carried.

"But you will come to a country where the stranger is suspect, and in the place where the silver seed lies guarded no stranger may enter at all; and the guard is threefold—a circle, and within it a second circle, and within that a third circle. You may stain your skin till it is as dark as mine, but you cannot speak in the tongue of that people, neither do you know their ways. And if you would attain your end by violence, you will be one man against a myriad of men. So that if you go, two things are certain. The first is that you will never even see the silver seed, and the second is that you will die very soon."

"Have you no better help for me than this?"

"There may be another way. You said truly that this is a great matter. It is one that must be weighed well with long thought. I will, if you please, go back now and ponder upon it. And to-morrow at this time I will come again to you."

So I gave him a present and let him go, his robe curiously swollen with many oranges that he carried.

And next day he came back to me and said: "There is one way, and one only. It may bring you what you seek but it is not sure. If you would take it, two things will be necessary. The first is that you must trust me utterly, more than most men will trust their brothers. Secondly, the cost will be great, so that of all your possessions there will be but little left to you."

"You are sure that it is the only way?"

"It is the only way."

"Then I will take it. Tell me of it."

"You cannot go, but I can go for you. Also, I am very willing to go. Twenty years have I been a stranger in this little place, and my own country calls me. I know the tongue of the people and all their ways. Moreover, I myself have been of the innermost guard of the temple, and know much which is hidden from most men of my race. If there is any man on earth who can get the seed of the tree of death, then I can get it. But I must be able to buy men, and they are such that a small present will not tempt them."

"When will you return?"

"In the ninth month from the day that I start you should have the silver seed either at my hand or at the hand of a sure messenger."

"If I trust you whom at least I know, that may be well. Must I trust also a messenger whom I do not know?"

"You may do so without fear. For he will not receive the last half of his reward until he has delivered the seed into your hands. Moreover, he will know that if he is treacherous, his own life and the life of his dearest that he leaves behind him will be forfeited."

"It is a great journey, and you are old."

"I still have strength, not having spent myself with too much labour. Moreover, there are two that travel speedily—the young man that goes to his beloved and the old man that returns at last to his native country."

"You have no fear that you will be robbed? For you will carry with you much wealth."

"If I went with a train of laden camels, travelling as a rich merchant, then the danger would be great. But my wealth will be hidden in a belt about my body and I shall seem to be a poor man. There is indeed the chance that death one way or another may overtake me, but both you and I must take that chance."

"How do you know that you will find the silver seeds? Since it is known that they are evil, may they not have been destroyed?"

"No, for it is known that the evil must die of itself, and they who would destroy it will make yet worse evil that shall fall on their own heads."

"When you yourself planted that seed in the garden of your wife's lover, was it then guarded in the temple? And if that be so, how came you to be able to make these great gifts and so get possession of it?"

"The temple was triply guarded, and I myself was of the innermost guard. But the seed was not there then, neither was the nature of it known—save to me only—until two years after I had planted it. In quite another way did I obtain that seed, and I beg that you will not ask of it, for it was shameful to me."

Many other questions did I ask of him, and to all he had a ready answer. But I showed little judgment, my mind being filled with thoughts of my beloved. And in all things I did as he bade me.

Then for many days I sold my possessions until the black man said: "It is enough," and afterwards I journeyed with him for three days to a town where there was a great bazaar, but our business was not in the bazaar, but at the house of the principal merchants. For we bought diamonds, emeralds, and pearls. And among the pearls there were two that were twins, being perfectly alike in size and shape, in weight and colour. And when he secured this treasure into the belt that he would wear, he left out one of these twin pearls and placed it in my hand, bidding me to keep it with the utmost care.

"For," he said, "I am an old man and it is more likely that I shall choose to die in the land of my fathers. The messenger that I send with the silver seed will take the great oath of my people, swearing that he will be guilty of no negligence, and no treachery, and no disobedience. If any man takes this oath and breaks it, then in the whole earth there is no place where he may hide from swift and terrible vengeance. For this reason no man of my people will take this oath unless for a great reward."

"It is justice," I said.

"Therefore I give him one of the twin pearls when he sets forth. And when he arrives and places in your hands the silver seed, you will give him the other. Then he will return and show me the two pearls, and that will be the sign that he has performed his oath, and I shall have written for him quittance of it. So he will sell the pearls and get himself a wife and a house, and I myself may die in peace."

And he found a brown-sailed boat that went up with a favouring wind to the next village carrying sugar-cane. And making a small payment to the owner of the boat, he stretched himself upon the sugar-cane and so was carried out of my sight. All the day he would sleep in the boat and at night he would leave the boat, and purchase an ass, swift and sure-footed, and ride all night. And so he would go on, by this way and that: taking the best that chance offered or his wit could devise, until he came to his journey's end.

IV

On the day that the black man went I made my computation. My house and my walled garden were left to me, and there was store enough for another month. All else—herds and fertile land, and the treasure that I had of my fathers—was changed into little stones, and these stones were being carried away from me round the belly of a black man whom I should never see again. In another month it seemed that I who had hired others to work for me must myself work for hire.

To most men these would have been black thoughts, and they would have rent their garments and cursed their own folly that had brought such ruin upon them. But to me all this was a source of joy. "Now truly," I said, "of mine own will have I made a great sacrifice, and in the end I shall have my reward."

And that evening, as my custom was, I waited to see my beloved come up from the river. And as she passed me she made a sign that I should wait. And having set the water-jar down in her father's house, she came back to me.

It was the first time she had spoken with me since the night when we heard of the tree of death and afterwards sat by the river together. True, I might have spoken to her, but 1 feared lest by being too importunate I should lose such favour as I had in her eyes.

"These last days," she said, "I have heard much foolish talk about you and about the old story-teller. Those that know a few things, yet have not the key of them, must always guess wrongly. But I have the key; would you hear what I know?"

"Your words are to me the sweetest music."

"Some say that the black man has gone to tell his stories in other villages, that for one story he may receive many gifts. Others say he pays a visit to his own country, and others say that he goes to examine for you some house or land that you are minded to buy in place of that which you have sold. Certainly he is gone, and another will sleep in his hut this night. It is true that he has gone to his own country, but I know that he goes to get for you the silver seed, though you declared to me that you would go yourself, even if it cost you your life, so great was your love for me."

And then I told her all, as I have set it down, explaining that I had indeed been willing to go and why that could not be. And she said:

"If a man risk his life for a woman, that is his greatest praise of her. But if he buy another man to risk his life, that is a greater wisdom for him.

Yet in other respects you have not acted wisely. For the old man may die, or he may be a thief; and even if he live and be worthy of trust, he may fail to get the silver seed; and even if he gets it, he may fail to render it to you. So that if the measure of your folly be the measure of your love for me, I am still commended, though with a lesser praise. Meanwhile, there will be none to tell me a story, making the cool evening pleasant for me. Moreover, that which you have given to get me you cannot give again to keep me. Also, my father has scolded me, and—"

Here she stayed, and her brow cleared, and she laughed.

"Take no heed of these words. If you are destined for me, I shall certainly love you very much. It is this heavy air that makes me say bitter things to you. Nor is it I alone who am troubled by it. The river itself is troubled—fretting and tossing—and there is anger in the setting sun. Somewhere to-night there will be havoc and great misery."

And therein she spoke the truth. For that night the earthquake came, awakening me from a deep sleep. Scarce can the fringe of it have touched the village. In my house two jars were shattered and I felt the earth move under me; but three mud-huts were brought down in ruins, so that there was much praying and screaming until the dawn came.

I judged that the full force of the earthquake had spent itself in the desert, so when the dawn came I saddled an ass and rode into the desert to see what had befallen. And since the air was now fresh and serene, the ride was pleasant to me. And presently I saw that the outline of a great rock had changed from what it was aforetime. So I rode up to it. And then I saw that the rock had split, revealing the entrance to a tomb.

I dismounted and went in a little way, but it was so dark within that I could distinguish nothing. And I went back to my house and said nothing of what I had seen, lest some others should forestall me.

And that night, when the village slept and all was at peace, again I rode out, taking with me a spade and a good lantern. And all the night I spent in that tomb.

I think it was the tomb of one of royal blood. It had many chambers with marvellous paintings on the walls, ranged on each side of the entrance hall, and from thence there were fine wide steps that led downwards, but somewhat encumbered with sand and fallen fragments of the rock. And never had I seen such treasure—cups and platters, rings and figures, all of the purest gold. And there were also ornaments of precious stones.

Much of this treasure I had buried that night in another place, marking the spot in a way that none save he who set the mark could have the skill to see. And on many of the nights that followed I buried further treasure. And I had none to help me, for I could trust none.

So once more it became necessary for me to go to that great town. By night I loaded two camels with treasure, hiding it so that it would appear that they carried forage only. And even so I travelled in great fear, with my dagger ever ready to my hand, and urging the camels to their greatest speed.

But it was appointed that I should arrive safely. And I was well received in the houses of the principal merchants with whom I had traded before, and so disposed of my treasure.

Thus by chance all that which I had given up, in order that I might have the silver seed and thereby the heart of my beloved, was restored to me again, and at first I was well content.

But afterwards my eyes were opened, and in great anguish I saw what had befallen me. For of my own free will had I made sacrifice and it had not been accepted, and that which I had given was returned into my hands again. What reward, then, could I hope?

"Without doubt," I said, "the earthquake overtook the old story-teller as he went through the night, and he is buried beneath fallen rocks or is drowned in the river. And the desire of my heart is taken from me."

And that very night I spoke with a man who, as he travelled towards the village on the day after the earthquake, had met the black man. Thus vainly do we fit our keys to the door that is ever locked. That which is written, is written, and that which will be, will be. So that now I no longer dared to forecast either my happiness or the manner of my suffering. I folded my hands and waited.

Once more in the evening my beloved spoke to me.

"They speak of you in the village after this manner," she said. "They say that you sold much and that now you buy much, and that in the difference of the price you have your advantage. This is the wisdom of fools who speak, not having the key. But I have the key. I know that, when you sold, the black man took it away with him, so that I even marvelled if my father would willingly give me to one who had become poor. Whence, then, have you the means now to buy so much? Either you lied to me, and the black man bore no wealth of precious stones in his belt, or you have worked some great magic. And if it be the first, then the black man will not send you the silver seed, for it was not his habit to do much for little, nor are you destined for me. But if it be the second, then I beg that you will show me how to work the same magic, that I may make my father very content and also buy for myself a new robe and a bracelet of gold."

"Neither have I lied to you, nor have I worked any magic. Since you gave me your secret, and have kept close in your own heart what I have told you so far, I will trust you yet again. It was destined that I should find a great treasure, making up for all that I had bestowed on the black man. Ask me no more of this now, but tell me why you wish for a new robe and a bracelet of gold."

"I have a cousin, and she is beautiful, but not so beautiful as you think that I am. Also the time has come that she must be married. Neither she nor I know who her husband will be, but she is obedient and will leave the choice to her father. Undoubtedly he will choose a rich man, and there will be a very great festival of the marriage, lasting all the night through, with music and dancing-girls. Surely I shall be bidden to the festival, and I would not be ashamed there. But my father is not rich, neither does he ever find anything."

"Then it is you who must find."

"What shall I find?"

"A purse hidden in a basket of pomegranates. And this basket of pomegranates I will send to your father's house soon after the hour of sunrise to-morrow."

"Listen," she said. "Your love for me is as the desert, and my love for you is not yet even as one grain of sand. Will you still send this gift?"

"I will still send it."

She said that, if it were known, the tongues of the malicious would speak evil of her, and, therefore, it would be a secret. And she was pleased, just as a child may be pleased with a little gift. She had said truly that she was still very young. She laughed and played with the maidens of her age. And neither for me nor for any other man had she one thought of love.

Yet even then love slept deep in her calm eyes, as the fish with golden scales lies sleeping at the bottom of a deep pool. And the time of awakening was near.

V

He that enjoys knows how swift the passage of time may be, and he that awaits an event knows how slow it may be. But at last eight months had passed since the departure of the old story-teller, and he had said that in the next month—the great month of fruition—I should receive the silver seed of the tree of death—if, indeed, I ever received it.

So now in every footstep I seemed to hear the sound of an approaching messenger, and in every sound to hear my name called. My blood grew hot as with a fever and my sleep left me, so that for the greater part of the night I paced in my garden alone.

All night on the ninth night of the month I heard in the distance the sounds of music and revelry. It was the wedding of the cousin of my beloved, and there was a great festival. But towards dawn the sounds died away, and I paced to and fro in my garden. And suddenly, as I passed the door in the wall of the garden, I heard a little sound, and I was called by my name. But it was not the voice of any messenger that called. It was the voice of my beloved.

I opened the door and bade her enter. She came in without a word, wearing the new robe and the golden bracelet. And in the gray and awful light of the dawn her face seemed still wondrous beautiful, and yet changed.

"You are weary?" I said.

She made a sign of assent.

"Yes," I said, "the marriage festival was long. All night I have heard the music. Your eyes tell of your weariness." And I spread a silken carpet for her under a tree that she might rest, greatly wondering that she should come to me in this way.

She knelt on the carpet, bending her body and covering her face with her hands.

"I have not been at the festival," she said. "Oh, I have much to say and there is not one word of it that you can ever forgive. Yet promise to hear me to the end, and then—then do with me as you will."

Then my heart fainted and doom sang in my ears. And there was a long silence before I could say: "I will hear you to the end."

And now she stretched herself at full length on the rug, her hands clasped behind her head. And she spoke like a tired child that repeats a long lesson.

"Yesterday," she said, "at sunrise I went down to wash myself in the water of the river. And when I had put on my garment again and risen up, I was aware that a youth came towards me, riding upon a white ass that was bedecked with silver ornaments. And he dismounted and looked long at me. He was darker than we are, yet not so dark as the old story-teller. And I read in his eyes that which I have read in yours and in the eyes of other men. I knew that he desired me. Every day a beautiful woman may read that language. Yet it moved me not, and it was as if there were a mist before my eyes.

"He named you and asked me where he might find you, speaking in our tongue but slowly, as one but newly accustomed to it.

"I said: 'If you follow me, I will take you to him.'

"'And afterwards?' he said. 'For you are more beautiful than any woman on this earth, and it is for you that my love has waited.'

"I laughed, for there was still the mist before my eyes. Besides, such a speech was daring and sudden, since he now saw me for the first time. 'Afterwards,' I said, 'will be as it will be. Meantime what seek you with this man?'

"He turned his eyes from me, as if he feared to look on me. 'It is forbidden to me,' he said, 'so much as to speak of it.'

"Now, whether you believe it or not, it is true that in the next words which I said I had no intent but to vex him a little. Was not the mist still before my eyes, so that I could not judge aright? Was I any more than the thistle-seed caught in the wind of destiny?

"I said, still laughing: 'You love me, and yet you refuse the first thing that I ask of you?'

"And now he looked long at me again, breathing deeply, and suddenly he thrust his hand into his robe and drew forth something that glistened.

"'Since you ask it,' he said, 'behold! I go to render this to him.'

"And so he stood before me, holding in his hand a ball that was not of silver but of the colour of silver, and in the ball there was life and death. Thus was it determined in the beginning, before the stars were set and before the earth was shaped. The mist passed from my eyes and I saw that there was no beauty like his beauty. And when he spoke his voice was dearer to me than any that I have ever heard. And never had there been such love as now burnt my whole being.

"'See!' he cried. 'I have broken the great oath, and for that death will come soon upon me. My hours are numbered, and yet if they be hours of love, the price is small. Do I not love you? Do I not worship you?'

"My head drooped and my eyes fainted, and I sank down on my knees. 'Lord of my heart!' I said. 'Lord of my life!'"

And now she turned over on her face, and her whole body was shaken with weeping.

For a few moments I remained silent, and then I said: "Have you ended that which you would say to me?"

"No, no!" she cried. "No, no!"

"Speak on, then," I said, "and I would beg you to speak quickly."

Now she rose to her feet, and thereafter she spoke standing, holding to the trunk of the tree as if for support.

"He had come by the way of the desert, and the night before he had come to the great rock. And finding a great tomb in the rock, he had rested there for the night, and there he had left his gear, setting forth with the white ass to find you, and so to complete his mission.

"Little thought had he now of that mission. And since already people were astir in the village he took me back with him to the tomb in the rock. I rode and he ran by my side, and in less than an hour we were there alone with our love in the cool dusk of the tomb.

"And when it drew near to the evening I was afraid lest my father should send out on all sides to seek me, and haply I should be found with my lover. So I arose and went to my father's house, and when he demanded why I had been away so long, I said that I had been helping in the preparation for my cousin's festival. Moreover, I put on my new robe and the gold bracelet on my arm, and said to him that I now went to her wedding. And he was content, and disposed himself to sleep, for he is old and feeble and unsuited to a night of revelry.

"And so in breathless haste I went back to my lover, knowing that our hours were but few, and that eternity could scarce contain our love. Until an hour ago I was with him, and then it was necessary to see you. And I came near the latticed door of your garden, and, hearing your step, I called to you. And so I come to the very heart of the matter."

Here, pausing, she looked intently at me. And presently she went on speaking.

"There is neither anger nor mercy in your eyes. They have become like the eyes of a stone image in a temple—eyes that change not and see not. Hear me now to the end.

"He has broken the great oath, and the punishment is sure. One will come to him—he knows not when, but it will be very soon—and will say to him: 'Show me the twin pearls that are in all things alike, for this is the proof that you have fulfilled your oath.' And if he has them not, then must he be slain instantly. And, further, in that far country from whence he came the life of his mother will be forfeited, for she was the surety for him in the great oath. And shall not his death be also mine?

"He has but one of the twin pearls, and the other is in your keeping. So that now you hold in your hand three lives.

"It may be that you will say to yourself that I was very young, and that when I tempted him to break his oath I knew not what I did. And you may say further that your hatred is against destiny, and not with these thistle-seeds that the wind of destiny has swept together. If that were so, and you gave me the twin pearl and let us depart with it to his own country, then in all the words of praise there is none that is worthy of such great nobility.

"But in that I ask, it may be, more than any man can give. So, if you still desire me, I will remain here. And if you would have me as a wife or as a slave, I will be ever faithful and obedient. And I ask no reward but that by some instant messenger you will send the twin pearl to my lover, that he may go in peace. And I myself will see him no more at all. Do with me as you will, but let not his blood be upon my head. The fault was mine. Moreover, he has in part fulfilled his oath, for by me he sends to you the seed of the tree of death. I pray you to answer me."

It is very truth that until then I knew not what I would answer. But as she spoke she drew from her garment that silver glistening ball, and held it out to me, and I took it. It was still warm with the warmth of her beautiful body.

In a moment I had buried my dagger deep in her body. She fell at my feet, and a shudder went through her, and she was dead.

I became quite calm again, and my mind was as clear water, and my heart beat steadily and quietly. I knew just what I would do.

I dug a deep grave for her in a corner of my garden. Then I drew forth the dagger, wrapped her in the silken carpet, and so buried her and the silver seed with her.

I made the earth smooth over her, and cleaned my dagger. And at last it was all so ordered that the garden looked even as it looked the morning before, and there was no trace of that which had been done. Neither had any eye beheld it.

And then I rode forth to the tomb that I had found in the great rock, and that the woman's lover had also found. But there, even as I feared, I came too late, and my work had been done for me.

The man lay dead in the entrance to the tomb with a knife in his throat. The bundle of fodder that he had carried for the ass had been spread out like a couch, and beside it were a jar of water and a brass cup. But the white ass bedecked with silver ornaments was no longer there; and I supposed that the man who had slain him had taken it, but he had not taken the twin pearl, for that lay on the open hand of the dead man. There

I left it. And I left the dead man to the vultures and jackals. And I saw that all the time the messenger journeyed from that far country another had travelled close behind him, watching to see if he fulfilled his oath, and with the power to slay him if he broke it.

And after that I went back to my own house and lay on my bed, preparing for myself that which I believed should be my last sleep, merging itself in the end in death. But the drug that I took failed me. Sleep, indeed, I obtained, but at noon on the following day I waked again. And in my sleep it was revealed to me that not at this time, nor after this manner, should my death be. There were to be yet two years of waiting for me, while the silver seed woke to life where I had set it, even in the very heart of death.

VI

It was said in the village that my beloved had fled with a man of another race—for the two had been seen together—thus bringing shame upon her father's house. It was also said by others that the river had taken her, for she was accustomed to wash herself in the water of the river. And some said one thing and some another, but none said the truth, nor did any accuse me.

And as the tale of the months grew, I became greatly changed. No longer could the beauty of any woman move me, nor could any enterprise attract me. Had fabulous wealth been within my reach I would not have put out my hand to it. I was almost without wishes, save the wish to be alone. Never was there a guest in my house, nor the sound of music, nor laughter. Long and sweet sleep at night had left me, and I slept fitfully at strange hours, haunted always by dreams that seemed so real, that waking I scarce knew whether I was awake or slept, nor which was the substance and which the shadow.

Waking or sleeping, the thought of her whom I loved was ever present with me. I longed to call her up from death that I might tell her how nearly I had come to forgiveness, and how slight a thing in the end had driven me to madness. It grieved me that she would never know that. There was no longer any jealousy or rancour in my heart towards her. She had been ever as she had said, as thistledown caught in the wind of destiny.

After the first year of waiting, I sometimes saw her as I walked in my garden in the cool of the evening. She came and vanished again, like smoke scattered by the wind. And as the second year drew on, the vision came more frequently and remained longer with me. Even I heard her speak. She stood beneath my orange-tree, and she opened her robe wide and pointed to the wound in her breast.

"You have hurt me," she said. "How could you hurt her whom you loved?"

And at last the day came when the tree of death should rise to twice the height of a man, and should drink my blood, and should die again, and all betwixt a sunrise and a sunset.

The sun was not fully risen when I examined the earth over her grave. None other but myself was permitted to come into that part of the garden, and it was with my own hands that I had kept it free of all chance growth. And I saw now that there were in the earth crevices like the picture of the sun's rays, and through the centres of these something hard pushed its way. It was rounded at the top, and it was dark green and crimson intermingled, and on the surface of it were little drops of moisture as though it sweated with the struggle to get through.

Then I went back through the empty garden to the empty house, for on the day before I had sent forth those that waited on me. And I bathed myself and put on a white robe, and then I saw to it that the doors were securely locked, and came back to the tree of death. It had risen now to the height of my knee, and it was still a single shaft tapering upwards, and it seemed to me that a light vapour came from it. And sitting down I watched this great miracle.

When it was the height of a man many stems separated themselves from the main stem, save at the base where they were joined to it, and these lolled outwards and grew no more. But from these side stems a shower of tendrils began to descend, writhing in the air as if they had been serpents. And looking closely I saw that each of them was covered with little mouths that opened and shut continuously. But the centre stem grew upwards tapering still, but carrying at the summit a curious mass. This increased in size, and I knew that from it would come the flower of the tree.

It was the hour of noon. I withdrew myself a little and still watched. From the side stems the rain of tendrils descended continuously, and they covered the ground so that over the place where I had laid her there was a moving sea of green and crimson. And shortly after noon the heavy mass at the head of the stem separated into three pods; the skin of them was like clear, thin silk, and they had veins like the veins of a man. I could see them swelling more and more, and that something white seemed to be struggling within them, and the top of the stem rocked to and fro a little as if in agony.

So far all had gone on in silence. But suddenly the skin of one of those pods was rent from end to end, and in the rending it made a sound like a woman that is hurt. From the burst pod there leapt a white flower of gorgeous beauty, greater than I have ever seen, and from the flower there fell a cloud of gold dust, sparkling in the sunlight, and the perfume of it, even at the distance where I stood, was of almost intolerable richness.

Then I cried aloud the words that came to me:

"O tree of love!" I cried. "You whose roots have devoured and taken into your being all that I have loved on earth, now take me also, that at the last we may be mingled together, and after the anguish and evil of life there may be peace. O tree of love and death, I come to you!"

And I went forward slowly and knelt beside the tree, looking upwards. And twice I heard that cry as of a woman that is hurt as the second and third flower burst forth. The clouds of gold dust blinded my eyes, and the heavy scent suffocated me. I fell at full length among those ramping tendrils whose little mouths sought my blood. And the last sleep came.

I have written this, I who have been long dead, so that my bones are dust and for countless years my name has been forgotten. And I have written in a strange language and in a strange land, and by the living hand of one whom I know not.

Not on the Passenger-List

I had not slept. It may have been the noise which prevented me. The entire ship groaned, creaked, screamed, and sobbed. In the staterooms near mine the flooring was being torn up, and somebody was busy with a very blunt saw just over my head—at least it sounded like that. The motion, too, was not favourable for sleep. There was nothing but strong personal magnetism to keep me in my bunk. If I had relaxed it for a moment I should have fallen out.

Then the big trunk under my berth began to be busy, and I switched on the light to look at it. In a slow and portly way it began to lollop across the floor towards the door. It was trying to get out of the ship, and I never blamed it. But before it could reach the door a suit-case dashed out from under the couch and kicked it in the stomach. I switched off the light again, and let them fight it out in the dark.

I recalled that an elderly pessimist in the smoking-room the night before had expressed his belief that we were overloaded and that if the ship met any heavy weather she'd break in two for sure. And then I was playing chess with a fat negress who said she was only black when she was playing the black pieces; but in the middle of it somebody knocked and said that my bath was ready.

The last part turned out to be true. My bath was even more than ready, it was impatient; as I entered the bathroom the water jumped out to meet me and did so. Then, when the bath and I had finished with each other, my steward came slanting down the passage, at an angle of thirty degrees to the floor, without spilling my morning tea, and said that the weather was improving.

There were very few early risers at breakfast that morning, but I was not the first. Mrs. Derrison was coming out as I entered the saloon. I thought she looked ill, but it was not particularly surprising. We said good-morning, and then she hesitated for a moment.

"I want to speak to you," she said. "Do you mind? Not now. Come up on deck when you've finished breakfast."

She was not an experienced traveller, and had already consulted me about various small matters. I supposed she wanted to know what was the right tip for a stewardess or something of that kind. Accordingly, after breakfast I went up, and found her wrapped in furs—very expensive furs—in her deck-chair. I could see now that she was not in the least sea-sick, but she said she had not slept all night. I moved her chair into a better position, and chatted as I wrapped the rug round her. I confessed that with the exception of an hour's nightmare about a fat negress I also had not slept. As a rule, she would have smiled at this, for she smiled easily and readily. But now she stared out over the sea as if she had heard the words without understanding them. She was a woman of thirty-four or thirty-five, I should think, and had what is generally called an interesting face. You noticed her eyes particularly.

"Well," I said, "the wind's dropping, and we shall all sleep better to-night. Look, there's the sun coming out at last. And now, what's the trouble? What can I do for you?"

"I don't think that even you can help," she said drearily, "though you've done lots of kind things for me. Still, I've got to tell somebody. I simply can't stand it alone. Oh, if I were only the captain of this ship!"

"I don't think you'd like it! Why, what would you do?"

"Turn round and go back to New York."

"It couldn't be done. The ship doesn't carry enough coal. And we shall be at Liverpool the morning after next. But why? What's the matter?"

She held out one hand in the sunlight. It looked very small and transparent. It shook.

"The matter is that I'm frightened. I'm simply frightened out of my life."

I looked hard at her. There was no doubt about it. She was a badly frightened woman. I resisted an impulse to pat her on the shoulder.

"But really, Mrs. Derrison, if you'll forgive me for saying so, this is absolute nonsense. The boat's slower than she ought to be, and I'll admit that she rolls pretty badly, but she's as safe as a church all the same."

"Yes, I know. In any case, that is not the kind of thing that would frighten me. This is something quite different. And when I have told you it, you will probably think that I am insane."

"No," I said, "I shall not think that."

"Very well. I told you that I was a widow. I wear no mourning, and I did not tell you that Alec, my husband, died only three months ago. Nor did I tell you, which is also the truth, that I am going to England in order to marry another man."

"I understand all that. Go on."

"Alec died three months ago. But he is on this boat. I saw him last night. I think he has come for me."

She made that amazing statement quietly and without excitement. But you cannot tell a ghost-story convincingly to a man who is sitting in the sun at half-past nine in the morning. I neither doubted her sincerity nor her sanity. I merely wondered how the illusion had been produced.

"Well," I said, "you know that's quite impossible, don't you?"

"Yesterday, I should have said so."

"So you will to-morrow. Tell me how it happened, and I will tell you the explanation."

"I went to my room at eleven last night. The door was a little way open—fixed by that hook arrangement—the way I generally leave it. I switched on the light and went in. He was sitting on the berth with his legs dangling, his profile towards me. The light shone on the bald place on his head. He wore blue pyjamas and red slippers—the kind that he always wore. The pocket of the coat was weighed down, and I remembered what he had told me—that when he was travelling he put his watch, money, and keys there at night. He turned his head towards me. It came round very slowly, as if with an effort. That was strange, because so far I had been startled and surprised but not frightened. When the head turned round I became really frightened. You see, it was Alec—and yet it was not."

"I don't think I understand. How do you mean?"

"Well, it was like him—a roundish face, clean-shaven, heavily lined—he was fifteen years older than I was—with his very heavy eyebrows and his ridiculously small mouth. His mouth was really abnormal. But the whole thing looked as if it had been modelled out of wax and painted. And, then, when a head turns towards you, you expect the eyes to look at you. These did not. They remained with the lids half down—very much as I remembered him after the doctors had gone. Oh, I was frightened! I fumbled with one hand behind me, trying to find the bell-push. And yet I could not help speaking out loud. I said: 'What does this mean, Alec?' Just then I got my finger on the bell-push. He knew I had rung—I could see that. His lips kept opening and shutting as if he were trying hard to speak. When the voice came at last, it was only a whisper. He said: 'I want you!' when the stewardess tapped at the door, and I did not see him any more."

"Did you tell the stewardess?"

"Oh, no! I did not mean to tell anybody then. I pretended to be nervous about the ship rolling too much, and managed to keep her with me for a long time. She offered to fetch the doctor for me, so that I could ask him for a sleeping-draught, but I wouldn't have that."

"Why not?"

"I was afraid to go to sleep. I wanted to be ready in case—in case it happened again. You see, I knew why it was."

"I don't think you did, Mrs. Derrison. But I will tell you why it was, if you like. The explanation is very simple and also very prosaic."

"What is it?"

"The cause of the illusion was merely sea-sickness."

"But I've not felt ill at all."

"Very likely not. If you had been ill in the ordinary way, the way in which it has taken a good many of our friends, you would never have had the illusion. Brain and stomach act and react on one another. The motion of the boat, too, is particularly trying to the optic nerves. In some cases, not very common perhaps, but quite well-known and recognized—it is the brain and not the other organ which is temporarily affected."

I do not know anything about it really, and had merely invented the sea-sickness theory on the spur of the moment. It was necessary to think of something plausible and very commonplace. Mrs. Derrison was suffering a good deal, and I had to stop it.

"If I could only think that," she said, "what a comfort it would be!"

"Whether you believe it or not, it's the truth," I said. "I've known a similar case. It won't happen to you again, because the weather's getting better, and so you won't be ill."

She wanted to know all about the "similar case," and I made up a convincing little story about it. Gradually she began to be reassured.

"I wish I had known about it before," she said. "All last night I sat in my room, with the light turned on, getting more and more frightened. I don't think there's anything hurts one so much as fear. I can understand people being driven mad by it. You see, I had a special reason to be afraid, because Alec was jealous, very jealous. He had even, I suppose, some grounds for jealousy."

She began to tell me her story. She had married Alec Derrison nine years before. She liked him at that time, but she did not love him, and she told him so. He said that it did not matter, and that in time she would come to love him. I dare say a good many marriages that begin in that way turn out happily, but this marriage was a mistake.

He took her to his house in New York, and there they lived for a year without actual disaster. He was very kind to her, and she was touched by his kindness. She had been quite poor, and she now had plenty of money to spend, and liked it. But it became clear to her in that year not only that she did not love her husband but that she never would love him. And she was, I could believe, a rather romantic and temperamental kind of woman, by whom many men were greatly attracted. Alec Derrison began to be very jealous—at that time quite absurdly and without reason.

At the end of the year Derrison took her to Europe for a holiday. And there, in England, in her father's country rectory, she met the man whom she ought to have married—an artist of the same age as herself. The two fell desperately in love with one another. The man wanted to take her away with him and ultimately to marry her. She refused.

There is a curious mixture of conscience and temperament which is sometimes mistaken for cowardice, and is often accompanied by extraordinary courage. She went to her husband and, so to speak, put her cards down on the table. "I love another man," she said. "I love him in the way in which I wished to love you but cannot. I did not want this and I did not look for it, but it has happened to me. I am sorry it has happened, but I do not ask you to forgive me, for you have nothing to forgive. I want to know what you mean to do."

His answer was to take her straight back to New York. There for the eight years before he died he treated her with kindness and gave her every luxury, but all the time he had her watched. Traps were laid for her, but in vain. He had for business reasons to go to England every year, but he never took her with him. When he was away, two of his sisters came to the house and watched for him.

And yet, because in some things a woman is cleverer than a man, and also because the feminine conscience always has its limitations, during the whole of those eight years she corresponded regularly with the other man without being found out. They never met, but she had his letters. And now she was going back to marry him.

It was, perhaps, a little curious that she should tell all this to a man whom she had known only for a few days. But intimacies grow quickly on board ship, and besides she wanted to explain her terror.

"You see how it was," she said. "If a dead man could come back again, then certainly he would come back. And when one begins to be frightened the fear grows and grows. One thinks of things. For instance, he crossed more than once in this very boat—I thought of that."

"Well, Mrs. Derrison," I said, "the dead cannot and do not come back. But a disordered interior does sometimes produce an optical illusion. That's all there is to it. However, if you like, I'll go to the purser and get your room changed for another; I can manage that all right."

It was not a very wise suggestion, and she refused it. She said that it would be like admitting that there was something in it beyond sea-sickness.

"Good!" I said. "I think you're quite right. I thought it might ease your mind not to see again the room where you were frightened, but it is much better to be firm about it. In fact, you had better take a cup of soup and then go back to your room now, and get an hour's sleep before lunch."

"I wonder if I could."

"Of course you can. You're getting your colour back, and there's much less motion on the boat. You won't have another attack. You've had a sort of suppressed form of sea-sickness, that's all. And I can quite understand that it scared you at the time, when you didn't know; but there's no reason why it should scare you now when you do know."

She took my advice. A woman will generally take advice from any man except her husband—because he's the only man she really knows. She was disproportionately grateful. Gratitude is rare, but, when found, it is in very large streaks. She had also decided to believe that I knew everything, could do everything, and had other admirable qualities. When a woman decides to believe, facts do not hamper her.

She was much better at lunch and afterwards. Next day she was apparently normal, and was taking part in the usual deck-games. I began to think that my sea-sickness theory might have been a lucky shot. I consulted the ship's doctor about it, without giving him names or details, but he was very non-committal. He was a general practitioner, of course, and I was taking him into the specialist regions. Besides, naturally enough, a doctor does not care to talk his own shop with a layman. He gave me an impression that any conclusions to which I came would necessarily be wrong. But it did not worry me much. I did not see a great deal of Mrs. Derrison, but it was quite obvious that she had recovered her normal health and spirits. I believed that the trouble was over.

But it was not.

On the night before we arrived, after the smoking-room had been closed, old Bartlett asked me to come to his rooms for a chat and a whisky-and-soda. The old man slept badly, and was inclined to a late sitting. We discussed various subjects, and amongst them memory for faces.

"I've got that memory," he said. "Names bother me, but not faces. For instance, I remember the faces of the seventy or eighty in the first-class here."

"I thought we were more than that."

"No. People don't cross the Atlantic for fun in February. It's a pretty light list. It's a funny thing, too—we've got one man on board who's never showed up at all. I saw him for the first time this morning—to be accurate, yesterday morning—coming from the bath, and I've not seen him since. He must have been hiding in his state-room all the time."

"Ill, probably."

"No, not ill. I asked the doctor. I suppose he don't enjoy the society of his fellow-men for some reason or other."

"Well, now," I said, "let's test your memory. What was he like?"

"You've given me an easy one as it happens, for he was rather a curious chap to look at, and easy to remember in consequence. A man in the fifties, I should say; medium height; wore blue pyjamas with a gold watch-chain trickling out of the pocket, and those red slippers that you buy in Cairo. But his face was what I noticed particularly. He's got a one-inch mouth—smallest mouth I ever saw on a man. But the whole look on his face was queer, just as if it had been painted and then varnished.

"He was bald, round-faced, wrinkled, and clean-shaven. He walked very slowly, and he looked as if he were worried out of his life. There's the portrait, and you can check it when we get off the boat—you're bound to see him then."

"Yes, you've a good memory. If I had just passed a man in a passage, I shouldn't have remembered a thing about him ten minutes afterwards. By the way, have you spoken about the hermit passenger to anybody else?"

"No. Oh, yes, I did mention it to some of the ladies after dinner! Why?"

"I wondered if anybody besides yourself had seen him."

"Well, they didn't say they had. Bless you, I've known men like that. It's a sort of sulkiness. They'd sooner be alone."

A few minutes later I said good-night and left him. It was between one and two in the morning. His story had made a strong impression upon me. My theory of sea-sickness had to go, and I was scared. Quite frankly, I was afraid of meeting something in blue pyjamas. But I was more afraid about Mrs. Derrison. There were very few ladies on board, and it was almost certain she was in the group to whom Bartlett had told his story. If that were so, anything might have happened. I decided to go past her state-room, listening as I did so.

But before I reached her room the door opened, and she swung out in her nightdress. She had got her mouth open and one hand at her throat. With the other hand she clutched the handle of the door, as if she were trying to hold it shut against somebody. I hurried towards her, and she turned and saw me. In an instant she was in my arms, clinging to me in sheer mad, helpless terror.

She was hysterical, of course, but fortunately she did not make much noise. She kept saying: "I've got to go back to him—into the sea!" It seemed a long time before I could get her calm enough to listen to me.

"You've had a bad dream, and it has frightened you, poor child."

"No, no. Not a dream!"

"It didn't seem like one to you, but that's what it was. You're all right now. I'm going to take care of you."

"Don't let go of me for a moment. He wants me. He's in there."

"Oh, no! I'll show you that he's not there."

I opened the door. Within all was darkness. I still kept one arm round her, or she would have fallen.

"I left the light on," she whispered.

"Yes," I said, "but your sleeve caught the switch as you came out. I saw it." It was a lie, of course, but one had to lie.

I switched the light on again. The room was empty. There were the tumbled bed-clothes on the berth, and a pillow had fallen to the floor. On the table some toilet things gleamed brightly. There was a pile of feminine garments on the couch. I drew her in and closed the door.

"I'll put you back into bed again," I said, "if you don't mind."

"If you'll promise not to go."

"Oh, I won't go!"

I picked her up and laid her on the berth, and drew the clothes over her. I put the pillow back under her head. With both her hands she clutched one of mine.

"Now, then," I said, "do you happen to have any brandy here?"

"In a flask in my dressing-bag. It's been there for years. I don't know if it's any good still."

She seemed reluctant to let go my hand, and clutched it again eagerly when I brought the brandy. She was quite docile, and drank as I told her. I have not put down half of what she said. She was muttering the whole time. The phrase "into the sea" occurred frequently. All ordinary notions of the relationship of a man and a woman had vanished. I was simply a big brother who was looking after her. That was felt by both of us. We called each other "dear" that night frequently, but there was not a trace of sex-sentimentality between us.

Gradually she became more quiet, and I was no longer afraid that she would faint. Still holding my hand, she said:

"Shall I tell you what it was?"

"Yes, dear, if you like. But you needn't. It was only a dream, you know."

"I don't think it was a dream. I went to sleep, which I had never expected to do after the thing that Mr. Bartlett told us. I couldn't have done it, only I argued that you must be right and the rest must be just a coincidence. Then I was awakened by the sound of somebody breathing close by my ear. It got further away, and I switched on the light quickly. He was standing just there—exactly as I described him to you—and he had picked up a pair of nail-scissors. He was opening and shutting them. Then he put them down open, and shook his head. (Look, they're open now, and I always close them.) And suddenly he lurched over, almost falling, and clutched the wooden edge of the berth. His red hands—they were terribly red, far redder than they used to be—came on to the wood with a slap. 'Go into the sea, Sheila,' he whispered. 'I'm waiting. I want you.' And after that I don't know what happened, but suddenly I was hanging on to you, dear. How long was it ago? Was it an hour? It doesn't matter. I'm safe while you're here."

I released her hands gently. Suddenly the paroxysm of terror returned.

"You're not going?" she cried, aghast.

"Of course not." I sat down on the couch opposite her. "But what makes you think you're safe while I'm here?"

"You're stronger than he is," she said.

She said it as if it were a self-evident fact which did not admit of argument. Certainly, though no doubt unreasonably, it gave me confidence. I felt somehow that he and I were fighting for the woman's life and soul, and I had got him down. I knew that in some mysterious way I was the stronger.

"Well," I said, "the dream that one is awake is a fairly common dream. But what was the thing that Bartlett told you?"

"He saw him—in blue pyjamas and red slippers. He mentioned the mouth too."

"I'm glad you told me that," I said, and began a few useful inventions. "The man that Bartlett saw was Curwen. We've just been talking about it."

"Who's Curwen?"

"Not a bad chap—an electrical engineer, I believe. As soon as Bartlett mentioned the mole on the cheek and the little black moustache I spotted that it was Curwen."

"But he said he had never seen him before."

"Nor had he. Curwen's a bad sailor and has kept to his state-room—in fact, that was his first public appearance. But I saw Curwen when he came on board and had a talk with him. As soon as Barlett mentioned the mole, I knew who it was."

"Then the colour of the slippers and—"

"They were merely a coincidence, and a mighty unlucky one for you."

"I see," she said. Her muscles relaxed. She gave a little sigh of relief and sank back on the pillow. I was glad that I had invented Curwen and the mole.

I changed the subject now, and began to talk about Liverpool—not so many miles away now. I asked her if she had changed her American money yet. I spoke about the customs, and confessed to some successful smuggling that I had once done. In fact, I talked about anything that might take her mind away from her panic. Then I said:

"If you will give me about ten seconds start now, so that I can get back to my own room, you might ring for your stewardess to come and take care of you. It will mean an extra tip for her, and she won't mind."

"Yes," she said, "I ought not to keep you any longer. Indeed, it is very kind of you to have helped me and to have stayed so long. I'll never forget it. But even now I daren't be alone for a moment. Will you wait until she's actually here?"

I was not ready for that.

"Well," I said hesitatingly.

"Of course," she said. "I hadn't thought of it. I can't keep you. You've had no sleep at all. And yet if you go, he'll— Oh, what am I to do? What am I to do?"

I was afraid she would begin to cry.

"That's all right," I said. "I can stay for another hour or two easily enough."

She was full of gratitude. She told me to throw the things off the end of the couch so that I could lie at full length. I dozed for a while, but I do not think she slept at all. She was wide awake when I opened my eyes. I talked to her for a little, and found her much reassured and calmed. People were beginning to move about. It was necessary for me to go immediately if I was not to be seen.

She agreed at once. When I shook hands with her, and told her to try for an hour's sleep, she kissed my hand fervently in a childish sort of way. Frightened people behave rather like children.

I was not seen as I came from her room. The luck was with me. It is just possible that on the other side of the ship, a steward saw me enter my own room in evening clothes at a little after five. If he did, it did not matter.

I have had the most grateful and kindly letters from her and from her new husband—the cheery and handsome man who met her at Liverpool. In her letter she speaks of her "awful nightmare, that even now it seems sometimes as if it must have been real." She has sent me a cigarette-case that I am afraid I cannot use publicly. A gold cigarette-case with a diamond push-button would give a wrong impression of my income, and the inscription inside might easily be misunderstood. But I like to have it.

Thanks to my innocent mendacity, she has a theory which covers the whole ground. But I myself have no theory at all. I know this—that I might travel to New York by that same boat to-morrow, and that I am waiting three days for another.

I have suppressed the name of the boat, and I think I have said nothing by which she could be identified. I do not want to spoil business. Besides, it may be funk and superstition that convinces me that on every trip she carries a passenger whose name is not on the list. But, for all that, I *am* quite convinced!

The Reaction

Ernest Purdon had served his apprenticeship, passed his examinations with a little luck and not much margin, and was qualified to dispense medicines. He was now an assistant at one of Myer and Co.'s myriad shops. This particular shop was in Dunnivan Road, Whitechapel. It was not a sweet neighbourhood, and hardly a day passed when Mr. Purdon was not asked to do something absolutely illegal. Such a proposal never even tempted him. He flicked the dirty, folded note back across the counter, and told the man or woman to go away. He had a conscience. Why, he went to church every Sunday morning with Ethel and her mother.

During business hours he was pontifical and impressive. He wore a fairly good black coat, and his hands were very white. He took care of his finger-nails, and his signet-ring was genuine. He was under thirty, but when he assumed his gilt-rimmed pince-nez you felt at once that he had only to look into it. He even had a local reputation. Clumsy, ill-dressed men, earning more money than our Mr. Purdon ever did or could, lumbered up from the docks and addressed him with great respect. John Mace, ship's steward, was a walking testimonial.

"You go up to Myer's in Dunnivan Road," he would say, "and get a fair-haired bloke with eyeglasses. Can't miss him. He knows. Cured my leg. Took a pal of mine and sobered him up, so that he was fit to go aboard, in about record. Beats the doctors, to my mind."

It had been Mace himself and not a pal of his whom Mr. Purdon, fear and suggestion concurring, had sobered with such rapidity. But Mace was not a pedantically accurate man in any respect.

Out of business hours Ernest Purdon was much less pontifical and impressive. Myer and Co. did not overpay their assistants. Purdon lived at a cheap boarding-house, run by an experienced, iron-faced lady who had worked out to a small fraction what was the least she could possibly give for the money she took, and never gave more. The food was of the worst quality, the rooms were not clean. Purdon had a well-founded suspicion that five mornings out of six his bed was not made but merely camouflaged. But still it was cheap. Purdon, who had no expensive vices, managed to put by a very little money. Also, though he did not know it, he was heartily afraid of the iron-faced lady. He would not have dared to say that he was dissatisfied. He had once ventured to complain that the window of his bedroom would not remain closed.

"You surprise me," said Mrs. Bowes. "I should have thought that if there was one gentleman in my house to appreciate the value of fresh air, it would have been you, Mr. Purdon, being practically on the borders of the medical profession."

He gave up. But the nights in November were cold, and he made a device of his own with a piece of stout wire to keep that window closed.

He had been engaged to Ethel nearly a year. Sometimes he wondered if he were really engaged to Ethel, or to Ethel and her mother, for they were inseparable. He was well aware that Ethel was much more attached to her mother than she was to him. The mother, Mrs. Ratton, with Ethel's help ran a stationer's shop in Hampstead, which she had inherited from her deceased husband. They lived over the shop and did fairly well out of it. Every Sunday Ernest Purdon called for them, went to the morning service with them, and returned to their home for the midday meal. When it was finished, the same conversation nearly always took place, the responses coming with much the same regularity as the responses in church.

Purdon said: "Matter of fact, this is the only decent meal I get in the week."

Mrs. Ratton said: "If not comfortable where you are, why not change?"

Ethel said: "That's what I always tell him."

And finally Purdon said: "Oh, well, you never know."

Once a month he took Ethel and her mother to the theatre. They always chose the piece, and he found to some dissatisfaction that it was only too often Shakespeare. He had once ventured to suggest that he should take Ethel alone.

"Why," said Ethel brightly, "what has poor Mamma done?"

And Purdon protested lamely that of course he had taken it for granted that poor Mamma would come too. She did.

Purdon found life dull, but was not very discontented. It was of no use to cry for the moon, and if he lost Ethel he might not get another. He recognized that he was not popular with the ladies—not like his friend Harry Bates. Bates was a man of good appearance and manner, knew how to talk, and was sometimes dryly humorous. He was in the same profession as Purdon and no better qualified. But he was making considerably more money. Bates was not employed by Myer and Co., but by a man who kept a very well-known and very discreet druggist's shop in Mayfair. Wealthy young men, suffering from the night before, consulted Bates, took what he gave them, and were not ungenerous. Some of Bates's caustic sayings were quoted in the West End clubs. Well, Bates had promised that if ever he saw an opening, he would give his friend Purdon a lift. That might happen at any time—it had not happened yet.

II

It was growing dark on a November afternoon, and the lights in Myer's shop in Dunnivan Road were already lit. John Mace peered in. At the moment, Ernest Purdon was talking to an old woman with a shawl over her head. He held a phial of tablets in his hand. The old woman spoke of a sense of tightness in the chest, and Purdon tapped his own chest with his white fingers sympathetically. He quite understood. Then he tapped the phial. Two of those before each meal would probably remove the inconvenience. She purchased the phial and left the shop. Mace entered at once.

"Back again, Mr. Mace," said Purdon genially.

"Yes, sir. Got in the day before yesterday. There was a little thing I wanted to see you about."

"Well, well, what's the trouble?"

"It's not trouble exactly," said Mace, pulling out a bulky pocket-book and taking from it a small package in oiled paper. "It's this sample. I don't know what it is, and I want to know. I was wondering if you could tell me."

"We're pharmaceutical chemists here," said Purdon, "not analytical. If you want to know just what this stuff is, you'll have to take it to an analytical chemist, and I may as well warn you that you may have to pay a pretty stiff fee for it."

"I don't want to go anything beyond five shillings," said Mace. "I've reason to know that you're a good deal cleverer than the usual, Mr. Purdon. I've no doubt if you cared to take that home with you, you could tell me something about it by to-morrow evening. I don't say everything. I only want a general idea. Because I've reason to believe it might be pretty good."

"How do you mean? Where did you get it from?"

"Got it from a negro who died of pneumonia this trip and was buried at sea. He wasn't the ordinary sort. Mr. E. Matthews he was on the passenger-list, and letters after his name. An educated man I should say, and got money. Travelling in the first-class, he was. There weren't a lot of people wanted to talk to him, and he talked to me. Showed me this powder, and said he was going to make a fortune with it. That was all I could get out of him, and he was taken ill next day. If you'll take that home with you and look into it, I'll go to five shillings and chance it. You might find out something, or you might not."

"Very good," said Purdon, and slipped the little packet into his waistcoat-pocket. "See you to-morrow evening."

When he got back to the boarding-house he went to his bedroom and hung his overcoat and hat behind the door. He might have hung them up downstairs, but the boarding-house was one in which mistakes frequently happened, and Purdon was taking no risks. He took off his black business coat, brushed it and hung it in the wardrobe, and put on a light jacket. Then he took from his pocket the little packet which Mace had given him, and opened it. It contained a brown powder which was not of a regular consistency. Some of it was the finest dust, and some of it was much coarser, and there were even little unbroken lumps in it. The smell of it was terrific and unrecognizable. He had not the slightest notion what the stuff was. He tried a couple of simple tests, in order that he might have something to talk to Mace about. He found that the powder was easily soluble in water, and that it was alkaline. The whole thing did not take him five minutes.

He did not propose to investigate any farther. The stuff simply stank, and he wanted to get it out of his small bedroom. Even when it was gone he would have to leave the window open for half an hour before the place was fit to sleep in. The window looked out at the back of the house, over a small blackened yard that Mrs. Bowes called a garden. Purdon picked up the paper with the remainder of the powder, intending to throw it out of the window.

And then accident came in. As Purdon tried to undo that wire device of his which kept the window shut, he scratched the thumb of his left hand deeply, so that the blood came. And as he pushed the window open, a gust of wind blew a little of the fine powder over his bleeding thumb.

"Damn!" said Purdon. He went to his washstand and washed his thumb carefully. He heard the church clock outside strike eight. Then his eyes grew dark and his head swam. He groped his way to his bed and flung himself on it. And there for an hour he lay unconscious of his actual surroundings.

And in that hour he lived a whole year of the most perfect happiness.

It was nine o'clock when he became aware that he was lying on his bed in his own sordid room at the top of the boarding-house. But for a minute or two a thought persisted that he must have been unconscious for a year. Then he reflected that, if that had been so, he would have been found in his room, and would have been removed. He pulled out his watch; it was still going. He could only have been there an hour. It was marvellous, that time extension. In that one hour he had been through the countless incidents of a wonderful year—a year in which quiet bliss and triumphant ecstasy had alternated.

At a quarter-past nine Purdon saw it all, and began to be frightened. That brown powder was dope, and the accident to his thumb had practically given him a hypodermic injection of it. There was no dope like it in the world. Any man would spend his last penny—would five his soul—for a year such as Purdon had just been through.

But Purdon had never taken any form of dope before and, in his profession, he had seen something of it, and of the ghastly effects of it. That very day a little, shivering old lady with untidy hair had come into the shop with a prescription that was obviously and preposterously bogus, and had burst out crying when Purdon had tossed it back to her and told her not to come there again unless she wanted to be handed over to the police. Dope was appalling. Even now, with the memory of that great year still vivid in him, he had not the slightest inclination to renew the experiment. He could not have renewed it. He had no more of the drug in his possession.

Perhaps a man who has by accident taken a hypodermic injection of uncertain strength, of an unknown and potent drug, may be pardoned for feeling nervous. Purdon felt nervous. He did not know what the stuff might do to him. He might be taken ill in the night. Locked up in his room he had an ordinary eight-ounce medicine bottle filled with brandy. He kept it for emergencies, and had had it for two years. He got it out now and put it on the table by his bedside. He undressed quickly and got into bed. He did not suppose he would be able to sleep. Even if he did, he felt sure that he would awake on the following morning with a splitting head and tremulous nerves, possibly even unable to go to business. And that would not do him any good with Myer and Co.

He fell asleep almost immediately and slept quite peacefully till seven on the following morning. He had no headache at all. He took his pulse and temperature and found them normal. If anything, he felt better than usual. It was almost as though some of the happiness and confidence of that wonderful dream-year still lingered in him. His recollections of the dream-year had grown very vague. He could recall that several beautiful women had been very much in love with him, that men had respected him, that crowds had cheered him, that he had done many things exceedingly well which in real life he could never have done at all. But the picture was blurred. The very effort of trying to recall it seemed to make it more indistinct.

He went downstairs with a very good appetite for a very bad breakfast. It was in the train on his way to business that the great idea came to him. He must get the rest of that drug away from Mace. The negro had been quite right—there was money in it.

III

Throughout the day Purdon kept a very close eye upon himself. He took his pulse and temperature frequently. He could find no departure from the normal at all. He had never been better. He did his work well and easily. And all through the day that scheme grew rapidly in his mind. He was going to get the stuff away from Mace. At any rate, he was going to get some of it. Enough for his purpose.

It was shortly after six that Mace came in.

"Well, sir," said Mace eagerly. "Got any news for me? Spotted what it is?"

"Well," said Mr. Purdon, "there's not been much time. For that matter, you didn't give me nearly a big enough sample for a proper analysis. Still, I can tell you something. The stuff's in a very crude state, and full of impurities."

"Full of—?" suggested Mace.

"Impurities. Dirt. That would have to be put right before it could be used. The thing is a gum-resin—like gamboge or asafœtida, you know." (Purdon had not done much in the way of analysis, but he had done enough to show him that the stuff was not a resin.) "How many hundredweight of it have you got?"

"Hundredweights? Didn't I tell you? He carried it about with him in his hip-pocket. He'd got it in an old half-pound, flat tobacco tin. There's just over six ounces of it. What would that be worth?"

"In its present state, probably nothing. If it had been properly manufactured, it might have been worth a shilling or two. But you would never find a buyer."

"Then what did the nigger mean by telling me he was going to make a fortune with it?"

Purdon laughed.

"Well, your friend was a sick man, and may have been light-headed. Besides, what does a nigger know?"

"But I told you he was an educated man. Letters after his name."

"There are quite a number of people who have letters after their name, to which they are not entitled. I've known it happen in my own profession. Besides, all these niggers are superstitious. If you want me to tell you what I really think, it looks to me as if it were some kind of a crazy charm that he was carrying for luck. Not that it seems to have brought him much. But what made him give it to you?"

Mace appeared slightly embarrassed.

"Between ourselves, he didn't give it to me. I took a fancy to it. I wouldn't touch his money or jewellery. I never do. But a little thing like this that would never be missed, that's different. I expect you're right about it. The stuff's no good to me now I've got it. Worse than no good, because I've got to settle with you. What do I owe you?"

"Look here," said Purdon. "As a chemist, I don't like to be beaten. If you'll hand over the tin to me, that will give me enough to make a complete analysis, though in any case a crude gum-resin like that wouldn't be worth much. If you like to hand it over, I'll charge you nothing for my time and the drugs I've used so far, and I'll slip you a couple of shillings for yourself. You'll get a drink out of it anyway."

"Suppose I can't do better," said Mace hesitatingly.

"I know you can't," said Mr. Purdon lightly. "But if you like to try, I'm not stopping you."

"All right," said Mace, and drew the tin from his pocket and pushed it across the counter.

Mr. Purdon opened the lid and glanced at the contents. "Two shillings," he said, and dropped them into Mace's hand. "Good evening, and don't forget to drink my health."

Outside in the street, Mace paused and looked back into the shop. He saw Purdon take up the tin, wrap it in paper, and put it in the pocket of his overcoat, which hung behind the screen. Mace did not like the expression on Purdon's face. As he walked slowly away, the truth dawned on him. That blighter in the black coat had done him.

Why, there could not be a doubt of it. Purdon had wanted the stuff for himself. Chemists' assistants had no money to burn. Purdon didn't throw away two shillings on buying a little puzzle for his amusement. Oh, no, not in this life. Purdon knew all about it. He said he didn't, but he did. Why, you only had to see his face as he put the tin in his pocket. That nigger knew what he was talking about. There was money in it, and Purdon had found out where the money was.

Mace turned into the aristocratic seclusion of the private bar of a public-house. He ordered a drink and thought things over. Purdon had got the stuff now, but Purdon left his shop at seven, and Mace was not dead yet. That clever young man might not have it all his own way. Mace himself was clever enough in one or two little things.

Meanwhile Purdon's scheme went on rapidly. It seemed one dose of this new drug produced no bad after-effects at all. No doubt if the dose were repeated many times it might be injurious. Indeed, Purdon felt sure that it must be. But that drug would never go out of his own possession. It would be for him to say how many doses a customer might have. There was nothing illegal about it, for the law did not even know of the existence of such a drug. There was nothing even immoral about it. Purdon meant to do no harm. He would sooner sacrifice some of his profits than do any harm. All the same, the profits would be enormous. Ethel and her mother would be surprised. They would not have to be told everything, of course. Ethel's mother would be certain to ask questions. He would not tell her to mind her own business; he would simply say that in the course of chemical study and research he had come upon a discovery of commercial value, about which he was not at liberty to say more. It would make a difference. Ethel's mother had seemed at times almost patronizing. There would be an end to anything of that kind.

The first thing to do, of course, was to get into touch with Harry Bates. Through him he would be able to get just the right *clientèle*. The shop where Bates was employed had a great reputation with the big racing men and the stars of the theatrical world. Such people had money to spend and were willing to spend it. Purdon felt confident that they would have to spend it if they made but one experiment with the dope that gave you a year of paradise in an hour. Yes, as soon as he got back to his boarding-house he would write to Bates and make an appointment with him. It might not be wise to put down too much in actual writing.

At seven o'clock Purdon left the shop and made for the tube train. The crush on the platform, as usual at that hour, was terrific. As he struggled into the carriage he caught sight of Mace close beside him, and tossed him a little joke on the crowd. Once in the carriage he looked round for him again, but Mace had apparently been unable to fight his way in. And that was unlike Mace.

IV

Purdon hung up his overcoat, brushed and put away his business coat according to his usual routine, and turned to go downstairs again to write his letter to Bates.

But after all the night was not cold. It was a muggy night—unusually warm for the time of year. If he went downstairs the chances were that he would find the writing-tables all occupied. Even if he found a place, there were men and women in that boarding-house who were too much interested in other people. They found themselves accidentally in such a position that they could glance over the shoulder of the letter-writer. Purdon decided to write his letter in his own room. He took his writing-block and fountain-pen, sat down, and began as follows:

DEAR HARRY,

I want to see you to-morrow if possible. I want your help. And when I say help, I don't mean money. On the contrary, I shall be able to pay very handsomely for—

Why, some of that powder must have been spilt in the room. He could smell it. He had not noticed it when he first came in. But now there could be no mistake. It grew in intensity. He would have to open the window before he could finish the letter.

He looked up from his writing-block. Outside the church clock struck eight, and at the same time there was a rattle of a chair being moved in the room.

As he looked up he saw opposite to him a gigantic negro, wearing a light tweed suit, sitting astride a chair with his arms on the back of it, and his chin on his arms, watching Purdon intently.

For a moment Purdon was not much perturbed. Mrs. Bowes was not averse to making money from all nationalities and all colours. And this might be a boarder who had recently arrived and had mistaken his room.

"Begging your pardon," said Purdon firmly, "I think you've made a slight mistake. This is not—"

He stopped because the negro had suddenly vanished. And then, in a flash, he knew the truth. That paradise dope had its reaction. This was the beginning of the reaction.

He put down his writing-block, put his fountain-pen back in his pocket, and crossed over to the tiny looking-glass on his dressing-table. He could see that he looked ill. It seemed to him that his face had perceptibly changed. And then in the looking-glass he saw brown fingers come slowly round his throat. He felt them touch him and begin to press tightly. He made an effort and broke away. The negro in the light suit was standing opposite to him, laughing noiselessly.

Purdon decided on his line of action. The thing to do would be to lie down on his bed, close his eyes, and remain absolutely quiet until the whole thing had passed off. The only thing was that he dared not go past that negro in the light suit who stood opposite to him.

Once more the negro vanished. Now was his time.

He approached the bed, and from under it an arm shot out, and a hand gripped him by the ankle. This time he tried in vain to break away. He stood there sweating with terror.

This lasted for some seconds. And then suddenly the negro shot out from under the bed and sprang to his feet. He was not laughing now. He was breathing hard, and he looked like murder. Purdon noticed that the giant wore a double watch-chain, with a bunch of seals pendent from it, over his protuberant stomach, and that there was an enormous diamond in his emerald-green necktie. There were diamond rings, too, on the brown hands that now slowly approached Purdon. Purdon felt himself unable to move.

The hands clutched him by the waist, raised him in the air, and then hurled him forward.

He fell with a crash and did not dare to get up again. He lay there with his hands pressed tightly over his eyes, in order that he might not see anything more. And deep in his mind was the conviction that he was lost—lost for ever—lost in this world and the next. He could still hear the negro's panting breath.

Then all was still. Slowly and timidly he raised himself and looked round the room. It seemed to be quite empty. A picture had been torn from one of the walls and lay on the floor with the glass broken. He supposed he must have clutched at it as he was hurled through the air. He waited some little time before he dared to cross the room to the locked drawer in which he kept his brandy. He took the glass from his washstand, poured out the entire contents of the bottle, and drank it at a draught. If only that would steady him sufficiently he would be able to get downstairs and send somebody to fetch a doctor for him. He would have to tell the doctor everything. That could not be helped.

Again the awful stench of the drug filled the room. Sickened with it, Purdon staggered to the window and tore it open. Instantly a furry hand shot across the window ledge, a great chimpanzee lumbered into the room and crouched. Another followed, and another, and another. One of them was crouched before the door, so that there was no escape that way. They all had old, philosophical, weary expressions, and they all had their impartial eyes fixed on him.

The largest of the apes picked up a piece of the broken picture-frame, looked long at it as though he were trying to probe its secret, smelled it, broke it in two, sighed deeply, and as he scratched himself with one of the pieces fixed his eyes again on Purdon.

Purdon was backing along the edge of the table. It chanced that his hand knocked over the empty medicine-bottle.

The sound seemed suddenly to break up the melancholy calm of the chimpanzees. Their eyes became animated and angry. Their mouths twisted. One after another they put their hands on the floor, swung their bodies through their long arms, and advanced upon him.

Purdon tried to scream for help. His mouth opened wide, but no sound came. Desperate with terror, he flung the water-jug and the looking-elass at them. He picked up a chair and lashed out wildly with it till it broke in his hands. They leaped at him and got him down.

"Death—thank God!" thought Purdon.

And instantly he was sitting up and listening to Harry Bates. Harry Bates was not there. Purdon saw nobody in the room but himself, seated amid the furniture wreckage.

But the voice of Harry Bates was there—a resonant, confident bass.

"A thousand pities you didn't come to me at the very first," said Bates. "I could have warned you. I know about the stuff, and have seen two cases. Cocaine is a baby's toy to it. After one hypodermic, the reaction lasts as long as life lasts. Life doesn't last long, because suicide is inevitable. The sooner the better. No human being can stand the damned torture of it. No known drug touches it. Nothing can alleviate it. Good-bye, Ernest. The window's open. It's a seventy-foot drop. It won't take more than a few seconds."

Purdon rose and walked as a doomed man towards the open window. It chanced that he nearly slipped upon a fragment of the broken picture-frame. He staggered into the closed door of his room, and clutched at his overcoat hanging there to save himself from falling. Why, there it was. The drug itself would save him. For a time, at any rate. And he had a tin full of the stuff in the pocket of that overcoat. In a few moments he would be back again in a year of paradise. He began to search in the pockets of the overcoat. Through the open window he heard the clock strike nine.

He searched very carefully, but the tin was not there. His pocket had been picked, and Purdon knew just when it had been done. Mace had taken it. That was why Mace had never got into the train. Mace was welcome to it. Purdon had no wish ever to see the stuff again. He went to the open window and drew in deep breaths of the cold, refreshing air. He was still feeling very shaky. He had knocked himself about, and was sore and bruised, but it was nothing that could be called real suffering. The awful depression had gone. There were no more delusions and his mind seemed clear and logical. The reaction was over, and he knew it. His dream that he would make a fortune out of the drug was over too. And it did not seem to him to matter. He decided to sit down for half an hour or so and rest. After that, he would clear up his room, as best he could, and get a long night's sleep.

But now he heard voices and footsteps coming up the stairs. The loudest voice was that of Mrs. Bowes, enjoining silence on the others. Purdon could also recognize the whining voice of William, a weak old man who did the boots and knives, and looked as if all his life he had never done anything else.

There was a pause, and whispering on the landing outside the door. Then Mrs. Bowes's bony and decisive knuckles rapped twice.

"Come in," said Purdon. He recognized that the chance was coming to him to be quit of Mrs. Bowes for evermore, and he welcomed it.

Mrs. Bowes entered alone. She left the door ajar, and her reserves were marshalled outside to rush to her support if necessary. Purdon caught the suppressed giggle of a nervous maid. Mrs. Bowes looked—it was almost habitual with her—like avenging justice.

"What am I to understand by this, Mr. Purdon?" she said.

"Understand by what?" said Purdon, with a sudden calm courage.

"Pandemonium, Mr. Purdon. Ladies and gentlemen, living under my roof, saying that murder was being done upstairs. You ought to be ashamed. Look at the state of the room. Oh, look at the breakages."

"The breakages will be paid for at a fair valuation," said Purdon. "If you want to know, I have been experimenting upon myself with a potent and unknown drug—my own discovery, by the way. Men of science must make these sacrifices."

Mrs. Bowes picked up the empty medicine-bottle and sniffed at it.

"Potent and unknown drug," said Mrs. Bowes sardonically. "Not so very unknown. I could put a name to it. Just what I expected. Well, this is a respectable house, and—"

"You had better be careful, Mrs. Bowes. If you dare to imply—"

"Oh, I'll tell you what I imply fast enough. I imply that I'm giving you notice to quit this house at the end of your week."

"That all?" said Purdon. "I've been thinking for weeks past that the place was a bit low class for me. Of course I'll go. Let me remind you that the law knows how to deal with slander. And now, Mrs. Bowes, I should be obliged if you would get out of my room."

"Nothing but my strong sense of duty could ever have induced me to enter it," said Mrs. Bowes, and retired in good order.

Purdon was pleased. The right words had come slick to the tip of his tongue. He had told that old girl off properly. He wondered a little how he had done it. He need not have wondered. Reaction also has its reaction. Sudden cessation of acute suffering raises the spirit of a man.

V

"Well," said Ethel's mother, "you've given Mrs. Bowes notice, and I'm glad you have. But as to seeking for other lodgings, what I say is, why need you?"

"Well," said Purdon, "one's got to live somewhere."

"No doubt. But I've talked this all out with Ethel. It's for you to say, of course. I think you said £79 13*s.* 4*d.* was what you'd put by, and no doubt it does not seem much on which to face the responsibilities of life. But look at the facts as they stand. There need be no question of setting up a second establishment. This house is big enough. Besides Ethel's room, there's the spare room which is never occupied. You see, you have been engaged for a year. Ethel is an attractive girl, though I say so. But naturally she does not get any younger. At present there are two young men who are after her, madly in love with her."

"If you'll kindly give me their names and addresses," said Purdon, "I think that's a matter that I'm competent to—"

"Oh, don't you worry. Ethel knows how to take care of herself. She can put a man in his place all right. But there's the advantage to yourself from an immediate marriage. You'd be better fed, better looked after, and it would cost you less money. I should be glad to have you here too. Often and often Ethel and I have thought of spending the evening with friends and hardly liked to, leaving the house empty. Of course, if we were leaving a man here, there would be no cause for anxiety."

"And Ethel agrees?"

"You know as well as I do how shy the girl is. I'll say this much—I think you could persuade her."

"I'll try," said Purdon.

He was entirely successful.

The Missing Years

Sylvia Hetheril was the only daughter of James Hetheril, solicitor of Iddenside. She had one brother, Charles, seven years older than herself, who had been articled to his father and after his admission had continued to work in his father's office. The family lived together in a picturesque old house half a mile outside the town; the garden, in which Mr. Hetheril took a great interest, sloped down to the banks of the river Idden. Every weekday morning at half-past nine the father and son walked into the town to their office. They did not always return together. Sometimes Mr. Hetheril would return an hour or two earlier, to work in his beloved garden, leaving his son in charge.

Sylvia was beautiful and intelligent, and she thought a great deal more of her intelligence than she did of her beauty. Her father, whose ideas were a little old-fashioned, had not permitted Newnham. But Sylvia subscribed to a library in London which specialized in works of science, and studied hard. The science master at the big school in Iddenside helped her, and she was by far his most advanced pupil.

Somebody said one day to Sylvia's mother that Sylvia was perfectly charming.

"Well," said Mrs. Hetheril, "Sylvia's a good girl and a good daughter, but I do wish she were rather more like other girls. I don't want her to be vain, but really she never seems to think about clothes at all. Shopping actually bores her. If she hadn't me to see after her, she'd be—well, she'd be an absolute scarecrow. Books, books, books! She works far too hard. She prefers to play tennis with somebody who can just beat her. If she takes the punt out, it's to see how far she can get in a given time. Too strenuous altogether—I tell her so."

"She's the picture of health in spite of it," said the friend. "And she's very much admired."

"What's the use of it? It's my belief that she will never marry. She will be quite friendly with a man—till he falls in love with her. Then she's finished with him. I've seen it time after time."

One evening in June Sylvia's brother Charles, shortly after his return from the office, came into the library and found his sister at the writing-table.

"Sweltering evening," said Charles. "I'm going down to get a bathe before dinner. Coming along?"

"Don't think so," said Sylvia. "I had a swim this morning, while you were snoring. I was going to finish this library list and then stroll down the road, and post it."

Charles produced a letter from his pocket.

"Good," he said. "Then you might stuff this into the box for me. I meant to give it to the boy to post with the office letters, and forgot the damned thing."

"Right-o," said Sylvia cheerily.

Charles passed out through the open French windows, and went down the garden towards the boat-house, whistling as he went.

Suddenly a change came over Sylvia. She put her arms down on the table and rested her head on them. Her eyes closed. She was not asleep, but she was in a day-dream. It was delightful and it was new. Nothing of the kind had ever happened to her before. She was filled with happiness. She had forgotten library lists, and letters, and the room in which she sat. It seemed she was in a wood at twilight with a crescent moon above her. For nearly twenty minutes she remained motionless.

And then she suddenly started up, a little frightened. What on earth had happened to her? Feverishly she finished her library list. There would be just time to get to the pillar-box and back before she went up to dress for dinner. She put on the hat and gloves that lay on the table beside her, and snatched up the letters. Was there anything else? Yes, there was an envelope with bank-notes in it—a quarter's dress allowance. Her father would be annoyed if she left it lying about. She put it in the little bag she carried.

And then she hurried out of the house, expecting to be back again in five minutes.

Her father, mother, and brother sat down to dinner without her. It was not a very unusual occurrence, for Sylvia was sometimes a little unpunctual. It was expected that she would enter any moment, breathless, smiling, and apologetic.

As he finished his soup her father said, rather peevishly: "Where's Sylvia? I mean to say, what's she doing? She knows the dinner-hour. Reason in all things."

A maid was dispatched to find Miss Sylvia. Miss Sylvia was not to be found. There was definite evidence that she had not gone up to her room to get ready for dinner.

"She told me she was going down the road to post some letters," said Charles. "Probably she met some friends and they've collared her for dinner. She'll be telephoning directly."

By the end of dinner Sylvia had not returned nor had she telephoned. Her mother began to grow very anxious.

Mr. Hetheril said it was really too bad of Sylvia. Charles telephoned the Ingates and the Morrisons. Sylvia was not there, but Mrs. Morrison had seen her posting letters and had spoken to her. Sylvia had seemed quite well and happy. A little later Mr. Hetheril went to the police-station. At ten news came of her. She had gone up to London by the 7.20 train. The booking-clerk knew her by sight, and could describe the dress she was wearing. She had no luggage with her, and had to hurry to catch the train. There were two down trains that night by either of which Sylvia might return. Charles met them both, but she was not in either train.

Two days later the portrait of the missing girl appeared in the principal London newspapers with a full description. Several people wrote and claimed to have seen her on the evening of her departure, but none of the claims would stand investigation. Mr. Hetheril then offered a reward of £1000 for information which would lead to her recovery. This also produced nothing but a great number of unsatisfactory letters. Some weeks later the body of an unknown woman was taken out of the Thames, and it was thought by the police that it answered to the description that had been given them. Charles went up to London and saw the body. It was not his sister.

At the end of a year Sylvia's father and mother had practically given up hope. Their loss had aged them both considerably. Charles was still optimistic. He said that Sylvia had no troubles, that she was in excellent health, and that if she pleased she was quite well equipped to earn her own living as a teacher. She had always been independent in character, and might have chosen this way to see how she could get along by herself. It was pointed out to him that it was unlike Sylvia to do anything so cruel, and that if she had done it, she would most certainly have been seen and recognized by scores of people.

But when Sylvia had been away two years, Charles was astounded one morning to receive a letter addressed to him in what seemed to be her handwriting. He tore the envelope open and took out the letter, expecting to find that after all the similarity of the handwriting had been merely a coincidence.

But the letter was from Sylvia. It was written from a London hotel and was very short. She said that she was perfectly well, and that she was returning home late that evening. She thought it better for Charles to break this news to her father and mother. She could not tell them where she had been, or what she had been doing during the last two years. She had absolutely no recollection of it. She hoped that they would not ask her about it, because it worried her.

After a family consultation it was decided that her father and mother should go up to London to fetch Sylvia back, and a telegram was sent to her to tell her to expect them.

Sylvia could tell them very little. Four days before she had found herself in London, without luggage, without anything, except the clothes she stood up in, and with a handbag in which she found money. There was nearly £100 in notes, considerably more than she had in her possession when she left home. At one of the big London stores she had bought everything she required, had it packed in a couple of suit-cases, and had then taken her room at the hotel. She wanted time to pull herself together, time to decide what was the best course to take. She had finally decided to write to her brother. She was perfectly well, and she did not think she had been ill or unhappy during her absence. Her mother noticed that Sylvia was well and expensively dressed, and asked if she bought those things in London.

"No," said Sylvia, "I was wearing them when I came to London. Please don't ask me any questions. I would tell you if I could remember. It's all gone. Those two years have been missed out of my life."

Her eyes filled with tears and the subject was immediately changed.

But Sylvia has not told her parents quite everything. On her arrival in London she had noticed that she was wearing a plain gold wedding-ring. She had taken this off and hidden it. Later, she buried it in the garden.

She was not distressed with any further questions. This was in accordance with advice given by the family doctor. It had been, he thought, a case of secondary personality in which all recollection of the first personality had been lost. It was to be hoped that this secondary personality would not return, and meanwhile it would be better that her mind should be as undisturbed as possible, and that some sort of unobtrusive watch should be kept over her.

Mrs. Hetheril made two little discoveries that she did not mention to Sylvia. The dress that she had been wearing on her return bore the mark of a fashionable draper in Helmstone, and the linen was embroidered with a monogram, and the monogram was quite distinctly S.M.

Sylvia quickly took up again the threads of her normal life. There was much talk about her in Iddenside, which she detested, but gradually the wonder of her absence and her return was forgotten. She continued her scientific studies as before. She acted as bridesmaid at her brother's wedding, and she herself refused two offers of marriage. At the age of thirty-two she died of pneumonia, following on influenza.

It chanced that the letter which Charles Hetheril gave to his sister to post was addressed to a business acquaintance temporarily resident at a hotel in Helmstone. As Sylvia walked to the post she knew that she must hurry in order to be back in time for dinner. The feeling that she must hurry still persisted, but she had quite forgotten why. It really annoyed her a little that Mrs. Morrison met her and delayed her. As she dropped the letters in the pillar-box the word Helmstone caught her eye, though she would not have said that she had noticed it. She knew now that she must hurry because she was wanted. It was something important. She had not the least hesitation as to the direction she should take. It seemed to her that she knew it without thinking about it. She took the road to the railway station and just caught an up train.

Helmstone, she said to herself in the train. You went to it from Victoria. A taxi would get her to Victoria in ten minutes. She felt that she really ought to have looked up a train for Helmstone. But she supposed she must take her chance. Again chance aided her. She had not to wait five minutes. Of course, when she reached Helmstone, she would not be at her journey's end, but she could take a taxi most of the way.

"Where to, miss?" said the driver at Helmstone station.

"Go up to the sea front, turn to the left, and drive on till I tell you to stop."

"Will it be far, miss?"

"Five or six miles, perhaps. I'm not sure. I shall tell you when we get there."

Sylvia sat back in the cab, a little impatient to be at her journey's end, taking no notice whatever of the streets of Helmstone. Presently Helmstone was left behind. A little later the lights of a village blinked at her through the windows of the car. At intervals she could hear the constant murmur of the sea.

Suddenly she sat up and tapped the glass in front of her sharply. The driver pulled up on the near side, a little surprised, for there was no habitation in sight.

"This is as far as I can go by taxi," said Sylvia in explanation. "I have to walk the rest of the way. It's not far."

Sylvia had impressed the driver strongly. He would have remembered her face and the dress she was wearing. He would have seen the portrait of her which appeared in the newspapers. He would have communicated with the Hetherils. But on his return journey to Helmstone his car collided with another and he was thrown out and killed.

Sylvia went up across the downs. Soon she saw in front of her the wood for which she had been looking. It covered about two acres of ground and there was a high palisade round it. She found the gate in this palisade without any difficulty. There was a notice-board by the gate, but it was too dark for her to read it, and she did not trouble about it. The board stated that the wood was private property and that the public was not admitted. It also gave a warning that the dogs at large in the wood were dangerous. Sylvia entered, closing the gate behind her. She had gone a few steps when a great mastiff leapt from a thicket and came slowly towards her, growling.

"Don't be so silly," said Sylvia to the dog. "I'm not going to hurt you. Just you come here at once."

It almost seemed as if the dog had recognized her voice. The growling ceased. He came up to her, sniffing suspiciously. Then he pushed his cold nose into her hand, and wagged his tail.

"That's right," said Sylvia, patting his head and then taking hold of the loose collar on his neck. "Now then. You take me by the nearest way up to the house."

Sylvia and the mastiff went on together by a grassy track to a clearing in the middle of the wood where stood a big brick-built bungalow. At some distance behind it there were outbuildings.

Sylvia rang, and the door was immediately opened by a manservant. At the sight of the man the dog began to growl again.

"Be quiet," said Sylvia to the dog, patting him on the head.

"You are Miss Sefton?" said the man anxiously.

"No," said Sylvia, "I—"

Suddenly a door into the hall opened and a man came out whom Sylvia had expected to see. He was young and very dark, and his expression was tragic. He was in evening dress with a short jacket and black tie. Sylvia turned to him at once.

"I had to come to you," she said. And then a wave of trouble passed over her. "I've lost my memory," she stammered. "Will you help me?"

"Of course I will," said the man quietly. "Come in here, won't you?"

He turned sharply to the servant. "Carter, see that a room is got ready for this lady at once."

The room into which Sylvia was taken was furnished as a library, brightly lit with electric lights. The top drawer of a bureau was open and the man went quickly to it and closed it. He made Sylvia sit down on a couch, and drew up a chair beside it.

"Now then," he said, "you're quite all right here, aren't you? I did not expect you and yet you came just in time." He looked at her steadily. "Almost exactly the same," he said in a low voice. And then addressing her again: "My name is Richard Mordaunt, you know. I wonder if you can remember what yours is."

"My first name is Sylvia. I'm quite sure of that, but I do not know what the second name is. I think I've travelled a long way to get here. I had to come to you. You looked just as I expected. But you'll be happier now, won't you?"

"Of course I shall. I suppose you've not dined?"

"I don't remember. But I'm not a bit hungry. I'm rather tired."

"That's all right," he said in his pleasant, musical voice. "You shall go to bed early. Mrs. Carter and her daughter Alice will look after you. But I think we must have some supper first. You see, I did not dine this evening."

He touched the bell.

"That was very foolish," said Sylvia, looking up at him and smiling. "Why not?"

"It didn't seem worth while. The condemned man does not always—"

He broke off as Carter entered. "Carter," he said, "supper in the dining-room as soon as you can."

"Very good, sir. I was already preparing it. Mrs. Carter thought it would be required."

"Sensible woman. And the room?"

"Alice is seeing to it."

"That's right. Send Alice here as soon as the room is ready."

As Carter left he turned again to Sylvia and pointed to the big mastiff who had followed her in and was now asleep on the hearthrug.

"You know, Sylvia," he said, "you're rather a miracle. That dog does not allow anybody but myself to touch him. A tripper from Helmstone was foolish enough one day to disregard the notice I put up and to come into my wood, and he got pretty badly mauled before I could get to him and take the dog off."

"He was quite gentle with me," said Sylvia. "He really showed me the way to the house."

Alice, a ruddy-cheeked, healthy-looking damsel, entered and said that the room was ready.

Mordaunt's eye caught the monogram S.H. on Sylvia's handbag, and he made up his mind quickly.

"That's right," he said to Alice. "Miss Harding has lost her luggage. But you'll do the best you can for her, won't you?"

When Sylvia had gone from the room, Mordaunt stood for a moment or two in deep thought.

"An absolute miracle," he said aloud.

He crossed over to the bureau and opened that drawer again. In it were two letters which he had spent the day in writing. One of them was to a Miss Sefton, and the other was addressed to his solicitors. On the top of them lay a revolver. He removed the cartridges from the revolver. They would not be wanted now. He tore the two letters across. Though the evening was warm there was a small fire smouldering in the fireplace before which the dog lay.

Mordaunt touched the dog with his foot. "Get out of the light, Leo," he said.

The dog rose obediently, and moved a few steps away. Mordaunt threw the torn letters on the fire and smiled as he watched them burn. The dog looked up at him inquiringly, obviously asking a permission.

"Yes," said Mordaunt, "you can go back. You ought to be out in the wood looking for people, instead of behaving like a pampered spaniel. But you've done a good work this evening, and you shall have your own way for once."

Soon after dinner Sylvia retired for the night. Mordaunt called to the dog, took a short stroll through the wood, and then he also went to his room. In the servants' quarters the event of the evening was being discussed by the Carter family. Mr. Carter smoked a cherrywood pipe and enjoyed a bottle of stout. Mrs. Carter and Alice listened to him as to the fount of wisdom.

"I don't pretend to understand it," said Mr. Carter, "but I'm glad of it. If things had gone on as they were going on, in another week my gentleman would have been either in his coffin or in a madhouse."

"And who do you take it that she is?" asked Mrs. Carter.

"Ah, there you're asking something. When I opened the door I felt certain she was Miss Sefton come back again. She's pretty well the image of her to look at. Then she comes into the hall, turns to him, and says she's lost her memory, and will he help her? Yet that dog behaved as if he'd known her all his life. She was pulling him about in a way that none of us would like to do. When I waited on them at dinner he and she were talking exactly like old friends. What's more, he called her by her Christian name all the time. First time I've heard him laugh or seen him eat a meal as if he enjoyed it for many a long month. Why, he's a changed man. But if you ask me to explain it, I can't. One doesn't seem to fit with another."

"Well, George," said Mrs. Carter, "I'll tell you an idea that has crossed my mind. The bit about her losing her memory and wanting him to help her may have been some sort of private joke between them."

"Don't you believe it, my dear. I saw her, and heard her, and she wasn't joking. What's more, he didn't expect her, or the room would have been ready. I suppose she didn't happen to say anything to you, Alice?"

"Well," said Alice, "she was very pleasant and talked quite a good deal. But she didn't seem to tell me anything, and of course I couldn't ask."

"I wonder now," said Carter, "as a point of etiquette, if it's all right for her and him to be staying alone together in a house like this."

"You seem to forget there's us. Of course, if we weren't here I should give notice instantly—what I mean to say is, I shouldn't approve of it."

Richard and Sylvia, to neither of whom the "point of etiquette" had occurred, met at breakfast next morning. Sylvia said that she had slept perfectly.

"And you?" she asked.

"I also slept well," said Richard, "for the first time for four months."

"I'm glad. And what are we to do to-day?"

"If you don't mind, I'd like to drive you into Helmstone. You see, you arrived without luggage. You will have to buy heaps of things."

"That will be lovely," said Sylvia. "I find I've got some money in my handbag, though I've no notion where it came from."

"Oh, you will have to let me be your banker while you are here. I shall enjoy the drive too. For four months I've not been outside my wood."

"Four months again," said Sylvia meditatingly.

"Yes, I shall tell you all about that very soon, I think."

"And after we've bought everything?"

"Then I suppose we must go to the police-station and try to find out who you are, and see if you can be restored to your relatives again."

Tears came into Sylvia's eyes.

"No," she said, "I don't want that. I don't know anything about my relatives. Perhaps I have none. It must have been something bad that made me go away. I won't do anything to find out who I was. I'm content to be what I am. You must promise me that you won't do anything either."

"Well," he said hesitatingly.

"I don't want to be a bother to you. If you don't want me here I'll go away, of course. But I'm not going back again to the place I came from."

"You cannot guess how very much I want you here."

"Then promise you won't try to find out who I am."

And after some persuasion he gave his promise. He knew it was all wrong, but he would have promised her anything and kept his word if it had been humanly possible.

For Richard had fallen very much in love with Sylvia, and she with him. It had happened instantaneously—at first sight.

Sylvia's mother had said quite truly that Sylvia did not care for shopping and was careless about dress. But the new Sylvia that had come into being enjoyed her shopping immensely and was particularly careful to choose things that would suit her. They lunched together at a hotel in Helmstone and drove back with the little car laden with packages. More were to be sent on later.

Sylvia was seen that morning by many shop assistants and by waiters at the hotel, but no description of her had yet appeared in the newspapers. It was not till three days later that her portrait was published.

Newspapers were delivered regularly at the house in the wood. For four months Richard had never looked at them because he had lost his interest in the world. He never looked at them now because he was too much interested in Sylvia. But Carter was careful to keep himself well informed. A really good murder was a great satisfaction to him. He would retail the newspaper account afterwards to his wife and daughter with his own theory of the case, and his astonishment at the ineptitude of Scotland Yard.

On the morning that Sylvia's portrait was published, Carter held a consultation with his wife and then brought the newspaper to his master.

"I don't know if I'm doing right, sir, but we thought I should show you this. Christian name is the same and there seems to be some likeness."

Richard looked at the portrait, glanced over the letterpress, and laughed.

The portrait in the newspaper had been taken from a bad and not very recent photograph of Sylvia. It was very hurriedly and badly reproduced. Richard honestly did not believe that this was the Sylvia he knew.

"Not a bit like Miss Harding," he said to Carter. "Thousands of girls have got *blond-cendré* hair and blue eyes. Thousands of girls are just about that height. Thousands of girls wear a dark blue coat and skirt. Besides, if the Christian names are the same, the surnames are different. Yes, it's all right to have shown it to me, but don't bother Miss Harding about it. Just put the idea out of your mind. You're too romantic, Carter."

Neither Carter, nor Mrs. Carter, nor Alice was quite convinced. There were certainly many points of coincidence, but when they looked at the portrait again they could see that it was quite possibly a portrait of some-body else, and decidedly it was not for them to interfere.

It was after dinner that night that Richard Mordaunt told Sylvia some-thing of his history. He was, so far as he knew, without a relative in the world. His income was derived principally from house property that he had inherited from his father. He owned several houses in Helmstone, and was rather sardonic about them. He employed an agent to look after his property and had himself very little taste for business. Six months before he had met Mabel Sefton at a friend's house. At the end of a month they became engaged, and the engagement lasted one more month. Then Mabel Sefton threw him over.

The four months which followed had been a period of increasing mel-ancholy, depression, and insomnia. He had shut himself up alone in his house, seeing nobody except his servants, and taking every precaution that his solitude should be uninterrupted. On the night of Sylvia's arrival he had decided to make an end of it all, and that life was not worth living. He had the revolver in his hand when Sylvia rang at the front door.

"And now?" said Sylvia.

"Oh, Mabel was quite right. I can see that now, of course."

"What was she like?"

"She was very much like you. Wonderfully like you. But you're better. Mabel was just a little bit metallic."

The night was hot and they strolled out through the French windows, taking the grass path through the wood. Suddenly Sylvia stopped short.

"Ah," she said.

"What is it?" said Richard.

"I've been here before. The wood was just like this with that crescent moon above. The line of the trees against the sky was just like that, and I was very happy."

"And you're very happy now?"

She did not speak, but pressed her lips together and bowed her head in assent.

"I, too," he said. He paused and quoted: "What are we waiting for, O my heart?"

And in an instant he held her in his arms.

*　　*　　*

They were married by licence as soon as possible in the village church. Sylvia's name was given as Sylvia Harding, and her age as twenty-two. She had no idea at this time what her real age was. A honeymoon of three months was spent in Switzerland, and when they returned again to England to the house in the wood the search for Sylvia Hetheril had been practically given up.

Richard had several men friends whom it now seemed that he had neglected too long. Besides he was very proud of Sylvia. He wished to show the treasure that he possessed. And so, for the next month or two, there were generally men staying in the house. Richard knew there would be questions, and he was quite capable of dealing with them.

"You know, Richard," said an old friend of his one evening as they sat over their port after dinner, "you always were a curious sort of cuss, and you've sprung a great surprise on us with this sudden marriage of yours. If I am any judge, you are very much to be congratulated on it. But may I ask one question?"

"Anything you like," said Richard.

"Let's see. Your wife's maiden name was—"

"Harding," said Richard—"Sylvia Harding."

"When did you first meet her?"

"We first met," said Richard, "under very romantic circumstances, about which"—he paused and smiled humorously—"we are both of us determined not to say one word to anybody."

"Ah, well," said his friend, as he refilled his glass, "you always were unsatisfactory and mysterious, and I suppose you always will be."

Sylvia's baby, a girl, named after her, was born just about one year after Sylvia Hetheril left her home. The younger Sylvia was a very gay and healthy baby, receiving much devotion from the entire household. Alice Carter became the baby's nurse, having developed a natural genius in that direction, and another maid was engaged to take Alice's place.

One evening, when the baby was about six months old, Richard said to his wife at dinner: "Sylvia, you don't look very happy this evening. Are you worried about anything?"

"Not worried exactly. But I've been thinking about something. You remember Mabel Sefton?"

"Good old Mabel," said Richard. "She did me a good deal better turn than she ever imagined."

"Yet when she left you, you grew melancholy. You were even on the point of suicide."

"You remind me of past follies. But you remind me too that it was you who saved me."

"If I died, or if for any other reason I went out of your life, would you again be tempted to do that?"

"I might be tempted. I should be as unhappy as a man could be. But I should never do it. Not now. I've got the baby Sylvia to look after, you know."

"Yes, I've thought of that."

"And apart from death, what reason could there possibly be that you should leave me?"

"When I came to you, you know, I had forgotten everything that had happened before. It seems to me that I had changed in some way, that I was not quite the same person. I did not want to go back. I did not want to be the person that I had been before. I made you promise, you remember."

"Yes, I remember."

"Well, the thing that has been haunting me is that something of the kind might happen again. I might suddenly remember the girl that I used to be, and quite forget the woman that I am now. Possibly somewhere or other, I have a father and mother living, and should want to go back to them. If that ever happened I want you to promise not to look for them."

"You ask a hard thing, Sylvia—an impossible thing. Why do you ask it?"

"Because I dread the conflict between the two people—the girl I was and the woman I am. The circumstances of neither would fit with the other. I should be confused. I think I should go mad. If you love me, promise it, Richard."

"Then I must promise it. It will probably never happen. I do not believe you can ever forget me. I do not believe you can ever forget the baby Sylvia. Still, there's the chance that the thing that happened once may happen again. I must see what ought to be done."

A few days later he brought her £100 in bank-notes.

"I'd like you, Sylvia," he said, "to put those in some pocket of that little bag you always carry. I don't believe you're ever going back to—to wherever you were before you were sent to me. But if you do, the change may come suddenly when you are alone, and you must have money with you."

When the baby Sylvia was just a year old, Sylvia came out of the house one morning with two letters in her hand, invitations for the weekend. She found Richard reclining at full length in a comfortable chair on the verandah. He had been reading a newspaper, but had found the exertion too much, and had put it down. He was very nearly asleep.

"Richard," said Sylvia, "who is the laziest man on earth?"

"Can't say. I'm not in the first three. I cut a tree down yesterday. Where are you off to?"

"Just going to the pillar-box in the road to post these."

Richard pulled a somewhat crumpled letter from his pocket.

"You might post that as well," he said. "I carried the damned thing about all yesterday and didn't remember to post it. Hurry up or you'll be late for lunch."

"Right-o," said Sylvia.

It was as she posted the letters that the change came. Victoria Street was the address on one of them, and it caught her eye. She went straight on in the direction of the village. She must certainly hurry, for her father was always annoyed if she was late for dinner. Suddenly she pressed her hand to her forehead. Where was she? This was not Iddenside. She must get back to Victoria at once. In the village she took the motor omnibus into Helmstone. She felt dazed and horrified. She looked at her clothes. That was not the dress she had been wearing when she went away. How long had she been away? It was not until she reached Victoria that her mind became clear at all. She knew now that she had been away for two years, but she did not know what she had been doing. Of her baby and her husband she had no recollection whatever.

Shortly after her death, Dr. Norton, who attended her in her illness, sat one evening talking over things with his partner.

"You knew poor Miss Hetheril, didn't you?" said Norton.

"Slightly. Didn't she go away in a mysterious way years and years ago?"

"She did. And I know now why she went."

"You don't mean to say—"

"I have not the slightest doubt of it. This is between ourselves, of course. Her people don't know. And it was not part of my duty to tell them."

Dr. Norton's partner knocked out his pipe in the fender. "And she seemed such a nice quiet girl," he said meditatively. "One never knows."

Sylvia was thirty-two years old when she died. Her age in the newspaper announcement of her death, and also on her tombstone, was given as thirty. This was done at her express request. There were, so she said, two years of her life that had been missed out. She had never had them. Somebody had taken them from her.

THE·SHADOW
OF·THE·UNSEEN

BARRY·PAIN·&
JAMES·BLYTH

The Shadow of the Unseen

by
Barry Pain and James Blyth

Chapter I

On the Eve of Freedom

Down the white road that leads from Cambridge to the village of Trumpington came the motor-car. It turned in at the gates of a modern house of some pretensions and up the semicircular drive. The girl, without a word, relinquished the wheel, stood for a moment on the step watching the chauffeur drive away, and then passed through the open door into the hall of the house, an orderly, well-appointed, and quite inartistic hall.

The girl flung aside her white canvas motor-coat and was taking off her cap and veil as a servant crossed the hall.

"Mr. Trotter in?" the girl asked, a little brusquely.

"Yes, miss. He's in. He was inquiring if you had returned."

The girl began to speak and broke off abruptly. There was Mr. Trotter coming down the stairs.

Mr. Willoughby Trotter, senior tutor of St. Cecilia's College, was a little man of fifty. His manner was slightly flurried, and he had a restless and nervous eye. An occasional and rabbit-like twitch of the face was characteristic of him. His fair hair had receded by the processes of time from his forehead. His was a dome-like forehead which so often goes with great education and little originality. You could have told he was perfectly respectable a mile off.

"There you are, my dear," he said, speaking rapidly. "So busy, so busy, so busy. The car?"

"Not a quarter of an inch of petrol in the tank. The idiot is filling up now. He'll be round directly."

"That was very, very wrong of him. It might have caused serious inconvenience. What would you have done if the car had stopped in the road?"

"Sat there while he fetched petrol from the nearest place. There wouldn't be anything else to do, would there?"

"No, my dear; no, I suppose not," he said as he shuffled into his thin respectable overcoat. "You can't imagine what's happened. At the very last moment I find that Mrs. Branksome was not asked. Her name was on the list, of course. The omission is inexplicable. I must go there now and explain as well as I can. And I'm due at the college at twelve. Really one hardly knows which way to turn."

The tremolo effect of the car was heard outside, cut by two deep coughs from the horn. Mr. Trotter darted forward.

"Carefully now," he said to the driver. "Very carefully, please!"

The hot summer sunlight streamed in at the front door and fell on the figure of the girl as she was standing in the hall. There was nothing of the hard brightness of the sportswoman about her. The face was beautiful, but too pale, and too heavy—the mouth a little too large, the expression somewhat sullen and contemptuous. Her eyes were dark and unfathomable. Perhaps it was in those wonderful eyes and in her beautiful hair that her chief charm lay. Men who met her found riddles in those eyes, and sought in vain for the answer.

She passed from the hall into the morning-room. A woman sat at the table, a paint-box by her side, illuminating something on vellum. She was forty, and did not look it. The red of her hair was quite natural, and also did not look it. She had always fascinated, and had always been petted. Her friends thought her versatile. And her enemies called her fickle. At present she was the intimate friend of Linda Pettingill Merle, the girl who now stood watching her.

"My lord, the senior tutor, has just left," said the woman without looking up. "Nothing becomes him so much as the moment of his departure, as some historian said, I believe."

Linda laughed, and came over to look at the work.

"I wish I could do that," she said. "I haven't got any gifts."

"You are one supreme and stupendous gift," said the woman. "Also this is not a gift. It's a trick."

"Where's Aunt Mary?" Linda asked.

"Cumbered with much serving, by reason of a forthcoming garden party in honour of the twenty-first birthday of Linda Merle. Also she is in great disgrace, both with the esteemed Uncle Willoughby—how that man must be esteemed!—and also with herself. She forgot to ask some woman who does not matter in herself, but has married a man who matters rather less. So Aunt Mary moans that she cannot forgive herself. Funny, isn't it. I don't think I've ever been cumbered. And I can always forgive myself. In fact, I'm about the only person that I can forgive. So while the storm rages I sit in this quiet backwater and complete my thank-offering for you to-morrow."

"Not really?" said the girl. "It's too sweet of you. I've been adoring it all the time you've been doing it. And there are pages and pages of it."

Mrs. Devigny put down her work and leaned back in her chair. "You must remember that I did it largely to please myself. I have always thought that 'The Blessed Damosel' ought to be illuminated on vellum. It screams for it. I can't see it any other way."

"Cara," said the girl, solemnly, "you're a fish—"

"Thanks," said Mrs. Devigny, drily.

"Fish out of water."

"And what are you?" asked Mrs. Devigny.

"I wish to goodness I knew," said the girl, with conviction.

"We'll come out into the garden," said the woman. "This afternoon a perfect hurricane of lawn-mowers begins, and I prefer gardens when the gardeners are less in evidence."

"Yes," said Linda. And bareheaded they went through the French win-dows of the room and down the bright weedless gravel path. The garden was much older than the house. The house had been largely improved by Mr. Willoughby Trotter. The deep shrubberies at the further end of the garden gave a peaceful shaded retirement. Here they sat down together.

"I suppose," said Mrs. Devigny, thoughtfully, "it's very wrong of me to laugh at Mr. Trotter, seeing that I'm stopping in his house."

"But you're not his guest. You're mine."

"True, oh princess of the beautiful hair. But then he's your uncle."

"Only by courtesy. My guardian really. I like and respect him, and I love Aunt Mary. But still, if one has any sense of humour at all, one can't help seeing—"

"Oh, quite so. Very much so. His obsession that he must do his best, and his delirious activities in consequence strike me immensely. As true as I'm a fair to middling woman, he said yesterday at lunch, 'This bread-and-butter pudding is burnt. But, alas! I can't see to everything.' Nobody, of course, ever expected him to see to it. It is simply that the hyper-conscientiousness of a senior tutor must assume every responsibility whether it belongs to him or not."

"Yes," said the girl. "And really he has managed all my affairs ex-

tremely well. He has obtained better rents for my marsh property in Norfolk than my father was ever able to get, and succeeded in letting the
house and demesne at Merlesfleet to a tenant who not only paid a good
rent, but kept the place up magnificently. He must have learnt a lot when
he was bursar. I could go down there to-morrow if I wanted to."

"And will you?"

"No. Of course not. I cannot leave on the first day of my freedom. It
would hurt Aunt Mary's feelings. Besides, I don't know what the place is
like. It seems very picturesque from the photographs. But photographs are
such liars. And it's awfully out of the way. There would be no society there
at all except what one brought down. Oh yes. And that wonderful ex-
parson that my uncle admires but cannot approve. No. We must travel
first—you and I. As soon as winter comes we and the other birds—"

"I was a fish just now," said Mrs. Devigny, sweetly.

"Don't mind. It's only wealth of metaphor. We migrate. Italy, Sicily,
Egypt. Que sais je?"

"It sounds delightful. I will come. We will go through many dry places,
seeking rest."

"You often strike me, Cara, as on the verge of being very serious."

"Yes," said Mrs. Devigny, simply, "and I always am. We have not quite
found out what we want—you and I. Personally I want you principally,
and I always enjoy travel. But what about yourself? Did your seasons in
London satisfy you? Does the learned but somewhat parochial society of
Cambridge satisfy you? You are the image of sweet discontent. I don't
know what to do for you."

"Thanks so much for not telling me to get married. I believe the sober
slumbers of my Uncle Willoughby are often conscience-haunted with the
fact that he has not got me married. Aunt Mary feels it too. I do know, at
any rate, that that is not what I want. Now I will give you a chance to
laugh at me. I feel that even if I could get everything I wanted it would not
be worth while. It is all for so short a time. One can't know any of the
things that one wants to know. I would give my very life to know whence
I come and whither I go. And I never shall know it." She made an impatient movement with her hands. "When one says these things they sound
crude and affected. But when one thinks them, and thinks them, and
keeps on thinking them—"

"I know—I know," said Mrs. Devigny. "I've been there. Sometimes I
wonder if some future generation really will know—know for certain.
They are tinkering about now at the gates of life, these men of science. Is

it a true dawn or a false? It generally is false."

"To-morrow," said the girl, slowly, "will be my twenty-first birthday. On those three tennis courts undergraduates and maidens will be knocking a ball about. There will be claret cup and lemonade. There will even, on this occasion, be champagne cup. Uncle Willoughby will be going with the throttle full open and the spark advanced. He will talk to nobody for long because it will be his instant and imperative duty to talk to somebody else. There will be plenty of laughter and lots of jealousy and private notes of the adorable gown of Mrs. Devigny. Undergraduates will try to talk like old men, and aged dons will try to talk as if the gaiety of the dog were not yet dead in them. Sooner or later they will go and say that they have enjoyed themselves. Then there will be dinner for the chosen few. Uncle Willoughby will drink my health and say as many appropriate words as he can remember. Afterwards, if it is fine, we'll come out into the garden, you and I. Everything will be quiet, and there will be the stars. They won't be laughing at us, and they won't be sympathising with us. The immeasurable pettiness of everything we do is nothing to them. Even the occasional greatness of some of us is nothing to them. Out there starward, where the knowledge lies, nobody cares. And down here nobody knows. And we care terribly."

"Yes. I ought to laugh at you," said Mrs. Devigny. She caught the girl's hand impulsively. "But I won't. I know you so well, you see. And—and— I haven't always been very happy myself. And you say, I'm on the verge of being very serious. How one fights not to go over the verge! And it's better to laugh than to cry."

They strolled slowly back to the house together. Mrs. Devigny returned to her illumination. Linda slung her motor-coat over her arm and went up to her room. For a moment she stood at the window, looking far out over flat country. Then she turned to her writing-table and unlocked her diary. There were but a few blank pages left. Slowly, and with long pauses, she wrote as follows:—

"Motored into Cambridge this morning for Aunt Mary, and had luck to get back, as that idiot Garnier had forgotten to fill the tank. That man can do absolutely nothing except talk French. And it's only the accident of his birth that makes him able to do that. Lots of preparations going on here for the tennis party to-morrow. I wonder if it's worth while to write down this kind of thing. No. I don't wonder. I'm quite sure it's not. I turn back the pages of this diary and the repetitions strike me most. It is just a little round that goes on and on, and every now and then there are such sentences as 'How sick I am of it all!' Or, in a humbler mood, 'If other people can stand it and apparently even like it, why can't I?'

"I think I shall not keep a diary any more. The trivial round is not worth record, and retrospection has its dangers. I have a horror of becoming morbid and bad tempered, and ungrateful to people who, after all, mean to be very kind. I fill these last few pages more from a stupid love of completion than from any other motive.

"After all there is still Cara Devigny. She understands me better than anybody else—better, perhaps, than I understand myself. Whatever happens she must be with me in the days of my freedom. Nominally, these days begin to-morrow. I have the control and management of my own property then. I begin to order my life as I like. In reality, I shall still have the advice of Uncle Willoughby to help me, and I shall still have its results to contend with. I simply cannot go on here. Neither can I be indecent enough to make the break at the first possible moment. Gradually Uncle Willoughby's influence will wane and Cara's will increase. I wonder whither she will lead me, or whither I shall lead her? Great though our friendship is there are barriers of intimacy which we have not passed, stories which we have not told, things which we have kept ourselves back from saying. This morning for the first time since I've known her she confessed that she had not always been happy. I knew it, of course, but she had never said it before. I had been blurting out a lot of nonsense about my own feeling—my hatred and fury at the inevitable limits—my doubts whether anything so transient as life is worth the fuss which we make about it. She was more sympathetic than I had expected her to be."

The song of perfectly satisfied birds came in bursts through the open window. She rose impatiently and closed it. Then she sat down again at the writing-table and began drawing on the blotting paper. She had not the slightest gift in this direction. The head that she was drawing came out unexpectedly with a hideous ape-like, semi-human character. She shuddered and blotted it over. Then she went on writing.

"This kind of thing must not go on. I must not think about it. I must not bother myself with inquiries which are bound to be futile. The present is here and I have got to make the best of it. There really are material things which I do enjoy. Some things that I eat and drink, some aspects of this flat country, old gardens, driving the car, pretty clothes. I think I will take cooking lessons—or learn German—anything which will help the prosaic side of me. One must be reasonable, and not give way to fancies. There were my ideas about music, for instance—that music is a language, and that if one could only understand it, it would tell us everything. It—"

Clearly and precisely on the stroke of one the gong for luncheon rang out. She closed the diary and went over to the glass, to see if her hair was tidy.

Chapter II

A Change of Plan

On the morning of her twenty-first birthday Linda Merle woke with a strange feeling of depression. It may have been that the anticipatory gaiety which her Uncle Willoughby had thought it appropriate to assume in his twittering way on the previous evening was responsible for this. But Linda herself, in after years, always claimed that a presentiment had been vouchsafed to her to warn her to tread carefully along the path of freedom which the passage of years now opened out before her. The sombreness of her self-communing was accentuated by the necessity for her cheerful reciprocity of the congratulations and expressions of good will which her Uncle Willoughby and Aunt Mary heaped upon her.

Mrs. Devigny was not yet downstairs. She was a great sufferer from insomnia, and her usual custom was to breakfast in her room.

Mr. Trotter presented material evidences of his good will in a dual form. His first offering was an advance copy in tree calf of "My Tour in Galilee"—his own work, and to be published at his own expense.

"It is not," he said complacently, "a book which I should care to place in the hands of every young girl. It is—perhaps it would not be too much to say—fearless. Fearless," he repeated, and snapped a piece of dry toast in his hand. "I can trust you not to misunderstand it. A certain breadth of mind may go with—(one more lump of sugar, my dear)—a firm faith in all that is essential. I have used my eyes. The book may possibly make some outcry."

In justice to Mr. Willoughby Trotter it may be stated that the book caused no scandal whatever.

Linda accepted her risk with appropriate gratitude.

His second present was more curious even than he knew. It was a cup of some transparent material, of a wine-coloured hue, heavily mounted in soft gold, which had obviously been worked by the primitive methods of the East. It stood about six inches in height, and the base carried a partly obliterated inscription.

"It's the loveliest thing I ever saw," said Linda. "What on earth is it made of?"

"Ah! You would never be able to guess."

He had been quite unable to guess himself when he bought it.

"The bowl is of amber. Old amber takes that colour sometimes. I got it from a Greek in Port Said, and remembered your love for what is curious."

Linda also received a diamond bracelet from Aunt Mary, a comfortable toneless little woman, the willing slave of her husband.

In virtue of the occasion Mr. Trotter during breakfast presented a close resemblance to the advertisements of "Sunny Jim." His one exception was when he referred to the second failure of Mr. Percy Belton, of St. Cecilia's, to obtain a pass degree. "Had I known it in time," said the senior tutor, "he should never have been asked for this afternoon."

It was a mere flash of severity, and had gone in a moment.

Perhaps the near appearance of his book as well as the occasion of his ward's birthday had exercised a mollifying influence.

Soon after breakfast Linda slipped upstairs and tapped at Mrs. Devigny's door.

"If that's Linda, come in. If it's not, I'm not here," came the answer in Mrs. Devigny's voice.

"All right. Then it's not me," said Linda, as she entered the room. "Why, whatever's that you've got there?"

Mrs. Devigny was sitting up in bed, in a dressing jacket of pale blue silk. On her breakfast tray on her knees there were some sheets of paper and a weird-looking toy.

"You are an untruther," said she. "You are, Linda. And you are twenty-one, and you've got to come here and be wished all the happiness in the world."

Linda embraced her friend, and returned to her question.

"Thanks, dear. Now, what really is that thing you've got there?"

"It's a fraud," said Mrs. Devigny. "Merely a fraud. Like most other things. They call it 'Planchette.'"

"I've heard of that," said Linda, eagerly. "It does mysterious writing, doesn't it?"

"Oh, no it doesn't. Not a bit of it. It's supposed to do mysterious writing, and simple children of the desert, like myself, get taken in. After all you can't expect much mystery for a shilling."

"Do let me try," said Linda, bringing a chair up to the bedside. "It won't work for you because you're too light-minded."

Linda put her pretty fingers on the board and for a minute nothing happened. Then, with an eerie scratching noise, the pencil began to write, "Many happy returns of the day," but was interrupted.

"Linda, you're shoving it," said Mrs. Devigny, in a shocked tone of voice.

"Of course I am," said Linda. "The silly thing wouldn't move by itself. And I thought it might as well join in the chorus with the rest."

"Linda Pettingill Merle," said Mrs. Devigny, solemnly, "you are a dishonest woman. Leave the house."

"I will, as soon as you'll get up and come with me. How dare you be lazy on my twenty-first birthday? We can have a lovely time together before the trial of the afternoon."

"I'm old enough to be your mother," said Mrs. Devigny, "and I expect to be treated with respect. But then one never gets what one expects. Vanish, and I'll be ready in one hour."

Seated in their favourite place in the shrubberies at the end of the garden, Linda turned suddenly to her friend. "I want you to tell me something," she said.

"Speak, oh, princess of the beautiful hair."

"Do you believe in Planchette at all? Did you ever believe in that or in automatic writing of any kind?"

"Seriously?"

"Quite seriously."

"Yes, then, I did. I do still. I've seen it. I know it. I can't do it. Perhaps if I kept on I might be able to do it. But what good would it do? These messages, from the unseen tell one nothing, The only problem in the world which is worth solution remains insoluble. Besides, I've been told that it's dangerous to play this game."

"Why?"

"I knew a girl once. She had your curiosity without your intelligence. She lent herself to things of the kind. Either she got results, or she lied. It was some time ago, and she died in the asylum."

"Don't. That's too horrible. But after all it does not follow. Was it a form of madness which made her think that she was getting at the great secret? Or was it her experiments which drove her mad?"

Mrs. Devigny shrugged her shoulders. "Look here, Linda, I've answered your question. Now tell me why you asked it?"

"It's nothing. At any rate, it's a perfectly ridiculous trifle. I was writing in my room, and as I stopped to think I began unconsciously to draw on the blotting paper. You know those heads that one draws. Of course I can't draw really. I can't translate anything modelled into the flat. One draws on the blotting paper just as some people twiddle their thumbs. Simply in order to move their hands. Of course I never know what the head which I am drawing is going to turn out like. This time it was a horrible thing. There was the ape in it, and the human being, and the Devil. The stupid thing made an impression upon me. One moment I thought how horrible it would be to see that. And the next moment I knew for certain that one day I should see it. I put a lot of blots over it to hide it. But I remember it still. I think—and this is worse—that I shall always remember it."

"That's quaint," said Mrs. Devigny. "But you couldn't make Planchette write."

"No, I was trying to, hard. I have got an idea that these things don't come that way."

"Wake up, Linda. This is the twentieth century. We must not be super-stitious."

"Cara," said the girl, thoughtfully, "can you tell me exactly where relig-ion ends and superstition begins? All my life I've been taught to believe in a Power of Good, and one of the strongest convictions in my mind is a belief in a Power of Evil."

"I won't pretend that this doesn't make me think," said Mrs. Devigny. "It does. I don't know what to say. This is not always present to your mind?"

"No; certainly not. But from time to time I've always had it. I remem-ber as a child trying to propitiate the Power of Evil—the Devil—if you like to call it that."

"What did you do?"

"Fantastic ceremonies. The things which only children think of. Some of them I could not tell to you or to anybody."

"Such feelings are less strong with you now?"

"No; not less strong, but less frequent. I wish they would go alto-gether. I want to be just exactly like other people."

"Oh happy other people if that were possible!" said Mrs. Devigny.

The talk drifted into other channels. A few minutes later Mrs. Devigny was being very amusing and slightly irreverent on the subject of "My Tour in Galilee."

"There was the cup, too, that he gave me. Come and see it."

Mrs. Devigny seemed interested in it, and examined it narrowly. "Do you know what it has been used for?" she asked.

"No. Do you?"

"Yes, I think so. Perhaps I'm wrong. No, never mind. We won't talk about it. I won't answer any questions. If I can't get mystery any other way I'll be a mystery myself." She said it with a smile, but neither the smile nor the tone seemed sincere.

The garden party was a great success. The tennis lawns were in excellent condition, for his feverish sense of his responsibilities made the senior tutor keep a close and intelligent eye upon his gardeners. The Mauve Hungarians played as well as usual music, which was about as bad as usual. The sets were made up as well as could be expected, considering that social and even academical distinctions had their effect on the invitations to play. Mrs. Devigny at the highest point of her fascination captured an advanced don. He was a change from the other type and he amused her just as much. It was a particularly delicious moment when he explained to her that he considered the attendance of anybody at a religious service to be cowardly and immoral—anti-moral was his pet word for it—but he attended college chapel because it was necessary for him to set a good example. She led him gently on to his most unheaving, rebellious, and iconoclastic mood, and then checked his exposal of the Vatican with the statement, entirely untrue, that she happened to be a Catholic. It is to be feared that she was slightly malicious that afternoon. But she refused an ice and accepted his apologies. Linda talked to everybody without distinction, and forgot for the time that anything worried her. It was somewhat late in the afternoon when Percy Belton, who on the competitive test never ought to have been invited, emerged, handsome and modest, from his victory in a single. He had the misfortune to stumble upon the senior tutor.

"I congratulate you, Mr. Belton," said Mr. Trotter. "I only regret," he added, with a distinct note of sub-acidity in his voice, "that you have never thought it worth your while to attain proficiency in certain other arts, of, perhaps, equal importance. Equal, I think, hardly overstates it."

Linda saw the young man, and he was quite good to look at. She saw that he was humiliated. She saw that he would give the eyes out of his head (fine eyes as they were) to be able to speak to her. So, as he had never been introduced to her, she went up and spoke to him. A few minutes later they were strolling in the direction of the shrubberies, and the young man was being quite simple and quite young.

She was inclined to like him in a kind of way, much as one might like a well-bred, spirited dog.

With him, of course, it was quite different. The sarcasm of the senior tutor had sunk into oblivion. He was talking to the girl about whom everybody raved, and he was talking to her because she had deliberately shown that she wished to talk to him.

"What are you going to do this Long?" she asked, carelessly.

"They won't have me here," he said, dolefully. And she suddenly felt that her question had been a little indelicate.

"No, I forgot," she said. "I always understood that you did not intend to take honours."

"Couldn't get 'em," he said, simply. "Of course, I've got to work. They are pretty sick about it at home, about my being spun again, I mean. They don't seem to understand what a lot of other things there are to do."

"There must be," said Linda, with conviction. "And one does not want to be too much narrowed down."

"I wish to goodness you would talk to my father," said the young man, with sincerity. "That is just exactly the kind of thing that he ought to have said to him. In fact, I've tried to say it myself. However, I've got to go to Calcote."

"And who's that?"

"He's a parson away on the Norfolk marshes, and he's supposed to have a special gift for dealing with the kind of man which I'm supposed to be. I've been there before. That was in the winter, though, when one could get duck and snipe."

"Get?"

"Yes. Shoot, you know. Of course, this time of the year there isn't anything but pigeons. Perhaps it's better so," he added with an air of settled melancholy. "Of course, it's not as it would be if anybody took a real interest in anybody. You see what I mean."

She saw with the utmost perspicuity, and switched off at once.

"What's the name of the place?" she asked.

"Oatacre-by-Merlham. Funny sort of name, isn't it?"

"Not to me. Merlham is my native place."

"Of course. You are Miss Merle—of Merlesfleet. Do you come from there?"

"Yes, I am Miss Merle. How clever of you to have guessed it, as we have never been introduced. Merlesfleet is mine. I don't even know what the name means."

"Oh, I can tell you that. It isn't often I can tell anybody anything. The 'Fleet' is the dyke which runs through the home park. They call all dykes connected with tidal rivers 'fleets' down there. Why, it's a famous place. Of course, you've heard about the witch who was drowned there more than a hundred years ago?"

She put one hand on his arm impulsively. "Tell me all about that, please. Everything."

"I don't know everything, and that's one of the reasons why I'm under a sort of cloud at present. But I'll tell you what I know. The old woman's name was Jennis, and she was known as a witch all over there—East Anglia, you. know."

"Why did they drown her?"

"Oh she was believed to have bewitched some one in Merlham village, so they tied her hands and feet together and threw her in the Merles Fleet to see if she could swim. She didn't."

"Horrible. Why, what a queer name Jennis is."

"Oh, there's a Judith Jennis living there now with much the same reputation—a granddaughter, or great granddaughter, or something. I believe she's a tenant of yours, by the bye."

"Oh?"

"Yes. She's got a funny kind of place. The Tower House they call it. I believe it was built first for the marshmen to watch where the duck settled when the floods were out on the marshes. It's a rummy round-built place; one room below and one above with a sort of a look-out on the roof. She makes some of her money by dairy business and the rest of it— the greater part—"

"Well?"

"Oh, I don't know. All the marsh people come to her. There may be nothing in it, I've heard some queer things though. I had a very good experience myself."

"Tell me about it."

"Well, there wasn't much in it. But it was curious. I was going down the river with my gun when I met her. She was having some bother with her geese which she wanted to drive home, and I gave her a hand. Before I left her she looked in a funny way at me and asked if I should like to know what sport I was going to have. I said I didn't mind. She told me that I should shoot something I had never shot before, and see a sight I had never seen before."

"And did you?"

"Yes. Absolutely true. All of it. I shot a bittern, an old 'buttle' they call it about there. They are precious rare in England, and at first I didn't know what I shot. Coming home along the wall of the Cut, which was frozen over, I saw an even stranger thing. Two dog otters were fighting on the ice in the middle of the Cut. They did not seem to notice me, and I might have shot them both if I had not thought it better sport to watch 'em fight it out. I'd got number four shot in both barrels—but this won't interest you."

"It interests me very much. And is the woman living there now?"

"I don't know. But she was the winter before last."

They had joined the crowd again. She turned to him apologetically. "There are such lots of people looking for me, you know. I hope I shall see you when I am down at Merlesfleet."

The young man sought for a compromise between the ecstatic and the respectful, but she was gone before he had found it.

A minute later she was clutching Mrs. Devigny by the arm.

"It's all settled, Cara. Everything is changed. We are both going to Merlesfleet. I will tell you why after dinner."

Chapter III

Merlesfleet

Linda sat at the writing-table in the morning- room opening letters. There was on her face a look of greater life and eagerness than it had worn of late. There was a tinge of colour in her cheeks now. Mrs. Devigny sat opposite to her and watched her. Otherwise Mrs. Devigny was doing nothing. But she did nothing with great grace. Her elbows rested on the table and her chin on her two hands. The sleeves fell back and showed her pretty arms.

"Cara," said Linda, "you manage to get along with less occupation than any woman I know."

"Yes," said Mrs. Devigny, "I am the laziest creature that has yet been bred in captivity. But as a matter of fact I was deeply occupied. I was thinking."

Linda produced a penny.

"You wouldn't like your bargain. What would you yourself think about a girl who had decided when her days of freedom came to remain with her guardian for a few months and soften the blow of her departure?"

"I never said anything so conceited," said Linda, indignantly.

"Don't interrupt. You're going to hear the cold truth about yourself.

You had bought Baedekers and studied Bradshaws, and driven the young men at Cook's office in Piccadilly half mad. As soon as you felt that your guardian could bear it you had mapped out a year or more of travel, and had decided to take with you a tired, ginger-haired old woman called Cara Devigny."

"I don't permit you to insult my friends," said Linda, with a beautiful assumption of the glacial manner.

"I've had to speak about these interruptions before; don't let it occur again. This same girl happens to meet a handsome undergraduate and learns from him that somewhere about seven thousand years ago an old woman was drowned in the ornamental waters of her ancestral mansion. All the plans are blown sky-high at once. The feelings of the guardian are accounted for nothing. An army of painters and decorators is put into motion and harassed by absurd and unreasonable demands. The elderly lady, with red hair, is ordered to mobilise. No time is to be lost. The girl must get down to the aforesaid ancestral mansion at once. Sounds reasonable, doesn't it?"

"Of course it does not when it's put like that. Do you mean any of it?"

Mrs. Devigny suddenly changed her manner. "All I mean, dear, is that I don't quite understand why you want to go. As far as I myself am concerned, so long as I am to be with you I am delighted to go anywhere between here and the hereafter, but I'm not sure that I see your point of view."

Linda tossed aside the last of her letters. "It's like this, Cara. I thought I could live here for a few months longer, and I find I can't. I am suffering from uncle-on-the-nerves."

"Seniortutoritis," suggested Mrs. Devigny.

"Good," said Linda, "here I have a chance of leaving at once without offending him. I go to prepare a way—to air the mattress, to order the band, to erect the triumphal arch. Then, when all is ready, he and Aunt Mary come down as my guests. By that time I shall have had a rest, and shall like them better. As for the witch, the thing that happened a hundred years or so ago doesn't matter much to me or to anybody else. But think of the things that are happening there to-day. There are simple people there who are going hand-in-hand with the unseen, like a child with its mother. The powers of Judith Jennis are as much a fact to them as the price of butter or the rate of wages. I want to see that. I want to see it immensely. Then, again, I think it must be a kind of homing instinct that calls me there. My people have lived there from time immemorial, and now suddenly I feel that I must be there too. Do you see? It's not so much that I want to go. There's a compulsion on me to go. I think—"

She stopped as the door opened and Mr. Willoughby Trotter came in. Mrs. Devigny rose at once.

"Now, now, now," said Mr. Trotter, "don't let me drive anybody away."

"I know you must have so much business with Linda," said Mrs. Devigny, "and I have so many letters to write myself."

She vanished gracefully.

Linda held out a letter to her guardian. "This is Tallant and Hogg, the electric light people. They are making the reduction for cash as you suggested, and accept the time clause. How on earth could I have got on without you! I did not know there was such a thing as a time clause."

"Well, well," said her guardian, indulgently, "young ladies are not expected to be versed in these matters. You would have found it very unpleasant if the place had been still full of workmen on your arrival. The reduction, too, is quite right. Most firms are only too glad to make it. Satisfactory to both parties. What I wanted to speak to you about particularly was——er—Mr. Laurence Hebbelthwaite."

"Yes? The ex-parson, I suppose? Nasty words, by the way. Sounds like ex-convict."

"You must not let that distress you," he said, with a somewhat fatuous misapprehension, "he relinquished his orders long ago. But I have not understood that he has ceased to be a Christian in the sense which a broadminded man would give to the term. Breadth without laxity (if I may so phrase it) should be the note of serious people in their attitude towards religion. There is a chapter in 'My Tour in Galilee' which bears somewhat on this. What I wished to say particularly was that I have had a letter from Hebbelthwaithe. He had heard, of course, of your going down to take possession, and he proposes to call on you. Says that he thinks himself old enough and ugly enough to call on any young lady. He always had that free and rather slangy way of expressing himself. I dislike it immensely."

"Is he very ugly?" asked Linda.

"That," said Mr. Trotter, reflectively, "is not a point which I have ever noticed. On the occasions when we have met he struck me as being a very large man. Far above the usual height, I suppose. Certainly taller than I am. But these are not essential points, are they? I know of nothing against his character. He is a man, too, of some learning, and has talent, perhaps somewhat undisciplined. He is well endowed, too, with this world's goods.

Not that that is a question which affects us, and, of course, you'll have a sufficient chaperon in Mrs. Devigny. Still, I thought I would put it to you. If you would prefer not to see him for any reason, if you wish to be alone, you have only to say so, and I will send him a line. I have, perhaps, some little facility for letters of this kind. As senior tutor it frequently becomes my duty to convey unpleasant information in as polite a manner as possible."

"Oh, no," said Linda, "do let him come; one does not want to be unkind. Say we shall be glad to receive him. Why, if he has money and a mind, does he want to bury himself in solitude in a marsh village?"

"That," said Mr. Trotter, seriously, "is a point which he has never explained to me. I have given him opportunities to explain it—I may say I have been careful to make the opportunities. It would perhaps have been in better taste if he had availed himself of them. However, he is a man in whom there is a demarkation, a definite line of reserve. He seems to be speaking freely and carelessly, but one never gets beyond a certain point with him."

A fortnight later Linda and Cara were on their way to Merlesfleet.

When it became known in the village of Merlham that the last surviving Merle was soon coming back to the home where her family had lived for centuries, there was, of course, no little excitement. Little Jimmy Buddery, the wizened custodian of the draining mill which kept the waters from the Merlesfleet marshes, expressed the feelings of the neighbourhood over his evening "pint" at the Tench and Teal.

"I'm somethin' glad ta l'arn as the young missis be a comin' down ta taake har rightful plaace at the Hall at last o' time. That'll dew a bit o' good ta us pore men. We hain't got a sight out o' the mean warmins what ha' been kapin' the lay warm for har. But p'raps a pratty young wench like har whew ha' got the blood o' the mashes in har weins oan't grudge a pint or tew ta ole men whew ha' knowed her faa'er an' har grandfaa'er! Ah! an' fudder back tew."

"Hare dee yew stop a min't, bor," said Bob Middleton. "Wha, yew maake yarself out as old as Methusalum."

Little Jimmy drank from his pint measure, and wiped his mouth on his fingers, and his fingers on the blue slop, which, together with a conical felt hat, made his costume famous for miles round.

"Well, howsomediver, I mind more about har parients 'an yew dew, Bob, bor. I reckon if she give any one lave to pick a few right sort runes" (mushrooms), "or gather a scoor or tew or hornpie" (green plover) "eggs, I ote ta be the one."

"Ah! Yew allust wuz a hungry-gutted ole mousehunter" (stoat), said Bob. "But theer! Iverybardy know as yew fare half innercent. Soo noo doubt yew'll fare ta be took care on."

"Ah 'thout that booy o' Judy Jennis's git fust saay. Tha'ss give out a'riddy as she's ta hev the prowidin' things for the Hall, an' that doan't dew ta intarfare along o' Judy, as some folk ha' found out ta theer cost."

At this several weatherbeaten heads were solemnly shaken in the kitchen, where the evening symposium of the village worthies was always held. The name of Judith seemed to impress them uncannily. They shifted uneasily in their seats.

A short pause in the talk permitted the unctuous puffing of shag smoke to be heard in the room. They took their pipes heavily, drew hard, and exhaled loudly.

In the corner was sitting a tall ungainly man, whose ragged coat was decorated with a number of pseudo medals, made of stamped pieces of tin and buttons covered with silver foil. The heavy humour of the place had conferred them on this poor half-witted fellow (who yet was not half such a fool as he was thought to be, for all his pride in the medals) in sarcastic recognition of his powers of foretelling the weather. His name was Billy Hart, but he liked to be called "Sir William," and half believed in his title.

He was the first to break the silence.

"D'ye mind when Judy put a some'at onta ole Hook o' Thousand Acre Holdin'?" he asked. "Ah! That wuz whoolly a masterpiece. I see myself when his hay-cart stuck right i' the middle o' the gate of his gre't foorty aacre mowin' mash. That didn't touch agin' the gaate nowheers, but though he called up t'ree moor hosses besides the t'ree he had i' the cart a'riddy, mewve it they coun't till he went an' axed the witch's paardon for mobbin' on her when he copped har takin' a stick or tew for kin'lin' out o' his wood stack. She git all the kin'lin she want now, without noo axin' nei-ther."

Bob shuffled with his feet and rose to leave the house. Before he went he expectorated into the empty fireplace. "That bain't up to much, talkin' about har," he said. "I ha' spat for luck, but I doubt ill ull come on yar silly tongue for all that. Yew ote tew ha' knowed better, Billy."

"If gennlemen can call me 'Sir William,' yew can," said poor Billy. "T'other day—"

"Tha'ss enow on't," said the landlord, abruptly. And the conversation returned to the approaching advent of the lady of Merlesfleet.

The Hall of Merlesfleet is one of the oldest buildings in the Eastern

Counties. Some antiquarians claim that the huge flint foundations of part of its western side date back as far as the rule of the Danes in East Anglia. But the greater part of the building, and especially the superb hall, is of the Tudor period. The more modern rooms are a mixture of Jacobean and Georgian architecture, and have a special interest in that their outside walls were mostly composed of the hard, rich-tinted Roman bricks which were distributed about the country-side on the demolition of an old Roman castle hard by. The front of the Hall bays itself out irregularly on a terrace, from which the home park sweeps down over a well-timbered stretch of grassland to the dense plantations of larch, silver birch, spruce, oak, ash, and elm, which are fringed to the westward by the growth of sallow alder and hazel, which screens much of the marshland lying along the banks of the Fleet from the park. The woods and thickets sweep round circuitously to the nor'ard till the Fleet marshes merge in the greater expanse of the Yare and Waveney valley levels.

The woods and undergrowth are full of wild life. Wild pheasants nest and rear their broods amid the tussocks of marsh grass along the cars and coverts. The hollow music of the ringed pigeon's call echoes throughout the venerable trees. In the soft nights of summer-time the moth-hawks rend the stillness of the woodland gloom with their raucous scraping cry, and flit through the leafy maze of branch and twig like some fantastic flapping ghosts of evil birds. Where the Fleet broadens to a pool, wild duck and teal breed in the rushes, and the drum of the snipe in spring and his hovering flight (so different from his swift angular darts at other seasons of the year) remind the old folks of the village of the days when it was no unusual thing for fifty couple of the pretty long-beaked birds to be taken in a single night in horse-hair springes laid in the marsh drains.

Away further to the nor'-west, where the Tower House still stands as sentinel on the border-land of upland and true marsh, the wail of the hornpie makes the air dolorous with its complaint. It is cheery to hear the shrill whistle of the red-legs remonstrating with the pessimism of their tufted kindred. But the hornpie knows whose eggs are the most sought after, and will not be comforted.

On the eastward side of the house is an old-fashioned garden, walled in by a ten-foot wall four feet thick, along which stone-fruit ripens to the western sun.

From the nor'-west end of the terrace, a footpath runs to a point where a mossy cart track passes through the dense wood to the stables and out-buildings at the back of the house, affording a way for the pony-carriage of the Hall to pass to the Tower House, which was at one time the house of the Home Farm. Under Mr. Trotter's management, the Home Farm house was now represented by a block of modern and model buildings, provided with the latest appliances of scientific agriculture, and capable of supplying the house with all farm produce, even when filled with guests. The old Tower House was let separately to Judith Jennis, as it had been to her forebears for almost as many years as there had been Merles at Merlesfleet. With this went grazing rights over a tract of marsh which sufficed to provide a living for her goats and geese. Mr. Trotter had always dealt leniently and charitably with her—and had never omitted to tell her so.

Her goats' milk cheeses were famous, and by these alone she might have lived. It was typical of Mr. Trotter that, with all his shrewdness, he never suspected the means by which she supplemented that livelihood. There was hardly a day on which she did not receive tribute from some peasant seeking the advice of the wise woman.

The servants and the luggage came down from Cambridge by train. Mrs. Devigny and Linda Merle drove down in Linda's new car. They arrived at dusk. Swiftly though they passed, little Jimmy Buddery saw them, and guessed their identity. He was the bearer of the news of their arrival to the coterie at the Tench and Teal.

"Ah!" said he. "They wuz a buzzin' along like a woodcarck afore a blow, an' though that din't fare cold they wuz wropped up a rum un. But theer, bors, they did look deelaightful! The young missis wuz a twiddlin' a little titty wheel. I rackon tha'ss what wark it. But theer, bors; yew'll ha'e ta see for yarselves!"

"Wha yew silly chump," said the landlord; "ta bain't that at all. Tha'ss what they steer by, saame as they dew aboord them theer steam drifters what fare soo poplar now."

"Well," said Jimmy, "yew may be right as ta that, though I see't an' yew din't. But if tha'ss so, what dew maake it whizz along?"

"Ah!" says the landlord, "theer I own as yew ha' done me."

Jimmy turned slowly round to all the others in the kitchen, with a smile of triumph wrinkling his face. "What did I tall ye?" he asked, contemptuously. "He doan't knoo noo moor 'an us uns. Gie's a pint, bor, dew. That theer rood engine whoolly druv the dust down my t'root."

Chapter IV

Looking-Glass Writing

The August sunlight streamed in the curious hall, the doors of which were wide open to the terrace. It was a large, square hall. The inside walls were of Roman brick, beautifully set, and uncovered by panelling, paint, or plaster. There were a few portraits in heavy frames, and some fine old French tapestry. But for the modern electric light fittings and the silken Persian rugs on the floor, it was practically unfurnished. It gave an effect of space, light, and colour, refreshing to Linda, sick of the cramped and over-decorated rooms of artistic London and the crowded ugliness of the provinces. There was no staircase. This led from the smaller hall beyond it.

Linda and Cara, their arms about each other's waists, came slowly across the hall through the gaunt, empty dining-room into the smaller room, where they took luncheon. Linda had left many arrangements to the care of Mrs. Devigny, and Mrs. Devigny was above all things modern and luxurious. That bread and butter pudding, the burning of which Mr. Trotter had considered as a personal stain upon him, did not appear upon the table. Everything was quiet, unpretentious, and exquisite. It had given Mrs. Devigny much thought. Linda would not have liked to take the thought, but she did like the results of it. She said as much.

"Personally," said Mrs. Devigny, "I put up quite easily with anything. I hate the Simple Life. I can't pretend that I really like Young Oxford or Underdone Mutton or Diseases. But I would cheerfully put up with the whole lot of them to be with you. If I have taken thought for to-morrow, it is because I wanted to see you in your proper setting. This suave, delicate, restrained kind of life—it is your atmosphere. You are so perfectly tuned—"

"Do not be an idolater and an idiot. If you talk like this, I will demand steak and onions, and I shouldn't like it. What are you going to do, Cara, when you have arranged everything, when you have no longer got any sphere for your artistic activities? Remember there is no society here."

"No," said Cara, "I suppose not. You will interchange functions with the different magnates who have called on you, but they are all too far away to make intimacy possible. Mr. Calcote has called; Mr. Belton has found us out and left his card; the ex-parson will probably call one of these days—that's about all. Yes, there's the local doctor, of course. But then, of course, there is always the local doctor, isn't there? 'Ca m'est égal.'

I had enough of society of one kind and another— chiefly the other—in my two years of married life. This is not the kind of thing which bores one. I love your house. I love your adorable marsh country. I wonder why the beauties of the marshes are not better known. Your English tourists must have hills. 'No hill, no beauty,' he says, and we may thank God for it. Almost for the first time in my life I am happy and placid and content."

"I am very glad of it," said Linda. "What will you do when the senior tutor and Aunt Mary come down?"

"Specks on the sun. They will vanish, and I shan't. I shall be very, very good to your Aunt Mary."

"She adores you already," said Linda, carelessly.

"I'm glad I didn't miss that target altogether. Well, I don't want to make phrases, but really I do like this very much."

"Boredom is waiting for you," said Linda. "At present you find many things to do, and they are the kind of things which you like to do. Also we shall not be here for the whole of the year, of course. But there must come a time when you will find that you have absolutely nothing to do."

"It has come! That is the glory of it. Have I ever shown you an over-mastering passion for occupation?"

"It is all the sweeter of you to have worked so hard and to have done so much for me. . . ."

"I can't even try to please you without pleasing myself far more. There are always books. Thank God, there is always music. Thank God just a lit-tle more, there is always you."

"You are just a little too enthusiastic," said Linda, drily. "Fortunately, your enthusiasms are rare. And when you are talking to me without wit-nesses you cannot expect me to go to the expense of a blush. It's just your way, and I know it. But look at the thing practically. There is an afternoon before us. What are you going to do with it?"

"Planchette," said Cara, without hesitation.

"It never worked before."

"Do you expect a Planchette to work in the house of a senior tutor? There are temperatures so low that the bacilli cannot live in them. I feel the atmosphere of it here. I am hedged in by the stupid belief of a thou-sand rustics. I join in their contempt of all that is not traditional. As you said, they walk hand in hand with the unseen. Planchette will work here, you will see."

"For me or for you?"

"For you, of course."

"Why?"

"Who was the child who propitiated the Devil with unseen, unmentioned, and unmentionable rites?"

Linda's pale face blushed crimson. She stamped her foot. "Stop!" she cried. Then she laughed: "What a donkey I am. I forgot you didn't know. Well, we'll try it. We shall get the afternoon sun in the south drawing-room. Let's go there."

"The sunlight's terribly healthy and purifying," said Cara. "I wish you could have thought of something slightly more morbid. There are such things as churchyards, you know."

They both laughed. Neither at this moment had the slightest belief in Planchette.

"Never mind," said Linda. "Bring that silly shilling toy along. And this time I swear by the beard of my grandfather that I will not cheat. If the thing does not work we will simply go without it. We will find Judith Jennis. We will raise the Devil in some entirely different way."

The Planchette was brought and tried. Mrs. Devigny put her hands upon it first, and met with no response. "I knew I should get nothing," she said, with a sigh, "I'm too metallic."

"Too electric," suggested Linda.

"Now you try," said Mrs. Devigny.

Linda drew up a chair to the table and put the tips of her fingers lightly on the board of the Planchette.

For a while nothing happened. In the lull of their babble, the clock on the mantelpiece took on a new and dictatorial tick. It commanded each moment. Slowly Linda sank back in her chair and her eyes closed, her hand still resting on the board of the Planchette. Mrs. Devigny looked uneasy. She waited a moment, and then came forward. It had been her intention to touch Linda on the shoulder, and to suggest that they should play at something else. Just as she raised her hand the Planchette began to move, and to move rapidly. There was no possibility of fraud here. Linda's eyes were closed, and if they had been opened they would have been staring up at the ceiling. Also Mrs. Devigny noticed with regret that the marks on the paper were unintelligible. They looked like letters, but she could make nothing of them.

The Planchette stopped. There was a dead pause of a few seconds. Then Linda opened her eyes. "It's no good," she said. "I can't do it. The thing won't stir as fraction of an inch for me."

"But it's done it," cried Mrs. Devigny, excitedly. "You must have been asleep. It has really done it. Just look at this." She held up the sheet of paper.

Linda smiled feebly. "There's something there," she said, "but what is it? I can't read it. Can you?"

Cara seized the paper. "No," she said, "it looks like letters, and yet . . . Wait! Wait! It's looking-glass writing." She rushed to the window and held the sheet firmly pressed to the pane. They puzzled out the writing together.

"The first words are clear enough," said Linda. "It is the cup."

"Then comes 'of the,'" said Mrs. Devigny. "But the last word? That's a capital S.'"

"Yes," said Mrs. Devigny, and snatched the paper from the window-pane. "Give it me."

"Give it me again," said Linda.

"It's not worth while," said Cara. "The fact of the case is that Planchette's writing is so bad that you can make it mean anything. The first three or four words were clear enough, but the rest might be anything."

"I want you," said Linda, quite seriously, "to give me that paper. Now, please, at once. I am going—"

The door opened, and Mr. Laurence Hebbelthwaite was announced.

All mystery fell dead at the entrance of that easy giant. The first thing which impressed Linda was that he was much younger than she expected. She had pictured him as a man of the same age as her uncle. He could hardly have been more than thirty-five. His manner was perfectly simple and natural, but all the time she realised that her uncle had been right. There was a point in this man beyond which one did not get.

Mrs. Devigny, an educated woman, tried to find his line, in order that she might take a decent interest in it. She was clever, and she ranged quickly from one point to another. He knew so much, and he was so absolutely natural, that she began to think it worth while to look at him. She saw a strong face, very near to being handsome, with eyes that cut like razors. There was the flash of blue steel in them all the time. Certainly, as the senior tutor had said, he was not very conventional, nor very literary. He used the words on his lips without hesitation. His spirits were boyish. His evident knowledge of the social world was welcome. His intelligent interest in every topic was interesting. "He brought the interest with him when he came," said Cara afterwards.

And afterwards she put down in writing a collection of the facts which she had learned in a very few minutes from a man who had never appeared to try to teach her anything. They were as follows:

1. The reason why the village children looked less healthy than the London children was because they did not get so much milk. Milk is money in the country.

2. The common about Merlesfleet was full of vipers. In spite of science, many village folk were prepared to swear that they had many times seen the female viper swallow its young.

3. That an analogy might be made between the three great masters of the nineteenth century—Richard Wagner, Robert Browning, and George Meredith.

4. That an eel has never been known to swim up stream.

5. That a mackerel often kills itself by striking against the net in which it is enmeshed.

6. That Judith Jennis ought to be taken out and shot.

He left two startled and interested people—one of them, Linda, followed him into the hall. "I hope you will come again soon," she said. "My uncle will be down here very shortly. You know him, I think?"

"Yes," he said. "What was that thing you had on the other table?"

"The one in the window?—Planchette."

"I thought so," said he. "It's simply a little toy, of course. All the same, I wouldn't play with it if I were you."

"Then what would you like me to do with it?" said Linda.

"Burn it," he snapped. "That kind of thing is not good for you."

There was a slight emphasis on the last word.

Linda laughed. "Quite sure? You see, you don't know me very well, do you? Is there any other article of furniture in the house you'd like me to burn?"

"I mean what I say," he said, angrily. "You do not know what you're doing."

Linda was rather angry, too, and she put a drop of venom on the tip of the dagger. "Oh, please," she said, with the sweetest of smiles, "don't talk to me as if I were a congregation."

"Good-bye," he said, quietly. It made her the more angry that there was nothing whatever in his tone or manner to show that the allusion had penetrated.

The servant closed the door. And on his innocent head the storm broke. "Don't do that," she said. "How can you be so clumsy. You must learn to shut a door quietly." And the man, who had closed the heavy doors as quietly as was practicable, was amazed. Linda went back into the drawing-room.

"Well?" said Linda to Mrs. Devigny.

"Oh, of course, I like him," said Cara. "He's a fairly strong kind of man, isn't he?"

"Strength," said Linda, "is sometimes another name for rudeness."

"But he wasn't rude, was he?"

"Not intentionally, I'll do him that justice. It was in the hall just now. He treated me like a confirmation class. That's all. I took the liberty of telling him so, or something very like it."

"You see the possibility, dear, don't you—that a thing of that kind said to him might be rather cruel?"

"I hoped it would be rather cruel," said Linda. "But I'm afraid it wasn't. The man was preposterous. What do you think he said? He told me to burn Planchette. That reminds me. Now, give me that paper. This has become interesting. I'm going back to it."

"Look here," said Mrs. Devigny. She drew out the basket from under the writing-table. In it was that sheet of paper torn into tiny scraps and the wreck of the Planchette. "Yes," she said, "I did it myself. These cheap toys break very easily. I should have spoken to you about it first. Am I to get a month's notice?"

Linda swayed for a moment, and then kissed her impulsively. "I'm afraid I've been in a bad temper," she said. "Take me out into the garden and make me good again. When we come back I'll write and ask that man to lunch."

Chapter V

The Face on the Blotting Paper

The August mist still lay heavy along the levels of marshland when Bob Middleton and "Sir William" Hart drew near the door of the windmill, with which it was the duty of little Jimmy Buddery to keep the marsh dykes down to their proper level. Bob was on his morning round to inspect the few sheep and colts which remained on the grazing land, although the lusciousness of the sweet May grass had long turned to sourness, and there was but little good left in the withered pasture. "Sir William" had chosen to accompany the marshman on his round, in order to inspect the various signs of marsh, reed, water, and sedge with which he boasted that he was able to predict the weather with certainty. He wore his string of medals outside his coat, and as the sun began to work its way through the veil of the mist, now drifting along in filmy swathes before an awakening breeze, it shone and glittered merrily on the tokens of the poor man's simplicity of soul. As the two approached the door of the mill, little Jimmy came out on to the river wall. He took the long pole in his hand with which the marshmen set the sails to catch the best of the wind, and as he tiptoed up to reach the regulating sail he looked like a monkey on a stick which had been pushed to the extremity of the toy.

"Hi, Jimmy, bor!" shouted Bob. "Ha'e ye got a drop of liquor? This hare thick o' the mornin' git onta my chest. I could dew with a drop ta warm my innards."

"Mornin', Barb, mornin'," said little Jimmy, stretching away over his head, without turning to look at his visitor.

"Wha'ss that yew, Billy, bor?" he added. He had heard the chink of the medals, and knew that Bob had brought a companion with him. "Well! What d'ye think on it? Shall us fare ta hey a drop o' rain afore night? The sun was wonnerful red when that set larse night."

"If yew waant ta ax me about my business yew can gi'e me my proper naame," said poor Billy. "If gennlemen can call me 'Sir William' that doan't bemane yew ta dew't?"

"I'm shore I ax yar pardon, Sir Willum," said little Jimmy, turning with a grin to where the other two were now standing against him. "Will yew, Sir Willum, kindly tell a pore maan if yew think as we're a gooin' ta hey a drarp o' rain ta swell the wheat afore it ripen or not? I ha' got half an acre on my 'lotments, and that'll make a differ o' far or five bushel whether we hev rain or noo."

"Sir William" looked carefully up at the clearing sky. Then he pulled some marsh grass from the foot of the river wall, raised it to his nose, and smelt it.

"I'll dew what I can for ye, Jimmy," he said. "But if ta doan't come, doan't ye blaame me. Ye see, I can't plaise iverybardy. But I'll dew my best, I prarmuss ye that."

Sir William often believed that he could act as the cloud controller. Mr. Willoughby Trotter himself had not a larger sense of his responsibilities.

"But what about that drarp o' liquor, Jimmy?" asked Bob, who knew that even in the twentieth century an occasional if rare anker of Hollands gin found its way up the river unbeknown to the revenue authorities, and also knew that if there were any to be had little Jimmy would have it.

"If yew want any liquor yew must wark foor't," said Jimmy. "Lor' blaame my ole heart alive, yew mashmen doan't never dew enow wark ta maake a bacon hog sweat."

Jimmy, as the "minder" of the mill, did not consider himself as a "mashman" pure and simple. If anything, his work was less burdensome even than that of Bob Middleton.

"I'll lay I dew t'ree times as much wark in a yare as yew dew in far," said Bob. "Yew niver dew narthen aside muddle about wi' that ole mill. What dee yew knoo about the deeak drawin'—the scoopin' out o' the drains wi' the half moon, the weed cuttin' wi' the crane an' the cairner? Blust! Wha' when the time come for settin' the mash ta rights in October, when all the things are off, that 'ud taake a bigger maan 'an yew, ye little warter rat, ta dew a man's wark on a one journey trip. Could yew mow the reed rands? Yar little arms hain't got enow sap in 'em to send the scythe t'rew the stiffenin' stems. Goo along wi' ye, dew, ye little dickey. Come yew on, Sir Willum. I must count them colts on the hornpie mash, and the sheep on the foul mash. Blarmed if I doan't believe another o' them cussed sheep ha' got drownded in a deeak. There'll whoolly be a mobbin'. That'll be the sacond this month. But ta bain't my fault. Sheep hadn't niver ote to be left down ta mash by 'emselves. There'll be the skinnin' ta dew, an' the meeat all wasted. An' folk ull saay as that's my fault. One, tew, t'ree, far," and Bob went on to count a large flock almost instantaneously, with the wonderful eye of his craft, which can sum the total of a huge gathering of distant animals which looks infinitesimal on the vast flat expanse.

But though Jimmy did not want to part with his cherished "liquor," neither did he wish his morning's "mardle " (gossip) to be cut short.

He sacrificed the former for the sake of the latter.

"Hare, waait yew a min't, Barb, bor," he said, querulously. "Yew doan't waant to be sa short-waisted. I doan't saay as I hain't gart a drop o' tew o' Hollands gin in the mill."

"Ah! I knowed yew worn't sich a meean warmin as yew maade out ta be," said. Bob, softening.

Presently Jimmy and Bob stood with vessels of transparent horn, quaintly carved with lines suggesting rustic revelry. "Sir William" had no gin. He said himself he could "dew a drarp o' bare, but hadn't noo hid for liquor."

"Well," said. Bob, raising his measure of Hollands, "hare's enow wind, an' not tew much warter."

"An' hare's planty" o' fowl and d——n the decoy," replied Jimmy, each of the men courteously expressing the wish which he knew would be the darling of the other's heart.

"An' hare's to the young missis at the Hall," said "Sir William," with an imbecile chuckle. He plucked a leaf of the arrowhead which covered the dyke at his feet with shapely foliage and the seed vessels and stamens of the faded blossoms, and, scooping up a mouthful of water in it, he drank. "I reckon as she's the best thing as Gord or the Black Maan ha' sent us uns this many a yare."

"Yew might ha' waited till yew could ha' droonk har health in good bare," said Bob. "That may bring bad luck in the water."

"Not Sir Willum's wish," said poor Billy, solemnly.

"Sir Willum's friends wi' warter, wind, an' weather. That'll help har, Gord bless har pratty faace an' kape it saafe from the bad things o' mash, river, an' deeak; from Hob o' Lantern, from witch, wizard, and the black man o' the mash."

"Ah! she's a pratty dallikit titty bit," said Bob.

"Ah," said Jimmy. "But gi'e me the one wi' red heer. She's my mark."

"Tha'ss yar maneness again," said Bob, laughing. "Yew think as har hid ud saave yew cools i' winter."

"Oh, yew hode yar n'ise," said Jimmy. "An' doan't yew forget what Judy Jennis said t'other daay about the young missis. What wuz't, Sir Willum?"

"Sir William," having been given his title, was in a good humour. He spoke eagerly, with the definition of detail which is only possible to the marvellous memories which many of these wrongly-named "innocents" possess.

"I wuz a hidin' unner the north wall o' the Fleet deeak," he said, "watchin' for a parcel o' teal ta settle agin the springes which I'd set for 'em. The sun wuz a'moost due west, an' the oony buds as still piped wuz the maavishes. Theer worn't a breath o' wind, an' I lay still as a water hin unner a pollard stump when a dorg's a' nosin' arter her. Prasently I heerd Judy come t'rew the larch plantin', an' oh! She come quick an' sorft as an otter t'rew the tussocks. I hadn't noo right to be wheer I wuz, an' I didn't knoo but what she might ha' got thick wi' the young missis, seein' as she taake har cheeses up ta the Hall. I didn't waant no bother, an' I kep' still. But she didn't see me, nor yit she didn't seem to see narthen. She wuz a starin' up at the sky saame as I ha' seed yew stare up at flightin' time on a sheer night, Bob, bor, when yew could hare the duck above yar hid, but coun't see 'em. She come ta the pool wheer har great-gran'mother was drownded, as they saay, an' she h'isted her arms up above her hid. For a min't or two she stood still. Then she said some rum rhymin' wuds which I can hare now:

> "'The maid and the witch dance hand in hand
> When the Black Man comes from the mash to land.
> Sister is she, and sister am I,
> And one must live, an' t'other must die—
> The ch'ice is the Maaster's. She or I?'

"When she'd said them rhymes she tarned an' went back agin inta the wood."

Jimmy and Bob looked at each other, and then at "Sir William," and frank, if incredulous, admiration shone in their eyes.

"He run it off prarper; din't he?" said Jimmy.

"Ah!" said Bob. "He ha' gart a sight moor sense 'an what some folk think. I shoun't wunner if he become as much of a mean as yew or me one daay. Wha, Billy, bor, yew'll sapparise some on 'em arter all."

Poor Billy, who had stood by with a pleased smile of satisfaction at the words of praise, changed his expression as he was called "Billy." "My name's 'Sir Willum,'" he said, and, turning away, he walked out upon the rand, where he soon disappeared under cover of a dense growth of reeds.

All unconscious of rustic comment, Mrs. Devigny and Linda Merle walked that morning in the garden of Merlesfleet. Linda heard for the first time what Laurence Hebbelthwaite had said about Judith Jennis. It had been said when she was in the room, but at a moment when her attention was distracted. Such moments of reverie were becoming more common with her.

"So Judith Jennis is to be taken out and shot, is she? And the Planchette was to be burned. But in the meantime you broke it up with the poker. Crimes of violence seem to be common in these parts."

Cara Devigny laughed. "But you know why I broke it. So long as it was just a game it was a shocking poor game, but it was nothing else. The other afternoon we touched on the abnormal. I know your temperament, and, as I've told you, I dislike diseases. Remember my great age, and let me at times do what is good for you."

"I did think I was grown up," said Linda, mournfully. "I suppose I shall never be grown up. I can picture Judith Jennis—very wizened and old and bent, with a tangle of gray hair falling over her face. She holds a great staff, and points with a skinny finger."

"One penny plain and twopence coloured," said Cara. "She makes excellent goats' milk cheeses at the prevailing market rate. No woman who does that can possibly have one tinge of the romance of the unseen in her composition."

"That's just where you're wrong," said Linda. "Here that kind of thing is an everyday matter. It is mixed up with the ordinary business of life. My keeper is a steady, sober fellow, not badly educated, considering that he is self-taught. One night he actually saw the Black Man. He was found in the woods senseless in the morning."

"There are more ways than one of becoming senseless," said Mrs. Devigny, drily.

"No, he hadn't," said Linda, eagerly. "I mean he wasn't. And he never has done."

"Sort those tenses out, and say it again slowly."

"What I mean is that the man is a life-long teetotaler. He has never suffered from fits. He has splendid health, and he has no more doubt that that night he actually saw the Black Man than that he has seen a grass snake take a pheasant's egg. He will tell you that both sights are unusual. But he does not doubt the reality of one more than that of the other. He told me about this himself, and he went on to speak about the head of game we might expect to kill this year. I tell you the two things are mixed up."

"That only means," said Cara, "that they've got the minds to muddle."

"Possibly," said Linda; "or the eyes to see. In these waste places out of the world, I believe one's vision grows just as one's eyes see further across the flat country."

"If you go on talking like that, I will telegraph for the senior tutor."

"Then I take it all back," said Linda, laughing, as they passed into the house together.

"I'm going to get on with my work," said Mrs. Devigny, firmly. "I'm going to break myself from the besetting sin of laziness. The vellum came down yesterday. Don't dare to come in the room with me. If you do I shall only talk to you."

"I have plenty to do myself," said Linda. "The responsibilities of a landowner are heavy on me. Now that I am here they all do their utmost to get at me direct, instead of sending in their appeals to Mr. Frederick. It's equivalent to saying that I'm weak. And I don't like it."

When Cara had gone, Linda paused a moment irresolutely, and then she did what she had known, half unconsciously, all the time she meant to do. She took the path to the Tower House.

The August sun was at its zenith when Linda passed from its glare (which made the firm rolled terrace burn on the sight like a fiery ribbon) to the cool green shadowed glamour of the woods, through which ran the cart track which wound its velvety way towards the Tower House—the old mysterious residence where lived Judith Jennis, whom the fall of circumstances and the influence of temperament had made a dominant feature in the girl's thoughts.

The invigorating perfume of the brier-rose had lost much of its pungency, but here and there, as she passed amidst the trunks of pine and larch, Linda caught a breath of faint fascination from the undergrowth which edged the boundaries of the more majestic woods, and which she knew, urban as she was, could come from no other plant but the sweet-scented hedge-rose. The dog-roses, which six weeks ago covered the old may and elder bushes with their fragile beauty, were dead. The seed vessels, ere long to ripen to scarlet, bore their pointed ovals modestly in unobtrusive pallor. Here and there woodbine still rioted. The honeyed odour of its clarion-shaped petals sent a shudder of ecstasy through the sensitive girl, and seemed to cheer her on the mission to the witch, on which her heart was set.

As she advanced into the depths of the dark-plumaged pines, the relief of the delicate larches became less effective. The further she went the more the dread of some indefinable danger obsessed her. She forgot the cheery promise of the brier-rose bushes, the pink and white attraction of the woodbine, and her thoughts took a darker shade as the weft of her surroundings shot between the woof of her nature, borne on the shuttles of the woodland glamour that never fails to appeal to all imaginative spirits. The gloom of the pines grew upon her, till her heart beat thick with fearful anticipation. She tried to laugh at herself for her feelings. "Am I going to be ill?" she said to herself. Then suddenly, "Ah! that's better!"

She paused as the woods opened to the left and permitted her to see the pool where the Fleet broadened to its widest and deepest, and where the teal and duck loved to nest amidst the rushes. It was the spot of the ordeal of Judith Jennis's forebear. But Linda did not know it, and her only sensation was one of delight at the bright glory of water and reed, seen from the background of the darkness of the venerable woods.

As she paused and stood, her eyes softening and brightening at the tender and beautiful seclusion of which the scene whispered, an anxious cock teal, keenly on the watch for human enemies, gave the distinctive "lupe, lupe" of his breed, and shot up into the sunlight, a blaze of green, purple, gray, and white.

Linda was following the swift flight of the shimmering bird with delighted eyes, when, from somewhere close behind her, in the deep obscurity of the woods, a horrible inarticulate cry, half human, half bestial, thrilled out a long discordant howl through the stillness of the noontide in the silence of the shade of woodland.

She had faced round in a moment. A hundred explanations flashed and vibrated through her brain. She breathed quickly, but she stood her ground. She had heard of animals which made such sounds. And of them she was not afraid.

As she peered into the dimness of the plantation her eyes fell on a stunted bush of whitethorn which was all overgrown with woodbine in full bloom. What especially arrested her attention was that the bunches of blossom had arranged themselves about the middle of the face of the bush, so as to form a wreath. The artificiality of this struck her, and held her gaze fixed upon it.

Suddenly the whitethorn shook, and under the wreath appeared a great white blob. Its horrible resemblance to a face startled her. Then, in a flash, she saw that it was really a face, with slobbering lips and expressionless piscine eyes.

It was a face she knew—a face she had seen. Her courage was gone now, and her reason was gone. Everything was lost but the frantic desire to get away from this hideous and loathsome thing. She ran as if she had been running for her life, and as she ran there rose behind her again and again that dreadful cry which had first prompted her to peer into the secrets of the dark woods. She did not stop until out in the sunlight she came upon Mrs. Devigny, who had strolled out on the chance of finding her, and literally fell at her feet.

"Cara, save me!" she sobbed. "It's that face. It has come back. I told you about it. The face on the blotting paper."

"You are all right, dear," said Cara, gravely. "There is no one near you but myself. You are in no danger of any kind. Come back with me now. You can tell me what frightened you afterwards."

Linda rose, clung to her, and with a great effort controlled herself. "Yes, yes," she said. "I'm all right now. I can't talk though, yet."

As they entered the house there rose upon the brilliant sun-lit air, muted by the distance and by the trunks of ancient timber and the screen of undergrowth, that strange animal cry.

"Good God!" said Cara. "What's that?"

"Down there, I heard it quite close to me," almost whispered Linda.

The dumb imbecile who helped Judith Jennis to tend her geese and goats drew back in amazement from the woodbine bloom that he coveted. Why had that beautiful creature been afraid of him? He did not know that his voice was not music. He had not guessed the horror of his face. He was capable of little thought. He only wished vaguely that she would come back. He would never frighten her again.

Midst the tall bracken which spread from the edge of the woods to the beginning of the Tower House grounds he lay for a long time in absolute silence, waiting. If she would come back again he would neither speak (he thought he spoke) nor show himself.

Presently he looked up. He had seen nothing. He had heard nothing. But he knew that Judith Jennis was calling him back.

Chapter VI

'I Have Known You All My Life'

Lady Blickling, of Earlham-Thorpe, twelve miles away, drove over to Merlesfleet one morning to see the daughter of her old dead friend. She was a dignified old lady of great age. She retained the full possession of all her faculties, and they were remarkably good faculties too. Of her temper it is less easy to speak highly; her servants never even attempted to.

"Going to give me any lunch?" she said, after her first half-hour's chat with Linda.

"Why, of course. I've got two or three people coming to-day. We shall be almost a luncheon party."

"Tell me who they are."

"Well, of course, there'll be Mrs. Devigny, who lives with me, and is my greatest friend."

"Is she as pretty as you are?" said the old lady, abruptly.

"Infinitely prettier."

"That will probably be untrue, of course. Who are the others?"

"There's Mr. Calcote, and Mr. Belton."

"Calcote the crammer, you mean. I know him; he's afraid of me. I've told him what the duties of a parson are before now. Belton I've never heard of. There's a village of that name."

"There is," said Linda, "but I don't think he's any relation to it."

A faint twinkle came into the old lady's eye. She chuckled inwardly, as she did at times.

"And there's Laurence Hebbelthwaite," Linda added; "and I think that's all."

The old lady looked rather keenly at the girl. Why could she not have said "Mr. Hebbelthwaite"? "That's a man, at any rate. And he's no more afraid of me than you are."

"But I'm terribly afraid," said Linda.

"What a lot of fibs you do tell, my dear. You needn't, because I like you. I always know at a glance whether I can stand people or whether I can't. The first time I saw Hebbelthwaite he was a quarter of a mile off, but I knew from the way he walked that he was all right. He's not like that dirty little Calcote. That man's paid to teach the Gospel, and that ought to be enough for him. He goes about grubbing for money by shoving algebra into a lot of silly boys. Of course, this being your house, I shan't be nearly as rude to him as I generally am. You needn't be nervous about that, my dear. This fits in very nicely: I shall just get back to Earlham-Thorpe in time for my Motherhood Class."

"What's that?" said Linda.

"Well, my dear," said the old lady, with that ghost of a smile still lurking in her bright eyes, "you see, I never had any children myself. That has given me plenty of time to make a study of the rearing and education of infants. So I hold these classes for poor young mothers, and teach them what to do to their offspring. They are all of them my tenants, and they've got to do what I say, or I'll know the reason why."

Linda laughed. "I'm sure of it," she said. "And what do you teach them?"

"To give their children more milk, even if their husbands have to do with less beer; to wash their brats more often, and themselves, too, for that matter; to keep their windows open; and to trust to the Church schools. I won't have Board schools. The Government may do what it likes. I simply won't have 'em."

"It sounds splendid," said Linda. "I almost wish I were qualified to come to the classes."

"Perhaps you will be one of these days. Mind, you'll have to be punctual. They've got to be in their seats at half-past three. I don't allow any slackness. I'm no stricter with them than I am with myself. If I ever am a minute late for anything it upsets me for three weeks, and then the people round me know it. By the way, I came here on purpose to quarrel with you."

"What for?" said Linda, with open eyes.

"Because you've got one of those nasty, dirty, smelling motor-cars."

"I thought," said Linda, "that I had got a nice, bright, smoothly-gliding modern car, which it was a pleasure to ride in. Were you ever in one?"

"Never," said Lady Blickling, firmly. "I shall never get into a motor-car, except it is to attend the funeral of the last horse. I disapprove of them utterly. They have ruined the country-side, and look at the damage they do. My carriage-horses are all right. But I've got a sweet little pony, who simply goes mad if he sees a car."

"It's a pity he wasn't properly broken," said Linda.

"Properly broken! Why I did most of it myself. What would you do now if you were driving that horrible machine and you met me in the governess-cart?"

"If necessary, stop the car, stop the engine, lead your pony past, and apologise."

"And that," said Lady Blickling, "would be the very least that you could do. You will hardly believe me, but I have met many cars whose drivers have not even done as much as that."

Lady Blickling, Mrs. Devigny, and Linda were seated on the terrace when the Rev. James Calcote and Percy Belton came up. Calcote espied her ladyship, and shied perceptibly. She received his salutations graciously. Belton was presented to her.

"Reading with Mr. Calcote, are you?" she said. "Then just you come and sit by me; I always like to meet Mr. Calcote's pupils. You see, I have known him for twenty years, and I can tell them stories about him that make 'em laugh every time they look at him."

Belton laughed there and then. "Really, really," said Mr. Calcote, nervously. "This subversion of all discipline—"

"Oh, you go away, Mr. Calcote. I'm not bound to help you to keep discipline. If you can't do that for yourself you oughtn't to be allowed to have pupils. I suppose you haven't told Mr. Belton how you bought that skewbald. Ah! that'll do to begin with."

Calcote smiled in a sickly way. "I must warn you that I shall give my own version afterwards."

"Twenty versions, if you like—all different. Mine'll be the funniest, though, because you see mine actually did happen."

The arrival of Laurence Hebbelthwaite saved Calcote for the time being.

Lady Blickling shamelessly abandoned young Belton, and began talking earnestly with Hebbelthwaite on the work that was being done on the river walls. "If it wasn't for these wretched steam-tugs and their strings of filthy barges, it would never have been necessary," she said.

"I hate and loathe all machinery," she emphatically added.

"But there you're quite wrong, you know," said Hebbelthwaite, coolly.

"I don't care; I won't have so much as a sewing-machine in my house."

Belton, released from Lady Blickling, flew to Linda, even as a needle to the magnet. Mrs. Devigny consoled and fascinated Calcote. His spirits revived. Belton must be kept away from that terrible old woman, and then all would be well. He would take Belton away early. Work would be a pretext. They all passed into the house to luncheon.

Calcote had congratulated himself a little prematurely. Lady Blickling told the story of the skewbald, not to Belton alone, but to the entire table. Calcote had received a private visit from the Bishop of the Diocese. In honour of this occasion, the skewbald had been purchased at a price which the crammer thought eminently satisfactory. Unfortunately, the skewbald had been the property of a market gardener, famous, as her ladyship said, for the regularity of his irregularities. The consequence was that when Calcote drove the Bishop out the animal stopped dead at every licensed house to which they came, and refused to move for intervals varying from five minutes to a quarter of an hour. The Bishop walked back. Lady Blickling's description of the Bishop's fury and of Calcote's apologies was realistic and amusing. Calcote joined manfully in the laugh against himself, and got in one solitary stab. "You've improved that ever so much since the last time that I heard you tell it. But I still think that your first version, ten years ago, was much the best."

"I got a terrible scare the other day," said Linda, speaking across the table to Hebbelthwaite.

"Did you," said he. "I'm sorry. I should have thought," he added, "you were more in the habit of frightening other people." Their eyes met, and understood humorously. Linda went on speaking, hurriedly. "Yes. I was down in the wood standing by the pool—they call it 'The Witch's Pool,' I am told." She recounted what she had heard and seen.

"That boy is pretty horrible," said Hebbelthwaite, "even when you know him. He's quite harmless, though. I don't know where on earth he would have been but for Judith Jennis. Of course, he does work for her of a kind. But he would never make a living wage anywhere else. She treats him well, and sees to it that others treat him well. Villagers who have made the mistake of teasing the poor boy have pretty generally suffered for it."

Mrs. Devigny's slightly drawling voice broke in: "But I thought, Mr. Hebbelthwaite, that you said Judith ought to be taken out and shot."

"I did. I still say it. She's a dangerous woman. She has inherited dangerousness. She does things that are not to be done."

"The superstitious people about these parts," Mr. Calcote began, but was rudely interrupted by Lady Blickling, who spoke to Hebbelthwaite.

"I know what you mean. If I were Miss Merle, I'd have that woman out of the parish."

"I don't think I understand," said Mrs. Devigny. "That belongs to the dark ages, doesn't it? You are not going to tell us that you, to-day, believe in witchcraft?"

"Certainly I do," said Hebbelthwaite, quietly.

Calcote laughed loud and long. Wine had made glad his heart, and given him a cheerful countenance. He was slightly encouraged. Nothing more than that. Lady Blickling turned on him.

"Mr. Calcote," she said, "you have been here, I believe, over twenty years, and during that time I dare say you have taught a great many things to a great many boys. But you seem to have learnt astonishingly little by yourself and for yourself."

"Possibly," said Calcote, "I was nearly thirty when I came here. My education was finished."

"What you mean is that your education had stopped. I believe you've not got one opinion in your head which you have not picked out of some book or some newspaper. You have never seen anything for yourself. I suppose you visit the poor of your parish?"

"With regularity," said Calcote.

"I'm glad to hear it; but it shows that they don't trust you. If they did you must have seen the kind of thing which is going on. Christians are taught to believe in a Power of Evil as well as a Power of Good. They are willing enough to assign this event or that to the beneficent act of the Power of Good. But they see the work of the Power of Evil and feel themselves bound to deny its existence; that, they think, would be superstitious."

Calcote shrugged his shoulders. "Unfortunately, Lady Blickling," he said, "there are many points on which we disagree."

"I hope so," said Lady Blickling, fervently.

"As to the correct and orthodox view of witchcraft," Calcote continued, "perhaps an ordained priest of the Church of England has more right to speak than a layman."

Hebbelthwaite felt a little sorry for Calcote.

"For that matter," he said good-temperedly, "I suppose you would find me in 'Crockford' if you looked for me. After all, it is perhaps a question of what one means by witchcraft. By the way, speaking of Judith Jennis, do you know that she has got a first prize for her goats' milk cheeses at Bungay Dairy Show? She's very pleased about it, I'm told."

"I hope she won't put up the price of them," said Linda, laughing, as the women rose from the table. "She supplies me regularly. You've just been eating one. By the way, we shall be on the terrace when you've finished your cigarettes. Bring them out there, if you like."

"Lady Blickling," said Linda, as they took their seats on the terrace, "you did tell me you were not going to be as rude as usual to Mr. Calcote."

"I did," said Lady Blickling, "and I'm proud to say that I kept my word. There were times when I was sorely tempted to be harsh with the little worm. You should hear me talk to him sometimes, when I let myself go."

"Heaven forbid!" said Linda.

"It doesn't much matter," said Lady Blickling, philosophically; "in a few years' time I shan't be here to keep him in his place. And I really believe that he'll miss me. We are such old and intimate enemies."

The men came out from the house. Calcote was still feeling sore. Belton was sulky and depressed. Linda had spoken very little to him. At the tennis party at Trumpington she had been quite different. She had seemed really interested. For half-an-hour or more she had been out of the crowd with him. Now she was civil enough. But there was not one special sign of favour. He told himself gloomily that all girls were like that. You could never depend upon them. They encouraged you one day and they froze you the next. Who the devil was this Hebbelthwaite, whom everybody seemed to make so much fuss about? His one grim satisfaction was that Calcote had certainly made an ass of himself. There is a pleasure to the young in a mentor's downfall.

"Mr. Belton," said Linda, pleasantly, coming forward, "I've hardly had the chance of a word with you all the time. Lady Blickling wants so much to renew her acquaintance with the Witch's Pool that we are all going down there. Will you walk with me?"

Mr. Percy Belton revised his generalisations on women, and said he would be awfully glad.

"Do you know," said Linda, as they followed behind the rest, "that you and Mrs. Devigny are the only two people who behaved decently at luncheon? Everybody else was fighting, including myself. We ought to have been spanked and sent to bed."

"I say," said Belton, "I wonder if you'd tell me something. I don't know if it's cheek to ask it. When Mr. Hebbelthwaite said something about your being able to frighten people, there seemed to be some sort of a joke on between you. I hate to feel that I'm out of a joke. What was it?"

"Nothing at all," said Linda, colouring slightly. "There was no joke whatever. I was rather bad-tempered with him the other day. That's all."

"I bet he deserved it," said Belton. "What had the beggar done?"

"Given me very good advice. Don't you ever do that; it makes me very angry at the time."

"Yes. But afterwards?" said Belton, mournfully. "I thought he seemed to get on all right to-day, anyhow."

"Mr. Belton," said Linda, "I believe you are the very youngest of God's creatures. Now we are going to talk about something quite different. What did you do all this morning?"

It appeared that Mr. Calcote had supposed that Mr. Belton had spent the morning in the study. As a matter of fact, the weather being fine, Mr. Belton had taken his gun along the rand to see if he could find a few home-bred snipe.

"I wish you'd shoot some for me," said Linda. "You can go anywhere on my marshes, whenever you like. I know there are teal at the Witch's Pool."

Then was Mr. Percy Belton filled with glory.

He was up at five the next morning after the snipe, and four couple went up to the Hall in time for breakfast. This was the more noble of him, as he was basely deserted on the way back from the Pool. He could have borne it more easily had it been Calcote who supplanted him. But it was Laurence Hebbelthwaite. And they did not return to the house by the same path as the others.

"I'm afraid I was awfully clumsy when I called on you the other day," he said.

"Stop," she said. "You are not to apologise; I said an unpardonable thing. And it has haunted me since. But—you'd like to know it, perhaps—Planchette is broken up."

"You did it?" he asked, a little eagerly.

"No, it was Cara Devigny. I want to tell you about the experiment which we made."

He listened gravely to her story.

"Yes," he said shortly, "I'm glad that Mrs. Devigny broke that up. Leave all that kind of thing alone. Don't try thought-reading or table-turning, or anything of the sort."

"This is all very well," said Linda, discontentedly. "But why, why, why?"

"There is no time to tell the story now. It sounds crudely melodramatic to tell you that you have an enemy. Put simply, that is what it comes to. If she hurts you at all, it will be through that side of your nature—through your curiosity as to the unknown. You have not got the nervous constitution for investigations of this kind; few people have. The more I puzzle over it, and I've puzzled over it for many years, the more I've come to the conclusion that there is a line beyond which knowledge cannot with safety go. It sounds absurd to be talking like this just after luncheon, doesn't it?"

"Why should you warn me? Why should you take this interest in a stranger?"

He looked at her intently. "I do not think you are at all a stranger," said he; "I think I've known you all my life."

On the terrace there was great, desolation. The Motherhood Class was at half-past three, and it was now three.

"Of course, my horses can't possibly do it," said old Lady Blickling.

"My car can," said Linda.

Lady Blickling was in plenty of time for her class, and some of her opinions have undergone a slight modification.

Chapter VII

The Tower House

The Tower House was a perfectly circular building some forty feet in height. Its curving walls were of old flint mixed with Roman bricks and that hard, lustreless mortar with which the old-fashioned builders defied the ravages of time and weather for centuries. Age had given the rough stone and mortar a smooth glossiness which the Roman bricks had won long ere they were torn from the great castle which once dominated the mighty estuary where now stretched that vast expanse of grazing land which is known to farmers all the country over as the finest for fattening store stock in the world.

The Tower House itself contained but two rooms, a winding stone stairway leading (with nakedness unashamed) from the ground floor to the upper chamber which Judith Jennis alone could enter. The area of the rooms was small, their diameter scarcely exceeding ten feet. But they were lofty, and gave no impression of stuffiness.

In the ground-floor room was a round table of oak, worn black with age and smoke. The table had spread food before many a marshman in the days when the dried dung of the stock upon the marshes formed the greater part of the fuel used about the marsh levels. This, and peat cut from the layers of fibrous grass roots from the boggy rands, sent up a reek of pungent smoke, which left its mark on many of the pieces of old furniture which may still be seen in the houses of the old families, handed down from generation to generation, never parted from, in spite of the too frequent poverty of their possessors. An old settle, as black as the table, and a three-legged stool sufficed Judith and her "innocent" lad for chairs. But facing the one poor diamond-paned window (where the glass, like the bottom thicknesses of bottles, distorted everything seen through it,) was a leathern-backed chair. In this Judith was wont to seat those who sought her advice and aid for hallowed or unhallowed ends. In the darkest curve of the room was a litter of straw, which formed the bed of Job Sacret, the "innocent" lad. The whole room was scrupulously clean.

What was in the upper room was known to Judith alone. No foot other than her own was ever permitted to climb the stone stairway. No eye other than hers ever saw what eerie emblems or implements of her art were kept in that barred chamber. At the top of the tower a trap door opened on to a lead roofing, affording a standing place for a look-out. There was a low uneven parapet which ran round the edge of the roof. From here in old days the marshmen who had lived there had peered out across the miles of flat marsh, dykes, and rivers, spying for the flight or settling of the huge parcels of fowl which came in from the North Sea when winter threatened, or for some familiar sail which gave promise of rich drink or tobacco that had escaped the eye of the revenue officers under the hatches of a Norfolk "keel-boat" or wherry.

On the south-western side of the tower, screened from the north and east winds, stood a long stable-like building made of wattle and daub, This was divided into two compartments, in one of which was the dairy, in the other the neat small stalls for "Bel," the big black Billy goat, and the five Nanny goats which provided the milk from which the famous cheeses were made.

The dairy was filled with the old-fashioned earthenware shallow pans for the milk. Judith did not believe in the modern zinc pans. Along the shelves stood curd baskets, and the presses and strips of linen which were used in the manufacture of the cheeses.

On the night of the luncheon party at Merlesfleet in the lower room of the tower Job was stretched on his bed plaiting rushes. It was one of his singular aptitudes with which Nature repaid him for his deficiencies. He was shaping a flower-basket with an ornamental boss upon it, but it was of no use to himself or Judith, and would have commanded no sale in the district. But this basket was not being made for money. Judith entered with a clatter of keys. She had just locked up the dairy for the night.

It is true that no one but a stranger to the place would have dared to touch anything that belonged to Judith Jennis. She watched the boy curiously, and made a quick sign. He put down the work in obedience to her gesture, but began to make the whimpering cry which showed that he suffered. Judith paused, made another sign, and he resumed his work with a grin of content.

She stood erect, looking out from the window. A half-moon was beginning to show above the trees which surrounded Merlesfleet. She was dressed much the same as any other Norfolk peasant.

Judith Jennis was a woman who would have been remarked in any society. She was thirty-four years of age, tall, and magnificently built. Her square shoulders, held back with almost masculine vigour, softened to feminine charm in the lines of the full bust. The face was striking, masterful. It was said that her brown hair, black in shadow, reached to her knees. At the moment she wore it low, in a heavy mass on her neck. Her eyes were large, and formed a potent factor in her influence. For all that, even as the eyes of the most savage animal, they could grow strangely soft.

Suddenly she stepped back a few paces from the window, yet five minutes passed before the tap came at the door. Job sprang to his feet and went out of the room. In a moment he returned with a young woman, carrying a baby in her arms. It was a woman with a pretty, weak face. Her shawl covered a wealth of pale fluffy hair. The eyes were desperate.

"Judith," she said, breathlessly, "I had to come tew ye."

Judith motioned her to the leather-backed chair. The tired woman sank into it. Judith remained silent.

"My heart fare nigh ta break. He passed agin me t'other night in Fleet Loke, an' he din't paay noo moor regard 'an if I wuz a sarvant. I bore the little un in my arms. But he niver once give a look ta see if ta wuz a bundle o' sticks or a baaby. What should a dew? What should a dew? I can't beer it noo moor. 'Tain't the brass as upset me. He gi'e me a planty o' that. 'Tis him—'tis him, the maan what held me in his arms an' tode me he loved me trew as I want, as my brist y'arn foor."

"What ha'e ye gart for me if I wark for ye? Yew ote ta knoo as I dew narthen for narthen. I'm the black witch, as the fools miscall me. Why should I dew owt for narthen?"

In strange contradiction of her words, she went to where the woman sat, and raised the veil from the face of the child she bore.

"'Tis a gal, ain't it?"

"Yes," said the woman. "As pratty a little wench as iver I see, though har faa'er woun't look at har."

"Will ye gi'e me the baabe? Will ye gi'e har oover tew me? To hev as my own. Ta call my darter, and ta l'arn an' rare as I pleease? Mine—ah! mine!"

The woman drew the veil over the child's face again, and shrank back from the eagerness of the witch. But Judith suffered no interruption. "Give har tew me," she said again, "an' I'll bring him back tew ye. I'll lead him ta yar feet soo as he'll maake ye his own trew wife. I'll watch for ye, I'll weave my charms about yew an' him ye love. What ye will, that shall be yarn. Oon'y this baabe must be mine. An' if I bring him back agin yew'll niver miss har. Yew'll be happy sucklin' another, wi' yar maan by yar side. 'Tis the price I ax. The oon'y price I'll taake."

Job crouched on his straw litter, watching the whole scene with meaningless eyes. From his birth he had never heard a sound.

The woman pressed her babe close to her bosom, and shuddered at Judith's vehemence. Then, with a little moan of agony, she rose from the chair in which she sat, and felt blindly for the door.

"I can't—I can't," she cried. "Oh, God! my pore little baabe! Yew an' me must goo; theer's noo moor hoop for ayther on us."

Judith stood for a moment silent and motionless. Then her hand reached out after the departing woman. Her bosom rose and fell in quick agonising gasps. She seemed as though torn by two influences. As the woman touched the latch of the primitive door, Judith's voice rose in a cry so mellow, so full of love and humanity, that it seemed strange to her herself.

"Stop! Stop!" she said. "Yew doan't waant to be sa narvous. I shan't hu't ye. Come yew back an' tall us all about it agin. Theer, theer! my pore wench; set ye down agin—set ye down agin. I oan't ax for the little mawther noo moor. I prarmuss ye I oan't. Set ye down an' spake ta me as one 'oman tew another. I've noo call ta be hard on one in yar plaace. Come, my pratty; Judy'll see ye righted."

The boy with vacant eyes began to chew a straw with philosophic contentment. He had finished his flower-basket. Outside the goats bleated.

They seemed uneasy, as though some strange influence were hovering about.

The woman stayed her moanings, and staggered feebly back into the chair. The veil fell from the baby's face as her mother sank weakly into the seat. It was a pretty child.

"Theer, theer," said Judith again, "I'll git ye a some'at ta dew ye good. Yew fare opset. That's whaat 'tis. Waait yew a min't."

She went to where the circular walls of the room projected in a shallow cupboard. This she unlocked, and took from it a bottle of Hollands gin, which Jimmy Buddery had paid her for a charm against the hob-o'-lanterns. For the first time Job's eyes lit up. He knew the taste of gin, and loved it. He made the crooning cry which was his form of request. But Judith looked him once in the face, and he turned again to inspect his flower-basket. The consolation he found there did not seem to be wholly adequate.

Judith poured out a measure of the pungent, oily-tasting spirit into an old silver quaich, which had been her great-grandmother's, and held it to the woman's lips. "Theer," she said, "sup it, sup it. Why, Briony Prettyman, yew might ha' knowed better'n ta think as I would ha' hu't ye, arter all the yares I ha' knowd yew an' yar sister, as is sarvant up at the Hall. Sup it up."

Briony Prettyman drank the spirit, and it brought new life to her exhausted frame.

The boy sank back on the straw. There seemed to be no hope of liquor for him, and the refusal of the gin had made him sulky. He always went to sleep when he was sulky.

Judith slipped up the stairs to the upper room. In a moment she came slowly down them again, bearing in her hands with the utmost care a little cup. It was a cup of some transparent material, of a wine-coloured hue, heavily mounted in soft gold which had obviously been worked by the primitive methods of the East. It stood about six inches in height, and the base carried a partly obliterated inscription.

She placed the cup on the round table, and drew the candle nearer to it. The shimmer of the light showed a liquid that moved in the bowl. The heavy breathing of Job Sacret was the only sound within the room. Without the goats had ceased to bleat. The silence hung heavily, and oppressed Briony Prettyman with a sense of foreboding. Her gaze was fixed by the change which was passing over Judith's face. The witch's eyes were dead to all but the shimmering liquor. in the cup. It seemed a long, long time before she spoke.

"I see," she said, and there was an odd solemnity in her voice: "I see the maan o' yar heart. A gre't fine chap, wi' bright, curlin' heer an' eyes like the river unner the blue sky o' May. His faace is one to win the love o' women. His sinews and his limbs are strong wi' the might o' health, good livin', an' good blood. Them as sees the bardy oon'y might warship him. But within he fare weeak, as weeak as a new kindled lev'ret. Courage he ha' gart, good temper, an' good nater. But the fire o' the Powers o' might, whether for good or evil, are not in him. Pore wench, pore wench, yar heart is wrung for maan's weakness! But not as his be wrung for longin'. As yew love an' bu'n for him soo he love an' bu'n for another. As yar heart fare torn, soo his heart crack and rend wi' wantin' what will niver come tew'm. His ears are deef ta yar cry. But give him time. Maybe, he'll hev his h'arin' agin when all is said an' done. The light is gone."

The shimmer within the cup died away, and as it died the light of consciousness revived in Judith's eyes. She passed her hand over her head, and turned to Briony.

The unhappy mother had understood but a part of the witch's message. But two things she had grasped with all the keenness of her love: one was that Percy Belton, the father of her child, was in love with another woman, the other was that at some future time there was a chance that he might come back to her.

"Dee ye think as he'll iver come back?" she asked Judith, with pathetic eagerness. "Ooh, Judy, dare, I love him soo. How long will ta be afoor he knoo whew love him best in all the warld? Can ye help me to call his heart ta mine, ta bring him to my bosom once agin? Hare, taake this—the laast thing as he give me with a kiss upon my lips an' with lovin' wuds from his tongue. Taake it an' welcome, if yew'll put some'at on tew him ta bring him back sune ta Briony. Oh, sune, Judy, sune."

Her quivering fingers held something out to Judith—something which glittered in the feeble candle light. It was a brooch, set with three fine emeralds, which Percy had bought for his love at a time when no price seemed too high to pay to give her pleasure.

For an instant, Judith's eyes glowed with greed. The stones leered at her with their beautiful evil green glamour. How fine they would look against that olive-skinned neck of hers. How they would wink and laugh beneath her strands of sombre hair. She started to hold out her hand to take the trinket. But again the lines of her face softened and changed.

"Noo," she said, withdrawing her partly outstretched hand, "I'll dew't for nowt, Briony. Some'at ha' spook ta me an' tode me as 'tis the Black Maan's will that I should sarve ye. See." She took up the cup from the ta-

ble, and poured out the liquid upon the brick floor of the room. "I sweer
it by the magic cup."

Briony's unstable nature was cheered by the witch's promise of suc-
cour. The agony of her passion was calmed. She began to look about her
again with the interest in petty things which is characteristic of weakness.

"Wha wha'ss that, Judy?" she said, pointing to the cup. "I see my sister
Tabitha t'other daay, an' she wuz a talkin' about some rummy cup as the
young missis at the Hall ha' gart. She see it in Mr. Thomson's pantry
t'other day when he wuz a shinin' up the gold, an' from what she said that
must be wunnerful like this. Young missis think o' deeal harp. She spook
to Mr. Thomson about it, as if that wuz maade o' dimonds. I rackon tha'ss
wuth a tidy lump o' brass."

Judith started and looked eagerly at Briony. "Tell me agin," she said.
"What wuz the cup at the Hall like? How did Tabby describe it? Had it got
letterin' on it like this?"

She showed the partly obliterated inscription on the base.

Briony, very proud of being spoken to on such familiar terms by the
witch, did her best to recall the exact words of her sister, who was a
housemaid at Merlesfleet. But she knew nothing of the inscription. However, she remembered sufficient to satisfy Judith that a duplicate of the
cup which she had inherited from her great-grandmother was in Linda's
possession. She was now anxious to be rid of her visitor. She again went
up to the barred chamber, whence she presently returned, bearing a few
shrivelled leaves and twigs bound together by the dried gut of an eel.

"Now yew must be a gooin'," she said to Briony. "But taake this hare,
an' bu'n a pinch o' the harbs tied up wi' sav en o' yar own heers every
night afoor ye goo ta bed. Then saay this: 'Man o' the mash, man o' the
ooze, send my lover back ta me. Gi'e my babe a faa'er, an' gi'e me the
maan o' my heart. I ax it by the power o' the mistress o' the black goot.'"

Briony fearfully took the charm, and muttering her thanks, she bore
her baby out of the room. Judith watched her close the door, and seated
herself on her oak settle. There was a smile on her face, which had something of triumph in it.

Presently she crossed to the straw litter, and watched the boy narrowly.
Yes; he would sleep some hours. She went up the stairs to her own room.

A few minutes later, Judith Jennis, veiled and robed as the Egyptian
woman has been from time immemorial, and is still to-day, stood on the
leaded roof and watched the stars. She drew a piece of chalk from the
folds of her garment, and, bending down, drew on the flat leads a large

circle. In the middle of it she stood and waited. Suddenly the whole marsh to the west of the Tower was alive with the croaking of innumerable frogs. It sounded as though the cordage of a fleet of ships were being drawn through heavy blocks. The deep, hoarse "baa" of Bel, the great he-goat, was heard from the stable. Bats circled about her, two or three of them at first, then perhaps twenty. Lights from the distant Hall could still be seen glimmering through the woods. She raised her hand towards them.

> "Come to me, sister o' my blood,
>   Drawn by the cords which ye feel not,
>   Driven by the driver that ye see not.
> One must live and one must die.
>   The chice is the Master's:
> Yew or I."

Now she went back to the lower room, dressed once more as a Norfolk peasant. Surely this time the spell would work.

Chapter VIII

The Sisters

The clock in the smaller drawing-room at Merlesfleet struck one clear note. It was half-past nine. Cara Devigny, in a maize-coloured tea-gown, leaned back in her chair and yawned very deliberately.

"Sorry I'm keeping you up," said Linda.

"Don't think you are," said Cara. "At any rate, you won't much longer. The fact of the case is that I am old and frail, and I am going to my bye-bye as soon as I have energy enough to stand up."

"I don't believe this place suits you one bit," said Linda. "The blowsy milkmaid was never your style.' But really, you're looking thinner and paler than ever."

"Nonsense," said Cara, "I'm as right as ever I was in my life. I'm full of energy, during the day at any rate. I'm renewing my youth. Only this afternoon I was wondering whether I would or would not marry Percy Belton."

"When did he ask you?" said Linda, maliciously.

"There speaks the voice of jealousy."

"I hand over to you freely," said Linda, "any copyright which I may happen to possess in him. He is quite a nice boy, and I like him. Beyond that I've no use for him. Take him and be happy. I will announce it in 'The Post' to-morrow."

Cara laughed, and stood up.

"If I were not old enough to be his mother, I'd think about it seriously. It's a sad thing that a woman of forty should feel that she's outlived herself, isn't it? She has got a lot of time to wait still." She peered at herself in the glass. "She needn't even look ugly enough to frighten the cab-horses. But she knows, or ought to know, that it simply—won't—do."

"How can you be so out of date, Cara? The woman of forty has the best time of the lot. In London at any rate."

"Civilisation has lots of morbid developments. Here the race is to the swift, the battle to the strong, and the love to the young. Good-night, Linda. I wish I were you."

"No," said Linda to herself, "I am certainly not going to bed yet." The heat in the room oppressed her. She opened the French windows and passed out on to the terrace, the tail of her gown caught up over one arm. If she had thought about her dainty white satin slippers she would have paused and gone back. But she thought only of the glory of the night, and wandered on at haphazard.

She was away from the terrace now, on the moss-grown track that led to the Tower House. She was vaguely surprised, but she had no feeling of nervousness or fear. What a noise those things were making down on the marsh to-night. Could that be the frogs? She stopped, startled, as the "hoo-hoo" of an owl sounded close over her head. She looked up and saw the browny-white shadow, black in contrast with the moonlight, swoop in gliding silence on some unhappy mouse by the side of the track. A moth-hawk flitted across the opening in the trees. "Jar-r-r!" it croaked. How strange and mysterious were these calls of wild life by night! She had never before experienced the charm of woodland by moonlight. A sense of propinquity to the unseen came upon her. Her heart beat quickly; she felt lifted up, buoyant with a certain anticipation that she was nearer that world she had long desired to visit than she had ever been before.

The cart track opened out on to a wide stretch of grass close cropped by Judith's goats and geese. Here for the first time she was frightened. Loud, deep, and hoarse came a sound which she could not recognise. The virtue had gone out of her. She fled to the door of the Tower House, glad of the friendly light which shone through the window. Some one was still sitting up there. It would be easy enough to make an excuse.

Ere she reached the door, it opened, Judith stood before her. In the light of the flickering candle there was a strange resemblance between the faces of the two women.

"I heerd ye comin'," said Judith, tentatively.

"Yes," said Linda, "I hope I don't disturb you. I was out for a stroll by myself. The night is so hot, isn't it? And then I believe I was half frightened by a queer sound of some animal."

"Twuz narthen but Bel, my goot. Oan't ye come in an' set ye down?"

"Thanks, so much," said Linda. A feeling of lassitude had come over her; she even wondered how she would be able to walk back to Merlesfleet.

"I've heard so much of the Tower House; it will be interesting to see it. Judith Jennis lives here?"

"Tha'ss whew I be."

Linda laughed. "I don't know why, but I always supposed that you were quite an old woman."

There was a rustle in the straw where Job was sleeping.

"What's that?" said Linda, again startled.

"Yew doan't waant ta be afeared," said Judith. "'Tis oony my booy Job. He bain't a gay ta look at. But he 'ouldn't hu't noobardy."

The straw rustled again as Job hid his face in it.

"Do you know," said Linda, "I'm much more tired than I thought. I even begin to wonder how I shall get back again."

The witch smiled. There was again that suspicion of triumph to be seen in her eyes. "Will ye drink a drarp o' milk?" she asked. "That'll dew ye good if yew can stomach it."

"Yes, I should like some milk," Linda said. "Thank you. I nearly always drink some before I go to bed."

Judith fetched a large jug from the cupboard, and poured it into an engraved glass. "Drink," she said.

What was there in the milk to make her so strangely drowsy that the room in which she was sitting, the figure of the woman before her, and all the incidents of the evening seemed to her like a dream? Suddenly she rubbed her eyes. "I've been asleep," she said.

"Yes," said Judith, looking guardedly at her. "Yew ha' been asleep."

"I must go now," said Linda. "I wonder if you would come part of the way with me?"

"I'll dew better'n that," said Judith. "Them little titty shews o' yarn weren't meant for walkin'. Look a hare; yew shall ride. Yew doan't waant ta be narvous; ole Bel oan't hu't ye, will ye, my bewty?"

Outside the door stood a great he-goat, entirely black, motionless as a statue. On his back a blanket had been folded.

The goat stood some four-feet-six at the shoulder, but the reach of his head, with its huge horns, curving backward over his skull, must have brought his height to at least another two feet. His coarse black beard nearly reached his fore-feet.

"Am I really to ride on him? Is he strong enough to carry me?" asked Linda.

"Wha he'd carry tew like yew," said Judith, laughing grimly. "He come of funny stock, he dew; theer bain't another like him in these parts. Stand ye still, Bel," she continued, as she helped Linda to take her seat on the great back. "Cop hoold o' his horns," she advised the girl. "Bel, doan't yer chuck yar hid about. Yew knoo how to carry a laady. Now, tha'ss right—stiddy."

The goat stepped delicately and sedately. Linda had never had a more comfortable mount. Judith strode boldly by the side of her goat.

"What a thing this will be to talk about in the morning," thought Linda. "It is almost like being a child at the sea-side again!"

Then suddenly it flashed upon her that it was not in the least like it—that all this was something that she had never known before.

And so they passed along the track, a strange group in the moonlight, Bel holding his head high and steadily, Linda shivering a little now in her thin evening gown, though not from cold, and beside her the majestic figure of the witch, triumph in her step, triumph still in her eyes when the moonlight lit their depths.

On the terrace, at a word from his mistress, the goat halted. Linda slipped down from his back.

"Good-night, Bel," she said, patting his neck. Then she turned to Judith. "To-morrow I will come and thank you."

The somewhat prosaic figure of Thomson appeared at the French windows. He was really getting a little anxious. Linda called to him, and passed into the house.

As soon as the girl's figure had disappeared, Judith leapt on the goat's back, with a wild laugh, which Bel seemed to share, and, at headlong speed, the two strange creatures went galloping along the moonlit track towards the Tower House.

Chapter IX

'The Man's Impossible'

Laurence Hebbelthwaite had built his own house to suit himself, and the largest room in it was the library. Here he followed the many curious studies which kept him quite satisfied to live alone in this village of the marshes. The room was not wanting in traces of other days. They were to be seen in the oar above the mantelpiece, in the silver cups that filled the big corner cupboard, and in the foils and gloves and dumb-bells that he still used strenuously. With the gloves he found practice difficult. There were few of his weight and reach. There was but little left of his collection of theological books. He hated more than anything else in the world insincerity and prejudice, and he had found few theological works which were free from the taint of both these. For the same reason he had a certain impatience with the works of modern science. Science was always closing doors which it had afterwards to open, and opening doors which it afterwards had to close. It was always coming to a conclusion before the end was reached. He was a man who worked by himself on his own lines and for his own satisfaction. He had considerable private means, and his ambitions were of a high kind. They demanded no immediate recognition from his fellow-men. They were careless even of an ultimate recognition.

Many of the shelves were filled with county histories, surveys, ordnance maps, parish histories privately printed, and written for the most part by country parsons, genealogies, and the special magazines issued in this interest. On the lowest shelf of all was a series of portfolios stoutly and uniformly bound, numbered but not lettered, each of which contained the documents which he had collected and the notes which he had made on some special subject.

This afternoon, with the quick decision of a man who mostly knows what he means to do, he drew from its shelf the portfolio which concerned the Merle family. His work in this direction had begun long before he had ever met Linda. It was partly, perhaps, in consequence of what he knew of her family and of that of Judith Jennis that he had written to the senior tutor of St. Cecilia's and expressed his intention of calling when Miss Merle came down to take possession of her property.

For the meticulousness in points of scholarship that Mr. Trotter displayed Hebbelthwaite had an honest admiration. For the rest of him he had a good deal of contempt. He did not like to see a man cramped and dwarfed by his manner of life as Willoughby Trotter was cramped. He did not like to see one side of a man's nature developed at the expense of the other sides equally valuable, or even more valuable.

Even his most intimate friends, of whom Hebbelthwaite had a few, admitted that he was as obstinate as a mule. His own line was the only line which he could or would take. Adherence to a party or deference to a school seemed to him, perhaps, something of the character of an ignominious surrender. If his self-confidence was balanced by an unassuming modesty, it was because the line of his studies had taken him into the regions where one man matters little more than another. And the same arbitrary but inevitable law crushes just and unjust alike.

He opened the portfolio on a large and unencumbered table, and glanced at his watch. He had just twenty minutes to look through it before he might expect a visit which Mrs. Devigny and Linda had promised him.

The history which he read there may be thus summarised:

Shortly before the last decade of the eighteenth century Everett Merle, of Merlesfleet, became the father of a natural daughter by a Judith Jennis. The daughter took both the first and second names of her mother, was not baptized, and was provided for somewhat parsimoniously by her father. The parsimony may be traced to the fact that Everett Merle had now sown his wild oats and had given Merlesfleet a legitimate mistress. He married Lady Susan Cottenham, third daughter of the Earl of Thetford, and broke off his association with his previous mistress. Lady Susan Merle seems to have been a woman of great charm, if the Romney portrait may be trusted. Her health was weak, and she was of a nervous temperament. It is possible, though Hebbelthwaite had never been able to ascertain it definitely, that there was a meeting between Lady Susan and the woman whom she had supplanted. Judith had the reputation of magical powers which was subsequently inherited by every one of the female descendants. The men were extraordinary for nothing except perhaps for their dissipation. There can be no doubt, at any rate, that Everett Merle believed that Judith Jennis exercised an evil influence over his wife, and that her malevolence was due in part to jealousy and in part to her desire to get some proper recognition of the younger Judith Jennis, her child by him.

A year after her marriage, Lady Susan Merle died in childbirth, and her husband put into writing his oath that Judith was the cause of her death, and that he would be avenged for it. He was fully avenged for it. He waited his time. He did not commit the banality of banishing Judith from the parish—a feat which would have been easily within his power.

For three years he watched her, fostering in every way her growing unpopularity, stooping even himself to drop here and there a hint. Judith Jennis became an outcast. No one would speak to the witch—no one would have anything to do with her. It may be that she studied to deserve her bad name, but the legendary traditions of her miracles cannot of course be trusted. It is possible that she knew something of telepathy before the word was invented, and something of the force of suggestion before the researches of the Salpêtrière or Nancy. There were documents, at any rate, now in Hebbelthwaite's possession, which might well have served for a chapter of Huysman's "Là Bas."

The end came with the death of a beautiful and foolish girl of the village. There was no evidence that she had ever had anything whatever to do with Judith, or that her death was due to other than natural causes. But the train was already laid, and the spark fired it. Everett Merle himself was present when, in the broad water of the Fleet, at the spot now known as the Witch's Pool, she was subjected to the popular ordeal. The result has already been recorded. The child Judith, dry-eyed not comprehending, only frightened, saw her mother drown.

It is a difficult point in the history that at this time the daughter cannot have been more than six years of age. In some way or other, however, she had received her mother's instructions, and when she grew to womanhood she was keenly alive to them. Everett Merle had murdered her mother. Sooner or later the Merle family should give blood for blood.

With the next two generations Hebbelthwaite came upon a mass of more direct evidence. It was clear that neither that six-year-old child nor her daughter took the people of the village into her confidence as to this vendetta. Occasionally, however, a word had been said, and some old marshman or some old servant of the Hall had quoted it. Hebbelthwaite went about among them, and knew them all. There is respect in the marshes for a good sportsman. Even his kindly heart and his open purse could hardly bring him into contempt. The portfolio contained more than one minutely-accurate description of conversations which Hebbelthwaite had held with such people bearing on the history of the Merle and Jennis families.

He had not exaggerated, and he said that he believed in witchcraft, with his own definition of the term in his mind. He had had very good reason for his strong though simple warning to Linda Merle to keep back from any development of abnormal powers, and any prying beyond the closed doors.

Reviewing that history as he did now, he was a little in doubt. His own opinions were fixed enough. But he doubted at the moment if the necessity were sufficiently urgent for him to give Linda the reasons on which they rested, and to communicate to her a chapter in her family history which had never been communicated to her, a chapter, moreover, of which for the most obvious reasons it was not easy for him to speak.

Hebbelthwaite believed in a personal Power of Evil, and that Judith Jennis was in a closer touch with such a power, perhaps by virtue of her ancestry, than any ordinary man or woman. That she had "sold herself to the devil," as the phrase of romance has it, he did not, of course, believe. But he drew no hard-and-fast line between the wonders for which science has found an explanation and those which as yet it has not even classified. Indisputably Judith Jennis had actually accomplished things which belonged to the latter category, as well as many others which he could more easily understand. He felt sure that she would shipwreck Linda if she could, and that that shipwreck would not be of the kind which comes within the cognisance of the law. Linda was clearly a woman with a temperament, influenced by surroundings, influenced by personalities. Judith had but to tempt her to play a dangerous game, to strain after that which is hidden, to cultivate that unnamed sense by which all of us do on rare occasions perceive it. He had himself known cases of people who had begun as sober and scientific investigators of psychical mysteries, and in spite of their armour and equipment had ended badly. One had undergone an utter moral degradation. Two others had crept back from an asylum to live a shattered semi-life for the rest of their spoiled days.

He made up his mind. Once and once only he had spoken at some length with Judith Jennis. Now he would see her again. "And twist her neck if necessary," he added to himself. He was sufficiently a student of human nature to know that the repetition of warnings to Linda would make them lose their value. They would seem like mere sermonising. He respected her independent spirit. He was an independent man himself. He was glad that she drove a powerful car and drove well; glad that she could lose her temper if she supposed for one moment that advice was presumptuous. He would not have had that different. He looked on that spirit as the salt of the earth, the thing that keeps us from stopping and decaying, the thing that makes for the movement onwards by which we shall be what we shall be.

For a moment his thought strayed from this point. He had been struck the first time he saw her at a kind of likeness between Linda and Judith.

He recalled the evidence, and he admitted that it was quite insufficient, that the ancestress of the one had come very deeply under the influence of the ancestress of the other. Could this be the reason why Linda was so eager a neophyte of that dark world which held Judith among its initiated?

He put back the portfolio in its place. He could see Judith, postponing his visit for a critical moment. He was not in the least afraid of her. He even counted on being able to influence her. What else was there he could do? Like some doctor in the dark as to his diagnosis, he might try to treat the symptoms as they occurred.

His butler announced Mrs. Devigny and Miss Merle. Mrs. Devigny had a quick eye, and she had taken in a great deal in the few moments that she had been in the house. Firstly, Mr. Hebbelthwaite was not living in the way which she had expected. She had supposed a cottage with honeysuckle, a clean old woman to wait on them, and considerable difficulty about the tea, with humorous apologies, humorously accepted. This, on the contrary, was almost metropolitan. Secondly, he understood furniture, and it was a subject which Mrs. Devigny had studied deeply. She recognised the quality of two or three of the more important pieces, and the absence of any rubbish. She began to wonder if there were any subjects under the sun which he did not understand. She talked on unperturbedly, wittily at times. But all the while she was conscious that her eyes rested either for a less or a greater time than was necessary on this man. It was absurd to stare. It was absurd to be shy. She prayed that Linda might not have noticed it.

Linda had flown at a big portfolio on a stand, and was turning over a collection of mezzotints.

There were some good things there. "Yes," said Hebbelthwaite, "I collected those in the days before the price of them went out of sight; I leave that alone nowadays. For one thing, I haven't got the time for it any more; I've taken up such a lot of other work."

"You are a universal expert, Mr. Hebbelthwaite," said Mrs. Devigny.

"Jack-of-all-trades and master of none," corrected Hebbelthwaite.

"When I first heard of you," said Linda to Laurence Hebbelthwaite, "it puzzled me to think how you could manage to live here, and what you could try to do with your time. Now I'm beginning to see. What's all that long row of portfolios on the bottom shelf?"

"Each one contains notes and papers and photographs of some subject that I have taken up. One of them, for instance, is concerned with the history of your own family."

"Do let me see it—now."

"No," said Hebbelthwaite; "not now. Perhaps I will show it you one of these days."

"Mystery-monger," said Linda, fiercely.

Hebbelthwaite laughed. Was she never to be able to make this man angry—never to be able to move him in the least? Percy Belton flashed into her mind. She could have produced any required mood in him in ten minutes.

Hebbelthwaite remained himself, unmoved. Very well, then, Linda would see. There was yet a shaft in her quiver.

"I went the other night to see Judith Jennis," she said, boldly.

"Ah," said Hebbelthwaite. "Let me take that cup for you; won't you?"

"I think," said Linda, "that the way in which you speak of that woman is wrong and cruel. There is nothing of the witch about her. She is simply a very kindly peasant woman. I was tired when I got to her cottage. She gave me milk to drink, and, what do you think? Afterwards I went back home on that great goat of hers."

"What?" said Hebbelthwaite, "on Bel?"

"How did you know the name of the goat?"

"Well," said Hebbelthwaite, "he's rather a remarkable specimen of his kind, isn't he? I've seen him grazing often. He doesn't like me; goes for me with the utmost regularity, whenever he sees me."

"Perhaps you have ill-treated him," said Linda.

"Not yet," said Hebbelthwaite, drily.

"He was perfectly quiet with me, anyhow. A most friendly animal. I wonder if there are any others in England as big as he is."

"I should doubt it," said Hebbelthwaite; "certainly there is none about these parts. I've made a study of Bel rather, and of Judith's other goats. These photographs might interest you."

He took from one of his portfolios a number of excellent photographs, whole-plate size.

"These are good," said Linda. "Do look, Cara."

"Who took them?" asked Cara.

"I did," said Hebbelthwaite. "I'm not a swell at it, but the professional who came down for me could never get near the brutes."

"Wait," said Linda in a flash; "you told me that Bel always went for you."

"He does, when he sees me. But one learns to approach wild life carefully under cover about the marshes. I should never have shot golden plover had I not acquired something of the craft. Bel never knew that he was being photographed until it was too late."

"And what did he do then?" asked Cara.

"He did his best," said Hebbelthwaite, "but as he won't cross running water it didn't amount to anything. I kept the Fleet between my precious camera and him."

Hebbelthwaite thought things over, when the two women had gone.

How splendid that girl looked when she was angry! What was the meaning of Judith's kindness? The old tag crossed his mind, "Timeo Danaos, et dona ferentes."

At some distance from. Hebbelthwaite's house Linda stopped in the road and stamped her foot. "I absolutely hate that man," she said, vehemently.

Cara smiled sadly. "Quite sure?" she said. "I don't think you're quite fair to him."

"You can't be fair to him," said Linda; "the man's impossible."

Chapter X

The Strewer of Flowers

The feathery blossom of the reeds which spread their tremulous density along the rands beside the river, between wall and water, had lost the rich purple lustre of summer, and were fading to the gray of early autumn. It was time for the marshmen to see to the cutting of those great swathes of reeds which would be dried and sold for thatching and fencing at the rate of 1s. per fathom, thus transforming what most people would consider barren bog into a source of considerable income. The work is hard, and a good man, with the specially heavy scythe which it requires, can earn as much as two pounds a week by putting in six reasonable days at piece work.

Little Jimmy Buddery was useless at the mowing of the rands, and he knew it. But he could superintend as well as any man from Yarmouth to Bungay. No one ever took any notice of his instructions, but the cause of wit which he was in others kept the stalwart arms of Bob Middleton and his mowing "mate," "Sir William" Hart, in the better fettle, by reason of the joy of the chaff to which the little man was subjected. The scythes always sang with a more cheerful voice when laughter shook the tops of "the mow."

One morning in late August little Jimmy stood on the wall against his mill, looking down to the rand where Bob and Sir William were standing, their scythe blades held out in front of them, the handles resting on the fibrous rand, their hones sweeping backwards and forwards over the shining steel.

Soon the edges felt satisfactory to the testing fingers. Bob and Sir William spat on their hands, took a firm grasp of their scythe handles, and sent out the curved steel swishing through the reed-stems. After five minutes at this (during which little Jimmy continued to superintend in a silent, unobtrusive way), Bob stayed the sweep of his arms, and Sir William stopped in sympathy.

Bob looked up at the little man standing perkily on the wall close by. "Doan't ye wish as yew had the boon and s'news ta dew a bit o' honest wark, bor?" asked Bob. "But theer; yew fare as yew wuz maade, an' Judy Jennis harself coun't gi'e ye moor ile in yar marrow than enow ta stand a garpin' while men as be men git all of a muck wash."

" Doan't yew talk sa loud about yar bit o' muscle," said Jimmy, grinning down from his eminence. "Yew 'ouldn't be much aside Maaster Hibbelthwaitery. Wha he drawed a colt out o' the deeak t'other daay as yew an' far moor o' yar soort coun't mewve. A pratty set a fules yew lot appared. He just copped hold o' the hid roop i' one hand an' the starn roop in t'other, an' give a h'ist, an' up she come. Wha yew bain't much moor use 'an I be alongside o' him. He dew fare whoolly a rum egg. I shoun't keer ta hey wuds along o' he."

"Ah," said Sir William, "tha'ss all very well for yew ta mob, yew spidery, skinnery little stoot. But that worn't doned without witchcraft. That theer maan be wunnerful set agin Judy, but I rackon he bain't much better hisself. My ole granny allust did saay as tew of a traade niver agreed."

"Doan't ye talk sa silly, bor," said Jimmy, with a sneer of the superior intellect which he believed himself to possess. "Maaster Hibbelwaitery be a gennelman. Whaat dew he waant wi' witchcraft?"

"Noo, noo," said Bob, wiping the sweat from his forehead with the back of his hand. "Jimmy fare right theer, Sir Willum. 'Tain't witchcraft. 'Tis the good wittles an' drink as gennelmen git as maake him sa strong. Wha I ha' heerd as some gennelmen eeat a matter o' tew or t'ree pound o' meeat at ivery meeal, not countin' the feesh an' buds an' rarbuts as they swaller for a relish."

"But he dew knoo a sight," said Sir William, unwilling to surrender his theory of witchcraft. "Wha, he've gart a soort o' clock as hang up in the

Hall agin the dooar as tall him pratty nigh as much about the weather as I can dew."

"Wha, yew innercent fule!" cried Jimmy, "tha'ss a weather glass. I ha' seed a some'at like it at the coostguard at Yarmouth."

"But he dew fare wunnerful set agin Judy," persisted Sir William. "He! he! Ha' ye heerd as that booy o' Judy's ha' brook out frash? I wuz arter my owan bizness agin the Witch's Pool t'other evenin'—"

"Did ye git them teeal?" asked Bob, anxiously. He had an eye on the fowl himself, but dared not take the poaching liberties on which Sir William ventured by reason of his reputed simplicity.

"Yew ax my fut," said Billy. "I wuz a gooin' ta saay as I see the young missis a walkin' t'rew the plantin', an' as true's Gord that theer Job follered har, hidin' behind the scrub till she come ontew a rush basket full o comfrey an' ragged robin as lay in the track. When she picked up the rubbishy muck I see Job look that pleeased as niver wuz. I ha' seed him moor 'an oncet arter har. He doan't let har see him, but I dew believe as he warship the wery mowld she tread on. He! he! He! Tha'ss a maasterpiece. Yew'd hudly ha' thote as he had gumpertion enow ta knoo a pratty wench from a store peeg."

"Doan't yew maake noo mistaake," said Bob. "Wha, Sir William, I ha' seed yew—"

"That'll dew—that'll dew," said Billy.

But his tormentor proceeded, and became Rabelaisian.

The new development in Job Sacret had not escaped the notice of Judith Jennis. At first she looked on the dumb devotion of her poor lad for Linda with a contemptuous indifference. But when she found him day after day neglecting her geese and goats in order to weave strange and beautiful rush baskets, and to seek far and near for the lovelier wild flowers of the season wherewith to fill these votive offerings to the woman whom she longed to bring to disaster, she grew irritated, and let him know in a way which she knew he could understand that his attentions displeased her, and that they were to cease. Job whimpered and whined in his piteous inarticulate fashion, but his mistress did not relent. He made outward submission. But inwardly the obstinacy of the imbecile was roused to opposition.

Why, he puzzled, should she object to his making baskets and filling them with flowers for Linda? She had seemed eager enough to do the girl service on the night when Linda first visited the Tower House. His animal cunning taught him to conceal his inward revolt. But from that time he watched with jealousy the association between the mistress of Merlesfleet and the witch, which gave promise of becoming more intimate.

Judith herself was content with the way in which her plans were maturing. She knew well enough, though Linda did not, that it was owing to the influence she had exercised from the look-out on the top of the tower that Linda's feet had carried her to the Tower House on the night when Bel first bore her weight. She thought that she had established her power over the girl so firmly that it would rest solely with her to choose the time and place for the final triumph—the climax of the vendetta which had lasted throughout three lives. Time and time again she plied her mystic rites, peering into the brimming cup, or testing her powers of divination in the convolutions of the shiny slime of the ooze made by the scouring of the ebbing Fleet. She would read the future in the writhing fronds of ribbonweed, in the flight of the bats, in the cries with which the nocturnal wild life filled the marsh by night. And ever she saw the same end. It was the reading of this real or imaginary vision which gave her unease. For it might be interpreted in two ways, one of which meant disaster to Linda, and the other a very different fate. What was coming over her that her eyes should see no clearer?

She tried to get into closer touch with the powers of darkness, with which she fully believed she could hold communion. Night after night she rode the great goat Bel along the woodland ways. Night after night she whispered her secrets to her familiar, and thought he heard. Bel seemed to understand. He never sped so swiftly as when he galloped towards Merlesfleet. His eyes never twinkled with such malicious mischief as when he saw Linda holding converse with the witch. There was consciousness in the glances of Judith and her goat when they met. They understood each other.

One night "Sir William," lying concealed behind a bramble bush from which he was watching a wire snare set in a hare's run, had his feeble wits more unsettled than ever by the vision of Judith, sitting on the black goat's back, speeding along the ride, crying out some words which had no meaning for him, but which he felt were the language of the Black Man of the marshes and his servants. He clutched his precious medals fearfully, as though the poor rumpery might act as a talisman against the evil eye. And he was so terrified by the sight that he forbore to name it even to Bob Middleton. Never after that night did he venture forth at night without the string of medals hanging about him. The pride he took in their possession gave him comfort. Surely, he thought, a man who had been so honoured, a man whom "gennelmen" had called "Sir William" might defy the powers of darkness if any one could.

Chapter XI

Two A.M.

"I can't see it," said Linda, petulantly.

Cara began to pull to pieces slowly and deliberately the begonia bloom which she had plucked. "But obviously, Linda, dear, I can't be your guest for ever and ever, Amen."

"I want you to be," said Linda, with a mutinous mouth. "Why not, Cara? Of course Uncle Willoughby and Aunt Mary will be here all September, and I know that's what you have in your mind."

Cara's eyes were fixed on the wounded blossom. That was so very far from being what she had in her mind.

"Seriously," she said, "it is not that at all. Honestly, I don't dislike them. They have sometimes got on my nerves. But that's nothing."

"You see," said Linda, "You give me no real reason. I had wanted you to remain with me till November, and then, when it got cold here, to come with me to Egypt. It was almost arranged."

"Hear the voice of the prophetess," said Cara. "I do not think you'll go to Egypt in November. You will go a little later, and not alone. But not with me."

"Mistaken," said Linda, promptly. "I know Uncle Willoughby did think about it. But he has quite decided that it will be impossible for him to be away in the winter again. The only thing I can think of is your health. You've lost your spirits. You never sleep. I saw a light in your room at two the other morning."

"And what were you doing at two the other morning? You must have been outside the house to have seen the light."

"I was," said Linda. "When I've really lost my temper as I did at Mr. Hebbelthwaite's, I get upset and can't sleep. I felt feverish, and thought a breath of fresh air on the terrace would cool me. That's how it happened."

She was barely conscious of her motive in lying in this way. She had been down to the Tower House, and had been with Judith Jennis that night.

Cara Devigny took the refuge that was open to her. Yes. She could with safety plead health. "It's delightful to be here," she said. "And I love this country. But I believe it doesn't agree with me. It's awfully vulgar to permit anything not to agree with one. I wish I didn't do it. I kept it in the background as long as I could. But, really, I think I should do well to go north. I've neglected my friends at Grantown for a long time."

"They don't deserve you," said Linda.

"No," said Cara. "They've never done anything particularly wrong. All the same, I think I must write and break it to them gently that I am coming. We shall meet again, you know, dear. Perhaps in a month. I'm neither going to kill myself nor marry myself. I shall still be available."

"I wish you would marry," said Linda. "If you stop here I will find some one for you—Laurence Hebbelthwaite, perhaps; or I'll get some one down from London."

Then Cara said the cleverest thing she had ever said in her life. She said, with absolutely the right inflection of voice, "I should prefer Laurence Hebbelthwaite. I'm quite inclined to like him as it is."

"He's a devil, and makes me furious," said Linda. "I seriously believe that I do some wrong things, and shall keep on doing them, simply because I will not be influenced by what he says, or by what he thinks, though he daren't say it."

"Is, 'daren't' the word?" suggested Cara.

"You know it isn't; otherwise I would be less angry. What other man do I know that would half tell me things and refuse to tell me the rest when I demanded it? He's brutally obstinate; he goes his own way. He doesn't care a pin's head what it is."

"Do you mean to give him up?" said Cara; "not to see him any more—not to invite him?"

Linda shrugged her shoulders. "Of course not. What can one do in a place like this, where the society is so very limited? I'm ashamed to say that he interests me in a kind of a way. It's not a pleasant—it only makes me lose my temper."

Cara wondered in her own mind for a moment what the effect would be if she said plainly to Linda: "You are falling in love with Laurence Hebbelthwaite. It is the first time in your life that this kind of thing has happened to you, and you do not yet understand it."

She did not say it; she went off to write a cheerful and frivolous letter to her future hostess in Grantown. She dropped it into the letter-box in the library, and went up to her own room. Of course, he loved Linda, even if he himself had scarcely guessed it yet. She flung herself down on her bed to think about it. She was very firm with herself; she would scarcely let her own thoughts speak out what had happened. She might suffer, but she would not be humiliated. Many men had fallen in love with Cara Devigny. She had had scant mercy for them. She remembered that now with something like remorse. Her plans matured rapidly. Once at Grantown, some further excuse of health might be made. She might perhaps get Linda to come to her. In any case if she could help it, she must not see Laurence Hebbelthwaite again.

Linda was also in her room. She was carefully comparing two cups. The bowls of them were of wine-coloured amber—so exactly alike they seemed that she tied a black thread on one of them to distinguish it. Then she noticed that she had tied the thread on the cup which belonged to Judith Dennis.

The night before she had felt beyond mistake the influence at work upon her. She had recalled her first visit to Judith. She had remembered what she had heard of the woman from Laurence Hebbelthwaite and from others. "But to-night," she had said to herself, "I shall not go. I am going out on the terrace because it is cooler and pleasanter there. But that is all. I am not going to Judith Jennis." An hour later she had knocked at the door of the Tower House. A strange scene followed.

A voice from within told her to enter. The outer door was ajar, and Linda pushed it back and went in, guided by the light from the room within. Here Judith sat at the table. Before her was the cup which she used for divination. Her eyes were fixed upon it, and she did not look up as Linda entered. "Yew ha' come then? Yew heerd the call?"

Linda did not answer. Her eyes were fixed on the cup. Surely that was her own cup. Yet she believed Judith to be incapable of a sordid theft. Also, if the cup had been stolen, Judith had had ample time to hide it before her entry.

"What are you doing there?" Linda asked.

"I'm a-tryin' ta read what the time ta come hev in stoor for yew an' me, wha'ss a-goin' ta come for yew an' me, what the ind ull be o' the taale as is writ for us tew uns. But I ha' lost my gift. My eyes are blinded. I can see narthen moor nor anybardy else."

It was the first open avowal of magical power of any kind which she had made to Linda. Laurence Hebbelthwaite had been right then. Knowing as she did that her best and safest course was to leave this woman, her curiosity to know the unknowable prevailed.

"Hare be the cup. But tha'ss not a mite o' use without the gift, noo moor 'an the gift be without the cup. Yew doan't waant ta be afeared," she said, as she saw the look of alarm in Linda's eyes. "Yew ha gart the very sister on't. Tall me, ha'e ye gart the gift tew?"

She rose from the settle, and, without a word, sank down upon it. She drew the cup towards her. "What is it that I shall see?" she said.

"The ch'ice is the Maaster's."

"I see nothing but the shining liquid in the cup. It is bright, like silver. It becomes so bright that your face, Judith, as you bend over me, is reflected in it. Now the surface is all broken up. It becomes clouds, rolling fast away, one after another. Wait—I see it. Yes," she said breathlessly, "I see it—a woman kneeling in the wet, long grass. She's quite young; I've seen her in the village. I did not know she had a child. She holds the baby up high. There are tears streaming down her cheeks. I can't go on. What is the matter with me?"

"Stop ye theer. Look agin. Theer's moor ta come."

"Yes," said Linda, "there is more." And, without describing it, shrank back with a shudder. The witch spilt the contents of the cup upon the floor. "Do you know the name of the man?" Linda asked—"the man to whom the woman was kneeling?'"

"Aah! I know well enow."

The name of Percy Belton was never mentioned between them. Linda took the cup, and turned it about in her hands. "I think," she said, "this is exactly like mine. Tell me where it came from."

"Tha'ss moor nor I nor anybardy can tall ye. That belonged ta my gre't gran'mother, an' I've heerd my mother saay as that come from distant parts. I ha' tried ta l'arn its secret from the cup. But ta worn't noo good. Oony sometimes, when I fare to gaze intew't, a axin' it where ta come from, I hare the sound o' music in the rewm—music like what I ha' heerd when I've been a-passin' the chutch at service time. I think tha'ss maade by the organ, or 'ammonium, or some'at."

"I'm going to take it back with me, if I may," said Linda.

"Wha that yew maay an' welcome. Though yew doan't know narthen on't, yew an' me wuz born sisters o' the arts o' the mash. All I hev is yarn. Yew hev the gift a'riddy. But theer's moor for me ta l'arn ye, sister, moor for yew ta know. Should a l'arn ye ta bind an' onbind?—ta charm love or haate?—ta call the wipers an' scaleless fish o' marshland tew ye?—ta see wha'ss a comin'?—ta bring evil ta them as ye haate, an' good foortin' ta them as ye love? Speeak, sister; would ye eeat at Judy's taable an' be sister with har in trewth?'"

"Why do you call me sister?" asked Linda.

Judith said nothing, but pointed to the reflection of the two faces in the dark glass of the window with the moonless night outside.

"Yes," said Linda. "I had noticed it myself. I seem to be frightened, like somebody who turns out of the road he knows into a dark wilderness. What is the price you ask for all this?"

"'Tis not mine ta make the price," Judith. "The ch'ice is the Maaster's. Of some he axes one thing, of others another."

"Who is the master?" asked Linda in a hushed voice.

"The Black Man o' the mash. His name may not be spook," replied Judith. "Should a gi'e ye a sign? Dee ye ax for moor'an the cup? Hist! I'll call Bel, my gre't black goot, an' he shall beer ye hoamward without leeadin' o' moortal hand. Alooan shall he beer ye hooam, alooan shall he retarn ta me. Yew doan't waant ta be afeared on him. He oan't hu't ye. One other sign I'll gi'e ye: I'll send ye a dreeam i' the night when ye lie sleeapin' in yar maiden bed. But not yet shall ye dreeam it. Oony if theer bain't noo other waay. Then shall ye l'arn whose is the ch'ice, an' that the loke ye ha set yar feet upon fare narrer. Theer's noo tarnin' out on't."

Without the door the sound of Bel's deep, hoarse call was heard. Judith led out Linda in a. dazed condition, still grasping the cup. Still scarce conscious of her surroundings, the girl mounted the goat. As soon as he felt her weight, Bel, with head held high so that she might stay herself by his horns, stepped noiselessly, quietly, rapidly along the moss-grown track in the direction of Merlesfleet.

Judith went back to her place on the settle. She held her hands on high, clasped together. "At last o' time!" she cried. "Har feet are in the springe."

Out from the straw-litter crept the uncouth figure of Job Sacret. He crawled on hands and knees, and clasped his mistress about the feet, making the querulous moan with which he craved a boon. He pawed at Judith's skirt, as a dog will do to attract his mistress's notice. With one imperious gesture she sent him back to his litter. He lay there whimpering.

At length the whimpering died out as the idiot-boy sank to slumber. All was still. There was a long silence. Then came sharp rapping of Bel's horns upon the window. Away in the distance the church clock struck two.

Chapter XII

Exit Percy Belton—Enter Mr. Willoughby Trotter

Some days had elapsed. The morning had seen the departure of Mrs. Devigny in apparently the best of spirits. In the evening Mr. Trotter and his wife were to arrive from Cambridge. Linda looked ill and distraught.

An inquiry or two, discreetly made in the village, had told her the truth of Percy Belton. The news came to her as with a violent physical shock. It filled her with disgust and repulsion. She had known, of course, that these horrible things happened, but they had never come into her sheltered life before. She could not bear the thought of him, nor the sound of his name. She was unjust, not unnatural, considering her upbringing and the life she had led. There had been no planned cruelty on Belton's part, no intention of harming any one. He had the sins of a nature at once weak and passionate; in truth, Briony Prettyman would still have been happy enough had Linda never crossed his path.

The remembrance of that last scene with Judith haunted her like a terrible nightmare. Twenty times she had been on the verge of sending for Hebbelthwaite, telling him the whole story, and frankly asking his advice. Twenty times her pride had stayed her. The cup had been sent back to the Tower House by Tabitha Prettyman. No written or spoken word accompanied it. Judith concealed her surprise.

"Ha'e ye heerd yar laady ax consarnin' Briony?" asked Judith.

"Yes," answered Tabitha, who had lost some of her native tongue. "That might ha' been a bad business for me. Briony was all right till that Belton come. Ha'e ye been able to lay a spell upon him? Briony told me what you promised her."

"Tha'ss for Briony ta tell ye," answered Judith. "Yew'll dew yarself noo good by bitin' moor 'an yew can swaller. Still yar tongue, gal. Know as such as me bain't ta be questi'ned like them as gits theer wittles on the land. What I l'arn from them as comes ta me I tall to noobardy. Goo! Be off wi' ye back agin. Ax Briony owt as ye wish consarnin' all things barrin' Me."

Tabitha hurried away in terror lest she should have offended Judith. A board school education and domestic service had emasculated her Norfolk speech, but had not undermined her faith in the magic of the marshes.

Before she sent the cup back Linda had again tried by daylight, by candle-light and by moonlight to read the future in it, and in vain. No more came the silver sheen on the water, or the rolling clouds, or the strangely vivid picture. Could the clear liquid which Judith had poured on the floor have had some special virtue? But Linda knew that she was in danger now and hesitated to ask.

Lady Blickling drove over in the afternoon in a glistening new 40 h.-p. Mercédés, of which she explained that she entirely disapproved.

"They are bad and abominable inventions, my dear," she said. "I got this one simply and solely because I live so far from you, and I am a little tender about my horses. I look upon it simply as a substitute for a nasty dirty railway train. In fact, if there were a direct line between my house and yours I would burn or sell the thing at once."

In the meantime her driver in the butler's pantry was giving his own version. "No," he said, in unadulterated cockney, "mine's not such a 'eavenly little plice as you might think, Mr. Thomson. On the one 'and, I don't no want no mark on my licence, and on the other 'and I've got to carry out my lidy's orders. It's 'Can't you go a little quicker, 'Arris?' It's 'Need you slow quite so much for them corners, 'Arris ?' She'd brike 'er neck mine in ten minutes if I'd let 'er. A fair old korf-drop. That's what I call 'er. Thenk you, Mr. Thomson. There is a bit o' chill in the wind drivin' against it. A little drop o' water with mine."

Harris sipped and continued. "Then there's the work! You see this is a new with 'er lidyship. I'm kept at it pretty well night an' dye. And yet she never speaks o' that car without d——nin' its eyes one wye or another. She's got some language, too. Oh, not 'arf! 'Infernal machine,' she'll sye, as as look at yer. 'Box o' smells,' is another of 'er elegant expressions. There's some rum uns among the errystocracy, I can tell yer."

"I believe you," said Thomson. "I well remember when I was first footman with the Duke of Chingford—young man 'e was then, 'e's dead now. 'Look 'ere, d——n yer eyes, James,' was 'is customary way of speakin' to me. After a bit I couldn't stick it."

Upstairs Lady Blickling was accusing Linda of being ill, and refusing to accept her laughing denial.

"You won't eat porridge for breakfast. You spend all your time in that mechanical dog-crusher with which you've poisoned this country, and you can't expect to be well."

"I've done some riding as well," said Linda. "On rather a queer mount," she added, meditatively.

"I ought to have been your mother," said Blickling, with conviction. "I'd have looked after you properly. I wouldn't have had any silly nonsense about giving you your freedom just because you choose to say that you were twenty-one. Mary Trotter is a good woman, but she's a fool, or she wouldn't have handed you over to that Mrs. Devigny. Yes; yes. I dare say she is a very kind and clever woman. But she has not got a firm hand. Now, I have."

"I wish you'd give me some advice," said Linda, suddenly. "I've got something on my mind, and I don't know what to do about it."

"Tell me," said the old lady, kindly, her expression changing to one of almost motherly tenderness.

"It's not very easy to tell," said Linda. "It's a horrible story."

Slowly and with difficulty she said enough to make the old lady aware of what she had learnt concerning Percy Belton and Briony Prettyman. Even as she was speaking the door opened.

"Mr. Percy Belton has called, madam. He is in the library," announced Thomson.

"Very well," said Linda, looking over her shoulder. Thomson closed the door.

"I won't see him," said Linda, feverishly. "I can't see him."

"But I can, my dear," said the old lady, grimly. "And I will. I shall have just a few minutes' talk with him, and you will not be troubled with him again. Let me see, the library is the second door on the right, isn't it?"

The light of battle was in her steely eyes as she passed out of the room.

Percy Belton went through the interview like a gentleman. He said very little. Lady Blickling's last words were, "You know you never had any right to come to this house. What business had you to come straight from your miserable intrigue to a house like this? Never come near to the place again; never. If you have a spark of decency in you, you will leave Oatacre altogether."

There had been many points on which the wretched boy could have offered a defence or made an answer. He attempted nothing of the kind. "It is useless to try to explain to you, Lady Blickling," he said. Then, erect, with white face and set lips, he left Merlesfleet. He never entered the house again.

Lady Blickling went back to the drawing-room. "I think I've arranged that amicably enough," she said. "You won't be troubled with him again."

"How I wish these horrible things didn't happen!" said Linda.

Lady Blickling shrugged her shoulders. "Life is as it is, my dear," said she, "and we've got to face it. I never turn my back on anything. There are people who do. There are people who won't see the ugly facts of life. They won't be shocked. They won't be hurt. Everything has got to be for the nicest in the nicest of worlds. They wrap themselves up in cotton wool, and spray it with eau de Cologne first.

"My dear," Lady Blickling continued, impressively, "some of these are quite good people in their own mean way. They are selfish; they are too tender with themselves. It is a belief of mine that the same God made them that made those ugly facts. But what could one expect in this case?

Young men are young men. And Calcote has no more moral restraint over any of his menagerie than I have over the tides of the sea. Well, we've threshed it out and settled it. Now I want you to come out on my car. It's a much better one than yours, if you can recognise any difference between two pestilences. It's on the hills where we beat you, of course. I took the Beeston hills, near Cromer, the other day, and you hardly knew they were there."

Her direction to the driver when he brought the car round was as follows: "Harris, Miss Merle is anxious to see what our car can do. No dawdling, please."

"Very good, my lidy," said Harris, with a despondent look.

A turn of the switch started the engine. Thomson, as he shut the front doors, chuckled internally.

The senior tutor of St. Cecilia's, accompanied by his wife and his valet, arrived that evening, and were met by Linda with the car. It was perhaps characteristic that Mr. Trotter travelled with his own servant, and Mrs. Trotter left her maid behind. Every piece of luggage was stamped or painted with the name and address of Willoughby Trotter, Esquire, in full. It even figured on his wife's dress-baskets. He was emphatically on his holiday. He had tried to temper the precisian with the sportsman. The admixture worked out in a Norfolk jacket of a pepper-and-salt material, tastefully combined with black gloves. He wore trousers at present. But there were knickerbockers in one of his portmanteaux. There were also gaiters. Gaiters cover a multitude of shins, as Mrs. Devigny sometimes remarked.

He was so busy in trying to get the senior tutor out of his mind that it was never entirely absent. But the train waited some time at Norwich, and he had with great deliberation taken a whisky and soda in the afternoon— a thing which he had not done since his last holiday. He had also purchased a packet of "Pride of the Harem" cigarettes, ruthlessly destroying the cover, with its chromographic voluptuousness, and transferring the contents to the chaste sobriety of his gun-metal case.

Aunt Mary liked the smell of tobacco, and said she wished he smoked more often in Term time. "A pleasant vice," he said, complacently. "A pleasant vice. My work is of a nature which makes it absolutely essential to keep the head clear. A man in my position has to deny himself much. Now, of course one can let oneself go a little."

So he let himself go. This is to say, he ate one quarter of a "Pride of the Harem," smoked one quarter of it, and dropped the remaining moiety out of the window.

It was not a smoking compartment, but they had the carriage to themselves, and he was absolutely reckless.

Linda was a little surprised to find how very glad she was to see them again. That note of prosaic respectability was the note to which she wished to listen now. It was a talisman to keep her from dangerous influences. She made the senior tutor talk about University affairs, and the part he had taken in them. He did not much want to talk about University affairs, and for the fact that there was indisputably the part he had taken in them. She was amused to find that he showed a real knowledge of farming, and his questions concerning the crops of her home farm were pertinent. He was not the absolutely perfect man. But it was a virtue in him that he generally knew fairly well what he was talking about. An imaginary competitive examination was ever before his eyes, and he always passed high up in the list. Thus for a little while all went peacefully. The influence of Judith seemed to wane.

Chapter XIII

The Death of Bel

Perhaps, on the whole, it was a good thing that Percy Belton had come under the lash of Lady Blickling's tongue. She had said some things to him which were cruel and unfair, but she had brought him to see himself from a different point of view. At first he was filled with nothing but a passion of resentment against Linda, against Briony, and against all women.

How could Linda have heard about it if Briony had not betrayed him? What had Linda to do with the things that he had done before he had ever met her? Had he been any worse than thousands of other young men of his age? He had not forgotten the woman. He had not left her without provision for her needs. Why should Linda treat him as an outcast, so abominable that she could not even to speak of him? As his resentment against her increased, his resentment against Briony left him. He believed the girl still loved him. He doubted if she would have betrayed him. It might be worth while to see her, at any rate. It was something to be loved.

It was something also for his poor young vanity for him to do the thing that he knew Linda and Lady Blickling did not believe that he had the courage to do. He met Briony again. He left her with a promise of marriage. Briony, assured that she had entered into eternal happiness, went in gratitude to the witch. It was wonderful, and Judith had done it.

As she left the Tower House, bearing her baby in her arms, she passed across the march by the river wall on which Bel was grazing, in the midst of his attendant seraglio. She had nearly reached the ligger over which she had to pass to the wall which would take her to the high road, when Bel looked up, and his deep hoarse call grated out with a threat which alarmed the mother. She had heard of late strange tales of a new fierceness which the great he-goat had been said to show. Instead of hurrying to cross the ligger, her footsteps faltered, and she stopped, nervously clutching her child to her bosom, and turning back to see if the menace of the croaking voice were to be followed by any attack. To her terror she saw that Bel had separated himself from the nannies and was coming with swift springing leaps across the marsh in her direction. Briony was never possessed of any great self-confidence. An emergency always found her at her worst, danger always sought out her cowardice, and took the strength from her limbs, the volition from her poor trusting brain. She stood motionless, breathing quickly, her arms quivering with such violence that the child was frightened, and began to raise its wailing plaint.

Bel came with a dainty, dancing gait, which would have been pretty to see under other circumstances, till he was within ten yards of Briony. Then he halted, and again baaed forth his hoarse challenge. He leapt with all four feet from the ground, his wiry, agile body twitching with excitement. He placed his forefeet stiffly in front of him, and bent his head so that the terrible curving horns pointed at Briony. With these he made little fencing movements, thrusting his neck forth and backwards with lightning speed. His saturnine eyes seemed to the woman to twinkle with malice. His long coarse beard seemed to her to bristle. By this time Briony was quite helpless. She could scarce raise her voice beyond a whisper, and the piteous cries for help which were strangled in her throat were not sonorous enough to reach any spot from whence aid might be hoped.

Bel gave a final passado with his horns, and with a snort pregnant with menace leap forward.

While Briony had been watching Bel, her back turned towards the river wall, Laurence Hebbelthwaite had been hurrying to her assistance as fast as his long legs would carry him. He had seen the danger from a distance, and ran forward in the hope that the goat's hatred of himself might serve to turn his attention from the woman and child.

"This way; over the ligger," he cried.

But Briony was too dazed to give obedience to his warning. Hebbelthwaite took the ligger at one stride, and threw himself in front of

Briony just as Bel came rushing forward, his horns lowered to transfix this human obstruction, which at the moment seemed so objectionable to him. Hebbelthwaite was both strong and active. He formed his plans on the instant, and as the goat was in the very middle of its spring he caught one of the black convoluted horns in each hand, at the same time taking a half step to one side, so as to bring his front on his enemy's flank. He knew the momentum of the animal's attack might be sufficient to break his wrists. But he also knew how tough and powerful those same wrists were, and he risked it in the belief that he had adopted the only means of saving Briony.

The strain on wrist and arm was terrible, and as the goat's body swung round the man's whole frame swayed till every muscle was tense with effort. But his hands held: the first point in the game was his. Still holding the mighty horns, wrestling with the frantic struggles of the goat, he called again to Briony to make her escape over the ligger, and this time he succeeded in getting the meaning of his words through the wall of unconsciousness which terror and nervousness had built. When he knew she was safe he meant to modify his plan of campaign. He had heard much of this great goat recently. He would make this a fight to the finish. It was for him now to assume the offensive.

In spite of all his efforts, Bel, with a terrific jerk of his head, accompanied by a simultaneous spring from all four feet, succeeded in freeing himself, and, as he drew back momentarily to renew the attack with greater effect, his eyes danced with delight and eagerness. At last he had his old enemy on the same side of the Fleet. The ligger would be no escape for Hebbelthwaite. It was only the running water of the Fleet which had kept the two apart so long. Before Hebbelthwaite had steeled himself to meet the fresh rush, Bel gave an exulting roar, and came hurtling at him. This time the goat was on his guard, and watched the hands that sought again to seize him. With a rapid toss of the head he evaded Hebbelthwaite's grasp, and, in a flash, brought his horns again to the correct angle for a charge in mid-air. Hebbelthwaite leapt aside, but not so rapidly but that Bel's left horn came with awful force against his forearm. He felt the sleeve rip, but in the heat of the combat he did not notice the stream of blood that flowed from the deep flesh-wound where the point of the horn had pierced.

The goat's success was his destruction. Had he caught Hebbelthwaite full, with both horns, he would have rebounded directly back on all four feet. But his left horn caught for an instant in the torn sleeve, and he received such a wrench as his neck was bent aside that even his fine agility could not save him from a sidelong fall.

In a moment Hebbelthwaite was on him. While he still lay on his side the man's hands again gripped his horns, and bent his head down to the marsh, while he defied the threat of the kicking hoofs by kneeling boldly on the throat beneath that rank, stinking beard. With a sudden twist he turned Bel on his back, and the goat's horns were thrust deep down into the soft soil of the marsh. Hebbelthwaite thrust and thrust, all the while putting forth every ounce of the great strength with which he was endowed to prevent Bel from gaining his feet by any springing action of his body or limbs. The goat struggled frantically. But the hold of the marsh on his horns put him at a disadvantage with the man. He seemed to know his hour was come, for there burst from his throat (choked and muffled as it was by the pressure of Hebbelthwaite's bulk) a series of hoarse, clamant cries. There came an answering cry in a woman's voice, and with Briony's screams were now mingled the cries of Judith Jennis, who came hurrying from the Tower House in the direction of the marsh. But she was still at some distance when Hebbelthwaite thought that he might venture to withdraw the grip of one hand from the goat. With rapid stealth he slipped his hand behind him into his pocket, from whence he brought a small pocket-knife, which would have been useless as a weapon previously, but which might now suffice to give the coup de grâce. He opened the largest blade with his teeth, and plunged it into Bel's jugular vein. A spurt of blood deluged him, the goat's struggles became more violent than ever as the last convulsions of his muscles heaved and shook even the weight the man who had killed him. Before Judith got to the spot he had groaned his last.

Hebbelthwaite rose from the neck, now loathsome and red with blood. His every nerve was shaking. His breath came in quick, panting gasps. For a moment he stood, looking in triumphant satisfaction on what lay at his feet. Then his eyes dimmed, and he fell senseless on the marsh beside his late enemy. The nannies were huddled together at the further end of the marsh. They had no heart to avenge their champion. It was not theirs to fight. But standing beside the senseless man was one whose heart was hot with rage. She longed to choke the life out of this man.

Briony and her child were not yet gone. "Run ye up to the Hall," cried Judith. "I rackon he fare hu't pratty bad. Dooan't ye waait noo longer. Yew'll fare all right. Run ye right away."

Briony gave one look at the man who had saved her life, and thought she would be acting in his best interests by obeying Judith's behests.

Soon she disappeared in the woods on her way to Merlesfleet. Judith bent down to touch Hebbelthwaite. His heart, she felt, beat strong. He was not much hurt. Ah! she would soon remedy that.

But even as she set about her purpose there came a shout from the river wall.

Little Jimmy Buddery had gone down to his mill to change the set of the sails to meet a slant of wind which had come with the afternoon. He had watched with great interest, but at a prudent distance, the combat between Hebbelthwaite and Bel. He had no mind to risk his body or his soul by interfering in a struggle with so fell a creature as the black goat. But now that Bel was vanquished he thought that there would be brandy or cordial of some kind brought down for the wounded man. And he saw no reason why, if there were anything to be got, he should not have his share.

He had never had any quarrel with Judith. Indeed, he had sought her aid against the dangers into which the hob-o'-lanterns (wills-of-wisp) might lead him, and had paid her what she asked. "Hi!" he shouted. "Should a come oover tew ye, Judith? I rackon that'll taake a maan's strength ta h'ist that gre't chap off o' the mash. Waait yew a min't, and I'll be alonger ye."

Judith saw that her chance was gone. "Yew can come if ye like," she said; "but I rackon yar little titty arms oan't shift him fudder 'an a yud or tew. But come if ye like."

Her voice sounded sullen.

Jimmy came toddling along with his little legs over the ligger. "I niver see a better fight," said he, complacently. "Fust I thote as th' ole goot 'ould ha' doned for Maaster Hebbelthwaitery, an' then I thote as Maaster Hebbelthwaitery 'ould prewve tew much for he. I doubt yew'll stand a pore chance o' gittin' any brass for yar loss—what I might call compensaation," he said, and his tongue rolled the long word about in his mouth deliciously. "If ta hadn't ha' been for Maaster Hebbelthwaitery that 'ould ha' been all up wi' pore Briony an' har little un. Wha'ss come oover ole Bel o' laate, Judith, bor? I niver see him sa shoort-waaisted afoor. He come for the pore gal like a lurcher arter a heer. Ah! he'd ha' downed har right enow, yew maay deepend on't."

"He shall pay me," said Judith, and she spoke as if she meant it.

Well," said Jimmy, "I shoun't advise ye ta paay noo brass for lawin' on him. When ole Gully shot Billy P'inter's bull as went for him on the path acrost the cock-na-hay mash ole Billy pulled him, but coun't dew narthen tew ritrn on account of his hevin' shot in salf-deefence. O' course I unnerstan' as Hebbelthwaitery wuz a tresparsin' on yar mash. But how come Briony theer ? That'll be a p'int, I rackon. If I wuz yew, Judith—not but I know well enow as yew ha' gart moor gumpertion 'an iver I shall hev—I'd take any brass as he may orfer."

Judith paid but scant attention to the little man. Her eyes were fixed on the prone figure at her feet. She let Jimmy ramble on and on, and only when she heard the loud grunt of a motor-horn did she bring water from the neighbouring dyke and lave the face of the unconscious man. She was still bathing his forehead when the car from Merlesfleet appeared at the opening of the woodland track which led from the Hall to the Tower House. Linda was driving.

Chapter XIV

Linda in Love

Hebbelthwaite slept at Merlesfleet that night.

"A terrible affair," said the senior tutor, complacently, at dinner. "Quite out of the usual run. Almost an adventure. What an extraordinary amount of life, I sometimes think, is going on round us of which we know nothing!"

"That poor woman did seem so grateful," said Aunt Mary.

"Yes," said Linda, colourlessly. In the last few hours she had gone through a great deal. Hebbelthwaite was the man that she had hated. He had been impossible. He had been a devil. She had said these things herself And now was agony to her, that she dined downstairs with her guests instead of watching by his bedside.

She had no cause for anxiety, really. The doctor had told her so. It was merely a flesh-wound, and unless it became septic there was nothing to fear. There had been a considerable loss of blood, certainly. He quite agreed with Linda that it would be better for a day or two that Hebbelthwaite should not be moved. He always agreed whenever it was possible. His temper was naturally mild. Moreover, he was a general practitioner, with his living to get.

Linda had known it all at the very first moment, when Thomson had translated into measured and respectful utterances the breathless appeals of Briony. She had known it, but she had no time to think about it then. The car had to be rushed out. Bandages and brandy had to be got ready. Two men had to be found strong enough to be capable of lifting him without jerk or violence. Even when she had found him, and brought him back to Merlesfleet, there had been still much to do. It was over now. He was asleep. And she, with all the poetry of her life burning her veins, had to listen to the kindly, interminable prose of Uncle Willoughby and Aunt Mary.

"Yes," said Uncle Willoughby, "I am not deeply versed in the law. But it seems to me that this woman Jennis may possibly put herself very much in the wrong. It may be necessary to take action. We shall see. She appears to have been keeping a dangerous animal, and the famous case of 'Fletcher *v.* Rylands' has, I believe, laid it down clearly and definitely that she has done this at her own risk. Mr. Hebbelthwaite would, I should think, have a claim for damages against her. It seems to me, too, that some recognition of his extremely courageous conduct would not be out of place. Now I come to think of it, I have met the editor of—"

"Oh, please don't!" said Linda, fervently. He wouldn't like it."

"You venture to speak for him?" said the senior tutor. "I gather that you have seen much of him lately."

"No," said Linda. "But anybody who had seen him once would know that was not what he wanted."

Would it never end—this terrible dinner? Trotter was taking a glass of the port. Unusual, but, on a holiday, permissible.

"Shall we leave Uncle Willoughby to his cigarettes?" said Linda, rising.

"It is not absolutely essential," said Uncle Willoughby.

The butler placed the lamp, the cigars, and the cigarettes before him. He looked at the cigars as if he might have considered them seriously. "A cigarette to-night, I think," he said.

Linda established Aunt Mary in the drawing-room, and said, boldly, that she must see if that poor man upstairs had got everything he wanted. Aunt Mary suggested amiably that perhaps she might be able to help. "Please don't trouble," said Linda, "I shan't be a minute."

Upstairs she questioned servants rapidly. She seemed to them to be in rather a bad temper. They had done everything she had told them. They had thought of one or two things for themselves. Tabitha had made valuable suggestions. But because Linda had managed to find one thing of which they had not thought, they were criminally careless, and dangerously idiotic.

Hebbelthwaite slept through it all peacefully. He had been very happy when he fell asleep. He had seen at last the change in Linda's eyes for which he had so long been waiting.

They played dummy-whist downstairs, and Fate of its mercy gave Linda the dummy hand to play. Even so she was not entirely free from criticism. "I should imagine," said the senior tutor, as he shuffled the cards, "that you have been rather neglecting your whist lately. You seem to me to have forgotten the leads. You no longer make accurate deductions from the cards played. That revoke, too!"

"I expect Linda's tired," said Aunt Mary. "She's had so much to do to-day. There's been so much excitement."

"I'm not very tired," said Linda, bravely. "What Uncle Willoughby says is quite true. It is difficult to get any whist nowadays. It's always bridge, you know."

The senior tutor did not play bridge, nor did he approve of it. "Bridge," he said, "to my mind, is simply a manner of playing the fool with the more ancient and noble whist. The assignment of a different value to the different suits, and the possibility of playing without any trump suit at all, are innovations which must inevitably tend to convert a scientific pastime into an affair of chance. It is precisely the game which I should have expected to be introduced in this present day, with all its rest-lessness, its craving for excitement, its neglect of any solid basis in the form of study and scholarship." He shuffled the cards more and more rapidly as his warmth on this topic increased.

"Shall we be getting on now, dear?" said Aunt Mary.

"Quite so—quite so; merely an expression of my opinions. Your deal, I think."

The game came to an end at last. Aunt Mary went to bed at ten; Uncle Willoughby adulterated a small bottle of soda water with a reasonable suspicion, not enough to convict, of whisky. "I never do it at home," he said apologetically. Then he pecked at Linda's forehead, and also vanished.

Now she could breathe; now she could think.

She went out on the terrace. The moon had been down for some time, but the sky was bright with stars. The heavy scents of harvest-time lingered in the cool evening air. The distinctive cry of an otter screamed out in the stillness. Once she had wondered at the sound, so like the wail of a baby. But Judith had taught her much woodland and marshland lore.

She looked upward at the light which would burn all night in the window of the room where Laurence Hebblethwaite lay. She was filled with a new happiness. Her whole body tingled with the gladness of being. It was enough to be alive and alone with her thoughts on this quiet and beautiful night. She was almost amused when she recalled the silly, fierce way in which she had struggled, her obstinate resistance to his influence. How good it was to give that all up now! What peace could touch the peace of this absolute surrender! And it had come into her life for ever, though nothing was said between them—yes, even though she never saw him again. This was the night for which all her life had been but a dull preparation. This was the night that would be for ever fragrant in her memory.

A feeling of gratitude seemed to be awake throughout the whole of nature. The crops were ripe for harvest, the fruits were heavy on the trees. The young birds were strong on the wing. Completion and rest and thankfulness went hand in hand. Words drifted into her mind, and she spoke them half aloud:

"We praise Thee, O God, we acknowledge Thee to be the Lord. All the earth doth worship Thee, the Father everlasting."

* * * * *

Hebbelthwaite, with his arm in a sling, came down to luncheon the next day. He was quite cheerful, his eyes sparkled slightly over the senior tutor, and he was, perhaps, a little more slangy than usual and with intent. "I'm awfully sorry for being such a beastly nuisance," he said. "It's a bit too silly to be knocked out of time by a rotten old billy-goat."

"Surely," said the senior tutor, "the feeling of awe and the association with the beast are more characteristic of the accident itself than of its effects."

"Right," said Hebbelthwaite. "But I thought you'd know what I meant. I ought to apologise to you particularly, Miss Merle, for destroying your favourite hack."

Linda laughed, said nothing, and kept her eyes on him. She spoke, however, when they were alone in the garden together after lunch. "You are not going back to-night," she said.

"Really," he said, "I haven't got a shadow of an excuse for giving you any further bother."

"You must do what you're told," said Linda, gravely; "your arm is not at all right. I've sent for your servant. He'll bring over any clothes or things which you want. The doctor's left it to me to settle whether you dine downstairs to-night or not."

"And will you let me?" asked Laurence, playfully.

Linda nodded. "If you're good," she said.

"Why am I to do everything you tell me?" asked Laurence. "You don't do very much that I tell you, do you?" His eyes twinkled a little.

"Don't go on with that," she said, breathlessly. "I'm ashamed. I'm going to be quite good now." He caught both her hands impulsively. She bent her head down, and away from him.

"Thanks," he said, and released her hands.

Then they tried to talk about the flowers in the garden. It did not seem to matter much what they said so long as each heard the voice of the other. A turn of the path revealed the senior tutor in the college blazer and a straw hat, a copy of the "Times" on his knees. In one hand he held a "Pride of the Harem." It was still well alight. Indeed this brand has the special advantage that it will burn freely without assistance from the smoker.

"A bit of a sad affair at the War Office," said the senior tutor.

"At the present moment," said Laurence, "I don't think I care twopence about the War Office."

"A somewhat extraordinary position to take up, is it not? Might I ask your reason?"

"Well, you see," said Hebbelthwaite, "it's such glorious weather, isn't it?"

Linda laughed irreverently.

Chapter XV

Compensation

Mr. James Buddery had intimated through Mr. Thomson that he wished to have an interview with Miss Merle. Called upon to state his business, he said that it was a matter of compensation.

"I will attend to this for you," said the senior tutor, rising from his garden seat. It was just the kind of thing that he liked, and he didn't know Jimmy.

"Thanks so much," said Linda. "It would be awfully kind of you. Sure you won't have some more tea first?"

"No, I thank you," said Mr. Trotter. And, leaving the rest of the party on the terrace, he made his way to the little study at the back of the house that was generally used as an office for the transaction of business relating to the estate. There, by order, little Jimmy awaited him, casting about in his ingenious, if perverted, mind, for a means of obtaining something to which he was not entitled.

"Good afternoon," said Mr. Trotter, shortly, as he sat down at the desk. His pencil was poised over a sheet of foolscap. "Your name, I think, is—?"

Little Jimmy stood just inside the door, his conical-shaped hat held in both hands after the manner of an offertory bag.

He smiled broadly, almost pityingly. "I'm Jimmy Buddery, I be. Wha iverybardy know that about hare."

"Name, I said," repeated the tutor, acidly.

"Jimmy Buddery," roared Jimmy, under the impression that his interlocutor was deaf, "what hev the mindin' o' the Tower House level mill. I rackon yew fare a trifle hud o' harin', maaster," he added.

Mr. Trotter swivelled round on his chair. "A little less noisily, if you please. Now, with regard to the claim which you propose to make?"

"Well, tha'ss like this hare," began Jimmy, "I wuz a standin' agin my mill a little arter far o'clock yisterday arternune. I'd been a trimmin' the saails for the slant o' wind to the norard, an' wuz a lookin' backwards a watchin' them theer goots o' Judy Jennis—"

"Will you come to the point please? Firstly, in respect of what loss or damage is this claim made?"

"Well," said Jimmy, twiddling his hat in his hand, "tha'ss what I'm a comin' tew. Yew can't bind afoor yew ha' reeaped, an' tha'ss noo good a po'rin out tay afoor tha'ss drawed."

The senior tutor drew out his watch and placed it on the table. "I give you precisely three minutes more," he said; "if I have not arrived at some intelligible account from you at the end of that time I shall not prolong the interview. You will have to go, and any further prosecution of your claim will have to take the form of a letter to Mr. Frederick."

Jimmy twiddled his hat a little more rapidly. He had no clear comprehension of the meaning of the senior tutor's exordium, but he gathered dimly that there was hostility in the air. He invariably met this by an assumption of frank innocence.

"Wha, lor, maaster," said he, "us pore min can't dew wi' he. If I don't fare ta unnerstan' what 'tis yew waant right off yew must escewse me. Ye see, I bain't noo scholard. I niver had noo book l'arnin', but yew'll find me as honest an' open-spook a maan as theer be in these parts. 'Tain't much I ax for what I doned, an' for what I ha' lost t'rew wishin' ta gi'e a hand ta Maaster Hibbelthwaitery when I seed him knocked oover by that blarmed ole goot. Wha, gentry'd niver miss the little as I ax. Come, maaster, gie's five shillun, an' le'ss saay noo moor about it. I oony waant wha'ss fair owin' tew me. Noobardy'll iver say as Jimmy Buddery wuz hoggish-gutted—noobardy."

"At last we come to a definite fact," said the senior tutor, more complacently; "I admit, and regret, Buddery, the educational disadvantages under which you labour. I note then that your claim is for five shillings. Now what was the damage which you sustained?"

Jimmy had observed the inclination to relent which the statement of his lack of education had aroused in the senior tutor. He regretted that he had not put the figure higher. "Well, maaster," said he, deprecatingly, "I said as we'd call it five shillun. But I doubt I shall be the loser by that. I rackon I'd best leeave ta yew ta dew the prarper thing. That wuz like this hare: I runned sa quick along the river wall ta git ta wheer the gennelman lay strook silly by the goot, that fust I bust my waaistcoot, an' the buttons flewed inta the deeak. Then, when I came ta the plaace, Judy Jennis hadn't narthen ta fetch warter in to hull in his pore faace, soo I gi'e har my hat, an' that hode a quart or moor—ah! a right soort o' hat that wuz for fetchin' warter in! yew'd niver find a better. I rackon that hat wuz filled saven or eight time afoor the young laady druv down in har rood ingine, an' that bain't up to much for a pore man's best hat to be sooked t'rew an' t'rew like that wuz."

"Damage in respect of waistcoat and hat," said the senior tutor, as he wrote it down. "Now, can you tell me why you expect Miss Merle to be responsible for this damage—if any was indeed sustained? The service which you rendered was to Mr. Hebbelthwaite. The responsibility perhaps for the fact that the service was required would seem to me to rest with Judith Jennis. Supposing, as I take it to be the case, that 'Fletcher v. Rylands' applies here."

"I doan't knoo ayther o' them gennelmen," said Jimmy. "Wha's the good o' Maaster Fletcher applyin'? Tha'ss me what lent the hat. Theer worn't noo Fletcher, as I see."

"What I want to know," said the senior tutor, as if he were speaking to a very small child, "is why you ask Miss Merle for this money. She is not responsible. It is a very delicate question who is responsible."

Jimmy left off twiddling his hat, and scratched his head instead.

"Well, o' coorse," said he, "I doan't oony waant what I thote as the young laady 'ould ha' been pleeased ta gi'e me. Wha, look yew hare, maaster," he continued, with some confidence, "I mind as when I wuz a brooshin' for har faa'er in the larch plantin' an' one o' his freends put half-an-ounce o' number six shot inta the calf o' my leg that wuz Maaster Marle as gi'e me the five pound compensaation, an' when I heerd as Maaster Hibbelthwaitery had been brote hare an' wuz a staayin' at the Hall, wha naterallie I thote as I should ha'e ta ax the laady o' the house for what wuz ewe me. Tha'ss how ta come about."

" I see, I see," said the senior tutor. "Legally, of course, I admit no claim whatever; but I dare say Miss Merle would prefer to settle the matter rather than that an invalid, a guest in her house, should be disturbed. Let me see if I can assess the damage. To begin with, produce the waistcoat."

Jimmy was wearing this article of apparel beneath his blue smock at the very moment. But he knew better than to admit this fact.

"Wha theer now !" said he, in a tone of the most intense mortification, "if I hain't been an' tore that up ta maake a scarecrow on my 'lotment. I'd niver thote as that 'ould be noo good noo moor. If I'd thote as a gennelman like yew 'ould ha' waanted the blarmed ole thing I'd ha' saaved it for ye. Tha'ss truth I would—willin' an' welcome."

"And the hat?" said the tutor, resignedly. "The hat? That hat you have in your hands bears some appearance of a recent immersion. May I take it that that is the hat?"

"Wha, yew maay taake it if yew waant tew, maaster," said Jimmy, a little ruefully; "but if yew dew I rackon five shillun oan't enow."

"What I mean," said the tutor, "is simply this: Is that the hat in which the water was fetched?"

Jimmy shuffled with his feet. His hopes, which had but a moment ago soared high, now began to droop. It was the hat, and he dared not deny it. Any one in the village would have informed the senior tutor that he had never had more than that one hat for ten or fifteen years past.

"Well," he said, "tha'ss noo good my sayin' as ta bain't the hat. Dee yew look ar it. That doan't fare prarply dry now."

The senior tutor raised his gold-framed pince-nez. "Thank you," he said, "I can inspect it sufficiently well from this distance. I notice that it seems rather cleaner than the rest of your apparel. What now was the original cost of this hat?"

"Aah!" said Jimmy, "that I can't tall ye. That wuz giv ta me as a token o' bes' respecks when I feeshed out a Lunnon gennelman as wuz oovertarned out o' a dinghey agin my mill. I stood on the rond and hulled the teeth o' my deeak-drawin' raake oover him at the risk o' my life. He said he niver see a better bit o' pluck in his life, an' gi'e me the best hat he could buy in Narwich as what I maay call a kind o' meementoo. Twalve yare agoo, that wuz, an' that wuz better'n iver ta wuz afoor Judy Jennis sp'ilt it wi that blarmed warter. That wuz wuth a deeal moor 'an a crown ta me."

"I should put the damage to your waistcoat and hat," said Mr. Trotter, "at considerably less than fourpence. If, however, you care to take that sum, and to sign a receipt in full discharge, I am prepared to hand it over to you."

"What, farpence?" cried Jimmy. "An' what about my time? Hare I ha' been tew hour an' moor a mardlin' alonger yew, an' yisterdaay arternune that took me off my wark at the mill. Farpence! Now doan't yew be sa ree-dickerlous. Noo, noo; a crown's my mark, an' I'm shore as a gennelman like yew 'ouldn't goo ta orfer me a farden less."

"Very well, then," said Mr. Trotter. "I may point out to you that the time which you have sacrificed in this extremely childish manner is already paid for by Miss Merle. Unless you can attend to your duties better in fu-ture I shall feel it my duty to recommend her to obtain a more conscien-tious servant. You can go, Mr. Blithery."

"Whaat?" cried little Jimmy, pulling up his bent back till it was almost straight. "Yew worn't a jookin'? An' yew call me a sarvant! The Commis-sioners pay me my waage. Now, look yew hare, guv'nor. I don't rackon as yew meaan noo harm. I rackon tha'ss iggerance as maade ye taalk sich fule talk, if I may saay soo 'thout offence. Us mill chaps bain't sarvants. Doan't yew maake noo mistaake. Whew yew be I don't rightly knoo. But I doubt as the young laady fare mistook in ye. I'm a pore man, I be. But iverybardy knoo little Jimmy Buddery, an' doan't miscall him out of his baptised name, as yew fared ta dew this wery min't past. An' noobardy knoo yew! Now yew goo an' ax somebardy ta larn ye the prarper waay ta conduck yarself an' then theer worn't be narthen moor hud about it. I shall git my crown an' shan't maake any onpleasantness. Wha, yew little skinny-shanked chump, I ha' 'hulled better min in the deeak afoor now for huf whaat yew ha' said ta me. I—"

Mr. Trotter's sole reply was to ring the bell. "Kindly see," he said to Thomson, "that this man leaves the place at once, and that he is not ad-mitted here again."

Little Jimmy turned to go. "Tha'ss all right, maaster," he said. "Yew din't want ta ax Mr. Thomson to tarn me out. Whew yew be I don't un-nerstan'. But us mashmen an' mill chaps bain't used ta bein' mobbed like that. Yew maay be right. Yew maay be wrong; I doan't knoo narthen about ye. But I rackon the young laady'll be for fair plaay. 'Tain't in har blood ta treeat a Buddery onjust."

Mr. Trotter deigned no further answer. He returned to the party on the terrace, and found Hebbelthwaite on the point of starting for the Tower House. Linda had offered to go with him. He was less abrupt than usual in his reply. "I wonder," he said, "if you would meet me at the Witch's Pool on my way back. You see, I must pay Judith Jennis whatever she wants for her wretched old goat, and I expect she'll be angry with me. It might be unpleasant."

"You are not to stop a long time and argue with her and exhaust yourself," said Linda.

"I don't argue half enough, said Hebbelthwaite; "it's a fault of mine. I don't know how I get to half my conclusions."

He would have continued, perhaps, but Aunt Mary, who had gone into the house to fetch her work, now returned. Hebbelthwaite strolled off in the direction of Judith's house.

He rapped at the door of the Tower House, and Judith herself opened it.

"Sorry I killed your goat," said Hebbelthwaite, shortly. "One of us had to kill the other, you see. I don't want you to lose by it. If you tell me the value you put on him I will pay it you."

Judith looked him steadily in the eyes. "Is that what yew've come hare ta saay?" she asked, with no shadow of expression on her face.

"Of course. Don't be silly."

"Then yew can goo back agin," said Judith. "Whaat can yew onnerstand o' the wally o' Bel? Noo, noo; goo yew back from wheer ye come; I'll see myself righted, doan't yew be afeared o' that."

"I'm not," said Hebbelthwaite, drily. "There is just one other point: you've been interfering with Miss Merle."

"Did she tall ye soo?" asked Judith, keenly.

Hebbelthwaite took slight notice. "There must be no more presumption of that kind. Drop it, see? Otherwise the Tower House will find another tenant."

"When yew see me goo ta seek Miss Merle, yew can tall me not ta interfare. When yew're the lord o' the Marlesfleet Manor yew can bid me leeave the Tower House. Ax har if I've gone ta har, or she've come ta me. Tell har as yew be riddy ta plaay the maaster oover har owan lands. Tha'ss all I ha' gart ta saay. Now yew be a gooin'."

Hebbelthwaite slowly and deliberately filled and lit his brier pipe. "I'm not arguing with you," he said; "I'm giving you some remarkably good advice. You'd better take it. You have nothing whatever to do with Miss Merle; don't forget that. Good afternoon."

He swung round in the direction of the Witch's Pool. As he passed the stack of coarse marsh hay which stood by the stable he saw Job Sacret, shrinking against it, hiding himself as far as he was able from the window of the Tower House. There was a look on Job's face which Hebbelthwaite never remembered to have seen before. His mouth was writhing and twitching most horribly. But it was not this slobbering abomination which chiefly struck Hebbelthwaite's attention, but the glare in those eyes which had erst been dead of all but animal life. There was a passion of hatred in them—of hatred which seemed to be directed against the Tower House or mistress.

"I wonder what that means?" said Hebbelthwaite to himself. He knew that Judith had always been kind to the boy. He did not know of the new devotion which had sprung up in him far stronger than his devotion to Judith. He little guessed how the cunning of the idiot had been able to read the awful hostility of Judith to the mistress of Merlesfleet.

At the Witch's Pool Linda was waiting for him. "I knew you couldn't be here before now," she said "But I love this place. Uncle Willoughby and Aunt Mary are writing multitudinous letters against time to catch the evening post out. Tell me, how much did that woman want for her goat?"

"Nothing in money. She replied that she would take it out of me some other way."

"And you believe in witchcraft, don't you?" said Linda suddenly.

" I do. I do not believe that this woman's witchcraft can prevail against a higher Power, and I am in the hands of the higher Power. I don't presume to guide it or to say what it will do. I know that Judith will not let this end without a struggle. But the good will prevail."

Linda had seated herself by the water's edge. She dipped her hand in the pool, and watched the sparkle of the falling drops. "I wonder," she said, "if you would mind telling me a great deal more about yourself?"

"It doesn't make me very proud to talk of him," said Hebbelthwaite. "My father was a parson, and everything was arranged for me. I was to take Orders. I might have known then, if I had formed the habit of thinking clearly, that I could not do it—that, at any cost, I should have refused. Well, I was young, and I gave way."

"When you resigned your Orders," said Linda, "was it because you had lost your faith?"

"No," said Hebbelthwaite, simply: "it was because I'd found it. That's what bothered people. They wouldn't see it. They wouldn't understand my belief in the Power of Good was all the stronger because I was too humble to dogmatise about it or to accept men-made dogmas. They called it atheism or agnosticism. When I avowed my belief also in a personal Power of Evil they called it silly superstition. How was I to help it? No man with a mind can really live among the people in these parts and understand them and their surroundings without coming to that belief. Judith's case is not the only one. There *is* a Power of darkness, and there *are* people like Judith who are more closely in touch with it than others. I have nothing to say against a sober and scientific investigation of the facts that puzzle us. But when I see women take up this thought-reading as an afternoon's entertainment with table-turning, with palmistry, with Planchette, with any of these efforts to approach the unknown in a wrong and flippant spirit, then I get angry. I got angry with you. And I hope you'll forgive me one of these days. But I'm not angry without reason. Investigation of that kind never brings out one new fact. It never helps us; it never sets our feet on the rock. It is a bewildering hob-o'-lantern, but it absolutely wrecks the people who go in for it. Leave it alone, for God's sake. Live out your life and do the best you can with it. But don't try to make the world beyond a parlour game for your idle moments. The world beyond also has its revenges."

Linda began to plait very neatly three strands of grass. "I think I know what you mean," she said. "I'm going to do what you tell me now. I suppose it was a kind of curiosity with me. It got a good deal of hold on me. I'm rather afraid of it. I fear that it will get a stronger hold still. I wanted to play with the outside edge of the thing, and I'm in danger of the whirlpool. It's all my own fault. I hardly know why I went to Judith."

"Probably because she made you go to her. The conditions of telepathy are not perfectly understood yet. I have just been warning her, but she'll make a fight of it. She will try make her influence the stronger. She is a splendid creature in many ways. I like the people who make a fight of it. She's sincere, too, and I like sincerity. She believes that at one stroke she may avenge an ancestral wrong. I'll show you all about it in my portfolio whenever you like. And she has a deeper and more selfish motive."

"What is that?" Linda asked.

"The words to describe it hardly belong to this century. The woman undoubtedly believes that she has supernatural powers, and that she has bought them at the price of her own soul. She also believes that she may find a substitute. Remember that she is a child of generations and generations who have held such faith. It has been taught to her as that unintelligible catechism is taught to young children."

"I understand," said Linda, playing with the plaited grasses, her eyes bent down on them.

"Why have you changed, Linda?" said Laurence. "You mistrusted me. I think you hated me. I really didn't want to make a show, I didn't want to assert myself. It began with no more than common humanity. I had studied your family history, and I knew Judith through and through as a dangerous woman. I am pretty tactless, and I have lived out of the world a lot here studying the things that interest me. Well, I made a mess of it; that's easy enough to understand—I can't be ass enough to miss that. But now it's all different, though I haven't done a single, solitary thing to make it different. You let me talk about my ideas. You've been most awfully kind to me. You—"

He stopped short. Linda's eyes were still fixed on the grasses in her shaking hand. There was a long pause before he continued.

"I'm going to say it," he said. "I have always loved you from the first time I saw you; I shall always love you. But as you said, you dearest woman, I will be good. With all my vanity, I can't find any reason why this should mean to you what it does to me. That any woman can love any man is a miracle, anyhow. I don't know how to talk about this kind of thing in the right way. I don't put it well—I don't make you see how it is within me. Oh, speak, Linda!"

She raised her eyes until they were full upon him. "If there were only any words," she stammered—and broke off. She swayed towards him.

Chapter XVI

Linda's Secret

Mr. James Buddery had borne his defeat with philosophy. He had tried many such things, and sometimes they came off and sometimes they did not. An intelligent man, with the care of a mill, should not lose a chance. What hurt him more than anything was that he had been "bested by a furriner." He was far too wily to expose himself to chaff by talking of his discomfiture. At the Tench and Teal he preferred to make himself of importance by a vivid narration of the combat between Hebbelthwaite and Bel.

Bob Middleton began to "put the grin on to him," by asking why he had not gone to "the gennelman's" assistance. But the majority of those present thought that this was in somewhat doubtful taste. Hebbelthwaite, though well known to them, and possessed of their respect, and even admiration, by reason of his sporting feats and his superb strength, was not of their blood, as was Jimmy. They could see no reason why the little man was in any way bound to jeopardise his life, perhaps more than his life, by rushing on an encounter of so terrible a nature. They listened to the story of the fight, and pledged the victor heartily. But they thought that Jimmy had done well not to irritate the powers of darkness by any interference with Bel.

"Tha'ss all very well for yew ta mob," said Sir William. "I rackon yew 'ouldn't ha' doned noo moor 'an little Jimmy. All on us ha' l'arnt as that fare tew risky ta goo agin Judy Jennis an' ote belongin' tew har. An' if Maaster Hebbelthwaitery coun't maaster th' ole goot whativer could little Jimmy ha' doned wi' his little titty boons?"

So Bob, being in a minority, ceased his jibes, and paid for a pint of "old" for little Jimmy, by way (as Jimmy might have said) of "compensation."

The next morning, on his way down to his mill, Jimmy suddenly encountered Miss Merle. She was wearing an expression of far more sternness than she actually felt.

"Good-morning, Jimmy," she said; "I've got to talk to you."

"Good-mornin', Miss," said Jimmy. "That allust fare a treeat ta me ta talk along o' one o' the rale old gentry. Lor, Miss, if I maay saay soo 'thout offence, yew look as pratty as a gay this mornin'."

"Never mind about that, Jimmy," said Linda, severely; "I'm very angry with you."

"Tha'ss bad h'arin'," said little Jimmy, taking off his hat and scratching his head. "Wha'ss wrong?"

"You came up to the house the other afternoon about some compensation, and you were very rude indeed to Mr. Trotter. He was my guardian, and he is my uncle—at least I've always called him my uncle. He consented to see you in order to save me trouble. When you are being rude to him you are really being rude to me."

Jimmy shuffled his feet and looked at the girl, whom he respected as only peasants respect the good old country blood.

"Well, Miss," said he, "that wuz like this hare. I niver see the gennelman afoor, an' he din't fare ta seem ta me like one o' yar fam'ly. An' he miscalled me soo that I might ha' forgot myself. I din't knoo as yew'd gi'en him leave ta miscall me like he did. I 'ouldn't niver ha' believed as yar faa'er's daughter 'ould ha' se pore little Jimmy Buddery miscalled. But I ax yar pardon, Miss, humble. Ye see, he's a furriner about hare, an' he doan't look up tew a sight. But theer, I rackon I oughtn't to ha' said that. I bain't noo judge o' gennelmen. I can put a weight tew a fat peeg as well as any maan. But I bain't noo judge o' a gennelman."

"There you are, Jimmy, you see," said Linda, "as you know nothing about a gentleman, you should be more careful how you talk to them. Mr. Trotter has done a good many things for me, and has been very kind to me. In future, you must never talk in that way to any one who is staying at the Hall. Mr. Trotter has been talking about writing to the Drainage Commissioners about you. He says he has noticed several little things which he thinks they ought to know. I'm going to tell him that you're very sorry, and that it will never happen again, and I don't think he'll write that letter. By the way what was it that you did want when you saw him?"

Jimmy stood silent for some moments. It was a bitter pill for him. He had no fear of any letter to the Drainage Commissioners. That worthy body would have resented as keenly as himself any interference by a "furriner" with any of their employees. But he loved the Merle blood, and would have died to save Linda any discomfort. Moreover, he longed to win back the place in her regard which he believed he had held before this unfortunate occurrence. He cast about in his wily mind for an answer to turn away wrath.

"If I'd know'd as he was a freend o' yarn, Miss," said he, "I'd niver ha' said a wud agin him. I thote he wuz a kind o' sarvant—I ax yar pardon, Miss, I meean ta saay as I din't knoo whew he wuz, an' I thote he wuz ta-akin' a sight moor upon hisseif than yew knowed on. I only axed for what wuz ewe me. If ta hadn't been for me, I rackon Maaster Hebbelthwaitery 'ould ha' been in a bad waay. I did what I could for him, an' I sp'ilt a hat as I plaaced gre't wally on. But theer, Miss, that doan't sigerfy. I'd sp'ile moor 'an a hat ta dew yew sarvice, or Maaster Hebbelthwaitery ayther."

"Why? Do you like him?" asked Linda.

"He's the finest gennelman as iver I did see," said Jimmy, feeling, instinctively, that he had struck the right chord. "He pulled a colt out o' the deeak what far strong min coun't mewve, an' he fote that blarmed ole goot as braave as a lion. Aah! Tha'ss a pity as theer bain't moor o' his soort about these parts. They doan't breed 'em like him in this hare new-fangled time."

"Now, Jimmy," said Linda, "what was it that you really wanted?"

"Whaat I axed foor, Miss, wuz a crown. But that doan't sigerfy. Not a mite. I'll saave up ta buy another hat. Doan't yew taake on, Miss. Little Jimmy'd dew it agin for narthen, any time. But that theer Maaster Trotter hadn't ote tew ha' miscalled me."

"But what did he call you?" asked Linda.

"He called me 'Blithery,' Miss," said Jimmy. And at the recollection his heart grew hot. He would have even surrendered the hopes of a crown which had again begun to spring up for the chance of retaliation on the senior tutor.

"There you are," said Linda; "he didn't know you, and he forgot your name."

"Wha, iverybardy knoo me, Miss," said Jimmy, in perfect bona fides.

"Yes, yes; everybody about here knows you. But this is a very learned gentleman, who doesn't live here; he is senior tutor of a college at Cambridge. I'm sure he never intended to offend you."

"Aah!" said Jimmy, suddenly enlightened, "I thote he wuz some'at o' that soort. A kind o' schule-maaster ta them booys up at college. Lor', Miss, if I knowed that, I'd niver ha' paid noo regard. Whaat dew that sigerfy whaat them teeachers saay? Theer, Miss, I axes his pardon free; he din't knoo noo better."

Linda fumbled in her purse. "That's all right, Jimmy. And you won't be rude to any guests of mine again, will you?"

"Niver, Miss," said Jimmy; "I niver knowed he was a guest o' yarn. I fare right wexed I should ha' doned it."

"Here's the five shillings," said Linda, "because it was quite right of you to come to help Mr. Hebbelthwaite." She paused a moment. "If you meet Mr. Trotter again, you must tell him that you're sorry, and—and— you needn't tell him, Jimmy, that I gave you this money."

Jimmy's face lit up with delight. He spat on the coins for luck before depositing them in his pocket. "Yew're a gennelman," he began. "Theer, whaat a silly ole fule I be; I meean as yew be a rale Marle, Miss. I thank ye hearty. As for Maaster Trotter, Lor', I'll ax his pardon if I see him. I doan't paay noo regard ta whaat a schule-maaster saay. That'll maake him happy an' that oan't hu't me. An' I oan't saay a wud about the brass. Not a wud. Yew doan't waant ta be afeared o' me. Thanky, Miss, thanky."

Linda went a little further along the road. At the church gate she saw Laurence coming towards her. The appearance of an accidental meeting was well maintained. What Laurence said was: "I was before the time, and I guessed you would come this way so I came on to meet you."

They took the bridle path which led up to the common. His eyes never left her. Now and again they met her look coming shyly up from under the long lashes. There was no word of love-making. None was needed in this moment. The happiness of each was transparent.

The common stretched down from the high-road to where the marsh-land spread its misty, shifting tones of brown and green along the valleys of the Yare and Waveney. The purple ling glowed in bunches, which distance made cushions of velvety softness. Patches of bracken afforded relief to the eye, the glow of ever-flowering gorse and the lingering yellow of broom lit up the more sombre spread of heather and bracken. Away on the rivers the great slate-coloured sails of Norfolk trading wherries bellied out before a pleasant breeze, or stretched hard and tight in a reach which brought the craft close-hauled to the wind. They seemed as though they were actually cruising on the marshes themselves, save where here and there the bends of the reaches or a break in the river-wall permitted the sheen of the flowing water to glisten in the sunlight. About the rands little ant-like shapes swayed to and fro. These were marshmen mowing the reeds.

Linda sat down on a hillock of mossy turf that rose among the ling. She drew in a deep breath of the scented air. "It is good for us to be here," she said, simply.

"Will they be away long?" he asked, as he took his place at her feet.

"I do not expect them back till after lunch. It's nearly all the property of St. Cecilia's about there, you know, and although, of course, he's not bursar now, he likes to see how things are going."

"And why," said Laurence, "did not the lady of the house accompany her guests?"

"She had letters to write," said Linda, demurely. "She had to reprove James Buddery for impertinence. I've done it, too," she added.

"How much did you give him?"

"Five shillings, and you're not to say anything at all about it."

They both laughed. Linda's eyes followed the sails of a cutter yacht heading up the Yare towards Cantley. She seemed lost in reverie.

"Now tell me all about it," said Laurence.

She told him in slow, measured sentences of her early days, her childish belief in a Power of Evil which must be propitiated; of the hideous face her hands had drawn by chance on the blotting paper; of the impulse when she first heard of Judith which led her to change her plans and to come to Merlesfleet at once. She referred again to her first visit to Judith. Then she spoke of the cup which her guardian had given her on her twenty-first birthday. Hebbelthwaite made her describe it minutely. He seemed interested in it.

"But," she said, "you haven't heard the strangest thing about it. I went a second time to Judith. Perhaps it was just because I was trying to resist your influence. I did try tremendously for a long time, you know. Judith has a cup exactly like that my uncle gave me—the very sister of it. She uses it for divination. There was liquid of some kind in it, and she made me look into it. At first it was like bright silver; then clouds came over it, and then I saw a picture in it very distinctly."

"What did you see?" asked Hebbelthwaite.

"I can't tell you what it was. It was something that does not concern us, and that I'd rather not speak about. But it told me a thing which had really taken place, though until I looked in the cup I had known nothing about it."

"Yes," said Hebbelthwaite. "But did Judith know?"

Linda thought for a moment. "I can't say for certain. Now I come to think about it, she might very easily have known."

"I thought so," said Hebbelthwaite. "Have you tried the experiment since, when you were alone?"

"Often and often." She smiled sadly. "I believe I did that, too, partly because I knew it would have made you angry if you had known it. That sounds childish, doesn't it?"

"No," he said, "I shouldn't call it that. And when you tried it alone, what did you see in the cup?"

"Nothing—nothing whatever. I tried with Judith's cup, and with my own too; but it was never any good. Now tell me, how do you explain all this?"

"I don't," he said, simply. "A few coincidences, a little telepathy, a little hypnotism, will make an explanation of a kind; but of what are we to say that these coincidences and this extraordinary power which Judith has over you are a manifestation? Well, I've told you already that I believe in a personal Power of Evil, and it never worries me greatly to leave some things unexplained. I have no scientific wish to fool myself into the belief that life has no more mysteries for me. All that you have told me is very strange, and I shall have to think about it. I'm frightfully slow at seeing things sometimes. Now tell me about the future. Is that all over?"

"Ye–e–es," said Linda, doubtfully.

"And why isn't it?" said Hebbelthwaite with a smile. "Don't be frightened, dear. Tell me all about it. Perhaps I can put a stop to it."

"Laurence," she said, "it's like this. Ever since I looked into that cup of Judith's I have felt the bond between us grow stronger. It is almost as if it were something sacramental."

Hebbelthwaite shot one sharp glance at her.

"Go on," he said.

"She said that she would give me a sign. Bel, the black goat—thank God, you killed him—came up to the door. He stood still while I mounted on his back. With no guidance from me he carried me to Merlesfleet, going as carefully and steadily as possible. Then, when I slipped off his back he turned and raced like mad back homewards again."

"Very curious," said Hebbelthwaite; "animals can be trained to do strange things. But the cruelty of their training sometimes poisons their tempers. What next? "

"She said there was a third sign; it was to come in the form of a dream. I think it was to be a kind of final test. It has not yet come. But it will all the more because I have never been near her since."

"And when it comes?" asked Hebbelthwaite.

"I don't know," said Linda; " I'm frightened. Perhaps it will drive me mad. Perhaps it will make me come back to her when I awake whether I will or no. And when I go back something else will be done, something horrible, something which will bind me for ever to—"

"Yes," Said Laurence, "to the Power of Evil. You are not to be frightened any more. The dream may come, but whatever its results may be, it shall not take you back to Judith again, I promise you that. In the end the Power of Good will prevail."

"Does it always prevail?" asked Linda.

"There are many worlds. We do not know whence we come, or whither we go. This life here is often perhaps only the middle of the story that had its beginning, and will have its end, elsewhere. Not always here and now, but somewhere, and in the end I do believe that Good prevails. Here I think the end will come soon, and that it will be good—mixed with evil, perhaps, but with the good prevailing. I do not often have presentiments; I haven't got the right kind of temperament for them. Perhaps what I feel now is more deduction than presentiment. It is not blind chance that has settled these things that have happened to you; nor is it blind chance that has brought me into your life, to my own great happiness. Linda, the end will be good."

"Say again that you promise me when that third sign comes it shall not bring me back to Judith."

"I promise you that, on my word of honour. However strong the impulse may be, you shall not go back."

"Sometimes," said Linda, "I've had a mad impulse to tell my uncle all about this. I see him telegraphing to a specialist to inquire into my health. I see him preparing a careful and accurate report of the whole case in which I shall figure as 'L. M., age twenty-one, of dependent means.' I see the strong line which he would take with regard to the tenancy of the Tower House. If I had never met you think I should have told him. I held back chiefly because it would have distressed Aunt Mary. He would have poured a stream of cold prose on to the fires, wouldn't he? Also, for a man of his kind to be mixed up with a thing of this sort would have made me laugh."

"You might have done worse," said Hebbelthwaite; "laughter is a fairly healthy thing. I can conceive the possibility, though, that the laugh would have been on Judith's side, and at the expense of your uncle. She is an extraordinary woman."

They rose from their place, and strolled slowly back to the bridle path again.

"Have you told him yet that I'm going to marry you?" asked Laurence.

"No," said Linda; "I think I am a very surreptitious woman. I don't want to tell him at all."

"You needn't," said Hebbelthwaite; "I'll do that."

"It would come to the same thing," said Linda, "so far as the look in their eyes when they next saw me was concerned. You know that kind of look? Curious, congratulatory, and surprised. For a few days longer we will keep it all secret to ourselves. I must see you every day. I live on your strength, you know. I have so much more to tell you, too, so much more to hear."

"How long I've waited for you, Linda! It seems strange that there was a time when you and I had never met. What can have been the use of it?"

"I know when my life began," said Linda; "it was when I drove the car down the moss-grown track towards you, not knowing whether I should find you dead or alive. All that went before was colourless."

They passed out on to the white high road. From the distance came the voices of rustic singing together:

> "Oh, the cows be a-gooin' down ta mash,
> An' the cream stand thick once moor,
>   An' the apple-buds are fillin',
>   An' the gals are gittin' willin',
> They're a-courtin' up the willage by the scoor."

Linda pretended that she had not heard any of it.

Chapter XVII

The Third Sign

Mr. Calcote had been tried in the balances and found wanting. The project of asking him to dine and to complete the whist-table afterwards had always been a little dangerous, for the senior tutor looked with no kindly eye on crammers. But Linda was sorry for the man. She did not hold him in any way responsible for Percy Belton's lapse. She had plenty of evidence, both from Belton and others, that the little man did his best with the very unpromising material committed to his charge. Lady Blickling had certainly been too hard on him. It was all very well to blame him for taking pupils. But the church did not give him enough to live upon without them.

It was not a success. The dinner passed off well enough. Calcote was a little in awe of the senior tutor when he met him in public. He had scathing things to say about senior tutors in the retirement of his own study. He made a good audience. He led Mr. Trotter gently on to the subject of compulsory Greek, and Mr. Trotter crowed and flapped around that subject for quite a long time.

It was at the card-table that his downfall came. Mr. Trotter became icily polite. His shoulders and eyebrows spoke for him. He was being shocked and pained. If the man had only proclaimed himself a novice, and apologised, it might have been tolerable. It was the attempt at a defence which led Mr. Trotter to observe that the game had apparently suffered considerable changes during the last month or two, and to express, a little ironically, his regret that he was not more up to date. It was additionally sad that the cards simply refused to allow Mr. Calcote to lose, and that during the whole of the evening Mr. Trotter never won a rubber.

"Very kind of you to have asked him," said Mr. Trotter, when Calcote had gone. "Of course, the dummy game is not the same thing. Played intelligently, very useful practice. But that is all that one can say for it. He's a pleasant little man, too. Naturally, his ideas about education and mine are somewhat at variance, but I have no doubt that in his own groove he does as well as he can. The only thing I regret is that he should ever play whist. No, no, no; I don't mind in the least. One must meet with players of every kind. But when a man makes almost every mistake known to science, and excuses himself on the ground that he is used to the American leads, and when it appears that he is totally unacquainted with these, or with anything else connected with the game, and that he is unwilling to learn, then one draws the line. That man must not play whist. He should try bridge, or snap, or something of that kind."

"You see, dear," said Aunt Mary, "it is rather difficult to find a man who plays whist nowadays, and there are so few people in a little place like this. I wonder, now, if Linda and I could think of some one better?"

"There's Mr. Hebbelthwaite," said Linda, quite coolly.

"Who?" said the tutor.

"Mr. Hebbelthwaite," said Linda. "Didn't you hear? It might be worth while to see if he plays."

"But I have played with him," said the tutor, eagerly. "As a young man, I remember his playing with me, and I remember that he was unusually sound. No brilliance—that I do not ask. He knew what he was doing. If he did make a mistake, he could be made to see it."

"Then he shall dine here and play whist afterwards every night of your stay," said Linda.

"Ah," said the tutor. "Now, my dear child, you are really spoiling me."

"Not at all," said Linda; "Aunt Mary and I will go round to see him to-morrow."

So it came to pass that on the next night Laurence dined at Merlesfleet. He was afraid, he said, that his whist was terribly rusty. But he had learned the game properly, and at one time he had played a good deal. Mr. Trotter expressed himself as being completely satisfied. That there was any under-standing of any kind between him and Linda Mr. Trotter never suspected for one moment. He had shrewd eyes for the things which he could see, but affairs of the heart did not come within that category.

Of course, Aunt Mary saw perfectly, because she happened to be a woman. But she was a wise and kind woman, and said nothing. She was, indeed, glad to see it. It mattered less then that the tutor's prosaic attempts to get his ward safely married had ended in failure. She had chosen for herself. Aunt Mary recognised that this was the only way in which a woman of Linda's spirit would make her choice.

After this, Aunt Mary became very tactful indeed. She played the part of the vanishing lady to such perfection that Linda occasionally had suspicions.

So for three days more the secret that was no secret went on, and Judith Jennis was almost forgotten.

On the night of the fourth day after Laurence had gone, good-nights were said, and Linda went up to her room. When her maid had left her,

Linda drew back the curtains from one of the windows that looked out on the terrace, opened it wide, and leaned out. She wore a kimono of barbaric colours. Her heavy hair hung down, fastened by a ribbon. The night was very still. The languorous heat of the day had hardly yet yielded to the cool touch of night. In the full moon she could see shimmering mist breast-high on the strip marsh that fringed the Fleet. Here and there the tops of the willows and alders on the further side sprang from it as from an island in some quiet and unknown sea. How good was to be alive on so beautiful a night! How good it was to be loved! How peaceful it was to have sur-rendered everything!

It was late before she got into bed, and switched off the last of the lights in the lamp on the table by her side. Sleep came to her very sud-denly, and very deeply.

And with the sleep came the third sign—the dream.

It seemed to her that she had awakened again in the dark room. One line of moonlight crossed it obliquely from the window, sparkling on the silver things on the toilet-table, throwing a distorted shadow of the case-ment on the far wall.

Boom—boom—boom! A great bell was tolling. It made so much noise that she could hardly make out what all the fluttering and scratching was in the dark corner of the room. Had some bird flown in? A bat, perhaps? She listened intently, straining her ears. Boom—boom—boom! the bell went on.

No, it was not a bird. It was something much bigger than that. She could hear it striking on the ground with its feet very rapidly, making soft thuds on the thick carpet. The bell stopped suddenly. As the last harmo-nies died away there came from the corner of the room a faint chuckle. At first she said that could not be an animal, and then she knew that it could not be human.

The thing came lolloping across the floor to her in a kind of grotesque dance. She could see nothing, but she could hear a pat-pat on the carpet; she could hear the breathing grow harder with the exertion. It seemed that she was fumbling for the electric-light, and could not find it. As she did so a wet, rough tongue licked her forearm. She screamed as the dream ended.

Yes, she must be awake now. The light by her bedside was switched on again. She supposed that she had done it in her sleep. Why was her mind so hazy? What was that awful sense of physical contamination that weighed her down? She must be going at once. She slipped out of bed in-stantly, and began to put on her white satin shoes. They were the first that came to her hand. She did not wait to dress. She would be sure to meet no one, and it was not cold. A thick dressing. gown—yes, that would be enough. She must go very, very softly, so as not to wake anybody in the house. Her hand shook as she lit the candle. Bearing it in her hand, she sped rapidly along the passage and down the broad flight of stairs. The front doors had too many locks and bolts. There were the French windows in the little drawing-room. That would be better. It would not matter if she left them unfastened behind her. They were all honest people about that part—all very honest people. The phrase kept echoing and echoing in her mind. All very honest people, she whispered again to herself.

She must be quick. There was no time to lose. There was that silk scarf which she had left at the Tower House. Judith was doing something with it. It was terrible. She must go at once and stop her. She would have to explain it to Laurence afterwards. It was really necessary that she should get that silk scarf—quite necessary. Again her brain played her a trick of repeating the phrase. "Quite necessary, quite necessary," said her little feet as they pattered along. She was on the track now which led to the Tower House.

Out from the wood came a masculine voice, good-tempered, encouraging, above all things natural. That was half the comfort of it. "Don't be frightened, Linda. I thought I might meet you."

A moment later Laurence stood with his arms about her. She pressed her head close to his shoulder, and lay there, saying nothing.

"Don't bother," he said, gently; "it's going to be all right. Never mind about any explanation."

She turned her head a little and looked up at him. "I think I was still half asleep," she said. "The dream came, and then I seemed to be awake. But I was not really awake. I had to go to Judith. It was about a scarf. She was doing something with it."

"Do you want to go to her now?" asked Hebbelthwaite.

"No, I want to stop just like this for a little while; then I shall be all right again."

For almost a minute they stood in silence. Then his quick ear caught the sound of sobbing. He began to stroke her hair. He had never seen it down before. "Don't cry, Linda, dear," he said. "There's nothing to cry about. What you do when you're half asleep doesn't matter."

"But that's not why I'm crying," she said. "It's you, you, you! Every night since I told you, you must have been out here waiting for me."

"Yes," he said, "every night. It's pleasant to be out on these hot nights.

You can't mind about that. I promised you, you know. Why," he said, with
a forced cheerfulness, "even if it had been winter I would have done t
gladly to hold you like this, you dearest woman."

Linda pressed closer to him. The chill wind of dawn rustled the trees.
She shivered slightly. He took off his big coat, and put it on her.

"Aren't you cold, too?" she said.

"No, not at all." He looked at her intently. The coat was buttoned
across her breast; her arms were not in the sleeves. They hung limp and
dead. Even so she could not look grotesque; her face was a very star of
beauty.

"I have never kissed you," he said.

"Do it," she whispered, and closed her eyes. "Kiss me now."

He drew her closer to him, and looked long at her. Then he bent over
her and kissed her on the mouth.

"Will you take me back now?" she said. "The burden has gone from
my mind. Judith has no more power over me, because, you see, you've
kissed me. Asleep and awake, I belong to you always now."

At the open French windows she paused. "If you feel the least little bit
nervous," he said, "you must ring for somebody. I won't have you frightened like this again."

She almost laughed. "I shall never be frightened again," she said. "How
could any one be frightened whom you love so much as that? I have
drunk of your strength." She pressed his hand between her two, and was
gone.

Chapter XVIII

The Wisdom of the Idiot

On the evening of the night which brought the third sign to Linda, Judith
Jennis stabled her goats early. Reserved and taciturn as she always was, as
the day faded to the "between-the-lights" of marshland her expression became even more sombre, her lips appeared even more grimly set than was
usual with her. As soon as the last glow of sunset had died away over the
rise of Reedham village her eyes turned again and again to the thick obscurity which was spreading over the reeking rands and fen land, and which
the rise of the full moon would change to a sheet of diaphanous gossamer.

Job Sacret watched her closely. His instinct told him that the woman
who had saved him from the workhouse was plotting against the other

woman whom his animal devotion worshipped as some unintelligible divinity. The idiot lad was more human in the irrationality of his blind worship than in anything else. Linda had never noticed him, beyond evincing a pitiful disgust at his uncouthness, a disgust which Job could read well enough. She meant to be kind to the poor boy, but the delicacy of her refinement was revolted by a human instance in so beast-like a form, and she could not cloak the horror of her eyes when they fell upon him.

Judith, on the other hand, had never shown repulsion. Her kindness had been hard and matter-of-fact. She had fed and lodged the lad as she fed and lodged her nanny-goats or her pigs, looking at him in much the same way, neither horrified nor attracted by him. For every reason Job should have adored Judith and disliked Linda. He did not trouble to diagnose his feelings. All he knew was that he worshipped the dainty lady from the Hall, and gave her humble thanks for merely existing. To think of her filled him with an ecstasy even surpassing that which gin afforded him.

And now he felt certain that Judith, the woman to whom he was bound by every law of gratitude, but whom he regarded no more than he would have regarded a dyke leech when weighed in the balance with Linda, was scheming, plotting some fell attempt on his bright deity. Though he was a congenital deaf-mute, he was able to follow the movements of lips speaking, and to associate them with the object with which they were concerned. On Linda's visits to the Tower House he had seen Judith's lips shape "sister" over and over again. And this evening he knew that they were again shaping the dissyllable, and that there was triumphant threat in every movement of them.

Ever since he had first distrusted Judith's intentions towards Linda, Job had watched his mistress from the cover of his litter of straw. To-night he crept into his bed as soon as he had eaten the scraps of food which Judith tossed to him when the milking was done, the; goats stabled, and the last set curds pressed into the cheese shapes.

Judith's eyes were very bright. There was a hard ribaldry in them which the boy had never seen before, and which frightened him more than any show of fierceness. They spoke of some inhuman malice about to be gratified. A glutton of souls, awaiting his next repast which he could hear being prepared for his maw, and licking his lips in greedy anticipation of his meal, might have looked like that.

Judith herself fasted, save a drink of some liquid which she took from the cupboard in the downstairs room.

As the night drew on Job saw her go again to where the open door let the bead of light from her solitary candle stream feebly out into the marsh, now growing beautiful in the moonlight. Again and again Judith stood in her porch and peered out down across the levels. Once Job thought he saw a dancing flame pass the thick window-glass. But he knew it was nothing but a hob-o'-lantern, and he was too familiar with the burning gases of the ooze to fear them.

A little after half-past ten Judith gave a sudden cry of exultation. The boy was peering through the strands of straw which covered his head. He was cautious not to open his eyes wide. He knew that the reflection of the candle on his eyeballs would betray his wakefulness to Judith, and that she would then take good care to keep him from her purpose.

Of the terror that was approaching Job's infirmity made him all unconscious.

In the silence of the night without came a faint pulsation. Had one of the goats got out of the stable? How it was galloping! But this was not going from near to far, but approaching at incredible speed from the distant marsh to the Tower House paddock.

The hoofs came nearer and nearer, and now thundered past, though Job heard them not. But he felt the vibration, and he shuddered though he knew not why.

It must be something bigger than a goat. Had the red bull again leapt the dykes? But the bull was always taken up to the land at night. What was that thing which Judith waved? Job recognised it. It was a silk scarf which Linda had left twisted round Bel's horns that last night when she rode him home. What was Judith doing with it?

Fainter and fainter the galloping feet swept over the paddock. They grew sharper, if more faint, when the paddock was crossed. They were on the track through the woods to Merlesfleet.

Why, thought Job, did Judith say again and again that word which he associated with Linda? The word was "sister," though he did not know it, and Judith had said:

> "'The maid and the witch dance hand in hand
> When the Black Man comes from the mash to land.
> Sister is she, and sister am I,
> And one must live, an' t'other must die—
> The ch'ice is the Maaster's. She or I?'

"And now it will be she!—she!"

Job watched the sibilants of her lips. There was a lot about Linda in what she was saying. Why could he not understand all? Why could Judith and other folk whom he knew convey their meaning to each other by moving their lips? They seemed to understand clearly and at once. Why could not he? Ah! If he, poor Job Sacret, might only do something for that dear vision which had taught him that beauty might be gentle instead of strong, that there was another radiance besides the gloomy splendour of his mistress—for, in spite of their likeness, there was that vast disparity between Judith and Linda which is only seen in two people who are in some ways similar.

Judith still stood at the door, letting the moonlight stream on her face, which was lifted towards it. She held her hands above her head, and her whole pose was one of infinite gratitude.

"At last o' time," she cried. "Granny! granny!—for yew, for me the curse ha' passed. If all goo well t'rewout the night the Maaster's ch'ice ull fall on a daintier mossel 'an ayther on us uns, an' yew an' me'll be free to room wheer we list. At last o' time the wrong shall paaid foor, an' the blood which took life but spilt noo blood shall be p'isoned by the kiss o' the Black Maan o' the mash. Ooh, ye sarvants of the night, dee yew waatch an' see the night pass as ta should! T'ree lives hev sarved the Maaster; is't not time for the ind? Is not the price paaid yit?"

Job had no notion of the meaning of her words. But he shivered. His animal instinct told him that there was some foul thing near, some horror which his sight was too human to see. Perchance it may have been one of those denizens of the Unseen which strike death to the terrified eyes of dogs in chambers where no man has ever seen aught of which to be afraid. Job's animal instinct served to warn him of some such presence, or to make him think that some awful thing was near, but either his human incapacity blinded his sight to what was there or cleansed his eyes from mere morbid imagination. He could see nothing but Judith. But oh! he could feel, and terror clutched him by the heart.

But, had he known the sentence, he might have said, "Perfect love casteth out fear," and surely his love for Linda was perfect, so purged was it of all grossness, so humble and devout a worship. He gathered his love about his heart, and warmed himself with it. His terror left him. Were it man, woman, or devil that threatened Linda, he would hazard his life to save her.

Judith came within the room and closed the door. There was a sprightly happiness about her which seemed to the lad almost painfully incongruous with his fears. But the strangeness of this mood kept him the more keenly on the alert.

Judith, still bearing the silk scarf in her hand, passed up the stairway to the upper chamber which Job had never hitherto been able to enter. In the ecstasy of what she believed to be her approaching victory, her final revenge for the wrongs of her ancestors and of all her race, her release from the bonds which she fully believed held her thrall to the "Black Maan o' the mash," she forgot that her cupboard was unlocked; she forgot to lock the door of her upper chamber on the stairway, and, when she thrust open the trap-door on to the leads she forgot to fasten it behind her.

Job saw her disappear up the stairway. She had taken Linda's scarf with her. She had murmured "Sister" derisively as she mounted the steps. Job knew better than he had ever known anything in his life that she was about to bring some terrible disaster on the woman he adored. His cunning did not leave him. As he had always hidden his thoughts and suspicions from his mistress, so he now concealed his resentment under a presence of deep slumber. Judith had paused but a moment to look at him as she passed him on her way to the stairs. He lay motionless, breathing heavily. He had never given her the least reason to suspect his revolt against her rule, to think for one moment that he would sacrifice her for the sake of Linda with no more compunction than he would have shown in killing a mouse-hunter. But as soon as she had passed out of his sight Job raised himself stealthily, and so carefully that there was no rustle of his litter to warn Judith that he had moved. His eyes fell first upon the open cupboard. Once Judith had experimented on him with some gin, twice or thrice she had dosed him with the spirit for medicinal purposes. Job loved the taste of it. He crept cautiously to the cupboard and drew out the stone bottle of schiedam which Jimmy Buddery had paid for the charm against the wills-o'-the-wisp. It had held a gallon, and was still half full. Job drew out the bung with his teeth, and, raising the mouth of the jar to his lips, took a long and satisfying draught.

He took another nip for luck, and then, exhilarated but not in the least intoxicated, but with every nerve abnormally alert and able, he crept swiftly up the stairway on his bare feet. He did not know that Judith had forgotten to lock her door. But he would probably have burst it open had he found it closed. It opened as his outstretched fingers touched it.

The moonlight came through the open trap-door, for the moon was almost at her zenith and was high over the Tower House. The chamber was so weird and strange that it would well have repaid more attention than the lad gave it. He only looked round once to see if Judith were there, and, finding that she was not, he went straight to the bottom rung of the ladder which gave egress to the leads on the top of the roof.

So silently did he move that the keen hearing of his mistress gave her no warning that she was being followed. When Job's head emerged from the trap-door he saw Judith standing with her back towards him on the curve of the Tower which was nearest to Merlesfleet. Her hands were held out before her in an attitude which might have been supplication but for the proud uprightness of her shoulders. Between her hands the silk scarf stretched tightly.

Job stealthily crept on to the leads.

He had never seen the marshland by moonlight before. In spite of himself, he stood one instant and gazed at the fleecy veil of mist that lay spread out to the west'ard and nor'ard, and followed the lie of it with his eyes till they fell on the deep contrast of the shadow of the woods and the glint of the moon on the quivering leaves of aspens and black poplars. Even he felt the view to be very fair. But it was not for scenery that he had ventured to climb into this forbidden region. There was Judith before him, unconscious of his presence, holding out Linda's scarf, hissing (he could see her lips moving as he stole a look at her profile) the name which was associated with Linda. And oh! how her expression screamed of relentless hate, of the satisfaction of unspeakable enmity.

Job's decision was rapid. Somehow he knew that from this eminence some evil spell was being woven for the woman he would perish to protect. What could he, a poor "innocent," do if Judith once discovered him there?—for his self-confidence did not reach so far as to tell him that his thews and sinews would prove far too much for his mistress in any merely physical struggle.

But what if he leapt upon her unawares, and bore her down, down that terrible descent? He would fall with her. He could not make a certainty of it otherwise. But what would that matter? His life was none too happy, and since Linda had given him an inkling of some better things than he had ever before dreamed of, his weariness with his existence had grown heavy upon him. His mind was soon made up.

Chapter XIX

When Day Dawned—The Inquest

Judith, unconscious of her danger, was exerting every nerve of influence which she was able, or thought she was able, to exercise over what Hebbelthwaite called the Power of Evil. She was lost in the passion of her spell. Now was the time when her fate would be decided for ever. If she could bring Linda to her, after the dream which she knew she had dreamt, she thought that Linda would take her place as thrall to the Black Man, and would set her free. Let her only come down to the Tower House now to-night, under that radiance of the moon which has from time immemorial been held in evil repute. And Linda was coming. She knew it. She could feel it.

The minutes passed. Judith had no sense of the lapse of time. All of her consciousness was rapt in the one attempt. Well, she would soon know.

Job crept a little closer to her. He could see the quivering emotion of her body. He could almost read the very thoughts which were filling her with an agony of suspense.

He was sure the time was come. It would not be safe for Linda if he delayed longer.

There was never a prayer on his lips as he sprang. He did not know a prayer of any kind, not even a prayer to the Black Man had entered into his course of education. But his whole poor nature went out on the wings of the night to where Linda was. Ah! if she could only know that he had done this thing for her sake! But she would never know that. She had hardly seemed to care about his flowers when once she knew who gathered them for her, and plaited the rush baskets which held them. But he could not complain of that. He knew that he was "innocent," "sorft," "a button short," "not quite all theer"—any one of the peasant terms would have expressed his feelings towards himself.

He gripped the leads with his naked toes, bent his body forward, and leapt at Judith with every ounce of strength which he could command. His arms clutched her round her neck and stifled the cry which she tried to give as she felt the throttling grip about her.

The two shapes shot forward over the edge of the Tower—forward, then a little downward. The upper part of the linked bodies swerved down with terrible suddenness.

Down, down, down fell the bodies, head-first, till they struck the hard yard where the fowls pecked for gravel, and lay there still and silent.

The sun rose over the woodland to the east. The goats bleated in the stable. The fowls came forth and pecked the gravel. One hopped upon the bodies. Some rabbits were playing near the yard, and wild birds played fearlessly near the still, shapeless mass.

The day had come again. But not for Job Sacret nor Judith Jennis.

*   *   *   *   *

After he had left Linda, Laurence went back in the cool dawn to his own house. His spirit was too uplifted for sleep. He changed, and bathed, and came out again. He took the road to the Tower House. Judith would be up early, attending to her goats. He would be able to speak with her.

He meant now to try gentler means. His whole being was filled with too much happiness for him to wish for anything else now that he was at last assured that this woman's power over Linda had gone. So far Judith had not known what he knew. Coming to her, as he would now, with perfect frankness, telling of his study of the history of the Merle and Jennis families, of his own belief in a personal Power of Evil, and of his belief in a personal Power of Good that must ultimately prevail, he might do some good. It was worth trying. He was prepared even to tell her of his love for Linda if that should be necessary.

He took the path along the river wall which led to the back of the Tower House, the same path along which he had run to the rescue of Briony Prettyman. To his surprise he noticed that the stable in which the goats were housed at night was still closed. He had heard their impatient bleating long before, and wondered at it. They must still be there and they should have been out on the marsh hours before. Judith was not a woman to oversleep herself. Besides, Job would have awakened her. She might be ill, and in want of help. The boy would be able to do nothing for her.

There was a flutter among the chickens as he came round the Tower. There, in the shingle-spread yard under a sunlight which seemed merciless, lay the bodies of Job and Judith. The hands of the boy were still round the woman's neck. For a moment or two Laurence hesitated, and then he pulled himself together. He drove back the fowls savagely out of the yard, anywhere. Then he bent over the two bodies and found the signs of death that he had known he would find. There were some details which he noted too horrible for description. They had fallen, then, from the Tower together. Was it really a fall? Why were the boy's broken arms still tight to the woman's neck? He recognised Linda's silk scarf in Judith's hand. Very carefully he disengaged it from her fingers, folded it, and put it in his pocket. Possibly he had no right to do anything of the kind. But for that he cared very little. Linda's name must not be mentioned at the inquest.

There was nothing more that could be done there. It was a matter for the police and the doctors. Once more he hesitated. He hardly liked to leave the bodies unguarded. The fowls had come back again. Where could he find a messenger? He passed again round the Tower and looked over the marsh to the river wall. Bob Middleton, stock dog at heel, was slouching along back homewards from his early morning round on his level. He was a little later on Sunday mornings than on week days. Hebbelthwaite hailed him.

Bob stopped, and turned in the direction of the hail with slow deliberation.

"Wha'ss up?" he roared. He was accustomed to conversing at a distance, and his voice carried easily across two marshes and a couple of dykes.

"Come here, Bob," shouted Hebbelthwaite, making a funnel of his hands. "There's trouble here."

Bob metaphorically pricked up his ears. Trouble has a universal attraction. "Whaaat!" he yelled, as he got down the river wall into the marsh and began to walk towards the nearest gateway in the direction of the Tower House. "Be theer anything wrong wi' Judy, or s't that warmin of a booy?"

He shouted as he walked with perfect ease.

Hebbelthwaite waited till he came up. He was hastily scribbling two notes on pages drawn from his pocket-book. "They're dead," he said. "Both of them. I think they fell from the top of the Tower together. Would you mind taking these notes—this one to Dr. Porthal and the other to Ash, the constable at Oatacre?" There were no police in the village of Merlham.

Bob looked at the shilling which accompanied the notes. "Wha'ss this hare foor?" he asked.

"Take it, Bob," said Hebbelthwaite. "I'm giving you a lot of work and on Sunday."

"Lor, maaster," said Bob, grinning broadly. "Yew hadn't noo need to dew that. I'd run far mile at any time to l'arn as Judy's did. Dee yew put it back in yar parkut. Yew lent us uns a haand when that theer coolt gart in the deeak. Yew doan't owe me narthen. Blarm, theer'll whoolly be a song about this in the willage. Fare ye well, maaster. I'll be a gooin'."

The bleating of the goats increased. Their udders, full of milk, fretted them. Hebbelthwaite knew what was the matter. His strong hands wrenched open the padlock of the stable door. Clean pails stood in readiness. He was used to animals, and they stood patiently as he milked them one after the other. From time to time he paused in his work to drive the fowls back again. He had found some sacking in the stable and covered the bodies with it.

As he returned to the front of the house the third tine he saw the doctor coming fast along the river wall. In the further marsh Judith's flock of geese plucked and plucked at the short-cropped grass. They were almost ready for the Michaelmas market. In the dykes some dozen of them were dipping and preening themselves, beating the surface of the water with their powerful wings, scuttling in play in and out the dykes, hissing and honking with delight at the glorious morning. They recked nothing of their mistress's fate, or of the death of their herd, the idiot boy. They had all that they wanted for the moment. They hissed angrily at the doctor as he leapt into their marsh, and followed him across with outstretched necks.

Doctor Porthal drew back the sacking from the bodies and bent over them for a minute or two. He looked up to the top of the Tower and down again. "Well, you see how it is," he said to Hebbelthwaite.

"Yes," said Laurence, "I suppose so."

"What were you doing round there at the back?"

"Milking her goats. Why should the poor devils suffer?"

"I see, I see," said Dr. Porthal. "Could you lend me a pencil? I must make a few notes for the coroner in case he wants them."

"Thanks," he said, handing back the pencil. "You've sent for Ash, Bob told me. But he can't be here yet. I'll come round and help you with the goats if you like."

In the sun, on the side of the road opposite to the Tench and Teal, almost the whole male population of Merlham gathered together. Bob Middleton had found time to shout out the news to little Jimmy Buddery as he passed through the "street" on his way to the doctor, and Jimmy did not fail to spread it. Every Sunday morning which is not hopelessly wet sees the group of men and hobbledehoys assembled at the corner by the inn as the day draws on to noon. It is the great village assembly of the week, and old and young come together and speak of and listen to strange tales which wile away the time until half-past twelve opens the door of the Tench and Teal and sets the good brown beer flowing from the casks into the earthenware mugs which are being eagerly demanded.

On this Sunday the gathering was even greater than usual. A great and terrible thing had happened to one who had been feared by every man or boy there. The women huddled together within doors, seeing to the midday meal. Those who had a husband easy enough to permit them to go to church in the morning did not fail to gossip of the tidings as they walked down Church Lane in all their pride of Sunday frocks and white starched petticoats. Before and after service the lane hummed with female clatter. But this was what Jimmy would have called "silly fule woman talk." Alone of all the village Briony Prettyman wept in her cottage.

The real discussion of the village went on opposite the Tench and Teal. Jimmy himself, in the unavoidable absence of Bob Middleton, was the hero of the hour. He narrated over and over again how he had once given Judith a bottle of Hollands for a charm against hob-o'-lanterns, and how the charm in question had succeeded in protecting him from the dangerous wiles of those enticing lights. He had rarely enjoyed himself more. He loved to rule the talk, and he grew quite petulant when Sir William broke in with a fresh interest, recounting how he had heard Judith's prophecy concerning the sisters and the Black Man o' the mash. He recited this with much gusto, and kept on doing so till Jimmy bethought himself of a way in which he might change the trend of his rival's thoughts.

"Bain't that wunnerful," said Jimmy, addressing his hearers en masse, "how pore innocent Sir Willum fare ta mind them wusses. An' that mind me, Sir Willum. When I heerd ye tall them afoor I thote as yew'd arned another medal. For I rackon theer bain't another maan in the willage as could ha' doned it. Hare, yew Tarm," he cried to a lad of sixteen, named Tom Nearboy, "run yew in an' ax my missus ta gi'e ye the medal as I maade for Sir Willum hare. That stand in the workshop agin the wice."

Sir William beamed with gratified pride. He forgot the tragedy, and looked eagerly after: the lad as he disappeared in Jimmy's cottage hard by. Presently Tom emerged with a star-shaped piece of tin, into which Jimmy had punched a hole and fastened a bit of silver thread.

"Hare ye be, Sir Willum," said Jimmy, handing over the worthless toy with an admirable burlesque solemnity; "taake it, 'ecos yew ha' arnt it by recollectin' Judy's wuds."

Sir William was conquered. Until the opening of the inn he sat in silence, rapturously regarding his new honours. Little Jimmy again held sway till half-past twelve brought on a topic of even more engrossing interest than the fate of Judith and Job.

For the next few days little was discussed in the village save the forthcoming inquest. The necessity for one of these functions is always regarded with mixed feelings by those of the peasantry who are liable to be summoned to serve upon the jury. This means loss of at least half a day's work, probably even a whole day's work, and the shilling or sixpence which the generous country allows each juror for his services hardly makes up for the loss of wage.

On the other hand, there is always the curiosity to inspect the body. In the case of Judith and Job there was an additional motive on each side. The terror with which the mistress of the Tower House had been regarded both acted as an attraction and as a deterrent. Most would have liked to look upon that face in death which they had never dared to confront in life. But all were chilled by a sense of reluctance to bringing themselves within the sphere of the witch's influence, whether she were dead or alive.

There was little talk of murder or suicide. Where Judith was concerned, nothing could surprise the people. How should they know what had happened? It might even be that the Black Man himself had flung his servant over the edge of the Tower House, and that Job Sacret was, after all, but a familiar. The general impression was that it would be well not to search too closely into the cause of death.

Little Jimmy (who had been warned by the coroner's officer that he would have to serve) expressed the feeling of the majority when he said, "I rackon as we'd best bring it in accidental death, or death by the wisitation o' Gord. If ta worn't by the wisitation o' Gord that wuz by the will o' the daavil, an' arter all I doan't speckilate as theer fare ta be a sight o' difference. I bain't a gooin' ta shove my nose inta noo shud as maay nose wuss than anybardy knoo on. Noo, noo; accidental death or death by the wisitation o' Gord ull satisfy the willage an' tha'ss what I shall woot foor."

After the evidence, circumstantial and otherwise, had been received, the coroner commenced his charge to the jury by saying, "If any of you gentlemen feel that open window you can move further into the room." He glanced at his watch on the table before him.

At one time he had thought it would be necessary to adjourn the inquest. But he no longer thought it necessary. He would direct their attention especially to the open gin-bottle found in the lower room of the house, and to the fact that the door of the dead woman's room was open, though, as a rule, it was kept locked. There had already been some signs of malevolence on the part of this afflicted boy. They had heard what Mr. Hebbelthwaite had to say as to that. It was possible, of course, that the woman had had to submit him to some little discipline, and had angered him. They must not, of course, judge this deficient lad as if he were one of themselves. It seemed to him almost certain that the boy had been maddened by drink, that Judith had opened her door to see what was the matter, hearing the noise below, and that she had then been pursued by this mad creature. She had sought refuge on the tower, but he had followed her too closely for her to be able to close the trap-door.

The jury took three minutes to consider their verdict, and returned it unanimously as "Death by the visitation of God."

The coroner raised his head sharply, and peered through his pince-nez. "Really, gentlemen," he said, "do you mean that? I can hardly take that verdict, and"—here he glanced at his watch again—"I have only ten minutes before I must start to catch my train. May I say accidental death? If you will not accept my view—"

Little Jimmy was the foreman. He looked at his brothers of the jury. They nodded: "We doan't objec' to that," said he. "Accidental death mean much the saame as death by wisitation. Let it goo at that."

Judith and Job were buried in that nettle-grown corner of the churchyard which is grudged to the unbaptised. No service was read over them. It was late at night that the crowd of awe-struck villagers watched this scornful interment of one who had been so great amongst them. They felt some bitterness on the point. The rigid parson had never been popular with them, and they had held Judith in far higher respect than they did him. Who was he thus to mutilate the rights of the dead? It was whispered that the expense of the funeral had been borne by the lady of Merlesfleet. Certainly flowers from the Merlesfleet hothouses were found on the grave the next morning. With them was a bunch of superb cactus dahlias, of which Briony had despoiled her garden. It was the only recognition which she could make for a kindness which she never forgot.

On the night of the funeral, Sir William went about his business begirt with his chain of medals, which he had come to regard as a talisman against all black magic. October was within a day or two, and he had received his usual order for early pheasants from a well-known dealer in game of the neighbouring market town. With his pan of charcoal and his packet of sulphur he crept warily through the Merlesfleet woods when the moon was bright enough to enable him to see the plump shapes of the long-tailed birds roosting in the trees in the plantations. He had been drawn by the birds to a point near the edge of the track which led from Merlesfleet to the Tower House, and had caught a sight of a fine old cock perched complacently not more than ten feet from the earth. He held his pan of smouldering charcoal high beneath the pheasant, and scattered the sulphur upon its glowing embers, waiting till the bird should be overcome by the fumes, and fall senseless at his feet.

Suddenly he heard the syncopated beat of galloping hoofs. They seemed to be coming along the track through the woods, and coming swiftly. There can be no doubt that he believed he heard these, and that he also believed that while he was watching, frightened, clutching at his medals, for what might come, a dark mass swept furiously by, which resolved itself to his wondering gaze into the form of Judith seated upon Bel. The air seemed to him to grow icily chill as the vision passed. He dropped the charcoal and fell in a state of stupefied terror at the foot of the oak on which the pheasant perched.

The story was all over the village the next day, and for long the pheasants which chose that part of the woods for their perches were safe from any unauthorised interference.

Chapter XX

Vicisti

Great was the love of Linda; great was her happiness, her sense of final certainty. But for all that Judith's terrible death brought her a shock and depression. She even asked herself if in some indirect way she could be at all responsible for it. It was fortunate that she had Hebbelthwaite with whom to speak on that subject. The steady prose of the senior tutor and the simple maternal affection of his wife were a comfort to her. Within a week she was herself again.

About this time, Hebbelthwaite called at Merlesfleet in the morning, and asked to see Mr. Trotter. Briefly, and with some dignity, he told him of his intention to marry Linda. "I hope, Mr. Trotter," he said, "the marriage may have your approval."

"Really! really! really!" said Mr. Trotter. "Do you know that this surprises me very much?"

"It surprises me, too, a little," said Hebbelthwaite.

"Do you know, Mr. Hebbelthwaite," said the senior tutor, "that during the period of my guardianship I did on one or two occasions attempt to arrange a matrimonial alliance for Linda, and with no success whatever. Amenable as she generally is to my wishes, I here found what I can only characterise as a distinct opposition. Yet now, without a word from me, she apparently settles the whole thing for herself. It is extraordinary."

"It is very extraordinary," said Hebbelthwaite. He went on to furnish the tutor with some of the usual particulars about himself. Much he would have had to say to a stranger the tutor knew already. When he approached with some delicacy and difficulty the question of his means the tutor interrupted him. All the bursar in him rose to the surface. "One moment," he said; "we should, I think, go carefully into this. You will not mind if I ask a few questions?"

Hebbelthwaite was able to satisfy him on these points. The tutor was already inclined to like him, and after some further conversation he decided that the marriage should take place with his approval.

From this to the conviction that, as a matter of fact, he had arranged the marriage himself took but few steps. "This might have been foreseen," he said to his wife when they first talked it over. Subsequent talk showed that it really had been foreseen. Aunt Mary, with her usual docility and kindliness, contented herself with discovering new virtues in Hebbelthwaite daily.

Linda had a small party down from London to shoot over her coverts, and this gave her the opportunity to introduce Hebbelthwaite to her friends. Merlesfleet wore a more mundane air now. Paris frocks flicked the gravel of the terrace where once the black goat Bel had stood immobile in the small hours of the morning as Linda dismounted. Quite frivolous people, a little curious of the story of the tragedy, were escorted by the senior tutor to see the quaint old Tower House. The goats and geese were gone by this time. The place wore an air of perpetual desolation. Already Mr. Trotter was making his plans. It had been offered to Bob Middleton, who had charge of the level, and Bob found six excellent reasons for refusing to take it, not one of which was the true one. The place was not in good condition, and Mr. Trotter doubted whether it was worth the repairs which would be required even if he could find a tenant. This was extremely unlikely. The place suited Judith and her forebears. It would have suited no one else, even apart from the cloud which now rested on it. Access to the main road was too difficult. The interior arrangement of the house was inconvenient, and the local authorities would have condemned it as a residence for a family. It was better, so Mr. Trotter thought, to pull it all down, turn it into grazing land, and let it with the marshes. Linda held strongly the same view.

Linda and Laurence took their full share in the gaiety of the house. It was good for both of them. The strange undercurrent of life which had once caught them so strongly had left them now to bask on the surface. Nothing was said by them of their faith, their souls and the hereafter of their souls. Much was said about what was to be done to-morrow by way of amusement. Laurence was a modest man and a good sportsman. He was liked for his own sake, even by men who envied him his good fortune, and would have had a kind of malicious pleasure in finding him inferior to themselves.

The little house party broke up at the end of the third week in October. A few days later the wedding was to take place, quietly, and in the village church.

It was during one of these few days that Linda and Laurence wandered out one afternoon along the river wall. The wind was shrewd and the tide high. They descended on the sheltered side of the wall, and sat down in the sun. Linda, her face between her hands, had been looking out into the distance. Suddenly she said, "It all seems so very long ago, doesn't it?"

"Yes," said Hebbelthwaite, "it seems very long ago. We have had the material world a good deal about us lately, haven't we? The existence of the other shrinks back into nothing. I've found time to think about the proportion of birds killed to cartridges used, and things of that kind. But one has only to sit out her quietly in the open to feel it come back again."

"I did feel that," said Linda. "I think that even with all the best that this world can give it seems at times an irritating kind of waiting-place. It is not what we are, but what we shall be. Shall I ever be drawn again, I wonder, so near to the outer darkness?"

"Never, I hope," said Laurence. "Even if it happened—"

"Yes," she said, "the Power of Good is the stronger. I had wandered into dangerous places, and I have been won back again. 'Vicisti, Vicisti.'"

There was a long pause. His keen eyes watched her beauty, transparently tender and spiritual. She turned to him half smiling.

"That is why you were angry with me, then? You foresaw what would happen, and you cared for me?"

"Yes," he said, "I cared for you, but I never foresaw what would happen. I was angry with any attempt of the kind you were then making. I am still angry with it. I hate to see a woman with the gift, if one can call it a gift, that Judith had, use it as she used it. I hate far more to see the woman of society, with her half-belief and her ignorant curiosities, trying to turn the communion of saints into a parlour trick."

"I wasn't quite that kind of woman," said Linda.

"You were not," said Hebbelthwaite; "I judged you wrongly. I often make mistakes. The line I took with you was very tactless. But I worshipped you all the time, you know. You see, I knew exactly what Judith's beliefs were. I knew, as you know now, what the history of them had been. I had feared no worse than that she might make of you a nervous wreck. It didn't work out as I thought. I fancy there was worse in store for you had you ever gone back to her."

"Do you remember how you used to watch in the woods every night for me?"

"It was not so long ago, really." He laughed. "Yes, those were the finest nights in my life. You can't think what a funny kind of satisfaction a man can get in thinking he is doing something for the woman he loves."

"But you did something; you saved me."

"No," he said, simply. "What was it you said just now? It was not to me that you spoke when you whispered 'Vicisti.'"

She nodded her head gravely. They rose and went back together again along the river wall. The sun was sinking. About the levels marshmen could be seen bearing their stools to their favourite spots for awaiting the evening flight of wild duck.

"Oh the comfort of you!" said Linda, suddenly. They spoke of the approaching wedding as they neared the house.

"It is really rather awful," said Linda; "it is only last night that I wrote to Cara Devigny to tell her about it. I suppose that lovers are selfish. Then, you see, we've had a few people here, and that has kept one occupied and driven things out of one's head. I've told her that we are going to be married with the utmost privacy—no bridesmaids, no anything. She'll forgive me for not having written before."

"She should," said Laurence; "I mean, it can't have been so long ago that she herself was going to be married, and had so many things to think of."

"Yes," said Linda; "but with her it was different. She wasn't very happy, you know, dear Cara."

Laurence tried to feel sorry for Cara. He failed even to be interested in her. "She is still quite beautiful," he said. There would have been more enthusiasm in his voice if he had been speaking of a well-bred setter. In truth, he had almost forgotten her.

Chapter XXI

Sorrow and Song

Her hostess considered that Cara Devigny was quite a good woman to have in the house. It was quite true that the men were sportsmen who were there for sport, and quite true that Cara Devigny did not care one halfpenny about sport. But it was also apparent that sportsmen preferred her to the woman who, from mistaken notions that it was necessary to share the masculine interest, persistently talked of that which she did not know. Cara jeered at sport, but she amused the sportsmen. She was charmingly dressed; she was bright, she had ideas. She never appeared till luncheon, and she always effaced herself at tea-time if she thought the men were tired with a hard day's shooting. But she was at her best at dinner and afterwards. She was certainly a success.

"But she is as hard as bricks," her hostess added.

The lady who was as hard as bricks sat at the writing-table in her room, and replied to the letter which she had received from her old friend Linda.

"Dearest Linda," she wrote. "I never was more rejoiced in my life. I like Mr. Hebbe1thwaite immensely. I am quite certain you will be happy with him. I always thought there was a chance of your marrying him when you seemed so angry with him. Those men win who can make us glad or who can make us savage. It is the insipidities who cannot make us anything that get left out. Briefly, a man has got to be a man, and I confess that this is not my own discovery.

"My dear, I am breaking my heart to know what the senior tutor is like at Merlesfleet. When you can spare a moment from more serious interests, you must write and describe that faithfully without the least trace of human kindness. You must not vitiate that portrait. It is my own firm conviction that he must pine and die if he is taken out of the academic air.

"Private though your wedding may be, I should fly at once to Merlesfleet, but for the fact that I am practically screwed to the floor here, until I leave with my other friends for Egypt. Do you remember my prophecy? Perhaps I got it mixed. Anyhow, I cannot help thinking that if I could once see the senior tutor in breeches with a gun tucked under his arm, I could die happy, with his photograph engraved on my retina. Life could contain nothing else quite so exquisite.

"You may be as sub rosa and sotto voce as you like about your wedding, but that is not going to prevent me from sending you a wedding present. I shall expect the usual lie from you about it But don't worry to acknowledge it yet. The curse of marriage is that in its initial stage it gives one too many letters to write. That is why I never married again. But, goodness only knows what Egypt may bring forth. At any rate, the man who took me in to dinner last night said that he considered the climate romantic; I made him say a lot of other things like that, and some of them were still better. They are a great comfort to me. They give me something to laugh about when I lie awake at night. Dearest and sweetest Linda, to be serious for one moment, I do wish you every happiness, and do believe that you will have it I am a frivolous idiot, but I do love you dearly.—Ever yours, CARA DEVIGNY."

As a matter of fact, she did not laugh much when she lay awake at night. That was the worst time for her. During the day she could, and did, insist on perpetual occupation. She did not give way to the temper of the woman who marries from pique nor to the self-deception of the woman who tries to drown the earthly love with the heavenly, nor to the cowardice that throws down the cards altogether. She played the game right through to the end, went on much as she had always done, and made a good many people happy. It was only when she lay dying some three years later that she realised what torture those years had been, and how merciful was the unsought relief.

The marriage of Linda and Laurence took place at half-past eight in the morning. Mr. Trotter appeared in a perfect frock coat, and a perfect silk hat. It was only one more disguise for him. At Cambridge, his appearance suggested a scholar and a gentleman. At the wedding he was a close replica of the hireling detective who guards the presents. He gave the bride away with sufficient dignity. She wore white because she liked that part of the matrimonial traditions, but Covent Garden had done absolutely nothing for her. There was not an inch of florists' wire anywhere about her. Hebbelthwaite wore the clothes that he meant to travel in. Aunt Mary wept a little in the front pew. It seems almost unnecessary to add that she wore brown.

The village had been given to understand Linda's wishes, and had respected them. Not one of the peasants was present in the church, though there was a perfect avenue of them outside the doors.

As the bride and bridegroom emerged from the porch some of the oldest among the local marsh men fired their great muzzle-loaders in the air.

Linda had been told that this was the old custom, and had hoped that it would be carried out.

At Merlesfleet, the car, with their luggage upon it, was in waiting. They sped away upon it with no professional driver to accompany them. The place at which they would spend their honeymoon had never been mentioned. At first, in answer to the many inquiries of her friends, Linda said that it was a funny thing, but it was one of those places whose names one simply cannot remember. Laurence suffered from the same forgetfulness. Even that good man, Mr. Trotter, was not in the secret, although he had wished to be. Aunt Mary, on the other hand, had prayed that she might not be told. "I should only let it out," she said. Her diagnosis was probably correct.

There was a great feast at Merlham that night. The great barn of the model farm had been transformed for the occasion. The whole of the private way which led from the high road to the farmhouse, and thence to the barn, was ablaze with Japanese lanterns.

"Lor'," said Mrs. Bob Middleton, "bain't them theer lanterns as pratty as gays; I niver seed narthen like 'em afoor. Howiver they bu'n sa bright 'thout catchin' afire git oover me. But that dew fare bewtiful, an' noo mistaake. Tha'ss a'moost as good as the firewucks I see at Narwich at Dimond Jubilee time, an' tha'ss a fack."

A good band had been engaged, and occupied a platform at the far end of the barn, where they played strenuously whenever they were required, and sometimes when they were not Mr. Trotter had promised to preside, and he put his whole soul into it. He was in full evening dress, because the dignity of the occasion demanded it. But he drank beer out of an earthenware mug to show his simple, good-hearted fellowship. "Not more than a quarter full," he had whispered to the hired waiter. The style of his costume was unfamiliar to some of the guests, and caused some good-humoured but slightly irreverent criticism.

The banquet began at seven. By close attention to the serious business of the evening, smoking time was reached by a little after eight. Mr. Trotter now rose from his place, and rapped three times on the table with the black handle of his knife. The noise gradually died down. The squeaking voice of little Jimmy Buddery, which had hitherto been making more noise than any other in the barn, was heard crying aloud, "Silence! doan't yew hare the gennelman a knockin'? Blust! Hain't none on ye gart moor breedin' 'an a cross-bred peeg? Hode yar n'ise. The gennelman waant ta hev a h'arin' along o' us uns."

Mr. Trotter had prepared his speech very carefully. In his strenuous desire not to get above the level of his audience he had composed it mostly in words of one syllable. Perhaps the only mistake that he made was the too frequent introduction of rhetorical questions. His audience did not understand that these were an oratorical artifice, and obliged him on each occasion with prompt and hearty answers.

"My good friends," said Mr. Trotter, "I think you all know what it is I want to say. We are met here in joy and mirth. We fill the cup" (he waved his empty mug recklessly), "our hearts are glad. Why?"

"'Cos our bellies fare full, maaster," cried little Jimmy, who had filled and emptied the cup many times.

Mr. Trotter permitted himself an indulgent smile. "That may be one cause," he said, clinging frantically to the style of the first reader. "But I can tell you one more. What did we see on the morn of this day?"

There was a chorus of answers in reply to this. Many of them referred to the marriage. But Bob Middleton cried out that he had seen the first immigrant fowl of the year as he was on his level "deeak drawin'" the "fust o' the mornin'." "Aah!" cried Jimmy. "I see theer wuck in the mill deeak yisterdaay arternune." Sir William (who was gay with all his medals ostentatiously displayed) thought that the time was propitious for the narration of his personal experiences. "I see an ole otter in the oozier plantin'," said he; "that wus just arter sunrise. Tha'ss the fust time I ha' seed one theer for thutty yare. Tha'ss whaat I see this moarnin'."

The indulgent smile again sunned itself on Mr. Trotter's twitching and ascetic countenance. "Yes," he said, "I see you all know what I mean. I need not make a long speech, need I?"

One voice was heard to reply, "Noo, noo—leeast said sunest l'arnt." But the politer manners suppressed it. The cry, "Tha'ss as yew pleease, master," prevailed. "Goo yew on. That doan't sigerfy. We ha gart our bare an' bocca an' noobardy doan't waant ta paay noo regard 'thout he like."

Then Mr. Trotter got bang down on to the right note. "I want you," he said, "to drink the health of one whom it is not too much to say we all love."

There was a great shuffling of mugs at this, and shouts of "Miss Linda, Gord bless har!"

Mr. Trotter raised his mug dramatically. "To the health of Mr. and Mrs. Hebbelthwaite!" he shouted.

His final lapse from the style of reading without tears was pardonable. You cannot get Hebbelthwaite into a monosyllable. He raised the mug to his lips, and presented every appearance of one who drank deep.

Every figure seated at the long trestle tables leapt to its feet. Men and women, girls and boys, all stood up together, and all blended hearts and voices in one mighty shout of enthusiasm. Cheers such as no town ever hears echoed through the vast barn, and rioted up among the dim oak baulks which traversed the tops of the walls from side to side. The hired waiters had filled every mug on the table with either beer or lemonade. No drilled regiment could have presented a more solid front of charged vessels than did the long lines of peasants. But there was little mechanical discipline about them. A distinctive and honest individuality could be observed in each voice. Shouts and cries leapt and echoed in a discord which was yet pleasant to hear.

Mr. Trotter stood amazed. He had an inclination to stuff his fingers in his ears, for the rough, uncultured sounds struck upon his hearing at first with physical agony. But there was something in the tumult which attracted him. He forebore to deafen himself, and listened. Soon he grasped the meaning. This shouting, this orgie of enthusiasm, was the note of the devotion of the peasants for the blood of the family which had been the father of the patriarchal community for centuries. It was the vow of allegiance, the homage of inherited affection and respect.

The eyes of some of the women were wet with tears. They scarcely knew why. It was the same feeling that comes over them when the soldiers are marching out of the town and the band is playing "The Girl I Left Behind Me"—the same feeling that shook so many when the state coach passed at the Jubilee of Queen Victoria At a signal from Mr. Trotter, the band began the National Anthem. As the chorus of it swelled upwards, Mr. Trotter slipped out of the barn. He had yet another duty to perform—to open the servants' ball at Merlesfleet.

Here there reigned a different atmosphere—an air of formality so great as to be almost terrific. Mr. Trotter, with a mechanical accuracy of step and great conscientiousness, danced with Mrs. Dodge. Mr. Thomson piloted Aunt Mary through the Lancers with not less care than he would have given to a slightly top-heavy ice-pudding. Then Mr. and Mrs. Trotter retired, and the atmosphere cleared perceptibly. Dancing was also going on at the barn, where the long tables had been removed.

*　　*　　*　　*　　*

Everything was quiet now. The last of the revellers had long since gone home. The pale dawn crept up, and its light came almost sardonically on the swinging Japanese lanterns, in which the candles had burnt out. The first rays of the sun sparkled on the rime-frost which lay on the thatch of the great barn.

Then the silence was broken by the tramp of feet and the sound of many voices. The gang of house-breakers passed through the farm-yard on their way to the Tower House.

Epilogue

The pale and thin young man whom Lady Blickling, on her car, had just met had passed her deliberately without a sign. "Stop, Harris," said her ladyship, imperatively. "Turn round and catch that gentleman up." Harris looked dubious.

"The lane's a bit narrer, my lidy," he said.

"Then open that gate and back her into that field. Don't be so childish."

The car stopped as it overtook the young man. Yes; he was very shabby indeed. "You don't seem to remember me, Mr. Belton," said Lady Blickling, sharply. Then she turned to Harris. "Stop the engine, Harris. Get out and go up to Mrs. Durrant's cottage, and see if she has taken the medicine I left yesterday."

Harris vanished obediently. Percy Belton looked a trifle obstinate. "You forget, Lady Blickling," he said, "that you once gave me to understand that you did not know me in future."

"Stuff and nonsense," said Lady Blickling. "You're coming back to lunch with me now."

"Pardon me," he said; "but I'm not."

"Oh yes, you are. I can't discuss it all in the road. And I shall have to see if you will be likely to suit me before I could definitely give you the post."

"I'm not coming," he said, doggedly.

"Look here," said Lady Blickling; "you were man enough to do the right thing at last, and I know what it has cost you with your father. You've got more than your own pride to think about now. You've got a wife and a child to keep, and a very pretty wife she is. Don't you be unreasonable."

"Very well," he said, with a slight twitch of his lips, "I will come."

A few days later saw his appointment as agent and steward to Lady Blickling's Oxfordshire property. For work of that kind he was admirably suited.

Laurence found an opportunity to purchase the amber cup which Judith had used for purposes of divination. The black thread which Linda had tied on it was still there. He spent a long time on a comparative study of the two partly-effaced inscriptions. Both cups are now restored to the place from which some sacrilegious person had stolen them more than a century ago, and to their original use.

Each cup now bears its inscription restored. Underneath, in Latin characters, a single word is engraved: "Vicisti."

THE END

CPSIA information can be obtained at www.ICGtesting.com
Printed in the USA
BVOW080715280911

272313BV00005B/264/P